# Fated

## A.S. Roberts

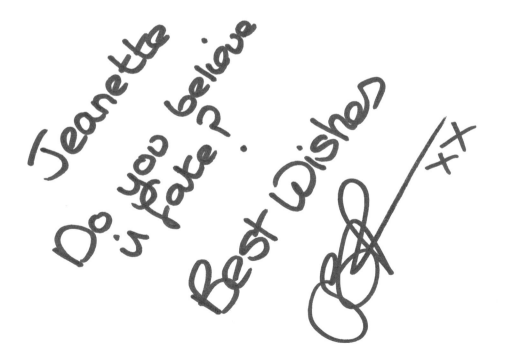

Jeanette

Do you believe in fate?

Best Wishes

xx

A.S. Roberts

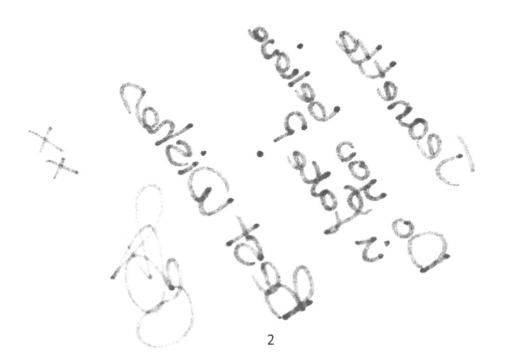

Fated

Edited by Karen J
Proofreading by The fireball fillies
Beta read by The fireball fillies
Cover art by Marisa of Cover Me Darling
Cover Model – Stuart Reardon
Photo by Golden @FuriousFotog
Formatted by Brenda Wright, Formatting Done Wright

Playlist

# Chapters

A.S. Roberts

This book is dedicated to my husband. He has stood with me every step of our journey together. Thank you for always being there, inspiring me, when others have failed to do so. I Love you and the team that we created together.

To our boys, the loves, of my life. Let this book inspire you to follow your dreams!

This is also dedicated to my friends, new and old. I believe in fate and always have. Thank you for helping me to create the story that has gone around in my head for years!

From proof reading, to beta reading, teaser creation and just for simply being there, for me to ask advice off.

You know who you are!

Love you all x

'Never love anyone who
treats you like
you're ordinary.'

Oscar Wilde

# 6 years previously

What sort of person isn't able to attend the funeral of their only parent of any consequence?

Me, I was that sort of person.

I had suffered a sort of breakdown, the doctors concurred. Emotional stress and exhaustion they called it.

Pathetic my mother called it.

I was standing finally on very sodden soil, constantly having to move my feet, listening to the repetitive squelching noise my black boots made in contact with the mud. I repeated the movement over and over, in order to stop them being consumed into the ground. The very ground that now held my dad. All the while, I was struggling to choke back the tears, which threatened to fall. Continuously I rubbed my hands together, to keep them warm.

Although it was August, the weather was obviously empathetic and had the same thoughts and emotions as me. The skies continued to darken over and the rain fell in a heavy, sluggish drizzle.

I was finally here, wrapped in a heavy coat and my own grief. Audibly sighing, my eyes ran over and over the words on the headstone.

Michael Paul Jones
Born 26/10/66
Died 29/07/09
Loving husband of Carol

But there was no mention of me on there, his only child.

In the world of my stepmother, I didn't exist. She hadn't given birth to me, so therefore I was insignificant.

I caught my breath, trying to swallow a gulping sob. I conjured up picture memories in my head. At least he had finally managed to tell me he loved me, even if it was only the once, and on his deathbed.

I looked up to the sky and watched the clouds travel unhurriedly overhead. Closing my eyes, the droplets fell; they hit my face and grouped together, finally running down my neck in rivulets.

The sadness I felt was completely overwhelming.

Never be the unwanted pregnancy of two people who hate each other's guts, would be my advice to anyone.

From behind me, two hands came forward. They gently rubbed up and down my arms, trying to formulate a soothing sensation

*'Sweetheart, you know we are here for you, don't you?'*

The gentle voice of my aunt came through to me. I turned to her, my aunt and uncle swaddled me up in their arms. There we stood, clustered together for several minutes.

*'Come on, Frankie,'* I heard my cousin JJ speaking and as my aunt and uncle pulled away from me, he took their place and pulled me in tight against his side.

'Let's go home.'

I managed a fragile smile in answer, staying as close to him as was possible, wrapping my arm tight around his waist. JJ gave me the strength I had always felt I lacked. I was so pleased he had come back from America. His presence here today meant everything to me.

I was last to walk down the well-worn path to the front door of my aunt and uncle's small, but very homely, terraced house. The old wooden gate shut with a bang behind us. Flexing and contracting on its very antique, rusted spring.

'Frankie love.' The raised voice of our next-door neighbour broke me out of my melancholy thoughts. I raised my eyes from the cobbled path. She came out of her front door quickly; obviously she had been awaiting our return, twitching the net curtains. Her arms were laden.

'These came for you, my dear.' She handed me a large, beautiful bouquet of mixed flowers, the colours of which seemed like a rainbow on such a wet day. Her face showed concern for my obviously distressed appearance. She ran her hand fleetingly up and down my arm.

'Oh thank you, Norah' I took the bouquet from her. Puzzled as to where they had come from, I pulled the card from the small envelope and started to read.

A person's strength isn't shown
by how much they can take
before they break.
A person's strength is shown
by how much they can take
after they have already
been broken.
X

# Present day

# Frankie

My sudden intake of breath awoke me with a start; both of my hands gripped the armrests. I released my fingers and flexed them over the soft, velvety material. Glancing around quickly, I checked to see if anyone had noticed.

Please, I prayed, don't let me have been talking out loud. Bella had often told me that I did, when sharing halls at university. With relief I realised my secret was safe, after taking another quick look around me. Everyone was either asleep or very much occupied with their own business. Thank God. I expelled a very loud sigh.

My pulse was still preposterously fast, banging and throbbing against my eardrums like a bass drum. I breathed in slowly, just willing my body to calm down. From previous experience, I knew just what I looked like after having my favourite erotic nightmare. But in this very public place, I felt very reluctant to share the view. Placing my palms against my cheeks, I felt the heat, they were still flushed and the throbbing need between my legs was only relieved by crossing over my jean-clad thighs and squeezing them tight.

The passing stewardess smiled at me 'Can I get anything for you, Miss Jones?' shaking my head I smiled back, not trusting my voice just yet. I tried to focus on the aircraft noise and not my heart rate.

It made me feel foolish, that eighteen months on, my one and only meeting with him could still leave me feeling like this. I wasn't a stupid teenager for Christ sake and we didn't even have a proper conversation.

*I mean I don't even know his real name.*

But whenever I closed my eyes his presence wrapped around me like a favourite blanket, the smell of his cologne expensive, fresh and clean, like the ocean. In mock inhalation, I closed my eyes again and settled back into the extremely comfortable first class seat, allowing myself the pleasure of reliving our only meeting, as I had hundreds of times before.

My aunt, uncle and I had flown to California, my only other time outside of England, to attend a meeting at Coronado, a US Navy SEAL base. The memories stirred mixed feelings, harrowing and exciting, within me. We had been flown out courtesy of the US Navy to hear the verdict of an enquiry into my cousin JJ's death.

Continuing my train of thought, I took a deep breath and swallowed. Even now I still had difficulty believing JJ was gone.

The wallpaper in the waiting area, outside the room where the enquiry was being held, was imprinted on my mind; heavy green flocked print, to go with the solid mahogany polished chairs that we sat on. I could still smell the lavender furniture polish, obviously overused as it was almost headache inducing. All the while we waited, for the internal enquiry to run its course.

Thank God for the large, arch-shaped windows in the building, otherwise the room would have been as dark as the mood that surrounded everybody within it. When the enquiry finally adjourned and the servicemen filed out, my aunt and uncle were asked to enter the room. Inside they had been delivered the verdict by the commanding officer.

I had sat outside, wringing my hands together in disbelief that we were even here. I had lost track of time, sitting and waiting. JJ only an interpreter, not a military man, and only 27, was gone. The mission in Afghanistan had gone wrong and had been aborted. The officer in charge had asked for an extraction, but too late for JJ. We were here to see if anyone's poor judgement had cost my cousin his life.

I had sat looking down at my royal blue shift dress, hands tucked underneath my thighs, crossing and uncrossing my feet, encased in matching blue pumps. Slowly becoming aware of some of the witnesses, who had just vacated the enquiry. Studying the small tightly gathered group, who were stood chatting; my awareness had prickled at the sight of one man. He stood slightly apart from the rest. He wreaked dominance, which just screamed for my attention. His large masculine frame was almost Greek God like, my dad would have described him as built like a brick outhouse, and I stifled a giggle.

*Seriously. What the hell was wrong with me?*

Honestly, *emotional wreck* should have been hung on a sign around my neck! I was sure I was losing it big time. I was going from tearful to giggling, like an adolescent school girl.

Resuming my study; the broad shoulders went down to a small waist, creating the perfect V shape. His hair was almost black, and he had a deep cleft chin. His lips were sinful looking, full and heart shaped. Not the sort of lips a man should have. A Greek God encased in uniform, it doesn't get any better. Bella would kick herself when she knew she had missed such a sight.

I really needed to get a grip and remind myself just exactly what I was here for. No one in their right mind would want to exchange places with me, having lost their surrogate sibling.

I think I had first noticed him because the hairs on the back of my neck had stood to attention. I remember raising my left hand and rubbing my neck underneath my long brown hair. I continued to stare because he was fidgeting with his white gloves. He hadn't looked like the sort of person to struggle with nerves or embarrassment, far from it in fact. From 10 feet away he had slowly lifted his gaze, from the floor to me and from the moment my eyes had fallen into his emerald green pools, they had been held captive and I was trapped. I remember even now, physically stopping to breathe.

He had made his way towards where I sat; walking with assured confidence. Watching him, I could see how he could easily bring a large crowd to a complete standstill. My top teeth had bitten down onto my bottom lip in apprehension.

*He tucked his peaked white cap under his left arm and continued towards me, his dress shoes making a clicking noise on the much worn, hardwood floor with every step. His cologne started to permeate my nostrils.*

*"Frankie?" he questioned gently, in the deepest voice I had ever heard, looking straight at me and standing so close I could have touched him.*

*"Y-yes," wondering how the hell he knew my name, and even if he knew who I was, only my family and friends called me Frankie and not my given first name of Francesca.*

*"I'm Jabby, I was in charge of the mission JJ was part of," he paused and inhaled deeply, trying to gauge my response. "I wanted to say how sorry I am, well all the team are," he said, gesturing towards the small group behind him. 'JJ was a great guy and a good friend. We wanted to bring him out with us alive, but I guess that wasn't to be," he sighed and moved his feet slightly waiting for my response.*

*"Were you exonerated?" I questioned, tilting my head slightly to one side, gesticulating towards the closed room, which now contained my aunt and uncle. I was still staring deeply into the green pools of his eyes, noticing now we were closer, that they contained amber flecks. I couldn't have looked away, even if I had wanted to.*

*How could I be so affected by the man who had possibly caused the death of my cousin? Standing up from my seat and establishing a position in front of him, I tried to give the impression that I was in control of my senses at least. I still had to look up, as even though I was tall, I still only came up to the height of his shoulders. My body was my own worst enemy and I felt my nipples pebble inside my bra.*

*His gaze shifted down further to my breasts, almost instinctively. Like my body had sounded a bloody horn to get his attention.*

*What the fuck? My confidence evaporated immediately and I shook my head trying to dislodge my thoughts. I fisted and clamped my hands to my sides, as they were aching to reach out and touch the Greek God.*

*"I was," he replied, re aligning his eyes with mine, "At least by the Navy..." he cleared his throat and paused, "If there is ever anything I can help you with? I mean anything; you only have to contact the liaison officer." Our conversation was interrupted just then by the return of my aunt and uncle" Frankie?" my aunt interjected, looking between me and the 6ft 4in God that stood in front of me.*

*I caught hold of her hands and reluctantly broke eye contact with Jabby, what the hell kind of name was that anyway? My aunt looked emotional and I hugged her briefly." It was an accident, Frankie" I heard my uncle say.*

*I had taken my first proper full breath then, since I had first clapped eyes on Jabby.*

*"I would like to offer my sincere apologies, and tell you of my deep regret...." He paused, swallowed and carried on, "JJ was like a brother to me and I am so sorry for your loss," his green eyes started to mist over and the amber flecks all but disappeared.*

*"He may have been like a brother to you... but he was my cousin, my surrogate brother." I caught an unexpected sob from the back of my throat, and clasped my right hand over my mouth. He moved his hand suddenly and held my forearm. I could feel the heat and when his fingers started to move, all be it slightly, I could feel his calloused skin abrading mine. My whole body responded, as though he had lit the touch paper to my soul. I don't know how long our eyes held each other's gaze again in mutual understanding. The moment eventually broke.*

*"Sir, Ma'am," Jabby saluted them, "Frankie," he nodded at me and then turned to exit the building. Walking away, replacing his cap*

*on his head, straightening it slightly as soon as his feet hit the outside. I was captivated just watching him put his white gloves on. I watched him move them down each of his long fingers. He turned to look at me only once, before he disappeared from view along with the rest of his team.*

*Why the hell did it feel like my whole future life was walking away with him? Mentally I chastised myself for being bloody ridiculous. It must be the emotions of the day.*

*Get a bloody grip Frankie.*

My memories were broken just then by an announcement on the aeroplane.

*Ladies and gentlemen, we are now two hours away from landing at JFK New York; we do hope you're enjoying your flight with us.*

Shifting slightly in my seat made me realise that just thinking about him had brought back the throbbing in-between my legs and had also made my knickers very damp.

*For God's sake Frankie, think about something else eh...*

I mentally slapped my face, to shake myself out of my favourite pastime, dreaming of my Greek God with the stupid bloody name.

Standing, I made my way to the toilets. After locking the door, I stared at myself in the small mirror, splashing water on my cheeks to take away the heat. I allowed myself to talk out loud. 'Frankie Jones, you really need to start living in reality land! For God 's sake, you're a grown woman. You have a good career and a brain, start acting your age.'

Leaning forward onto the vanity unit, I stared into the mirror. The reflection wasn't bad. Not stunning or anything, but not bad. Long brown hair, large, dark brown eyes, that were often commented on and a curvy figure. Not a model's but half decent, not quite up to my mother's exacting standards, but OK. I needed to start living in the here and now. It had been a long time since I'd had a man, the one and only man in my 24 years, and that was quite obviously the problem. It needed to be fixed, and fast I thought, I wasn't experienced enough to know. Another reason to be looking forward to seeing Bella, if she couldn't sort me out no one could, I thought with a chuckle.

Sitting back down, I concentrated then on why I was flying to New York. The new job was exciting and I could hardly believe my luck, to have been headhunted for it. The salary and package was excessive, but then it needed to be as the job would only last a couple of months. The offer took into consideration leaving my country and family, well my aunt and uncle, behind. The best part was going to be, being with Bella again after eleven months apart. I thought about her for a few minutes, I was so proud of her using her degree in journalism and working at the New York Post of all places.

*We came from a small coastal town in England, and well just look at us now.*

I picked up my kindle, to while away the last two hours of the flight, but after trying for at least ten minutes to lose myself in a good book I gave up, and decided to sit and check out the opulence of my surroundings.

*Who would have thought it, me Frankie Jones flying first class?*

I had only ever had one trip abroad before; I knew this was way beyond my usual means. We weren't a well-off family, and although in the last year I'd had some lucky breaks this had to be the best break yet. I put my earpieces in and relaxed into my music.

I felt the drop in temperature almost immediately the plane door opened. I pulled my black parka coat around me, feeling pleased that I had gone shopping for the coat and snow boots, Bella had insisted I was going to need. After all, she had experience of being here and I had only recollections of seeing New York in November on English TV. I vacated the plane and joined the rest of the first class passengers heading towards arrivals.

I heard Bella before I saw her, 'Frankie, over here,' she shouted. Her voice carried over the hustle and bustle.

I caught sight of her then, all blonde hair and flailing arms, waving above her head. My best friend was simply gorgeous and I realised in just that minute how much I had missed even the sight of her. A few steps and screams later, she pulled me into a massive hug. Clutching on to each other as though our lives depended on it, we jumped up and down.

'Gorgeous girl, I can't believe you are finally here, New York isn't going to know what's hit it this weekend. Have I got a plan!' she said, with a huge grin and a twinkle in her blue eyes.

I stood back slightly, to take a good look at her. Using Skype just hadn't cut it. She stood taller than me by a couple of inches; this is how we had first met at school. We were the tall girls, the ones who had freakishly hit adolescence way before anyone else. Our friendship had seen us through multiple boyfriends and break-ups, family problems and bereavements. Although I had to say, the boyfriends and break-ups were mainly on Bella, whilst unfortunately the family problems and bereavements were on me.

'I can't believe I'm here,' I said, gazing around at JFK arrivals.

19

'Well you are, so let's go. The first surprise of the weekend is our lift. You are so not going to believe how we are going home this afternoon.' She motioned towards a black limo waiting outside of arrivals. Turning towards me, she stopped, grinned and waggled her eyebrows laughing.

'OMG, Bella,' I shouted, 'you shouldn't have.' Grabbing hold of her arm and linking mine through it, I pulled her quickly towards the beautiful car.

'Oh I didn't, this is one of the perks of your new job.'

The very large driver of the limo waited patiently outside of the vehicle. As we walked nearer he smiled a genuine smile, 'Miss Jones?' he questioned, I nodded opening my mouth in amazement.

'Edwards, Miss Jones,' and he lifted his hand to shake mine. 'While you're in New York, I am going to be your driver,' with that, he opened the door to the limo for Bella and me to get in. I had never seen the inside of a limo before and faltered on the threshold for a few seconds, admiring the leather seats and a champagne bucket awaiting us. Edwards very competently stowed my luggage in the boot.

'It's got to be said Frankie, I don't think I have ever seen you speechless before,' Bella retorted. We both jumped in on the bench seat and roared with laughter. Just being here with Bella made me so happy, we laughed over nothing in particular, and that left me clutching my sides and realising this was just what I needed, a complete change.

Our laughter was broken by the sound of music. 'What the hell's that?' enquired Bella.

A light lit up the inside of my handbag. Fumbling inside, I pulled out the iPhone that had been supplied with my new job. The music was indicating an incoming text message. We both instinctively started chair dancing along to the beat. Bella was still roaring with laughter, as we recognised the track as *Welcome to New York* by Taylor Swift.

*Welcome Frankie!*

*I do hope your journey was as pleasant as possible. You will by now have met Edwards. He is one of my most trusted drivers and is at your disposal from now and all the time you are here with us in New York. He is under instructions to take you back to Bella's apartment this afternoon. Although if you change your mind and would like to stay in the accommodation offered with your position, please let me know and we can move you immediately. That would please me greatly. I wish you an enjoyable weekend with Bella.*

*I thought the text tone was appropriate!*

*Keep safe*

*Yours Alex Blackmore*

*CEO Blackmore industries*

'So, tell me about your new job?' asked Bella, literally lying on top of me, trying to read the text over my shoulder.

We sat back, warm in the limo, drinking the champagne provided. Talking as if we had never been apart and I explained how I had been head hunted.

Back in England I had been working at Foxworth House. I provided physiotherapy for injured service personnel. It had been an awe-inspiring experience, but too damned close to home after losing JJ. I needed a change and jumped at the chance to come to New York to be with Bella.

'Well, Bella, I'm going to be physiotherapist to Nathan Blackmore, do you know the Superbike rider?'

I watched as Bella's eyes widened with disbelief, her tongue jutted out through her teeth to lick her lips. 'Wow, you don't say, he's yummy with a capital Y.' She stretched out, crossing her legs at the ankles and placing her hands together on her stomach, interlinking her fingers. 'Mm mm, what I could do with a man like that,' she spoke, but I wasn't sure if she was still talking to me, or just out loud. 'No wonder we get the limo ride home, Miss Physio to the rich and famous.'

I slapped her thigh playfully. 'You have me at a disadvantage; I have no idea who he is really, apart from the medical records I received last week explaining his accident and subsequent injuries.' Shrugging my shoulders, I shook my head and looked at Bella, waiting for answers.

'You are untrue, where have you been, bloody Antarctica? Well let's put it this way,' she grinned at me, 'you won't be disappointed. Put that iPhone to good use and Google a picture of him.' It took me just a few minutes to do so.

Bella was fanning her face with her right hand and laughing at the expression on my face as I magnified the image on my phone of Nathan Blackmore. The picture showed a tall, dirty-blond haired, gorgeous man. He had, well, half had on his white bike leathers, the sleeves were tied around his waist. It revealed a naked, well muscled, lean, tanned, tattooed torso. But it was his face. He wore a cheeky lopsided grin and with oddly recognisable sparkling hazel eyes, the complete package seemed to give you the idea of a very bad boy.

'Mm, mm, mmmm!' left my lips. She was right I wasn't disappointed.

We settled again hardly speaking, but holding hands tightly, enjoying the excitement and the closeness of our friendship. We sat back just watching New York slide past the windows of the limo. The second bottle of champagne we found in the fridge went down slower than our first, and I relaxed into the comfort of our friendship and the leather upholstery of the limo, and started to doze.

# Chapter 3

'Frankie, Frankie, wake up,' I vaguely heard, but it was the sharp elbow I received from my so called best friend, straight to the middle of my ribs, that brought me back to the land of the living. 'When we have finished here, we are SO having a chat.'

'Finished where?' I replied, looking out of the limo window into a green park area. Gingerly I rubbed at my ribs.

Edwards opened the door and extended his hand to first help Bella and then me out. 'Miss Jones, Mr. Blackmore asked me to show you the accommodation available to you, in case you might want to use it.'

I glanced at Bella and shrugged my shoulders at her, 'Erm... OK.' My English politeness was obviously taking over. Because all I really wanted to do was to get to Bella's apartment in Hoboken.

Bella stood beside me in stunned silence; it was a day of firsts, as I don't think I had ever witnessed it before. I followed the gaze of her eyes to the magnificent building in front of us. 'You don't know where we are, do you,' she lowered her voice so only I could hear her, hopefully, 'the green area is Central Park and this is 5th Avenue,' she sounded awe struck. I sort of had an idea that this was possibly a good place to be living, but other than that the address went straight over my head.

We followed the very large frame of Edwards as he entered the foyer of the building. He stopped to have a quick conversation with the security guards and motioned us through to the lift furthest away from the entrance. 'This is the elevator we have to use, as it's the only one that goes straight up to the penthouse level,' he looked down at us expecting at least a modicum of understanding.

'The, where?' Bella almost screeched, grabbing me by the arm and gripping me so tightly I could feel her long finger nails through my coat. 'Bella' I whispered, trying to pretend that this happened to me every day. We almost danced into the lift.

Edwards just looked amused and glanced at us both. The lift rose quickly and stopped suddenly; we all disembarked into a large square marble hallway. I took in my surroundings, the cream marbled floor, a central arrangement of greenery and the four solid oak doors each placed next to a corner. We followed Edwards to the left and after he had swiped the key card, he held the door open wide for us to enter. 'I'll leave you to it ladies, have a good look around and meet me downstairs in the foyer when you are ready,' and with that the door closed behind him.

The room was enormous, with floor to ceiling windows overlooking New York; I stood still, taking the beautiful place in. The seating area was central to the room, to reach it you stepped down, leaving the dark hardwood floors behind and stepping onto a luscious, expensive, cream carpet. The cream settees were positioned in an L shape, pointing towards the corner window and the spectacular view of the park. The room was finished in tones of browns and creams, with the piece de resistance being a free-standing, open fireplace.

'WooooHoooo!' Bella ran quickly past me and jumped onto the nearest settee 'Will you just look at this place, Frankie.... Is this for real?' I couldn't help smiling when I saw the look of glee on her face. 'How big is it? Could we both stay here?' she waggled her eyebrows at me, a telltale trade mark of Bella's when she was excited. She used her left hand to sweep away the hair, that running and jumping had caused to fall onto her face.

Three doors led off the main room; upon further investigation we found a kitchen and two symmetrically huge bedrooms with en-suite bathrooms.

'Could we?' I questioned Bella, 'what about your apartment?'

'We could stay here for as long as your job lasts and then go back to mine afterwards, I mean it is closer to my job, which would be nice not having the commute for a while,' her convincing argument came out so quickly. The words almost tripping her up in her haste to get me to say yes.

Frowning, I pursed my lips together, thinking, 'Oh, bloody hell, why not?' She was in my arms almost immediately and together hugging, we jumped up and down. The doorbell sounded and then the door swung open. Edwards appeared in the doorway, almost filling the void with his frame, carrying my luggage 'Am I wrong?' he questioned, smiling at both of us.

'No,' I replied, smiling back at him, 'bring it in please.'

Edwards took Bella back to her apartment in Hoboken so she could get her stuff. I made an overdue call to my aunt and uncle back home, to put their minds at rest, and to tell them of mine and Bella's good fortune and new address.

*Strangely my aunt wasn't at all surprised, which was unusual as she normally questioned everything?*

Oh well never look a gift horse in the mouth.

After I had unpacked and showered, I sat down on a settee with a cup of tea. You can take a girl out of England, but not England out of the girl, I thought laughing to myself.

On the coffee table in front of me was an envelope, I hadn't noticed it before. The stationary was blue and expensive looking. Opening it, I read;

*Hi Frankie*

*No don't worry; there will be no additional music to accompany this. I am pleased you like the place enough to stay; I hope you and Bella will enjoy your time here.*
*The building is safe and I know you will be in good hands. It is ideal for your physio sessions with Nathan, as he will be in the next apartment to your left from sometime on Sunday.*
*If you need anything, please let me know.*
*Yours Alex*

*Christ, was I that predictable to Alex, I corrected myself Mr. Blackmore?*

I ran my fingertips slowly over the beautifully composed handwriting.

Getting up and going to the door, I glanced across the empty hallway; looking instinctively for the door mentioned in the letter. I heard the lift coming up and waited for Bella to arrive. Doing so, I caught an unmistakable masculine scent of a fresh, clean, ocean smell. I must be delusional; no, more than delusional... I really needed to get a grip. Pulling myself together, I waited for Bella.

We spent a further couple of hours settling in. Bella had so many clothes, it took an age to find them all a home, and some even encroached into my wardrobe. Finally, we sat down, in an exhausted heap, wearing our pyjamas. 'Sexy, huh?' I laughed.

'Oh, that's reminded me,' Bella stared at me, 'talking about sexy, care to share the interesting dream you had in the limo earlier?' Her blue eyes stared into mine, 'Good old Jabby again, I can't believe you haven't moved on, Frankie? Horny, much?' she laughed.

I shoved her over away from me and the take away pizza.

Sighing and chewing my bottom lip I began, 'All I have to do is close my eyes, Bella and he's back,' I told her about my embarrassment on the plane. She sat shaking her head at me in disbelief and amusement, stuffing an oversized slice of pizza into her daintily sized mouth.

'More now than ever before, you need a man!' I could always trust Bella to say it just how it was, whether I liked it or not. 'Well this maybe your first night in New York, and we are in with a pizza, but tomorrow you are so out with me! Let's see if we can create some new erotic memories, eh?' Her grin was positively catching; I knew she meant business.

I swallowed hard, in anticipation and dread.

## Chapter 4

The beads of sweat ran down my spine, literally racing each other. The music was so bloody loud that I could feel the vibrations inside my chest. My feet were on fire in my new ridiculously high, black, fuck me heels. Why the hell I had let Bella convince me to buy them, I didn't know. I shook my head and tutted, my mouth twitching in the corners with a smile.

I surveyed my surroundings in the second club Bella had got us into that night, resting the curve of my backside onto the only vacant bar stool I could find, and let out an 'Ahhh'.

My eyes were immediately drawn back to my best friend; she knew how to have a good time. She was currently strutting her stuff and gyrating all over her latest conquest, in the middle of the dance floor.

*Shit she was good.*

Her tight, short red dress attracted a lot of attention, but given the height of heels we had on, and our already tall stature, we were actually taller than most of the men here. This fact hadn't gone down well with a lot of the insecure Napoleon complex types. I was already picky in my choices, but we had narrowed the field even bloody further.

She was gorgeous, waist-length, blonde hair, with a figure any model would kill for, but with boobs! Why she ever wanted me as her wing woman, I would never understand, but would be forever grateful for. So much for erasing my Jabby thoughts, I was too tall to be approached by most men and was now receiving only the attention of the more drunk variety.

Turning to the bar, I awaited my turn. Holding up two fingers I gesticulated to the barman, 'Two Southern Comforts, doubles please, on the rocks, and two slippery nipples.'

'Sure thing.'

I felt every bit the tourist, as I listened to his American accent.

He placed the drinks down on the bar and took my cash. I was still having difficulty with the currency, all being the same colour. It reminded me of play money from when I was a child. I turned back around to search out Bella. When I caught her eye, I started waving frantically, nudging a group standing next to me.

'Sorry,' I said, shouting over the pulsating music, and smiled my apology.

But it was all slightly too late, as one of the guys in the group fell to the floor, letting go of the crutch that minutes before had been stabilising him. He looked up from the floor, but luckily laughed out loud, a full booming deep laugh. Thank God, either he's a happy drunk, or he has a sense of humour.

*Who the hell comes to a club on crutches?*

'OMG,' I said as I clutched my hand over my mouth. 'Can I get you another drink,' after seeing the empty glass in his left hand, and the sight of his obviously recently spilt beverage, down the front of his expensive, white dress-shirt.

'English, eh? You sure know how to make an entrance, lady.' He spoke whilst being helped up and onto my now vacated bar stool. 'I'll have a JD please, not any of your crappy shots,' thrusting the empty glass under my nose, and visibly wincing in pain.

Bella arrived just in time to watch me hand his newly bought drink over. Properly looking at him for the first time, face to face, God he was tall I thought, given my ridiculous heels, and the fact he was perched on a bar stool. What I saw in front of my eyes was breath taking. Shoulder-length, messy, dirty-blond hair and sparkling hazel eyes. He was wearing a day's worth of stubble. He smiled a slow sexy grin that lit up all of his face and produced a dimple either side of his mouth. 'Well hello, beautiful, or should I just call you chocolate drop? After seeing your gorgeous brown eyes,' he raised his left eyebrow at me in question.

I stared, with my mouth wide open, not saying a word, realising I had just met/ pushed over the subject of the picture from my iPhone, my new client, Nathan Blackmore.

A few of his group parted to allow a petite, dark-haired girl through. 'Oh Nate, baby, are you OK?... YOU NEED TO BE MORE CAREFUL!' she shouted after turning to face Bella and me, pointing a chipolata shaped finger at us.

'Whoa, hold on a minute, girl, get your facts straight,' shouted Bella fronting up to her, 'It was an accident... And you need to call off your Jack Russell,' she said reaching out and patting Nathan on the chest, her hand lingering much longer than needed.

'Candy, enough, go back and dance,' he expelled, glancing down at Bella's hand and the movement in her fingertips.

'Are you sure, Nate honey,' she drawled. I could feel my face puckering into a picture of distaste. My face was good at giving away my thoughts and was always getting me into trouble. 'Yeah go dance, Candy, if you know what's good for you,' shouted Bella. Candy turned back to the dance floor, after receiving a nodded silent permission from Nathan.

Nathan had interrupted my thoughts then, by roaring with laughter. 'Who let you two fighting English girls out tonight?'

'We don't need permission to be out, from anyone, unlike your stray dog,' Bella snapped back.

Nathan laughed, 'goddamn, I like you two, you say it like it is, and that is fucking refreshing.' He pushed the fingers of his left hand through his unruly hair. That act alone got Bella relooking at Nathan, she then turned to me and I raised my eyebrows, pulling together a tight-lipped smirk.

'Oh bloody hell; you're Nathan Blackmore, Aren't you?'

'And there it goes,' he replied. 'The refreshing truth just flew out the window, now you know who I am. So on that note, I bid you goodnight, blonde and sassy,' he said, nodding at Bella. 'Chocolate drop,' he turned to look at me. 'See ya around.'

I could feel myself biting into my lower lip, we watched him grab his crutches and slowly hobble away, to re-join his group of friends. We turned back towards the bar and savoured our drinks in silence. Not daring to turn around in case we were caught staring at the very hot Nathan Blackmore.

'Bloody hell, that's going to be embarrassing on Monday morning, isn't it?' Bella nodded at me, downing the residue of her Southern Comfort. 'Christ, way to go, Frankie, you just tipped your new, very wealthy client on his arse,' she exclaimed, bursting into laughter.

*Quite frankly I didn't know whether to laugh or cry.*

We had spent most of the day shopping and sightseeing. I was very suddenly aware of just how knackered I was. It must be the jet lag, or the stress, or probably my consumption of alcohol.

'Do you mind if we call it a night, Bella?'

'Hell, yes, it's just got interesting.' She took a good look at me, 'Oh OK, I can see you've had it, let's go home... There's always next weekend,' she said and hugged me close.

When we exited the club, I was so pleased to find Edwards waiting for us at the curb. We'd had too much alcohol to question how he knew where we were. Leaning back into the comfortable seats, I swore I could smell Jabby's cologne.

# Chapter 5

I held my mug of tea with one hand, and stretched out my other palm; I flattened it on the freezing cold glass and felt an involuntary shiver run over me. Standing staring out from our penthouse apartment was a novelty for me. I loved watching the New York day going past in front of my eyes. It was Monday morning and I had twenty minutes until my first proper appointment with Nathan, frankly, I was dreading the embarrassment of it.

I stared out of the window and lost myself in thoughts of yesterday. We had a lazy start to the day and then had explored our surroundings. Just so I could get my bearings. Now knowing how New York smelt and sounded, I loved it. I understood fully why Bella wanted to be here more than anywhere else, and I realised that it wasn't just because of her job. But the highlight of Sunday had to be the arrival of a humungous bouquet of flowers, for me! I looked over at them again. They rested on, and took all the space of the coffee table, blue and lilac roses. Picking up the card from them, I started to read it again.

Hi Frankie
Just a small gift to celebrate your new job!
We are really pleased you are here. Hope tomorrow goes well, if not, let me know
And I'll kick my little brother's ass!
Yours Alex

Well that had shocked me; I thought with a laugh. I had thought all along that Mr. Blackmore must be a father or maybe grandfather. Big brother... Interesting?

For the first time, I had replied to Alex.

*Thank you so much for the gorgeous flowers, roses are my favourite!*

*How did you know? I'm looking forward to starting tomorrow.*

*Thank you for the opportunity*

*Frankie Jones*

My phone had pinged back with an immediate response.

*You are more than welcome! Don't let Nathan give you any trouble. He can be a cocky little arsehole at times*
*Speak soon*
*Yours Alex*

Bella and I had started our Monday morning with a freezing cold run around Central Park; where else indeed? I thought, hugging myself with excitement and rubbing my hands up and down my almost bare triceps. We had shared fresh bagels for breakfast, another NYC moment, and then Bella had left for work. 'It'll be fine,' she had shouted over her shoulder, 'you're going to charm the pants off him,' she grinned, 'and if you don't, I sure the hell will.' With a well-aimed shot, I had thrown a cushion at her, her smirking face and the closing door.

Ok, time to put on my big girl pants. I left our apartment, taking myself off to the left and pressed the doorbell. I waited a few seconds, which seemed so, so much longer.

'Yep, coming!... Man on crutches, going as fast as he can.'

The door opened and my gaze drifted upwards to take in the bare chested sight of Nathan. And boy what a delicious sight he was. *Christ does the man ever wear clothes?* He leant casually on the doorframe using his left forearm. His right leg was up away from the floor and he had one crutch embedded into his right armpit. His numerous tattoos covered the majority of his upper body. It took me a few seconds to take in the fact he was only wearing antique leather wrist cuffs and old grey sweat shorts. God help me they hung so low I could make out the start of a very well defined V. I took in a deep breath and forced my gaze into his sparkling, very amused eyes. He knew exactly where I had been gazing, so hungrily.

*Bastard!*

'Unbelievable, if it isn't one of the fighting English girls,' he swung his body out of the way and moved his left arm with an open hand, indicating that I should enter. I could see the humour creasing his face, so much for not being recognised.

'So, chocolate drop, can I get you a coffee?'

'Can I have a glass of water please; hmm... Where would you like me to put my mat? Is the physio table set up somewhere?' I had replied, glancing around the apartment's main living space, but not finding what I was looking for. Trying to mask my embarrassment, with my professionalism and galloping speech.

Nathan's apartment seemed to be a mirror image of ours, only larger. Instead of a corner view of Central Park, the floor to ceiling windows framed it like a painting. The colour scheme wasn't the same as our browns and creams, it was blacks, greys and chrome. It screamed masculinity. Various black and white photos festooned the sides and walls. Taking a better look, I realised they were mainly of Nathan, on his motorbike, holding and kissing cups, snowboarding, bungee jumping, surfing and various other extreme sports. It was a wonder I hadn't been called in before. He was quite obviously the ultimate adrenalin junkie. One photo caught my attention, my eyes kept lingering on it, I don't know why, perhaps because the three men in it were all grinning. The photo showed the men somewhere up high in the mountains, in ski attire. It was Nathan, I had squinted closer, and another of the men looked like he could be his twin brother? The final guy stood in between them both, with his arms around their shoulders. He was slightly taller with dark hair and he wore ski goggles.

'Seen enough?' He drawled suddenly from directly behind me. For someone on a crutch, he could sure move around quietly. I broke my glance away from the photo.

'Sorry, always being told how nosy I am,' I grimaced at him. 'I have read your notes and...'

'Whoa, we need to sit and talk first... all work no play is definitely not what I goddamn live for,' he said shaking his head. Nathan plonked himself down on the black leather settee, and he dropped his crutch on the floor in front of his feet. Carefully he repositioned his right leg on the table in front of him. The skin was pink and you could see the long scar, from ankle to knee. It showed where he had recently been operated on, after his accident. The leg scar didn't hold my attention for long though, slowly, all too slowly I had let my gaze wander up his long limbs and over his comfortable, well-worn, grey shorts. I found myself involuntarily licking my lips as I took in a well-defined V and the smattering of fine hair on his abs, just below his navel, leading to well, I knew where...

The chuckle deep in his throat made my eyes shoot up to his suddenly. My face burned with embarrassment. He knew exactly what I had been looking at.... again. He patted the settee wanting me to sit.

*Christ what the hell was wrong with me?* I needed to stop gawping at the client.

'Hey, chocolate drop, I love a girl that can still blush... another thing I find very refreshing. Anyway, tell me a bit about you and I will tell you some stuff about me.' He looked back up at me with his penetrating stare and ran his left hand through his unruly, just fucked looking hair.

Sitting down on the very edge of the leather settee and picking up my bottle of water, I sipped at it. I took a deep breath, I hated talking about myself.

*I wondered where to start?*

What could I possibly tell him, that he would find remotely interesting, Mr. Hot motorbike, sex on legs/crutch, who from the look of the photos on the wall, had been everywhere and done everything and got the T-shirts to prove it (although he obviously didn't wear them). I hooked my hair behind both of my ears and sighed.

'Well until recently I have been working, looking after injured soldiers...'

'Yeah, Alex told me,' he nodded 'we have a lot of respect in our family for servicemen and women, but what about you?... who is Frankie Jones? And what makes her tick?' I looked at him sitting comfortably; both arms now up, and out along the top of the back of the settee. The position showed off his well-defined pecs. My God, he truly was magnificent. Was he flirting with me? I was so mousey in comparison, it wasn't possible.

*Maybe he was this interested in everybody?*

Or maybe just the women he came in to contact with. Or maybe he was just winding me up, just enough to make me blush and feel very uncomfortable. I looked at him again, but no, he really genuinely appeared to be interested in me!

'Well I'm 24, come from a small town on the South coast of England, lived at home with my aunt and uncle,' I was hardly drawing breath now and continued on my never ending path of boringness, but somehow I couldn't rein it in. 'I have a degree; my favourite animals are dogs.'

A loud laugh suddenly exploded from Nathan and his whole body convulsed forward, emphasizing his well defined chest and stomach muscles.

'You are so cute! Where the hell did he find you, you sound like you're being interviewed for Miss World.' I started laughing too, he was right, and what the hell was I rambling on about?

'Sorry, I get a bit tongue tied, I am not so comfortable talking about me,' my face contorted into a grimace.

'No problem, chocolate drop, my turn. I ride motorbikes for a living, I am 28 years old, and I am one of four. I have two brothers and a sister. I dropped out of high school much to the disgust of my mother, but then she's disgusted at everything I do,' he nodded again 'so it's not a surprise. I also love dogs.' He stopped then, looked at me and we both laughed. Ok he was trying to make me feel comfortable, and I appreciated it, I did feel more relaxed now.

'My mother despises me, too; I don't meet her never ending requirements as a daughter, so we have that in common.' Nathan stopped smiling and pondered in thought. 'Long story?' he questioned, and I nodded in response and clasped my hands together in my lap.

We chatted for a while, and I realised the last time I felt like this with a guy, was talking to JJ. I had unknowingly curled my legs underneath me, relaxing into the expensive, very soft leather that moulded itself to me. A feeling of melancholy gently slipped over me.

'OK, if you show me where the table is perhaps we can get started,' I changed the subject suddenly, trying to shake the feeling away, but glancing at Nathan I could tell he had noticed my change in mood. Gratefully I realised he wasn't going to ask why. So sex on legs was a sensitive guy as well, this must be too good to be true.

'It's in the spare bedroom,' he raised his left eyebrow at me.

'Oh OK,' I blushed.

'And there it is again,' Nathan laughed, looking pleased with himself, 'you're so cute when you blush, don't worry I won't molest you, well not unless you ask me to,' he smiled, showing me a beautiful lopsided grin and dimples.

Grabbing his crutch from the floor and pulling himself up onto it, he moved with well practised ease, to show me the way to the spare bedroom. Pausing to grab a remote from a side table he pressed a few buttons and music started to play. I recognised it instantly as a Nickelback track, OK now we had a similar taste in music, too. I couldn't wait to see Bella later and tell her all about Nathan, I almost skipped into the bedroom behind him.

We started working through the various exercises I already had planned for him. Feeling really pleased I had done my homework previously. The time passed quickly and he worked hard with me. A feeling of satisfaction travelled through me.

'If you carry on working this hard, we'll have you up and about in no time.'

'I will be ready for the start of next season,' he didn't ask a question; it was stated to me as a fact.

'When is that?'

'February, Phillip Island in Australia,' came the reply.

'OK, we'll see what we can do.'

'OH-I-WILL-BE-BACK-ON-MY-BIKE... whether this fucking thing is alright or not.' This was the first time I had even seen the remotest sign of irritation from Nathan and he slapped his right thigh in disgust.

I passed over the exercise plan to him, 'Well I will do my part of the deal and you can do yours, at least twice before tomorrow morning, when I'll be back,' pushing my index finger into his chest.

'Hmm, I love a woman in charge,' he muttered whilst getting off the physio table and once again throwing a wicked grin my way. I couldn't help but smile back.

I made my way towards the door. Freezing as I got there because it suddenly swung open and walking in wearing an oh too short skirt, a top that literally just held in her noticeably fake boobs and the tallest fuck-me heels I had ever seen, was the Jack Russell, Candy. Surprisingly she still looked like an overgrown child, even wearing the prostitute's clothing.

'Nate honey, oh there you are.' I watched as she sashayed herself over to him, completely ignoring me and dropping her various shopping bags on the way. She attached herself literally to every curve of his body. Surprised by the fact he could still balance, on his one crutch with her weight hanging off of him, I quickly passed him crutch number two.

I knew as he looked at me my face had, as always, portrayed to Nathan exactly what I was thinking. She really was everything I hated in a woman. She was everything I wasn't and would never lower myself to be. Putting my sneer away and uncurling my flared nostrils, I shouted a goodbye from the door.

'See ya, chocolate drop,' rolled off his tongue. And just before the door closed behind me I heard, 'Right babe, we got some exercises to do,' looking back I was just in time to see her sucking his face enthusiastically, he still had his eyes open... the bastard looked straight into my eyes and winked at me!

The blush came, but too late for him to witness, thank God. The door had slammed shut.

# Chapter 6

My bath water was wonderful; I slipped under until the frothy bubbles came up over my shoulders. A deep appreciative sigh left my lips and I closed my eyes. I had music playing in the background. My taste in music was eclectic. It always expressed everything I hadn't the words to do.

This afternoon I had been shopping, Bella would be mortified that she hadn't been with me. But it was an afternoon well spent. I couldn't believe the amount of free time this new position was going to offer me. Edwards had agreed to drive me to a second hand store, much to his disgust and a rather animated phone call to, I presume, Alex. He had tried to convince me that I could shop elsewhere and charge it to Blackmore Industries, anything we needed could be charged.

I had stuck to my guns and just said I wanted a few bits to make the apartment feel like home and they didn't need to be expensive. We had left the second hand place with a few cushions, some dried flowers and a canvas depicting a heart made of sticks laid out on an empty beach, it reminded me of home and was nothing fancy, but I loved it, I knew Bella would too.

Once I had placed the few bits around the apartment, I had decided to make an English dinner of beef stew and dumplings, ready for Bella's return from work. It was cold out and I thought it was appropriate.

I had run a deep bath and turned on my music. After stripping off I lay in the biggest bath I had ever seen and luxuriated in the bubbles, awaiting her return. A ping on my phone snapped me out of my thoughts and I dried one hand haphazardly on the nearby Egyptian cotton, raspberry coloured towel.

Grabbing my phone, I opened the text message. My right hand quickly flew to my mouth to suppress a laugh. In front of my eyes a picture opened of a very dishevelled looking Candy, it sure looked like she was leaving in a hurry and Bella had snapped her coming out of the penthouse lift, God knows how? Underneath the picture she had written.

JACK RUSSELL ALERT!!!!!

Laughing out loud I wondered why she was leaving so hurriedly. Just then my phone pinged again.


*Hi Frankie*

*I have just spoken to Nathan. He tells me the first appointment went well. I hope you left him in enough pain today, he will rethink wanting to get back on his bike? Ha-ha. Sorry about his choice of companion today. I asked him to refrain from sharing these with you. But that's little brothers for you!*

*I do hope you enjoyed your shopping trip? Please remember anything you need I will be only too happy to provide for you, we have accounts at many of the stores in New York.*

*Have a nice evening.......unfortunately my evening will be spent in a conference call to Japan (but that's business for you)*

*Speak soon*

*Yours Alex*

*CEO Blackmore Industries*


*Hi Alex*

*The first appt went well and I left Nathan with exercises to do before I return tomorrow. I think he had other exercises in mind though! Lol.*

*He was fairly worn out and achy when I left but not enough I don't think to put him off his motorbike. Don't worry about his companion we have met before and I am not easily squeamish.*

*It was really kind of you to offer to buy my shopping, but I am paid enough already!*

*Hope your call is short. Have a nice evening*

*Frankie*

I pressed send, just as I heard Bella shout out an arriving hello. Calling back,

I had let her know where I was. I looked at the sent text again, shaking my head.

What on earth had come over me to send such a casual reply to my employer? There must be something narcotic in these bubbles. How would he take my reply? I didn't have to worry for long.

*Well she certainly makes me squeamish!*

*I didn't realise you had the misfortune to have met before? Sounds like a story you will have to tell me at a later date.*

*Do try to hurt him more tomorrow will you? I could do with the help at the family business.......only joking, he would be useless. I'm hoping the call is short too.*

*Yours Alex*

*CEO Blackmore Industries*

Relief washed over me, he seemed quite relaxed about it. I found myself wondering about him. I suppose he probably wasn't too much older than Nathan. My thoughts were interrupted by Bella bouncing into my bathroom.

'God, she looked awful, did you get the text I sent to you. I suppose her being here today means you didn't manage to seduce the lovely Nathan?'

'No, although it's got to be said I wish I could have, he really seems like the full package.' I proceeded to tell her about how comfortable he had made me feel, our similar taste in music. But I saved the wonderfully low-slung, grey shorts until last.

'Here.' I reached out to take the very large glass of wine she was passing my way. Listening to her as she started to sing along with Pink's *U and UR hand*, I had playing.

'Can I smell beef stew? I do hope I wasn't imagining it. I have had a shit day at work, only made better by the fact I was coming home to you. Beef stew would erase the bloody day completely,' she expelled a deep sigh, kicked off her heels and sank down onto the raspberry coloured, floral armchair, placed in the corner of my bathroom.

'So tell me, do you fancy the lovely Nathan? If you do, we so need a plan... I know how long it's been since Luke.'

'I don't know Bella, he's gorgeous, but I'm not like you... as you know I have only ever been with Luke and I don't find this whole relationship thing very easy at all.'

'Bloody hell! That's the problem right there,' she sat up quick, as if to emphasise what she was saying, 'who was talking about a relationship, Frankie. You just need to be screwed by a man who knows what he's doing. Unlike the excuse for a man, Puke.'

Laughing at her nickname for Luke, I started to fidget in the bath, realising that the temperature of the water was dropping, or was it because the temperature of my body had risen with the embarrassment of being told I needed to be screwed? Bella passed me my bathrobe, leant down and retrieved her heels, 'How long until dinner?'

'Oh give me fifteen minutes,' I answered.

I spent ten minutes drying and creaming my body. My long hair, I brushed through and left to dry naturally. It would mean it would be wavy, but I could tame it tomorrow before I went to Nathan's next appointment. I quickly put on my very comfortable fleecy PJs. Walking to the kitchen, humming and feeling the under floor heating beneath my bare feet. I proceeded to fill two big bowls of stew; cut up some crusty bread and took my offerings out to the sitting area. 'Here you go,' I took a look around the room unable to find Bella. Sitting down I picked up the TV remote and switched it on, looking for a chick flick to share. Filling my mouth with the delicious goodness and smacking my lips together for effect, I suddenly heard a deep baritone voice behind me.

'Mmmm... smells damn good, do you have another bowl you could share with your poor neighbour?' the resonating voice came from behind me.

I closed my eyes instinctively. 'I'm not really dressed for company.'

'Get over yourself!' shouted Bella.

'Help the guy out, his overbearing brother got rid of the very lovely Candy today,' well that came out subtly sarcastic, but that thankfully only I would recognise, 'and she was going to make him dinner, too. As she was got rid of, so not to embarrass you, I think we owe him some English stew.'

I checked out the masculine presence in the room, he was wearing old, faded jeans and an even older T-shirt, stretched out magnificently across his chest, but surprisingly nothing on his feet.

'Of course, I'll get you some, sorry I was just a bit concerned about my rather scruffy attire,' I smiled at him then, and slowly he hobbled around to sit down.

'Ignore her, Nathan, what she really means is, she doesn't want you to see her in what she normally wears to bed.' I narrowed my eyes at Bella as she sat down next to Nathan and laughed, openly checking out the magnificent specimen that was Nathan Blackmore.

'But, Bella, I sleep naked,' I retorted, thinking two could play at this game.

'Ladies, lovely as the conversation is, I am a red blooded male and I really need... some food, pretty please. Now what are we watching tonight then?' Shaking my head, I left for the kitchen to fill another bowl, for the rather gorgeous male sitting in my new apartment in New York.

*I should pinch myself.*

The three of us spent a very companionable evening, watching movies, eating my stew, sharing a few beers and laughing. I couldn't remember having such a relaxed time with a male, except for years ago with JJ. Nathan had the most infectious laugh and he loved to mimic people. I was beginning to feel very at home.

'I know you have just fed and watered me, and shared the best film I have ever seen,' he raised his eyebrows in disgust. 'But I have to ask, what the fuck is with those hideous dried things that sort of resemble dead grass?'

Bella's beer bottle jerked away from her lips and she laughed, spraying some of her mouthful over Nathan. 'I was just thinking the same, how old are you, Frankie? You obviously cannot be trusted to shop by yourself.' Feeling chastised I glanced at my arrangement of second-hand, dried flowers, bought earlier that day. Although it went against every grain in my body I burst out laughing with them. They were right it was vile. I probably had only bought them to prove a point to Alex about second hand thrift; thank God he hadn't laid eyes on them.

'And why the fuck are you women always covering me in alcohol?' Nathan flicked some of the sprayed droplets back at Bella and she giggled shamelessly. It was very obvious she was starting to see some of his attraction.

45

Leaving Bella and Nathan deep in conversation, I took the dirty dishes to the kitchen. I started loading them into the dishwasher. This should be hilarious, having never used one in my life. It can't be that hard. After moving the dishes around several times, I finally managed to turn the bloody thing on, promising myself to wash up in future. Raising myself up I caught sight of my iPhone, which I retrieved from the kitchen worktop, remembering hearing an earlier ping.

*Unfortunately, the business call was anything other than short.*

*I hope your evening was fun. Dinner smelt great from the hallway.*

*Don't let my baby brother take advantage of you both........make him go home soon!*

*Yours Alex*

*CEO Blackmore Industries*

I chuckled to myself; oh God was this his way of letting me know I had stunk out the whole of the penthouse floor?

*Sorry Alex! About your long call and the stench in the hall!*

*Frankie*

Stupidly, I hadn't thought Alex might also live here. Another ping sounded an incoming message; hastily I pressed what I needed to read the reply.

*Frankie*

*I never said it stank, did I?*

*I love home cooked food, even if it is English!!!!! Ha-ha*

*Remember to Make Nathan go soon and please inflict lots of pain on him tomorrow.*

*Yours Alex*

*CEO Blackmore Industries*

Walking back into the living area, I took in the beautiful open fire and the lights of the city beyond. We had no curtains for the windows.

*Who needs to shut anything out from this high up?*

It was clear that my very presence was interrupting the now flowing conversation between two very animated people. Somehow Bella's legs were now thrown over Nathan's lap. His hand was running up and down very gently on her shin bone. *Mmmm... interesting.* I raised my eyes questioning her, sniggering inside. She smiled shyly back, shrugging her shoulders.

*Shyly?*

'Your brother is intent on trying to get me to inflict pain on you,' I said showing them my iPhone, jiggling it from side to side in my hand, 'and he also wants you to go home soon.' Nathan looked at my smirk.

'Fucking dominant control freak,' he ran a hand through his always just fucked looking hair. 'He can never just butt the hell out, big brothers who'd have em... eh?'

Bella sat up quick, realising what Nathan had just uttered. I shook my head at her, she couldn't protect me from everything and he wasn't to know.

'So Alex lives here, too?'

'Yeah, symmetrically to my apartment,' he waved his hand behind his head in the right direction. 'I assumed you would know that, as he employed you? Not that he is here that much, always working, you know the type. Thinks he damn well knows everything, overprotective and overbearing. He spends his life trying to father the rest of us... which is a fucking joke as he is not even two years older than me.'

God I thought, having imagined an older family member in the first place. Now that brought his age down to what? Thirtyish?

'Well I had better do as I am told; can someone please pass my crutches? I left them leaning on the back of the couch.'

'Since when do you obey orders? You really don't seem the type,' Bella jumped up, looking more flustered than I thought I had ever seen her. I watched her pass Nathan the crutches and I swear if you could visibly see the electrical current called chemistry, it was right there between the two of them, almost using the crutch as a conductor, arcing uncontrollably.

'You're right, sassy, I don't normally take orders from anyone, I do however like to give them.' Nathan had literally moved himself into the very oxygen she breathed. I felt like a voyeur. His voice had dropped an octave, 'But on this one and only fucking occasion, I have to concede he is probably right,' he put out his left hand and with his index finger and thumb lifted her chin. He gently kissed her on the tip of her nose. Bella stood transfixed to the spot, her face redder than when we had scarlet fever.

Nathan moved over to me. 'Thanks for the excellent dinner and company, chocolate drop; I'll be seeing you tomorrow.' I opened our door for him to exit, and he bent to kiss me on the cheek. Just like JJ would have done.

'See ya.'

I closed the door behind him, and I turned my gaze to Bella. I placed my hands on my hips. I was just about to start questioning her, when I heard talking on the other side of our front door. Being ever nosy and realising that I couldn't reopen the door now. I flung myself to the spy hole. Just in time to see Nathan hobbling, not towards his own door, but towards the door in the diagonal corner to ours. He was laughing loudly. Staring hard at the open door, I saw the largest hand I was sure I had ever seen, holding it open for him. Taking a further look I could see on the little finger, a signet ring. It held a green gem stone and looked like dirty silver, possibly titanium. Staring harder at the hand, I decided it had to be titanium; the hand was too masculine for anything else. I peeped until the hand and Nathan disappeared.

'What are you doing?' Bella made me jump back away from the door like a naughty child.

'Oh no, we are not going there after the little show I have just witnessed. What were you doing, lady?' I remembered to place my hands to my hips but my face broke into a huge grin. 'You looked like you were going to spontaneously combust, when the ever so lovely Nathan kissed your nose.'

'I am so sorry, Frankie, I know you like him and I would never shit on my own doorstep, but I couldn't help myself... it was like being reeled in.' Her blue eyes started to fill up. I could see she was struggling and she was wearing her guilty look. Not a look I had seen too often, as Bella rarely felt guilt about anything. She was a live and let live sort of girl.

'Bella it's OK.' I gathered her into a bear hug. 'It's not a problem, he reminds me of JJ, and we interact like siblings. I realised that today. So however wonderfully delicious he is and he is deeliiiicious,' I said emphasizing the vowels, 'I think on that, we and all the rest of the female population, 100% agree. He isn't for me; you know?' I sat back down and pulled her down with me.

'Thank God,' she sighed. 'I don't want us to fall out over a bloke, even if he is delicious with just fucked hair,' she closed her eyes and lay back on the settee blowing air through her lips.

'Yeah, right I've noticed that on occasion,' clutching a cushion to my chest 'and he keeps running his hand through it, too.' We looked at each other and burst into laughter.

'Why did you stare out of the spy hole? What caught your attention?'

'Oh I was looking at a hand.'

'What?' She screeched, throwing a hand to my forehead and pretending to take my temperature.

'A hand holding open the door for Nathan, I think it had to be Alex, you know my employer. But I couldn't see more than the hand. It was a nice hand though.' I think I sighed after that statement.

'Do you know; I think you may have jet lag or the dishwasher door dropped open onto your head earlier? A nice hand eh... I stand by my earlier diagnosis of, horny much?' she laughed at my discomfort.

'On the note of horny, can you do me a favour and not shag Nathan, then drop him from a high place on his balls. Whilst I am his physio, it might not go down too well with my boss.' I referred to the way Bella treated all the men in her life and pulled my face into a grimace.

'Yeah sure, anything for you bestie.'

The next couple of weeks flew by. We worked by day and spent some of our evenings with Nathan, who had become a part of the fixtures and furnishings, especially it seemed, when he was hungry. His leg was very slowly starting to show signs of increased strength. Some of the evenings Bella spent with us, other times she went out on dates. Much it seemed to Nathan's disgust.

I was receiving lots of texts from Alex, strangely enough 3 to 4 times a day and I looked forward to them arriving. We had a similar sense of humour. The trouble was I was sure if I went to see someone about this, I would be told I was mentally unstable. I was transfixed on my one Jabby memory, texts from a bloke I had never met and a very large hand wearing a titanium signet ring. If this hadn't had been me I was talking about, I would be advising the other person that they needed to get out more. This was precisely why I stopped sharing all of my thoughts with Bella. Then I didn't have to hear the words out loud.

*Stop thinking Frankie and get back to your book.*

This was another thing I didn't let Bella see too often, me immersed in a love story. With my latest BBF, as Bella would call them.

"Frankie, books are not real life, men in them do not exist in reality." I could hear her saying it like she was in the room with me.

*Hey, I have had enough bloody reality to last a lifetime; my books consumed me and took me to a better place.*

My phone sprung to life and snapped me out of my thoughts.

*Hi Chocolate drop*

*Are you at home?*
*I have an idea and need to speak to you*


*Of course, come over*

I stood up and made my way to the door, I knew it would take Nathan longer to reach me, so I propped the door ajar and went to the kitchen to put the kettle on. Keeping our doors open for each other was becoming quite a habit. The kettle had sprung to life with a low rumble; he wouldn't want tea, so I fumbled around in the fridge for something else.

'Hey,' I heard from behind me.

Glancing up from my crouched position, from behind the fridge door, 'Hi, you OK?' I noticed that his right leg was now gingerly resting on the floor. *Good progress.*

'Yeah, I just wanted to run something past you, you're English right?'

Laughing I looked at him quizzically.

'Yes, I believe so, last time I checked my passport,' I said slowly.

'You know what I goddamn mean, I've been thinking.'

Clutching my hand to my heart, I pretended to stumble backwards, smirking.

'Stop teasing and listen, please. Or I'll change my mind and leave,' exasperation hit his face.

'Sorry, too much time on my hands,' I lifted my hands up and showed him the juice I had retrieved for him and my otherwise empty surrendering hands. 'Please go on, I promise not to take the piss anymore.'

'Well this weekend my brother Alex, is playing rugby at a local club, you like rugby don't you, or are you one of those silly females that prefer soccer with supposed men falling down crying all the time?' he ran a hand through his hair, I don't know why he did it constantly. His hair would never be neat and tidy; it had a mind of its own and sprang up in the most peculiar places.

'I love rugby, and funny you should mention it, but I hate our country's national game, for the exact reason you described.'

'Good, I thought that perhaps you and Bella would like to come with me to watch the match. After they usually go out for a few beers and see where the evening takes us, what do you think? It's always a good laugh.'

We started to make our way back to the settees. I grasped my mug in two hands and blew on the top of the liquid, trying to make the tea cool enough to sip at.

'Sounds like a plan to me, I will just have to check with Bella, I'm sure she will be OK with it. I will sell it as a chance to meet some gorgeous men, that'll work,' I added smiling.

Nathan's eyes shot straight up to mine. 'Some of them are already attached. I don't want her throwing herself at them.'

'I know, but you know what she's like, she likes a bit of harmless fun.'

'Yeah I know what she's like,' I heard him almost whisper and I watched him run both hands through his hair in exasperation?

I didn't have time to question Nathan as my phone went off again.

*Afternoon Frankie*

*How did Nathan's physio go today?*

*Is your book going well?*

*I will be away a couple of days this week, with work. Any problems please make Edwards aware and he'll get hold of me.*

*I will try to keep in touch with you, as you lighten my day and my days always need lightening if you know what I mean.*

*Yours Alex*

*CEO Blackmore industries*

*Hi Alex*

*Yes, the physio went well and I caused Nathan much pain. But no seriously I can see progress which is good. Not as much as he would like yet, and I can see it sometimes makes him grumpy, but any progress this early is a good sign.*

*The book's great, I can't believe you remembered I was reading.*

*Hope you have a good trip wherever you are going. It would be lovely if you could keep in touch, just in case I need to talk to you about Nathan and I enjoy having a laugh with you too.*

*Frankie*

*I remember lots about you!*

*Talk later, heading into a meeting now*

*X*

*CEO Blackmore industries*

*He remembers lots about me? Interesting.* I turned my attention back to a stroppy looking Nathan.

'Sorry, just updating your brother. Telling him how hard you are working etc.'

'No you're good, I need a good evening out... this fucking leg of mine is getting me down,' he scrubbed at his face with both palms.

'You're too hard on yourself, we will get there, I promise.'

'Yeah.'

I looked at the very handsome but dejected face of Nathan. The hazel eyes didn't look as twinkly as normal and his posture showed he was quite obviously down.

'How about we get out of here? I don't know, take me somewhere touristy.'

He thought for a moment, running some ideas through his mind. He pulled at his chin, with all the fingers on his left hand. A slow smile broke out.

'Got it, is Edwards around to drive us? It's not far but with this leg we will need a lift.'

I texted Edwards, to check.

One hour later we were in a beautiful and very touristy horse-drawn carriage going around Central Park, heavily wrapped up against the strong November wind. A Scottish tartan rug spread over our legs. The air was fresh and bracing and just what we both needed. Nathan lifted his arm and cuddled me to him, it was comfortable, and once again he reminded me of JJ.

'I am a great fan of yours, you know, chocolate drop.' I felt his eyes burning into my cheekbone. He squeezed me to him closer, as if to show me. 'I sense a troubled background... ya know, when you've lived through one it's easy to recognise?'

I lifted my head slightly away from his comfortable shoulder. 'Who are you and what the hell have you done with the real Nathan Blackmore? You know player and bachelor extraordinaire. Doesn't take life too seriously, always a new girl on his arm.'

'I do have another side you know,' he exclaimed defensively, smiling his best panty dropping grin, poking at my ribs under the blanket with a finger from his spare hand. 'OK I will quit with the serious shit, just wanted to let you know I am always here to listen, since I have nothing better to do... until this fucking thing works properly again,' he had shot a quick glance to his leg.

'Don't worry, I will have a chat with Alex about allowing you your companions back in, I think the lack of sex is seriously damaging your health, and ageing you before your time.'

He laughed out loud at this; it was really pleasing to feel the air of depression lifting away. Our blossoming friendship definitely wasn't ready for my emotional baggage.

'There is no need for remorse... I'm still getting some ya know.' The left eyebrow lifted and the dimples came out to play, in all their glorious splendour. I slapped his arm and shook my head, almost squealing, 'TMI, Nathan.'

'Chat with my brother, eh? Bella has told me about this fucking daily occurrence, you do know he is a boring old workaholic, don't you?'

Luckily the atmosphere had changed, I could sense that now his mood had lifted, the teasing and joking was going to be all on me. It seemed a small price to pay.

It became an almost daily occurrence that after my breakfast, I would take a run around Central Park. Today was no different. I loved to have the space and quiet to think in. I loved looking up at the colours in the trees, they were so gorgeous. They almost seemed to be changing before my eyes. It did remind me of home and the autumnal season that I had left behind. Surprisingly enough, I felt no homesickness at all.

I made a point of phoning Aunty Jean at least every few days. Now there was only me, I appreciated how important it would be to her to have this regular contact. She seemed fine, although I could tell by the occasional crack in her voice, she was missing me. I tried to put myself in her shoes. Once, all four of us had been tightly packed into the small terrace. Now there was just her and Uncle Robert.

I started to make the turn back towards home. If I squinted, I could just make out the limo and the tall well built figure of Edwards, who seemed to be outside waiting. Then suddenly coming out of the large and architecturally, beautifully built building, appeared a large, dark haired male figure. He was very determinedly eating up the distance between himself and the car with large dogged strides. I stopped across the road, trying to get a better perspective and half heartedly began to stretch out. All the while I stared through the morning congestion of taxis, cars and buses. That must be Alex. I watched the well-built figure get into the limo and Edwards pull away from the kerb. All the while my gaze refused to leave the vehicle and it still declined, until it had completely disappeared from view.

# Chapter 8

I took a long shower in the biggest shower I had ever seen, part of my en-suite bathroom. It had two large shower heads and a built in bench seat along the opposite wall. I spent a long time lathering up my body in my favourite body wash, orange blossom. After rinsing out my hair again and shaving everywhere, I was just beginning to feel human again, my muscles only aching slightly now. Stepping out from the shower, I dried myself off and covered my body in the matching moisturiser. I inhaled deeply, loving the fresh citrus smell.

I heard the familiar ping and vibration of my iPhone.

*Chocolate drop*

*Alex has left on business. Unfortunately, as he is not here I need to go and sort out some shit at home. So I will have to take a rain check on my physio this morning. Can we make the appointment this afternoon instead? My latest x-rays have arrived back and I was hoping we could take a look together.*

*I should be back by 2pm, is that OK?*

*Nathan*

*That's fine Nathan*
*Knock on my door when you return*
*Where is home?*

*Yep will do.*

*Home is anywhere I am racing, or here at the apartment. It's only a figure of speech when I say home and am talking about my Mother's house.*

*She lives out in The Hamptons.*

*See ya.*

*We were obviously very much the same then.*

I hadn't seen Bella much in the last few days and had yet to talk to her about going out on Saturday. Quickly I sent her a text asking if we could meet for an early lunch and take advantage of the situation. We arranged to meet in a little cafe just along from her place of work.

I dressed in a good pair of jeans, my brown, knee length boots and a cream, eyelash jumper. I dried my long hair and put it up in a messy twist. I never wore much make-up and just applied my usual mascara and lip gloss.

We had been like ships passing in the night for the last week and I was dying to see my best friend. Her work just seemed to be getting in the way.

'Hey, gorgeous girl,' came a shout from the back of the cafe, 'over here.'

Waving back, I started to make my way through the very busy snack bar. One hug later and I sat down beside her on the bench, instead of the empty chair opposite her.

'Nosy, much?'

'You know me; always want to face the world for a bit of people watching.'

The hustle and bustle of people, shouting and laughing and waiters spinning around in the space of a fifty pence piece was exhausting, but uplifting to watch. It made me feel alive.

'Sorry I have been so busy with work, Frankie. It wasn't what I intended for your first few weeks here, really it wasn't.'

'No problem, Bella.' I said as I grasped her hand in mine, 'I'm sure it can't be helped, Nathan has been really good company.

Yesterday we spent the afternoon on a horse drawn carriage, and as you know he is never far away when there's a home cooked meal going.'

'Ermm... OK what you having?'

My phone pinged. *Did she just change the subject?*

*Hi Frankie*

*How are you today?*

*How did the physio go this morning?*

*Did the x-rays look OK?*

*Sorry about the twenty questions.........*

*Yours Alex*

*Skilful question master*

*C E O Blackmore industries*


*Hi Alex (skilful question master)*

*I am fine, thanks for asking. I am sitting having an early lunch with Bella.*

*You know a girl's gossip and catch up and of course a major people watch. I haven't seen Nathan yet today, he said he had to go home to your Mum's house, to sort out a problem. So we will meet this afternoon instead. That means I still haven't seen the x-rays yet.*

*I was just about to tell Bella that we almost bumped into each other today, outside of the building.*

*Maybe we will have to try that one day, actually meeting up?*

*Hope your journey was OK?*

*Frankie (gossiping queen and people watcher)*

Bella showed me the menu again, 'Come on girl, I haven't got all day, what are you going to order?'

'I fancy a proper burger with all the trimmings and chips. Oh yeah, and a big glass of root beer.' I couldn't get enough of the stuff, and drank it almost daily. Bella assured me the novelty would wear off soon.

'So who are you texting?'

I turned to her and gave her a look that invited her to guess.

'Oh, got it... Mr. Nice Hand,' she shook her head at me smiling.

I was quite surprised to not get a reply from Alex. I sort of looked forward to our banter. I felt a flush hit my cheeks, and worry started to rise up.

*Perhaps he thought I was flirting with him asking to meet? Well I suppose I sort of was, wasn't I?* I had to say he intrigued me and we always had a bit of fun texting. I needed to remember that I was the hired help.

'Penny for them?'

I looked at Bella now passing over my burger that had been delivered to our table in double quick time. Pulling a grimace, 'I have just flirted a bit by text with my employer and he hasn't replied.'

'What... Does he know what a delicious babe you are?... Don't concern yourself, his loss,' she shrugged her shoulders and proceeded to take a huge bite from the wonderful looking burger. I had to chuckle to myself, her smart Chanel suit and perfect hair and makeup didn't go with noshing on a huge juicy burger.

'Oh, on a different subject, Nathan wants us to go to a rugby match with him this weekend. Apparently Alex plays for a local side and he thought we might enjoy it. They have a few beers after and then sometimes go on to a club.' I looked at her with my best puppy dog eyes. 'Pretty please,' I said, pulling out the slice of steak tomato from the top of the burger bun, sucking the juice and seeds out and then dropping it unceremoniously to the edge of my plate.

'Oh go on then. You will need me as your wing woman for when you meet Alex, won't you?'

*Oh shit, she was right.* I hadn't thought about that. Well not much anyway, as when I did my stomach sort of turned over like the drum in a washing machine.

We tucked into our food then, Bella because quite simply she was running out of lunch hour and me because I was contemplating meeting Alex, and couldn't really hold a conversation. Strangely I couldn't eat all my lunch as my stomach kept churning.

At approximately 2:30pm my door bell rang.

'Just coming, Nathan,' I put down my kindle and quickly moved to the front door. Outside there stood another bouquet of flowers. I looked around, but apart from the noise of the descending lift there was nothing and no card either. Strange, I picked them up and carried them inside. I placed them carefully in front of the fireplace, maybe they were for Bella. Maybe from one of the many dates she happened to be seeing at the moment. I smiled to myself and sat back down. Nathan was late coming back.

*I hoped it wasn't a huge problem back home?*

I wasn't to see Nathan for the next couple of days. I also received no text from Alex. Both of which made my days feel quite sad and empty.

On the up side Bella spent the first evening at home with me. We had an all round girls' night and we drank too much Fireball, laughed too much, consumed far too much chocolate, not that I ever agreed there was such a thing as too much chocolate, and in between used every beauty product known to woman. Finally, we sat in the lounge painting each other's toe nails and trying not to laugh too much, in order not to crack the face masks we wore.

Pink was blaring through the iPod speakers from which my phone was connected. Bella was singing along to all the words.

'Oh yes,' she said, still butt dancing on the settee, 'As we are off to the rugby match on Saturday, at your request,' she lowered her eyes to mine. Looking quite alien in the green mask she wore, the cracks in it around her eyes only adding to the weird look, 'We are going on a double date tomorrow night,' she smiled her reassurance.

'And I don't get a say in this, I suppose?'

'Absolutely correct, gorgeous girl, you would attempt to talk us out of it, and frankly I am pissed off with the fact you are here in New York and spend most evenings in. Like a woman twice your age.'

She was right of course.

'So can I ask with whom you are intending we should spend the night with?'

'You're presuming a bit much there, aren't you?' she let out a laugh, 'I only said a date. I don't know, erotic dreams, texting a stranger, drooling over a beautiful hand and now expecting to sleep with a total stranger,' her eyebrows waggled at me in teasing delight. 'I say again, horny much?'

Sod the face pack and newly painted toenails, I set about her with a cushion from the settee. She was defenceless, laughing too much at her own jokes and lay back horizontally while I covered the nearly new cushion in green face pack.

The restaurant was posh; Bella had been right to talk me into wearing one of my better dresses. It was an aubergine wrap, which apparently showed off my curvy figure. Examining my surroundings and our company, I wondered why the hell I had let her talk me into this.

They were OK, as blokes went. The blond haired one who sat next to me was friendly and talked a lot about places he had travelled to and how much money he earnt in any given tax year. Unfortunately, he was not party to the fact that money doesn't really do much for me. Given that he was overly touchy as well, the whole dinner date was starting to wear very thin.

Trying hard to pull my face back together, as I knew it would be showing a pissed off/ bored expression, I heard a deep sigh escape my lips. My eyes shot up guiltily to meet the questioning gaze of Bella. My right hand clamped quickly to my mouth, whist I pretended to cough. I grinned at her, trying to placate the situation. She needn't have concerned herself; blond bloke hadn't noticed and was still animatedly talking about himself. I nodded and made all the listening noises he obviously wanted to hear.

My attention was on Bella now and how she had moved herself bodily against her date. God she was good; I didn't think I could ever be like her. I knew she wasn't really into him; in fact, I had only ever witnessed that phenomenon the once. When she had been really hurt, so now she was in love 'em and leave em' mode. It didn't worry me so much, as long as she was OK.

'So what do you think?' said blond guy who stared at me expectantly.

*Oh shit* ran through my mind. Not having a clue as to what I was supposed to be thinking about.

'Ermm...'

'We would love to,' I heard Bella say enthusiastically. She knew I hadn't a bloody clue what was going on. She was going to milk it for all it was worth.

'We would?' I replied questioningly, smiling sweetly at all seated at the table.

'Yes, we can go and watch the game at Will's house, on Thanksgiving, can't we,' it was stated as a given, so I fought hard to control my face, which had lapsed into a 'really' expression and I nodded unreservedly.

'Great, I will make arrangements and let you both know what time,'

'I hate to tear myself away from you,' I heard the curly haired guy, who was coupled almost to the point of being fused together with Bella, speak.

*I really must pay more attention...I really must pay more attention...*became my mantra; I couldn't for the life of me remember his name.

*Christ, the reality, am I really this unsociable?*

Ten minutes later and goodbyes were being said all round and I breathed a sigh of relief when I realised that the use of curly haired guy's name was not going to be necessary.

We sat back down at the restaurant table and after ordering another bottle of wine for the two of us, I awaited the barrage of abuse to begin. Bella threw her head back and began to laugh cathartically. Relieved I joined in, starting with a thankful giggle to begin with and then joining in with her full blown roar. The tears ran down my face.

'That has got to be the funniest thing I have witnessed with you, that poor man was completely smitten with you and you couldn't have given a monkey's arse about him. In fact, at points you looked almost comatose.'

'Comatose was not the look I was going for, I promise. He was just so, so not for me.'

'I hear you,' I watched her run her fingertip around the rim of the crystal wine glass.

'So what about this football date you agreed to, eh? To what's his name's, house?'

*Crying out loud, I can't remember his name now!*

'What's his name?' she bellowed, shocking a few of the other customers with the velocity.

'Frankie, have some more wine and loosen up,' I watched her fill up my glass with some more of the pinot grigio we had, post disaster date, treated ourselves to. I finally started to relax now it was just us. Again my mind started to wander.

I still hadn't heard from Alex. Nathan had sent a very short and to the point text this morning, explaining he was stuck at his mother's house, dealing with a problem. We arranged to meet at his early in the morning for his overdue physio and then travel to watch Alex play rugby, which was apparently an after lunch kick-off. This I was very much looking forward to, maybe I was more homesick than I thought?

'Come on, let's finish this bottle and call it a night shall we?'

I nodded in agreement, and swallowed the very smooth wine down.

It was a pleasant surprise to be met outside the restaurant by Edwards. Really this man was worth his weight in gold. We jumped into the welcome warmth of the limo and sped home. I was sure I could smell Jabby's cologne again, it must be Edwards. Maybe he happened to wear the same cologne? The thought didn't please me, but there had to be some sort of logical explanation. I would have to get closer to him and give him a sniff, next time I felt it was appropriate. I stifled a giggle, as if it was ever going to be appropriate to sniff Edwards. *Sometimes I really am a stupid cow.*

'Well, Nathan, these look really good.' I was holding up the X-rays to the portable light box and could see the fracture that Nathan had suffered was repairing well.

'So with a bit more work on your leg muscles, the strength will come back, maybe not to 100% but pretty close,' I licked my lips and nodded at him.

And there it was. I was treated to a full blown Nathan bad boy grin, dimples in full Technicolor. I could see why women fell at his feet.

'Yes,' he shouted and pumped his left fist into the air. 'So I can lose the crutches?'

'Well that needs to be checked by the orthopaedic surgeon, but probably really soon, you know, when you're in the apartment,' I started to shake my head, 'but probably not for longer periods of time on your feet.' I added in the last piece of information, but I could see he hadn't heard it. Nathan was the sort of guy that only heard what he wanted to. But his pleasure and relief at the good news was communicable. He pulled me into a tight hug and kissed my forehead.

'So how much time have I got to get ready for our outing?'

He released me and started to explain, 'It normally takes about an hour to get out to the ground, but as I still can't drive yet, we will take one of the family copters from the top of the building.'

'Copters, as in helicopter?' I questioned, raising my eyebrows up to him.

'Mm Hmm... have you ever been in one before?' He smiled at me.

'No.'

'You will love it, chocolate drop, flying takes no time at all to get there, it was all arranged to take Alex. But as he will be driving from my mother's house, I told him I would use it to come and watch anyway.'

'OK then, helicopter it is.' I made sure I sounded more confident than I felt. 'What time shall Bella and I be back here?'

'Say noon, and wrap up warm.'

'Yes Mum,' I said saluting him, although I wouldn't bestow that title on him, he was too nice. 'I have watched rugby before you know, in the cold and everything.'

'Sarcasm doesn't become you; you know, go and get ready. You need to give Bella plenty of notice, in case she is otherwise engaged.'

'Huh, right,' I made for his door. I really needed to ask what the hell was going on between them, there were definite vibes, of that I was sure.

'See ya,' came from behind me as I made my way back to the more feminine apartment that was Bella's and mine.

I found Bella sitting on the floor in the lounge area, staring at her laptop and chewing on a piece of toast. Totally immersed in whatever work she was doing.

'We have to be back at Nathan's by noon, how much longer are you working for?'

'I am just looking at some info... that's very interesting, I must say,' she quickly covered over her laptop by ¾ closing the lid, just as I made my way over to sneak a peek. 'Now, now,' she shook her head and smiled, 'confidential stuff on here.'

'Sorry, anyway Nathan is flying us to the ground in a helicopter.' I waited for the news to filter through.

'REALLY...! You do know how much I love your job and connections here, don't you?' She closed the laptop and jumped to her feet, grabbing hold of my forearms.

I did, and I was enjoying the perks, too.

At exactly 11:55am we knocked on Nathan's door. Bella was dressed to the nines; looking beautiful and somehow making it look like she hadn't even really bothered. I, on the other hand, although wearing good jeans and boots, had on one of JJ's old rugby shirts from Cambridge Uni and although I had tucked it in the top of my jeans it hung off me. I was comfortable, but extremely pleased I had taken extra time with my hair and make-up today, so at least I didn't feel too much like the ugly stepsister.

Nathan's door swung open quickly, to reveal a dressed down version of Edwards, complete with leather jacket. 'Ladies are we all ready?' he held the door open for Nathan who appeared wearing his panty dropping grin, directed straight at Bella, who openly swooned.

*WTF?*

I decided when we got home later, or as soon as we were not within earshot of anyone else, it was time to ask her some very pointed questions.

Nathan had his crutch positioned in its usual place, but I noted he was barely using it to support his weight. He was positively exuding happiness and excitement.

*Obviously good news from the surgeon then?* The four of us made our way to the lift that led up to the roof.

'OK ladies, we should be there in only about 10 minutes or so, do you have everything you need?' questioned Edwards.

After we nodded in response, he opened the roof door. God it was cold being so high up and outside. A bit scary too, as the wind had a quality and strength up here that could have almost blown you over. It reminded me of my favourite place near home. Edwards placed his arms around Bella and me and guided us towards the waiting helicopter. Opening the door he pointed towards the back seats, he then helped up a cross looking Nathan. We placed our headphones on and watched Edwards climb into the pilot seat, a man of many talents, so it seemed.

The nervousness in my stomach dissipated with the start of the helicopter blades. We moved away from the helipad and into a serene looking, clear blue sky. The view was simply breath-taking. Edwards was right with his estimation of time and only minutes later we touched down in a large green open field. After climbing out we watched Edwards take off again.

'Wow,' came from Bella.

'Come on let's go get a drink from the bar, before kick-off.' Nathan turned towards the car park and what looked like a very posh clubhouse.

Deliberately I slowed down, creating a little distance between myself, Bella and sex on legs in front of us. I placed my arm through hers, 'So care to tell me what's going on with you and just fucked hair?'

Bella's head spun around to meet my stare, 'Just a bit of fun, Frankie, that's all. Honest flirting, nothing more. Anyway we need to get you ready to meet the elusive Alex, don't we? Are you excited?'

I wasn't convinced by her answer, but Nathan had slowed up to wait for us and I could only nod my answer to her.

'What position does Alex play, Nathan?' I asked, drawing Nathan once more into our group.

'You do know your stuff then girls, unfortunately although I enjoy it I am not overly conversed in positions and such like on the rugby pitch... I do however know lots of other interesting positions,' he said grinning from ear to ear and lifting his left eyebrow, staring straight at Bella. She pushed him on the chest for good measure and placed her arm through the crutch less one, laughing.

*Harmless flirting? My arse.*

'I think he plays second row?' came from Nathan, his face was showing a frown, with a thoughtful expression. He was looking over his shoulder at me, as we carried on walking. 'He's a couple of inches taller than me, and a hell of a lot broader.

We had entered a very modern looking building, but I was completely blown away by what we found inside. The rugby club resembled a club you would find in England. It was as if it had been designed to be just that, heavy wooden floors, exposed brickwork with plaques and trophies displayed on them. The bar looked like it had been made of one continuous solid piece of wood and polished to a deep shine. But it was the smell that floored me, a smell that deeply resonated within me, 'Hops?' I said out loud to no one in particular. The whole place felt like home, warm and extremely comfortable.

'Girls, go and take a seat, what are you both drinking?' Nathan made his way to the bar and a small group of blokes having a beer. They welcomed Nathan with smiles, obviously asking how he was, as they kept glancing towards his leg. Bella and I made our way towards one of the semicircle booths that ran down two sides of the clubhouse, and sat on the dark green and very comfortable velvet seats.

'Well you must have had the heads up?' mumbled Bella, rubbing her hand over the velvet upholstery.

'Sorry?' I responded.

She touched JJ's old rugby shirt I was wearing, running her fingers lightly over the green and white jersey.

'Look around, this rugby team obviously plays in the same colours.'

I caught her drift just then, and grinning slightly I smiled at her, 'Oh yeah, what a coincidence.'

One of the guys from the bar was helping Nathan over to us, carrying our drinks on a tray.

'OK, so this is Brent,' he said as he nodded towards the smiling bloke who was now placing the tray on our table. 'Brent meet Bella and Frankie, Frankie is my physio and Bella is her very articulate friend,' he said with a twinkle in his eyes.

'Hi, pleased to meet you both,' his right hand had stuck out towards us and we shook it politely. Brent took a seat next to me and lifted his pint glass to his lips and proceeded to take a mouthful. After swallowing he looked at me quizzically and then again back at Nathan.

'The Frankie,' he questioned Nathan, raising both eyebrows in disbelief.

'Yep,' replied Nathan, 'The Frankie... the best physio in the world,' he said lifting his glass probably filled with JD, his drink of choice, and taking a large slug. A reverberating sigh leaving his lips as he gently placed the crystal glass down on our table with a clink. Nathan's eyes slowly lifted up from watching his fingers turn the glass in a slow methodical circle and met Brent's.

'OK, well I have to go get ready for the match now, it was great to meet you both, ladies,' Brent stood and climbed down from the raised booth, 'hopefully I'll get to see you after the match as well.'

I watched Brent make his way across the floor and felt like I had missed a whole unspoken conversation between the two men. Bella glanced at me and we shared a questioning look.

'Right, girls, we have approx. 45 minutes until kick-off,' Nathan stood slowly clapping his hands together with certainty. 'I need to eat. Can I get you both anything? They do a mean steak and kidney pie here.' He looked from face to face, tipping his head from side to side, 'Starving, hurry up.'

Bella and I both declined and Nathan slowly made his way towards the bar, again.

'So?' I heard from Bella, putting so much weight into that one questioning word. 'Don't you think that that was a little bloody strange?'

I shrugged my shoulders at her, not verbally replying because all I could concentrate on now was the doorway that Brent had just disappeared into. I sat sipping my root beer, wondering if the elusive Alex was already here and changing into his kit. I felt my interest notch up a level at the thought of the man naked.

# Chapter 11

The whole rugby ground had obviously been well designed. The stands were well sheltered, with comfortable, covered over seating in three out of the four. Someone had clearly spent a lot of money on it that was for certain.

It was just as well, the weather was the sort of cold that penetrated every layer you wore. I had to admit I was so looking forward to watching the match. I hadn't really been to many games since JJ had died and I acknowledged that maybe it was about time to move on and embrace the game we had always loved together.

The game got off to a slow start. Bella was screaming her head off next to me, much to the amusement of Nathan, who didn't seem to be watching the game much. Instead all his interest was on us, well mostly Bella. It always amazed me how men found it so amusing that we actually knew what we were talking about, in the mostly male dominated sport.

My eyes were on the game though, constantly trying to search out which of the second row Alex could possibly be. It was starting to be a very full on game and the play switched quickly from end to end. One of the forwards stood out to me though and my eyes were constantly pulled back towards the number five. He had to be the broadest one out there and was quite obviously the captain. I kept hearing his extremely deep voice shouting orders and encouragement. He always seemed to get himself into just the right place at the right time.

I was enjoying myself, but all too soon the game was drawing to a close. In the last few minutes of the second half, number five was hanging on the wing, just waiting for a pass. Once it came he took off, hogging the touch line, it was amazing to watch as this physically huge bloke barrelled his way through the opposition and sprinted towards the try line. He then turned to place the ball directly under the posts with one hand.

I was up and out of my seat, jumping and clapping. It wasn't the winning try as Alex's team lost the game. But in my mind I would replay it time and time again. My core tightened with the unexpected lust I felt for the number five. I watched his team clap him on the back and smiled.

Nathan had two fingers in his mouth, whistling an ear piercing shrill of a whistle. He punched his left arm into the air and shouted, 'Yes, way to go Bro.'

My stomach flipped itself over. Oh God, my hand moved involuntarily up to my open mouth.

*So number five was Alex?* I could feel Bella just staring at me; I sure as hell wasn't going to reward her by looking at her. I knew she would have on a shit eating grin, which quite simply I was refusing to look at.

The teams made their way to the edge of the pitch. Alex's team clapped the winners off. I still couldn't see him properly, because although he was one of the taller guys out there he was wearing a head guard. Oh well, I resigned myself to waiting until they had cleaned themselves up and found their way into the bar area.

It was so very welcome, walking back into the clubhouse. My face was bright red from the cold wind and had stung slightly as the warm air hit it. I unwound my scarf and removed my coat. I found myself making my way back to our original semi-circular seat and flopped down with a sigh. I glanced around, Bella was up at the bar ordering some drinks and a couple of the famed steak and kidney pies as the fresh air had made us ravenous.

A smile spread over my lips, she was openly flirting with the barman whilst ordering. Nathan on the other hand had his back to her, as he chatted with some other blokes who had also watched the game. He lifted the bottle up and down from his lips and every now and again shot a quick look at her, pursing his lips tighter together. If he kept on like this there wouldn't be any room in between them to actually drink the beer.

Jeez I needed a wee, quickly I shot a look around the bar area, just searching for the door I badly needed. I was fairly sure that I was a windblown mess. Old rugby shirt was one thing, a knotted mess of straw for hair was quite another. I saw the sign on the wall to the right hand side of the bar and made my way towards it, clasping my handbag as though it contained the crown jewels.

After a quick wee, I took a look at my reflection. Small amount of makeup was intact, check. My cheeks were flushed by the wind, but it gave me a healthy glow I surmised. A couple of brushes though my hair had it looking relatively good and not screaming "wild thing" anymore. I was good to go.

The bar area had certainly filled up with people by the time I made my way out of the ladies. I couldn't see our seating area. As I started to make my way towards the general vicinity, saying a very repetitive, 'excuse me please,' there was a strong smell in the air, of nicely cleaned men and the wonderful smell of quite expensive deodorants, shower gels etc.

I could just see the top of Bella's head now, her blonde hair moving to and fro. She was laughing, I recognised the head movement. I was a few steps away from finally reaching the table. Standing in front of it was a very tall, large, dark haired man. It had to be Alex. I felt excited and a little apprehensive all at the same time. I felt my pulse quicken, and a further rush of blood flowed to not only my face, but other parts of me as well.

His back was broad and very muscular, and although it was contained in a very tightly stretched, dark green, button-down shirt, you could see almost every line and contour of the muscles in his back, as his hands were obviously crossed in front of his chest. I had unwittingly slowed down to take in the sight. All I wanted to do was run my hands up his shoulder blades and press my nose to his spine.

'Here she is,' I heard Nathan speak.

I lifted my gaze up to meet Alex, in order to be introduced properly.

The very nice back slowly started to disappear from view as Alex almost hesitantly turned around to face me. I couldn't keep my head up for too long and started to take in the glorious site that was Alex. Old worn black jeans, that fitted him in all the right places, and the tucked in shirt, which stretched equally well across the very well defined abs. I slowly started to look up towards his face almost jumping up one shirt button at a time, in time with the beat of my heart. He must have uncrossed his arms now as they moved away from his chest and fell to his sides, his huge fists clenched. On his little finger I could see the large titanium ring, which I had spotted before. His well defined Adams apple bobbed up and down as he swallowed, was he nervous as well?

My tongue flicked out to wet my lips. Seriously what was wrong with me? It was like I wanted to eat him. I stifled the nervous giggle that wanted to leave my mouth.

I was pleased to note he had a couple of days of scruff on his face and a glorious cleft in his chin; finally, I made it to his eyes, desperately hoping I hadn't taken as long with my appraisal as I felt I must have.

I stared straight into the most gorgeous emerald green eyes and there stood in front of me, staring right back at me was... Jabby.

The hairs on my neck stood to attention, almost painfully.

# Chapter 12

'SERIOUSLY, what the FUCK?... Jabby?'

Physically I felt myself take a step back. I wasn't sure if it was from shock, or just a built in need to get away from the situation that was now presenting itself, right before my eyes.

I shot a look in Bella's direction, just in time to see the happy look she had been wearing slide off. To be replaced by one of sheer dismay.

Ok, so she was as shocked as me then.

Nathan on the other hand, was sporting a cocky grin and was leaning back into the comfortable seating area, arms folded across his chest. 'BINGO... I knew there was a bigger story to this, Alex? And I was correct. I would introduce you but it's quite obvious you two have met before.'

I held up my hand to Nathan, gesticulating for him stop.

'Shut the fuck up! Nathan, you know nothing... nothing at all. Why the hell couldn't you just leave this alone?' I heard Jabby shouting.

I couldn't listen to any more of the fucked up, so called conversation, and I proceeded with my usual flight response. Rushing from the bar at the quickest pace I could manage, I didn't even stop for my coat, and managed to bump into several people, in my haste to escape.

Oh my God, as soon as I hit the outside it was very evident I had made a huge mistake. The time had moved on and outside was slightly darker and very much colder. I wrapped my arms around myself, almost instinctively hugging. Just striving to keep the little bit of warmth I had left inside my body. Lifting my head, I looked up at the clear evening sky, trying to use its sense of calm to help my panic stricken mind.

'Frankie,' came from behind me; it came from the only voice I had heard in my dreams these past few months.

My head was very gingerly shaking from side to side.

'I don't know what to say to you.' I could still hear him, but I wasn't going to trust myself to turn around.

'Please, I need to know how you are feeling,' he continued.

Listening to his voice, it was easy to tell he was probably only a couple of feet away. His breathing was deep and calm, probably trying to control his anxiety.

'We need to talk,' his tone suddenly changed, from the concerned one almost pleading with me, to complete authority.

'Turn around... Frankie.'

I spun around with as much gusto as I could manage in my shocked state.

'Who the hell, do you think you are?' What gives you the right... to order me around?'

I wasn't going to stop, to let him actually answer any of the questions I was asking of him. I needed him to know and see exactly how this had made me feel.

'I don't understand... what the hell is going on?'

'How can I possibly be in your employ?'

My arm had now lifted and with every question I was happily stabbing my finger into the middle of his chest.

Why the hell was I even touching him? I didn't have a frigging clue, but only knew that with each stab on his chest, each connection between us, I found myself calming down slightly. I gritted my teeth and felt my forehead pull into a tight-lined frown; I forced my arms to my sides. I refused to let myself touch this... I had no bloody idea what this was?

My cousin's executioner?

My erotic fantasy?

My employer?

My control freak?

Swallowing deeply, I encouraged the bile that was rising to go back down. Maybe I should throw up all over his boots, Christ knows he deserved it.

'I don't know how to explain all this to you, Frankie,' he stood with his arms open and palms pointing upwards. His body language was trying to encourage me to believe that he was being open and honest.

'WELL. TRY. AT. THE. BLOODY. BEGINNING!!!!!' My voice was so loud and I almost didn't recognise it as mine.

'Right OK I will, but you have to hear me out.'

'I don't have to DO ANYTHING.'

Jabby/Alex took hold of my elbow and started to lead me back towards the clubhouse. I shook myself out of his hold and felt instantly emptier at the loss of his touch. It was times like this that I completely and utterly hated my traitorous body. These times always seemed to be because of him.

'OK I won't touch you, but we need to be somewhere warmer to have this conversation, before you start to go into shock. So do us both a favour and follow me... please.'

The please seemed to come as an afterthought, so control freak probably wasn't far wrong. Reluctantly I fell into step behind him, making my gaze settle nowhere other than the back of his head, several times it had tried to linger on his very squeezable backside encased in his jeans.

Bella was waiting for me just inside the door. With her was, it had to be said, a very mortified looking Nathan, who ran both of his hands through his hair over and over again.

'We are going in here to talk; I'd appreciate it if you didn't come in and allowed no one else to either.'

*He had to be bloody joking? Right?*

'Who the hell do you think you are?... Bella is coming in with me and looking at Nathan's face I think he needs to hear what the hell you've got to say, too.'

'Fine!' he forced the word out. He kicked open the wooden door with such strength and anger it banged on the inside wall causing the pictures inside the room to vibrate.

'Sit down everyone, please be my guest,' the sarcasm just rolled off his tongue.

*Good, I had finally started to get to him.*

We all entered a small office/reception area and the door closed behind us. Bella, Nathan and I took seats. I sat down on my hands as the compulsion to fidget with them was becoming all consuming. I gazed around the room, which was masculine in colour. The large furniture dominated the space, almost overwhelmingly.

I watched Alex walk slowly over to the bottles on a silver tray, he even moved like a God. I pinched the underneath of my thighs, reminding myself exactly what I was doing here. It certainly wasn't to check out the local talent.

'Drink?' Alex questioned us all. Obviously his good upbringing bringing out his politeness, even in this fucked up situation.

'Yes I'll have a fucking drink,' a very unsteady Nathan made his way over to the tray and proceeded to nearly fill a glass.

'I can only start by saying how sorry I am that you found out this way, Frankie.' Alex shot Nathan a seething look of derision.

'I can only hope you will except my apology, and believe the sincerity behind it.' Alex moved and sat himself on the edge of the desk facing us. He ran his hand slowly through his hair; and expelled a loud sigh. His long jean-clad legs stretched out in front of him and crossed at the ankles.

I had to stop myself from laughing. The resemblance of the mannerisms between the two brothers was comical. He paused placing his thumb in the deep cleft of his chin and the rest of his fingers curled up in a fist underneath, he was quite obviously thinking.

Remembering what I was doing here in the first place, I shot back, 'Are you sorry I found out this way, or sorry I found out at all?'

Alex closed his eyes and breathed deeply. When he reopened them I could see the amber flecks had widened.

*Oh, so I was making him angry was I?*

'I cannot tell you how many times I have run through my head the best way to tell you what was going on here,' he waved his arms around, 'but where to start?'

'How about at the bloody beginning, arsehole!' I was shouting again and really needed to get a grip on my overflowing emotions.

'You told me the day of the enquiry, if I ever needed anything from you to contact the liaison officer.' I was up on my feet now and seriously pissed off, taking slow punctuated steps towards him.

'Did I ever contact the Liaison officer?... No. I. Fucking. Didn't.... I don't need anything from you that's why!' My right hand flicked up quickly like I was swatting a nuisance bug, and slapped his face so hard I thought I would cry out from the pain it left behind.

The room was silent and Alex's eyes were downcast. I clutched my right wrist, squeezing to alleviate some of the pain and heat it now held.

I was sure that Bella and Nathan were still behind me, but I couldn't hear anything and I wasn't turning to check.

Keeping my eyes firmly on Alex's face I watched as he slowly returned my stare.

'No I understand that... but the trouble is I needed something from you,' his voice was calm and steady, it didn't match the bright red mark from my hand slowly seeping its colour through the scruff on his face.

He continued, 'My brother needed a damn good physio... he needed the best I could find and my investigations always came back to you.'

I was stood now with my arms crossed in front of me, shaking my head from side to side. I slowly turned to make my way out of this suddenly extremely claustrophobic room. Bella stood to accompany me. I placed my hand on the door handle and started to turn it, immediately appreciating the cold brass on my sore palm.

Just then I heard in that deep resonating voice I loved, 'But most of all...' He inhaled a deep breath, 'I needed your forgiveness.'

The door handle squeaked as I continued to turn it. I lifted my other palm and placed it onto the wood in front of me. I pressed my forehead to it and closed my eyes.

This deeply embittered person was not the person I wanted to be. God knows I had witnessed enough of this, in my own so called family. I had always refused to become like them. Releasing the door knob, I let it turn back to its original position and pushed the door shut, with a click.

'Gorgeous girl?' I felt Bella's hand lightly resting on my shoulder; she spun me round and gave me a hug. 'OK?'

I nodded to her and she sat back down, only this time next to Nathan. I watched her pick up his empty hand.

'I think perhaps Nathan and I will go back to the bar, and we'll wait there, is that OK... Frankie?'

I nodded my head slowly in agreement.

As they moved towards the door, Bella stopped suddenly and spun around, glaring at Alex, 'You need to sort this bloody mess out, and fast. I don't know what fucking game you're playing, but if you take on Frankie, you take on me too.'

They moved out of the door, Bella studying my face as she left. Just checking again, that it was OK to leave.

Alex had his back to me now and was standing, but with his shoulders hunched, leaning over the desk. They shook slightly. *Was he crying?*

'Right I'm listening. Perhaps you need to tell me exactly what's happening.'

# ALEX

All I can hear is the fucking ticking of the clock, on the wall directly behind me.

*Tick, Tick, Tick.* Just to remind me, I still hadn't had the balls to start this fucking conversation yet. God knows, I had done so often enough in my head.

OK so she was going to listen to me. Where the fucking hell was I going to start?

*Open your eyes and pull yourself together.*

I grimaced hearing my stepfather's voice in my head, something that I fought very fucking hard to always shut away, and leave back in the cupboard that he used to shut me in as punishment.

I lifted both hands from the table and pressed my index fingers into my temples and squeezed the dickwad out.

*You little cunt.*

*Just like your wretched, weak father.*

*The words always came with a kick or punch. But rather me, than them.*

I forced my eyes to open to the here and now. She was here and I really needed to sort out the clusterfuck Nathan had caused.

I had it all in hand; I was going to talk to her when the moment was right.

Who was I fucking kidding, I was good at sorting out everyone else, but me, well that was another story entirely.

I gave off the air of being totally at peace with myself, though. I presented a good poker face to the world. It's probably why the family business was so damn successful, I was the master of letting no one in. The English public school I was sent to, away from my family, had definitely helped with that. I had learnt the 'stiff upper lip' that the rich instilled in their children from an early age, and my American/English accent always won over the American business world. I could slip easily from a NYC burr into a fairly decent English inflection.

I stood and pushed my shoulders back, taking a huge calming breath. I could smell her, although that was nothing new, I could always smell the orange blossom she used. It was one of those smells I would remember for the rest of my life and it would always take me back to the first time we had met. My balls tightened; before I turned to face the music I adjusted them quickly.

*Fuck when had I become such a pussy whipped prick?*

'Thank you for staying and hearing me out, Frankie,' I turned when I spoke and took in the now calmer vision in front of me. She had sat back down on the couch in my office. I approached slowly and sat down next to her. My whole body screamed out to take her hand and try to comfort her. She and JJ had been so close and I wanted in some small way to show her how I understood.

I sat with my body positioned so I could face her directly.

She was an absolute vision. I noticed every time I saw her, how beautiful she was becoming. One of those women that grew better with every year.

She didn't see it though. Everyone around her noticed. I suppose that made her more attractive. The fact she had no need to flaunt herself, the fact that she didn't even notice how heads turned as she walked by. Unlike many of the women I had used over the years for my sexual release. She was a natural beauty. No false tits, shit on thinking that I had begun to gawp at her full, ripe breasts. I lifted my eyes suddenly, hoping she hadn't noticed. But of course she had and I heard her gasp, almost involuntarily.

*FUCK, I needed her.*

My balls that had hitched up earlier were beginning to ache like they hadn't been emptied in weeks. I was like a fucking randy teenager, and being near her made it better and worse all at the same time. I realised this was the first time we had ever been alone.

*Alex pull yourself the fuck together.*

I slid my hand over to hers and took her fingers into my gentle but firm grasp. There it was, that electric shock; I always knew it would be there.

*But fuck, I need to man the fuck up and quickly.*

She didn't pull away. Even though I knew she could feel the pulsating heat between us. I had seen the hairs on her forearm stand up, almost in surprise.

'They exonerated me, but it's not enough,' I began, 'I need to tell you what happened that day.'

Her eyes flew up from our conjoined hands to mine; I could lose myself in the very depths of them. The pupils were slightly dilated.

*Shit, I turned her on.*

I had felt the chemistry between us before. I had never felt anything like it before with any other woman. Sure, they knew which buttons to touch, so to speak, but this was like I was magnetised to her. My jeans became fucking uncomfortably tight as I fought with an ever growing erection. Thank fuck I was leaning over with my elbows on my knees. Hopefully it wasn't screamingly obvious.

'Our mission was just to observe... we needed JJ as usual to interpret with the locals. We were trying to gain any snippets of information...' I hated re-living this; God knows I did it enough in my nightmares. Needing to carry on with the explanation I closed my eyes, hoping to break the connection between us. My free hand went up to my forehead and I smoothed out my eyebrows with thumb and first finger.

'JJ was a professional; he knew what the risks were... But it was my fucking fault he died, we were led to an ambush and I took the decision to go there.' I couldn't hear anything over the sound of my own heart banging in my chest, and the deep gulping breaths I was taking, just to be able to continue with the story, in order to try and gain the vindication I so badly needed.

'We lost three of our team that day...' The pain in my chest was becoming excruciating and I coughed suddenly to try to relieve the tightness of it. Frankie hadn't spoken up to now but her eyes must have always been on me, I could feel them.

In my guilt I now couldn't meet her gaze.

'I should have protected them, my mistake cost them their lives... It was all we could do to bring them out of there with us.'

'I have apologised to your aunt and uncle several times, but I needed to do this with you. I know what a selfish fucker I am. I know how close you were, how proud he was of you. He spoke of you so often. He loved you so much,' I sighed. Jesus this was more difficult than I could have ever imagined. In business I was so in control, I knew how meetings were panning out and could alter the outcome, just by judging people's body language and altering my course appropriately. I lifted my spare hand and ran it through my hair, pulling slightly to cause discomfort, bringing myself back to the here and now and not what was going on with my crotch.

I looked down at our two hands as she squeezed mine tighter, by placing her other hand over the top. Finally, I lifted my eyes up to meet hers.

I couldn't help myself; the magnet just pulled me in.

Lifting up my hand I ran my fingers gently through the long brown locks of her hair. It felt so good falling in-between my fingers. Her hair felt like thick pieces of silk. She stopped breathing, her eyes never leaving my face.

My hands looked huge against the side of her face as I tenaciously brushed the back of my fingertips across her cheek bone and along her jaw. My thumb brushing over her top lip, taking in the reddish pink blush and wondering if her nipples and pussy were the same gorgeous colour, or if I could bring enough blood to them, to make them the same gorgeous hue. Her eyes closed and she began to shift ever so slightly in the seat.

*Was I really this sort of bastard?*

I had wanted her for as long as I could remember, and here she was pliant in my hands. It was the last coherent thought that ran through my head.

*Fuck I was going to have her.*

Grasping hold of her chin I lifted her face to meet mine as I came down to kiss her. She had to feel it. As our lips met, it was like being jump started. I was talking to myself, trying to get myself to take it slow. I knew she didn't have much experience with men and I couldn't fucking rush her.

Gently I ran the tip of my tongue along the seam of her closed mouth and sucked, oh so gently, on the fleshly pad of her bottom lip. She slowly and then suddenly all at once opened her mouth for me, her tongue jutted out to meet mine and she hesitantly joined me in our dance. I could kiss her forever and felt more like a fucking teenager than ever. Our kiss became more and more desperate. I heard the growls, which escaped my throat. I didn't think I had ever been so turned on in my life. My cock was screaming to be released from its confines.

Quickly I moved my hands to the top of her arms and lifted her easily onto my lap, shifting myself to the back of the couch. She sat down quickly on my hard on, obviously being taken by surprise at the sudden change in her position. I continued to kiss her, not giving her time to think, in case she realised what was going on, with the bastard she hated.

My cock felt so much relief from the pressure and heat of her pussy.

With every breath in I could smell her arousal mixed with her orange blossom body wash. It was fucking intoxicating. Her nipples hardened against the rugby shirt she was wearing, I could feel them through our two layers of clothing.

The need to see them was all consuming, to run my mouth over and around them, to flick at them with my hot tongue. I could hear her almost whining with need.

My hands started to slowly rub up the outside of her thighs. Over her backside, stopping to flex all of my fingers into her firm arse cheeks, I pulled her quickly forward, closer to me, needing more relief on my cock as she gasped and moaned into my mouth. Slowly my hands moved, they lifted up and over her waist moving in symmetry to each other. I found them at the base of her rugby shirt. Reluctantly I broke off our kiss.

Resting our foreheads together, 'I need this to come off,' my voice was almost unrecognisable with lust, 'I want you to tell me it's OK.' I hated asking the question and giving her time to think, but I would never take a woman against her will. Her body showed me she needed me, but fuck I am a greedy bastard, I want her head in it, too.

'Yes...' she whispered, her hands now running through my hair and pulling at the slightly long pieces on the top of my head.

'You want me, baby?'

'Yes! God help me.'

'God can't help you, but I sure fucking can... Holy Hell, what you do to me.' I needed to be in her and soon, I wanted to luxuriate in her and with her and take all day to do it, but here in my office I needed it fast and hard. I lifted the bottom of her shirt up and she raised her arms to help me. Not taking it over her head, I left it so she was momentarily blinkered with her arms stuck above her head. I pulled down the cups of her dark blue lacy bra together. Running my hands over both of her tits, they felt so heavy with her arousal. She moaned and it was like music to my balls. I felt her push down further onto me, trying to relieve her own ache. Her nipples were imploring me to take them in my mouth and suck.

So, I did. Her skin tasted sublime and the reaction was immediate.

'Oh, ALEX!'

Just hearing my name on her lips spurred me on. She knew it was me; she wasn't just lost in the moment. Continuing to suck and flick at her nipples I started to rock her into my cock by grabbing onto her hips. I needed to get off in her, but the compulsion to hear her come undone was growing. She was so fucking close, I could smell it, I could hear it in her breathing, feel it in her almost sporadic movements as she rubbed against my cock to increase her pleasure. But I needed to see it on her face. I wanted to watch her brown eyes roll into the back of her head, and to see the flush on her cheeks.

I released one of her hips and pulled at the shirt, to lift her out from her confines. Her hair was mussed, and it fell loosely around her shoulders. Her cheeks were as flushed as her lips and nipples. Her hands came down to my chest and she used the leverage to rub herself off on my cock, quicker, harder.

She was fucking gorgeous, I could feel the build up of my own release curling and uncurling at the base of my spine. Every moan and whimper she made, went straight to my balls.

'OH MY GOD!' she shouted and I quickly placed my mouth over hers to muffle her cries. I could feel every part of her stiffen and shake as her orgasm came and rolled over her time and time again, the rest of her sweet noises only for me as I licked and explored her mouth, pinching and rolling her nipples with both of my thumbs and forefingers. She seemed to go on forever.

I don't think my cock had ever been so fucking hard. I couldn't take anymore. My cock throbbed against its tight restraints, the heat of her pussy, her arousal filling up my nostrils and I ejaculated hard, inside of my jeans, without ever having had her hands on me, without even having the top button released.

*I....seriously it was like being on a first date as a kid.*

'FUCK...FUCK... What you do to me, baby.'

It was the most intense orgasm I had ever felt in my life. I clutched her to me as tight as I could without hurting her. The world slowly came back into view, but I didn't want to lose her to it just yet.

Suddenly the door burst open and I quickly rolled her off me and over to the side, away from the door. I didn't want anyone to see her in just her bra and jeans, with her tits exposed. They were for my eyes only.

*She is fucking mine.*

'Frankie?' I heard her friend Bella. I turned my head slightly and raised my eyes to hers, questioning her.

'OK, Frankie?'

'We're fine; close the door on your way out.'

'I'm not talking to you, you arsehole. Frankie?'

She didn't move out of my arms, which pleased me.

'I'm OK, Bella, please... I'll be out in a minute.' Her voice sounded so small, she never even looked at Bella, and she hid in the crook of my neck.

*Fucking hell she's ashamed.*

With relief I heard the door close; my body instantly sagged into the couch.

## Frankie

*Tick, tick, tick, tick*

The clock was almost telling me my time was over. Jesus Christ what had I done?

I slowly started to move, I couldn't look him in the eye, not just yet. What was I saying? … I couldn't look at him at all. The guilt weighed so heavy.

But I could feel him, boy could I feel him, the hardness of his body slightly pressed into mine, protecting me. His muscular arms wrapped around me. Me, pathetically clinging on to his bi-ceps, with both of my hands.

My aching swollen nipples were still hanging out of my bra. I felt so exposed, but still so turned on.

*Oh my God!*

*Oh my God!*

He wasn't moving at all, his body still felt weighty on mine. Every breath I took I could smell his cologne, the same smell that had haunted my dreams for so long, but with it a rather heady male muskiness that was pure Alex.

That was the thought that made me move.

Physically I pushed his body away from me, and he rolled over and away onto the other side of the settee.

I jumped up suddenly, I tried to replace the cups on my bra, and bend down all at the same time, to retrieve JJ's rugby shirt from floor.

'Don't over think this... Frankie,' reverberated his deep voice. Alex was now sitting up on the couch. He had leant forward now and I knew he was staring at me. In my peripheral view, I could see him turning his ring around over and over again.

*The ring, why hadn't I realised it before?*

It was the same ring I knew JJ had worn. I should have recognised it earlier. His eyes were now boring into the side of my face, leaving behind a cheek so hot you could fry an egg on it.

Finally, I felt the soft, almost comforting fabric of my shirt fall over me, covering up my traitorous body and removing it from his sight. I could speak then, now we were on an almost equal footing.

*I couldn't believe what I had just done on his lap.*

He witnessed me grinding my body into his cock and coming. My head was shaking very subtly from side to side. I wasn't sure if it was in disbelief or disgust with myself.

My one thought, which was paramount, was my body wanted to jump him again. Right here in this moment I wanted more of him, his smell, his hard body and his kisses. I had never been kissed like that; in fact, I thought they only existed in books. The books that I so loved to read. I lifted my right hand and ran my fingers lightly over the obviously swollen, claimed area of my mouth.

My thoughts silenced suddenly as he stood up.

Turning my head, I finally looked up at the man mountain.

Those eyes, they looked as though someone had lit them with a match, the green was on fire.

He started to unbutton his shirt. As the shirt fell away from his torso, it revealed everything I knew it would. Broad, well developed shoulders, huge traps running down from his neck, hard well defined pectorals, tattoos in various places and abdominal muscles that my tongue longed to lick, to try and follow the undulations. There was a spattering of chest hair, the all important V, and of course the happy trail leading down to his cock.

All the synapses in my brain start firing at once. As much as I wanted to, surely he didn't think now I had come to my senses somewhat, I was going to do it again?

'Frankie... calm down... when we have sex again... and we will have sex again, it will be in a much more appropriate place than my office at a rugby club. It will be somewhere we can lock the world out. Somewhere I can take my sweet time with you.'

'You sure are one cocky, arrogant bastard aren't you?'

'Yep,' he said, grinning from ear to ear, still undressing before me. My eyes watched the movement of his hands, undoing the brown belt on his jeans. The quick flick, which released the top button and I was now looking at a very tidy piece of manscaping.

*WHAT... the guy also goes commando?* I forced my eyes away, straight up to his very pleased smirk.

'But now I need to get rid of these clothes and take a quick shower, as much as I enjoyed... no I'll rephrase that,' his thumb and forefinger gently tipped my head back and he stared into my eyes, 'As much as I fucking loved ejaculating into my jeans, because of you and your sexy grinding motion... I don't want to be wearing my cum all the way home,' he winked at me, and released my chin. He turned and opened a section of the dark wood panelling that surrounded the masculine office. I hadn't even realised it was there. It was obviously a shower room.

At the sound of running water, I turned and performed my well practised routine again. I fled.

# Chapter 15

The light in the hallway made me feel worse. It was so bright, almost like a thousand spotlights had been turned on, especially to interrogate me. Thankfully it was void of people.

I knew the layout of the clubhouse was such that I would need to enter the bar area, in order to reach the ladies. With as much courage as I could muster, I pushed open the door.

Not wanting to attract anyone's attention, I silently made my way to the edge of the bar, to the welcome sight of the word 'Ladies' placed to the right of the door that I so badly needed to enter.

Once inside I leant my back on the cold wall and listened. Someone was obviously looking out for me. The toilet was silent and appeared to be vacant.

Making my way to the vanity unit on extremely shaky legs, I stared at my reflection.

It had to be said; I looked the best I had ever seen. My eyes shone so brightly. My cheeks were flushed and healthy looking. How ridiculous?

*So what I was saying was I was the best looking after rubbing myself off on a complete stranger's lap? The complete stranger, who led my cousin to his death.*

I looked down and started to wash my hands.

*Was I trying to wash away my guilt? Or the feeling of touching Jabby?*

I didn't know, but what I did know was I needed to remove my soaked knickers and then get the hell out of here and home. A quick exit was what I needed now.

I entered the cubicle. Undoing my jeans I pushed them down my legs and sat down with a sigh, my clit was still throbbing with need.

*What the hell was going on with me?*

I heard the toilet door open.

'Frankie?... are you OK?... I saw you come in. Come on, answer me.'

Letting out an audible sigh, my body sank further down onto the loo.

'Yeah, I'm in here, Bella; just give me a minute, please.'

I quickly removed my knickers and stuffed them in my jeans pocket. I pulled my jeans up and left my rugby shirt untucked, to cover up the now very evident bulge over my right hip. Lifting the lock, I opened the door and fell literally into a hug from my friend. She pushed my hair away from my face.

'Oh my God... what the hell did I just do?'

Bella smiled at me, 'I would say you just did one of the best looking blokes I have ever seen,' she waggled her eyebrows at me.

'BELLA... please be serious!'

'Frankie, I honestly believe you have to let this go. The bloke was exonerated; the whole thing was misjudgement, wasn't it?'

Pursing my lips together, I nodded slowly 'Yeah, I think you're right, but who the hell is he, thinking he can control my life?'

'That, gorgeous girl, remains to be seen. But I really do believe you need to at least stay here a while. See Nathan's physio through and see what happens. For once in your life I am going to be the friend, who doesn't let you run away,' she clasped both sides of my face and pulled me to her. 'Yes?'

'Yes.'

'Right come on, get cleaned up and let's get back to the bar.'

'Did you tell Nathan... what you saw in the office?' I lifted my gaze to meet hers in the mirror. She was examining her hair and face. I subconsciously ran my fingers through my own hair trying to make it appear tidy.

'Tell him what?... that I entered the office and saw his brother holding you in his arms, like all his Christmases and birthdays had come at once,' she smiled at me, whilst touching up her now fading lipstick.

'Really?' I stopped what I was doing and questioned her.

'Really,' her eyes bore into my own, trying to convey how strongly she wanted me to feel the word. 'Whatever he's got for you he's got it bad,' she finished pruning and held out her hand for mine. 'Come on let's do this.'

I took a deep breath and followed her out into the bar area.

The bar was much less busy now. We made our way back to our original booth. A quick glance around showed me that Nathan had been joined there by Alex and Brent. Nathan appeared a little worse for wear. Alex was refusing to take his eyes off me, as he turned the tumbler glass around and around in his two hands.

I couldn't meet his eyes, not just yet.

Nathan rather clumsily stood as best he could and grabbed me to him. 'Sorry, chocolate drop... I didn't mean to cause you any hurt. I just knew he knew you. And wanted to oust him... he's always so goddamn secretive!'

'It's alright, Nathan,' I patted his arm reassuringly, wanting him to sit, before he fell down in an intoxicated heap, at my feet.

'It's a real pleasure to finally meet you properly, Frankie. JJ talked about you all the time, I feel as though I already know you.' I looked towards the voice just in time to see Brent lift his beer to his mouth and catch the same ring on his left hand.

'You knew JJ?'

'I sure did honey, and it was an honour,' he cleared his throat obviously trying to disguise his emotions.

Still clutching Bella's hand, I glanced over to Alex. His forearms, in his now white shirt sleeves, were now on the table in front of him. But his eyes were still resting on me, trying to ascertain how I was feeling.

I smiled a small careful smile at him. I swallowed with the embarrassment of the pictorial flashes going through my head, of my latest orgasm.   He stood suddenly, lifting an eyebrow at me, questioningly. With his movement wafted over that cologne. The cologne that filled my dreams and now my reality, it seemed.

Bella almost instinctively dropped my hand as Alex came and stood next to me. His left hand reached out as he lightly ran his fingertips down, from in between my shoulder blades, grazing all the way down my spine, finally coming to a stop at the top of my bum cheeks. My body automatically jumped in response and my hips jerked forward.

I breathed in quickly, trying to disguise my response.   He stooped down to me. The scruff on his face bristled against the shell of my ear. I could feel his hot breath. It was all it took for my clit to start throbbing again. Then he whispered, 'Steady, baby, we have all night......'

*Jesus Christ what does this man have over me?*

Just then his phone rang, after checking the screen for the incoming contact details Alex took the call.

His deep voice affected me in ways I was just too naive to even contemplate. The hair on the back of my neck stood to attention. My blood pumped quicker around my body and my bloody nipples were so hard they were trying to force themselves through the lace holes in my bra.

'Right then, ladies and meddling brother of mine, we need to start making our way back to the city. Edwards is on time and will be landing in precisely 8 minutes.'

'You're travelling back with us?' I asked.

'Yes, Frankie, I am. I think we have some talking to do. Don't you? Now that we have finally... come together,' with the last statement the corners of his mouth lifted and formed his beautiful heart shaped lips into the start of a full on, bad boy grin.

The pull I felt as he poked his tongue out at me, wetting his lips in the process, was palpable. He left me feeling like a rabbit caught in car headlights. Paralysed I watched him casually run his hand through his wet hair. His preference was obviously to wear it flopped over slightly to one side; his hand seemed to check it out of habit. Even that small display left me breathless and weak at the knees.

The helicopter flight was quick and painless. I was quiet, not joining in the banter that was flowing between the others.

*What was Alex expecting when we got back to the penthouse?*

As much as I wanted, no needed him, I also needed to think about what had happened. What I really needed was to call Aunty Jean and have a chat. She had, all my life, managed to point me in the right direction and I knew she wouldn't fail me now.

The helicopter landed. We all clambered out. Alex had been brought up with good manners it seemed, as he helped first Bella and then me down. Once my feet had touched the roof, his hands didn't leave my waist and he pulled me flush to him. I couldn't believe how well I fitted against him. I couldn't deny myself and lifted my hands up onto his shoulders. His gaze was trying to penetrate my thoughts as he rested his forehead against mine.

'I can hear the wheels in your head turning, baby; I know a lot has happened this afternoon... I just don't want you over thinking this.' He moved slightly apart from me and gesticulated with his index finger between the two of us. Then he tapped his finger to my temple.

'I just need a little time.'

'Yeah... OK, as much as it pains me,' a deep sigh left those lovely lips that I couldn't take my eyes off. It was followed by an even deeper intake of breath.

'I do understand you need a little time, and I can give you that. But I won't let you fucking over think this... you are mine, baby; you have been for a fucking long time. I have wanted you so much, for so long,' he shook his head gently.

'Now that I finally have you, I sure as hell am not fucking letting you go. DO. NOT. EXPECT. ME. TO. LET. YOU. GO.' He used his thumb and fingers to lift my chin slightly and he slowly lowered his mouth to mine. The kiss was so gentle; his tongue licking the seam of my mouth almost begging permission to enter. I opened my lips to allow him access, and the kiss immediately turned from gentle to all consuming as we explored each other.  A shout from the open door of the lift broke us reluctantly apart.

'OK ... YOU GUYS, GET A ROOM!'

It had to be Bella, only she would refuse to bow down to an alpha male such as Alex.

Alex let me lead the way towards the open lift, where everyone else was gathered, just by placing a large hand to the small of my back. It made me smile inside, as I didn't want to break this connection with him just yet. Edwards being the consummate professional had not an expression out of place. Nathan and Bella on the other hand, had the biggest grins, having just witnessed our kiss and open display of affection or lust. I could hear them silently shouting I told you so, licking the tip of their index finger and moving it down through the air. To give us a one up signal.

Thankfully the lift being this crowded stopped it from being the lust filled space I knew it could be with just Alex and I inside. The doors opened at the penthouse level and we all made our way out.

'I'll help Nathan in, no problem,' Bella was now wrapping her arms around Nathan, and Edwards propped himself up and under where Nathan would normally bury his crutch. I watched as he appeared to bodily lift him up and the three of them made their way towards Nathan's door. The door opened and they disappeared inside.

This was the bit I had been dreading and wanting all at the same time. Alex hugged me to him, saying nothing at first. I consumed everything I could to memory, not knowing if I would ever be here again.

He made me feel safe.

He made me feel alive.

He made me feel longing.

He made me feel guilt.

But most of all, he made me feel.

'So tell me, baby... how long do you need?' He rested his forehead against mine and closed his slightly hooded eyes. He ever so slowly backed me into the wall beside my front door.

'I'm not sure,' I shook my head trying to convince him.

'Not good enough, Frankie... in order to give you the time and space you say you need, you have to give me a time scale to work to, a clear indication of when I can expect to take you to my bed.' Those green eyes I had dreamt of so often, widened and amber flecks started to flick through them. One eyebrow lifted in question to me. A growing bulge in his trousers pressed into my hip bone. A knowing smile threatened that beautifully shaped mouth.

*God he really is too good looking to be a male.*

'Can you give me a couple of days?' I tried to bargain with him, convinced I was still going to be at odds with myself even then, but I needed to break this connection somehow.

'OK... It's Saturday, I can give you till Monday evening, when I expect to have you over to my place for dinner.' He started to release his hold on me, and my body started to protest.

*I have no idea why this feels so right and so wrong all at the same time.*

I still couldn't answer him. It was a full time job just trying to control the feelings rising up inside of me.

'Yeah, Monday evening,' I finally agreed.

'I agree to not see you until then, but I do not agree to not contacting you, baby. I won't question you... but I will remind you how we feel when we are together. You do feel this, don't you?'

'Yes, I feel it,' my voice was small again as I owned up to his enquiry.

'OK, Frankie. Thank you for today, I am so pleased Nathan brought you to the rugby match, even if his timing is totally fucking shit,' exasperation seemed to get to him and one hand left my body and ran through his soft clean hair.

The moment was broken as Bella came out of Nathan's apartment grinning from ear to ear as her eyes fell upon us.

'Don't mind me,' she said as she entered our apartment, the door slammed shut behind her.

Alex hooked his fingers into the front pockets of my jeans and pulled me suddenly towards him. His mouth descended quickly to mine; there was no gentleness, no patience and no asking. His mouth forcibly invaded mine and after a split second of shock, my mouth joined him and we kissed like we might never do so again. He moved away from me, almost reluctantly it seemed. The handsome face in front of my eyes broke into a huge boyish grin.

'And these, must have been left especially for me?'

It took me a moment to become coherent once again; such was the kiss he had just blown me away with. But when my eyes became focused again I saw, much to my horror, my dark blue lacy thong hanging on his left index finger.

*OH MY GOD!*

I watched as he backed away from me, grinning from ear to ear. At the last moment he opened his door, lifted up my, I was sure still soaked, underwear and sniffed. A look of utter contentment stretched across that gorgeous face and he laughed a loud booming laugh.

'Till Monday, baby... so looking forward to it,' he winked at me and ducked behind the heavy wood.

## Chapter 16

As the door closed behind me I wanted to slide down it and sit on my arse, such was the feeling of utter physical and mental exhaustion that overwhelmed me. Standing not 5ft away from me was my bestie, holding two mugs of hot steaming tea.

'I think this is probably just what the doctor ordered,' she said with a grin.

'Yeah,' I said, taking my I love New York mug from her. 'I need to call Aunty Jean.' I left that floating in the air.

'Hmmm ... OK, you probably do. But first you need to sit down with me and give me all the details.'

I followed her down the step to our sitting area and sat down with a thump, curling my legs up underneath me. I placed two hands on my cup of tea, relishing the warmth that ran through me. Slowly my gaze lifted to her beautiful blue, enquiring eyes.

'So at least we know it hasn't grown over?' she laughed.

'What?'

'Your lady garden.'

It was all too much; I snorted when breathing in and spat out some of the hot tea I was in the act of trying to swallow.

'My lady garden?' I stared at her now, as she burst out in a giggling fit.

'Well you know, gorgeous girl, it hasn't been used in that long... I was seriously beginning to wonder if having had someone play with their balls in it once before, you had now decided it was a keep off the grass, sort of lady garden?'

I was sitting listening to all her euphemisms and shaking my head.

'How do you know if I used it at all, Bella?'

She moved closer to me, on the settee. 'Come on, spill.'

I proceeded to tell her. I told her the way Alex made me feel. I described the look in his eyes, as he had lifted me onto his lap, and the huge erection, which I had ground myself onto.

'Well that certainly has me hot under the collar,' she started to fan herself with her hand. 'That explains the position you were both in when I opened the door. He had rolled you off and away, to protect you.'

'What am I going to do, Bella; he has agreed to give me until Monday night to think.'

'You see, Frankie, that's where you and I differ. I don't really understand what it is you need to think about? I know he is part of JJ's history...' I could feel her searching for the right words to use. 'The bloke had an error of judgement, call it an accident, but he didn't deliberately cause JJ to die.' The atmosphere in the room sank down a level and she reached over to hug me to her, 'I am sure he lives with this, every day of his life, his other men wouldn't want to be around him if they felt he was really to blame, would they. And yet we met Brent today.' She picked up my hand from my lap and started worrying with it. She was also starting to very subtly shake her head.

'You have felt a connection to him, for like forever! I really believe you need to see what happens next and take a leap of faith. I have never had a guy look at me the way he looks at you, that's for sure... Right OK lecture over, drink your tea up and go and call Aunty Jean.'

'Yes, Sir.' I gave her a mock salute in a silent piss take. She made it all sound so easy.

After I took my now empty mug to the kitchen, I padded my way through to my bedroom, picking up the telephone en-route and I threw myself down onto the comfortable bed. Trying to work out exactly what it was I needed to say or ask Aunty Jean. But I knew I needed to do it quickly as it was coming up for 6pm here. Adding 5 hours on, she would be getting ready for bed. I closed my eyes and listened to the dialling tone stretching across the thousands of miles between us.

'Hello,' instantly I relaxed into her comforting voice.

'Hi, Aunty,'

'Oh, Frankie, how lovely to hear your voice, I was just making a drink and going off to bed. Are you OK darling?' And there it was the ball park question.

'I need to talk to you about something, but I can call back in the morning if you would prefer,' almost grasping the opportunity to cut and run.

'No dear, talk now. I am not often here in the mornings, Frankie.' Her voice stated.

'I met my boss today, Alex Blackmore. It turns out he is...' I stopped, unable to actually annunciate the words.

'I know who he is, Frankie.'

*Say what? Did she just say she knows?*

'Sorry, Aunty, I don't think I quite caught what you just said. Could you repeat it please?'

'You heard correctly darling. Your uncle and I have been in contact with him a few times now,' she stopped speaking suddenly. 'Frankie?'

'I don't know what to say, did you know I had taken this job from him?' My voice rose.

'I did love; he had asked us our opinion, on whether he should offer you the job in the first place.'

'Did he now? But no one thought, that just maybe, I should be included in this little conversation?' I hit back.

'Now stop it, Frankie, it wasn't like that, your uncle and I thought it would be a fantastic opportunity for you. You would get to be back with Bella. We knew how much you missed her. The job would be well paid and we knew he would look after you. If he had been truthful with you, I doubt very much you would have even considered taking the job. You need to move on with your life, JJ would want you to move on....' Just when I thought she had finished she added, 'Alex has always looked out for you dear, I feel he thinks he has some connection to you, and I certainly know you have a connection to him. I watched you at Coronado together. Every time we mentioned his name afterwards you would fight with feelings of disgust and yet at the same time, I could see you had other feelings for him too. Your face has always given you away.'

The silence was screamingly loud.

'I have feelings for him, Aunty Jean; I'm just not sure what those feelings are. It's why I phoned you today.'

'Life is short my love, if we remembered all the time that we could lose someone at any moment, we would love more strongly and without inhibition, without fear of the what ifs. Not because there is nothing to lose, but because everything can always be lost at any time.'

I had tears rolling silently down my cheeks, one chasing the other.

'Please, Frankie, you need to forgive him, and you need to forgive yourself. I am going to bed now my darling. Please phone me soon, I do so love to hear your voice.'

'Night, night. I love you.'

'We love you too; don't let the bed bugs bite.' I felt a smile tugging at the corners of my lips, hearing the words she always said when we were kids.

I should shower, but the bed felt too comfortable. I began to fall asleep, utter over thinking causing my fatigue.

# Alex

I leaned on the inside of my penthouse door, for what seemed like forever. I hated walking away from her, even though it was not my fucking choice. This was, it seemed, the very reason for my anger over this fucked up situation. This wasn't my choice. I slammed my hand back smacking the hard wood frame.

Ever since I had first been sent away from my family to England, even as an eleven-year-old, I had vowed to always be in control of everyone and everything I did, from that point on.

Yeah that fucking prick had to send me away. He knew after years of abuse at his hands, the tide was turning, when I had squared up to him after nearly reaching his height, and just finally having had enough of his crap. I squeezed my eyes closed to expel him from my mind, he had no right there, and I never allowed him to stay.

Slowly I slid down the door onto my ass, collecting my controller for the apartment on the way down from the hallway table. I could feel myself taking a few deep inhalations in my struggle not to reopen this fucking piece of wood and charge over to her and fuck her senseless. Pressing the buttons on the remote, I made the blinds come down that were in-between the layers of glass. I didn't want to see the fucking city lights tonight. What I really needed was her pressed up against the cold glass, butt naked, with the cold of the glass making her nipples so hard they ached for me to warm them with my hot, wet tongue.

*I am a fucking pussy whipped prick.*

I forcibly leaned my head forward onto my knees and dragged my hands through my hair in exasperation.

'Fuck you, Nathan!' His fucking timing stank; she wasn't supposed to know about me yet. Not with the shit hitting the fan back at the house, with Scott. But even in my fit of anger, I had to relent and acknowledge that I was relieved she knew. She hadn't taken it too badly and that was a fucking relief. I was hopeful I could keep her away from the other crap going on in my life. After all I was the master of control, except of course when my idiotic little brother tried to one up me.

With that thought I threw the remote across the hallway; it smashed as it skidded across the floor, spewing its guts over the grey marble. The very moment it stopped sliding and stilled was the moment the knock on the door came.

'Alex,' it was Edwards, not the voice I wanted to hear.

I stood suddenly grasping the handle and swung open the door. 'YES,' I definitely sounded more irate than I intended and I forced myself to quickly control my temper. Edwards remained resolute at my bark and stood firm, the only tell was the raising slightly of a questioning eyebrow.

'I just wanted to let you know that Nathan is now tucked up in bed, sleeping off his drink. Luckily, I had help undressing him, otherwise I would have just left him in the recovery position and let him sleep it off, uncomfortable or not. Anyway just wanted to let you know, and see if it's OK to go off duty now?'

'Bella helped?'

'She did.'

'OK... one thing, on your way out can you get George up with a new remote for the apartment, please. I dropped this one.'

'Of course, Alex. No problem.' I am sure I caught sight of a smirk, but let it go.

'Night.'

I decided to take myself off to the gym inside the apartment. If I couldn't fuck her out of my system, I would run and pound her out.

I changed into a pair of black running shorts, and dropped my clothes on the floor in my haste, with them I dropped the dark blue lacy thong I had acquired earlier. I resisted the fucking ridiculous urge to pick it up and inhale her scent again. That would have to wait until later, when I was sure I would need to wank at least once in order to get any fucking sleep at all. I did however relent and tuck them into the elasticated waist of my shorts. I couldn't leave them behind; they were all I had of her.

Turning on the wall mounted TV, and placing the headphones on my head, I tried to lose myself into the news that was on and I started up the running machine. Listening to the days latest and trying unsuccessfully to absorb what was happening as I felt my feet pounding ever quicker on the mechanical track. It didn't matter how fucking steep I made it, or how fucking fast I set it. Apart from my body screaming at me and the whole of my upper torso being covered in sweat, it was doing nothing to erase my goddamn thoughts of her. Finally, with what sounded like an animalistic roar I punched the stop button and leant on the handle bar, gasping for air. Stepping off the machine, legs shaking, I downed one bottle of water and tipped another over my head, I flicked the water off my face with a shake of my head. I pushed my messy hair up and out of my eyes.

I started to strap up my hands ready to use the punch bag.

Once ready I began to obliterate the heavy leather bag in front of my face, with a fast almost torturous rhythm. I needed to lose the mental picture of Frankie coming undone on my lap. My hard on throbbed in my shorts; I had been hard continuously since the helicopter ride and was going to need to fucking relieve it soon. The pain in my knuckles and the sudden onset of music around the apartment brought me to once more; I looked up in time to see George lifting up one arm in a gesture of goodbye from the other side of the glass wall that made up the gym. I was physically shattered and decided to call it a night.

Undoing the glass door, I concentrated more on the music that was now playing, it was an old song, but so damned appropriate. So appropriate I decided to text it to Frankie.

Picking up my phone from the bedroom floor, I sent her the text. Then I placed the phone down on my bedside table.

*Goddamn what the hell? I'm a pussy whipped prick. There was seriously no doubt.*

I made my way into my shower, stepping out of my running shorts as I went. Cock in one hand and her thong in the other. I allowed myself to take one sniff of her arousing scent and then carefully placed them on the hook that would normally hold a towel by the shower door. The water was warm as I stood underneath the strongest part of the spray, and I began to roughly soap up my body. Wincing occasionally as my hands ran over some of the bruising I had taken during today's match. I used the soap to briskly move my hand up and down my throbbing cock, while envisaging the picture of her coming undone on my lap. I jerked suddenly and all too quickly, as I knew I would, I came all over the tiles in the shower cubicle.

'Yes,' I expelled from between gritted teeth.

Leaning forward I turned the water to freezing and stood head bowed, leaning on my forearms, the water hitting the base of my neck and in between my shoulder blades. For the first time in what seemed like days my cock went semi flaccid, and semi, I realised, was probably all the relief I was going to get. At least, for the next couple of fucking long days.

# Frankie

I came to, because my mobile had just pinged with the sound of an incoming text. Through bleary eyes I tried to read what had been sent, it was from Alex of course, but somehow I knew it was going to be.

One sentence and a song title.

*I don't want to miss a thing – Aerosmith*

*Listen to this...please. It epitomizes everything I feel, right now.*

I fell back on top of my covers and searched out the song on my phone. After listening to it a couple of times I reluctantly sat up and swung my legs over the side of the mattress. My blinds were still open and it had grown dark outside. My room was bathed with just a few lights from the city glow. I had been asleep for an hour and my stomach was growling. Sleepily I made my way out to the living room, still clutching my phone to me.

Bella was curled up under a blanket, fire roaring and watching an old movie on the huge TV that dominated one wall. I recognised the film, but couldn't think what it was called, and quite frankly had better things on my mind than to analyse it further. Without even looking towards me she lifted up one side of the fleecy blanket, gesticulating for me to enter. I did as I was silently asked and curled up against her side.

'How are you doing?' she asked

'Well I had a chat with Aunty Jean, and here's the thing, you are so not going to believe it. She and Uncle Robert already knew about Alex.' I needed to look at her expressions now and untwisted myself from her side.

'You know, I'm not surprised, I've been thinking about it whilst you've been in your room and that makes perfect sense. They seemed almost happy for you to come over here. I know that sounds wrong, as they have always been supportive of you and want you to have the life you want. But she almost pushed you onto the plane like she couldn't wait to be rid of you. No that's come out wrong, although I think you know what I mean, don't you?'

'Yeah I do, funny you should mention it.'

Bella turned off the movie and gave me a hug. 'So what else did she say?'

'Well that I need to forgive Alex and forgive myself, and basically to get on with life as life is too short and all that.'

'I'm inclined to agree with her, gorgeous girl. Now enough about Alex, although I will say one thing and one more thing only. In the space of a few hours you don't call him Jabby at all anymore, you refer to him as Alex,' she nodded at me hoping I was catching her drift.

I let out a long sigh, all this constant thinking was wearing me out, but yes she was correct as always. I was only thinking of him as Alex now.

'Right now I need to eat, and after, I must go and check on the drunkard next door.'

'I tell you what Bella; let's make a quick omelette... well I'll make it,' I said laughing at her lightly, 'then we'll both go next door and check he's not lying in vomit.'

It felt so cathartic to have a laugh with my bestie, or was it because I had made a decision about giving Alex and I a go?

Once we were in the kitchen, I bent down and started pulling items from the fridge. Tomatoes, ham, cheese, onions, eggs and milk. God I was starving. Bella put the kettle on for a cup of tea and finding my iPhone I started playing the tune Alex had just sent.

'OK that's very fitting.'

'Yeah, isn't it?... Alex sent it a short while ago.'

'Told you, Frankie, whatever it is that huge hunk of a man has got, he's got it bad and it appears to all be for you.' We looked at each other now and I broke into a smile.

'I did tell you about him in all my dreams, and what he was like, didn't I? But I obviously didn't do him justice.'

I carried on mixing the eggs and milk and adding the ingredients. We moved around the kitchen almost pre-empting each other's movements. I put Aerosmith on repeat.

'Frankie, you were so funny when you came out and saw him for the first time. I mean before he turned around and you looked as though you wanted to deck him, just before that you looked as though you were going to eat him alive.' A laugh left her but before she continued she checked to see my expression.

'I know, laugh at my expense won't you.'

The omelette was just what I needed and after finishing every scrap on my plate, I ran my finger through the last little drip of HP sauce that I had brought with me from England, smacking my lips together. I drained the last of my tea, looking up to meet Bella's gaze.

'So, gorgeous girl, hot screaming orgasms obviously agree with you?... well they certainly give you an appetite anyway.'

'Enough, come on let's go and see the bloke you're lusting after,' I raised my hand suddenly to her showing her my palm, 'talk to the hand, don't even bother denying it, even I can see the chemistry between you two.'

'It's just...'

'No I don't want to know, unless it's the truth, and quite honestly I don't think you are even aware of the truth yet.'

'OK right... Yes, Nathan and I have a bloody arrangement, happy now?' she forced out.

'A bloody arrangement, what the hell is one of those?'

'Come on even in your virginal mind, you must have heard of fuck buddies?'

'OK, so let me get this straight, you and sex on crutches, with the just fucked hair, are fuck buddies?... good for you girl... I just hope neither of you get hurt at the end.' I was standing, leaning on the worktop, hands crossed over my chest, giving her a knowing look.

'Come on, Frankie... there you go again, over thinking everything and presuming one or both people in a perfectly adult agreement will get hurt. It doesn't always happen you know?' she had her hands on her hips, obviously trying to accentuate how strongly she felt.

I just twisted my head at her and offered a wry smile.

We made our way out from the kitchen and towards the front door.

'How are we going to get in to check Nathan? I don't think we've thought this through very well.'

Bella started waving a key card in front of my face. I had to relinquish, that maybe actually she had.

*How long exactly had she had a key to his apartment?*

It was cooler in the hallway. I couldn't help my eyes drifting to Alex's door. I fought with myself to concentrate on following Bella, who was walking in front of me, as she opened Nathan's door. She had obviously been over here quite a bit, as she could even find her way around the space in the semi darkness.

The bitch, we were so going to have to have a more in depth discussion about the fuck buddies understanding she had going on. I understood the concept. But I needed many, many more details.

I made sure to follow close behind Bella as we went as quietly as possible through Nathan's apartment, stepping behind her as we finally made it to his bedroom. The sound of snoring hit me first and

I tried not to laugh out loud. The smell of Jack Daniels hit next, it was obviously leaking out of him, from every available orifice. My eyes slowly adjusted to the dull light in the room.

Stretched out magnificently on his bed was a very naked Nathan. Luckily he was lying on his front, arms tucked under his pillow. Even drunk, he made a breath-taking sight.

'OK, perhaps you had better take it from here, Bella? Not sure he is going to want me seeing his bits.'

'I hear you, but how the hell am I going to turn him onto his side, all by myself, Einstein?'

'Right, but I'll help from his back side and not the front view.'

We carefully got ourselves into position on the bed. Trying to lift various parts of the famous superbike rider, who was like a lead weight in our arms. We were laughing out loud, at the mess and tangle of limbs we had all become. The more we struggled with the inert frame of Nathan, the more he fought back.

'Hey, Bella,' we heard from a slurring Nathan. 'You smell sexy, come here.'

'Just trying to move you, in case you're sick, Nathan, put your arm around my neck and lift yourself up slightly.'

I stopped touching Nathan and sat back, knees bent, bum on my ankles. It was a comical sight. It was great to relieve the pressure of the day. Nathan had hold of her around the neck and was trying to bring her down for a kiss. Bella on the other hand was keeping herself away, trying to manoeuvre him onto his side. For not the first time I felt like a voyeur. But it was too funny to leave just yet.

'I'm not as... drunk as... you make out, sassy.'

'Yeah, OK arsehole just move, so you're on your side, will you?'

Suddenly I became aware of movement behind me, from the door. A deep voice followed.

'Not quite sure what's going on here ladies, but do you need some assistance, while you manhandle my brother?'

I felt myself freeze, and just for a second, time stood still. Alex's fingertips found their way to the place between my shoulder blades and he ran them ever so slightly down my spine to the top of my bottom making my hips jerk forward in response, yet again.

'Alex, thank God. I just want him on his side, in case he throws up. But he's fighting me all the way.'

'Right cover up his junk for me and I'll move him. Maybe you would be better outside now, Frankie?' He said it as a given, obviously not wanting me to see his brother's junk, as he called it.

I made my way out to his living room and began to fumble around, feeling for some lights. Nervously, and trying to occupy my time now I could see, I begin to study all the black and white photographs Nathan had. I picked up the one which had previously interested me. Now I understood why, it was Nathan, Alex and what looked like their other brother? The sound of Alex's voice right behind me made me place the photograph down quickly. I spun around feeling like a naughty child for even touching it.

He was a glorious sight, standing to his full height, arms crossed in front of his chest. Sporting an amused, knowing smile. A T-shirt stretched across his broad chest and shoulders. I could make out a tattooed sleeve all over the skin of one of his arms. The same old jeans from earlier which were so worn and thin, I felt I could almost see through them and huge bare feet.

*You know what they say about men with big hands and feet? Really, I was going to go there now?*

I lifted my gaze to meet his smirk; he was obviously pleased that he had found me checking him out.

'I was wondering if you would mind putting on some coffee, Nathan has just fucking puked, at the moment he is in the shower being watched by Bella, but I need to get back to him... not quite the night I was hoping for,' he trailed off and I felt his gaze penetrating me.

'Yeah sure, no problem.' I started to move forward, expecting him to move out of my way, but he didn't and I literally walked into the man mountain. Feeling brave I looked up at him. His scruff was longer now and I allowed myself to run my fingertips over it.

Immediately his eyes lit up, with the amber flecks now dancing in them. He smelt so clean and irresistible as his cologne hit all my senses at once and I had to really fight hard, to even think lucidly. My thumb traced its way into the cleft of his chin. His arms closed tightly around me.

'I promised myself I wouldn't touch you when I saw you from the doorway, Frankie, and Then. You. Go. And. Walk... straight into my fucking arms,' he placed his face into my hair, and breathed me in. 'And fuck me if you don't feel fantastic there. I promised you I would give you the time you need even if it kills me... I gotta say... it is fucking killing me,' he was nodding his head as he spoke.

I continued to explore his striking features with my hand. He closed his eyes slowly and let out a sharp expel of air, from those heart shaped lips.

Suddenly his eyes flew open; he crushed my small frame to his enormous one. I could feel his erection, pressing into my stomach. Then all at once he pushed himself away from me.

'You're playing with fire, baby; don't start something you're not prepared to see through... to the end.' The look on his face was almost feral.

He spun around on his heels, and back towards Nathan's bedroom door, pushing his hands deep into the back pockets of his jeans. Gripping his arse cheeks, the same arse cheeks that I so wanted to grip myself.

'I have already decided,' I spoke to him, 'I don't need till Monday... I want you... I need to give this, whatever it is, a go.'

*Did that really come out of my mouth?*

I'd shocked myself. But the look on Alex's face was priceless as he spun back around so quickly. He vaulted over the couch in front of him in order to get back to me quicker. Upon reaching me he picked me up.

'Legs around my waist, now!' It wasn't a question it was a demand and bugger me if my body didn't comply immediately. My arse could feel his impressive erection, probing it. Our mouths mashed together and he kissed me like we had been apart years.

*I don't know, maybe we had?*

He held my body up to him, like I weighed nothing. His hands clasped around my back like a vice. Our tongues explored each other's mouths and lips like we were the very air each other needed to breathe. I had read about kissing till you were breathless before, and it seemed like I was going to find out exactly what that felt like, here and now. I only knew that in this very moment in time I needed to kiss him more than I needed oxygen to breathe. We eventually broke the kiss and he leaned his forehead to mine.

'You won't regret that decision, baby. I promise you.'

He broke the moment by swatting my arse with a hand that had just left my back.

'Jump down. Frankie and go make some coffee please; we need to sort out my inebriated little brother... And then you're coming home with me.' He winked at me and let me slide all the way down his body over his erection. Almost to remind me, just exactly why, I needed to go home with him later.

I didn't need reminding. Every hair on my body was on end and my skin tingled in all the places he had just touched me. My clit was throbbing and my jeans were soaked.

I watched him as he made his way to Nathan's door once again; he turned and mouthed at me.

'MINE.'

I flew out to the kitchen, just desperate to occupy my hands at the very least. My mind didn't stand a chance.

It proved to be a very late night/early morning for all of us, when Nathan had finally stopped hurling and we had managed to get him to take some fluids, we could at least start to relax.

Bella said she would stay with him and call if he started throwing up again. It seemed in his haste to drown his guilt over opening the can of worms; he had forgotten that pain medication does not mix well with too much alcohol.

It was 3am by the time we made it back to Alex's apartment.

# Chapter 19

I had never felt so wired in my life as we entered Alex's apartment. He closed the door behind us and for a split second I felt like running. Such was the feeling of utter panic rising inside of me. He was looking at me with that same feral, wild look, that his eyes took on and his whole stance had changed. I felt like his prey.

'Breathe, Frankie, just breathe. Nothing will happen here tonight, that you don't want. But you do need to relax.'

He moved towards what I could only believe must be his bedroom. He stopped in the doorway and held out his hand to me.

'Come.'

I only hesitated slightly and then found myself moving towards him. I slipped my, what seemed like tiny hand into his massive one and he walked us into the bedroom. The room was in semi darkness.

He held me to him briefly and then raised his left hand to cup the back of my neck whilst he placed feather like kisses onto and around my lips. His mouth left my mine and started to travel down and over my jaw line. He kissed and licked from the lobe of one ear all the way around to the other. His hand never left the nape of my neck. His fingers gently pressed into my hot skin.

My body felt like it was on fire, if he could do this to me by just placing his lips on me, what the hell else was going to happen tonight?

'I'm going to undress you now, baby and I am only going to ask once if that's OK with you.'

I nodded at him.

'Uh uh... I need the words, baby,' he resumed kissing my neck now and my heart was pounding so hard, I felt like it would leave my body. I couldn't even think straight, let alone speak.

He stopped suddenly. My neck felt bereft.

'Words, Frankie.'

'Yes, yes its fine, take all my bloody clothes off, I don't care, just carry on kissing me.'

The laugh that reverberated from him was one of the most joyful sounds I had ever heard.

'Arms up.' I lifted my arms on his command. He lifted off JJ's rugby shirt.

Suddenly I felt dirty, dirty that he was taking off the same clothes as I had been wearing yesterday.

'I haven't showered,' fell out of my mouth.

'And. You. Think. I. Care. Because?' He asked me this in between resuming the kisses to my neck, and now across the tops of each shoulder.

'You need to stop thinking, baby,' his voice was becoming even deeper.

I was beginning to shake in his arms now; the backs of my knees were starting to give way. Alex backed me slowly towards his bed and gently lowered me onto it. He stood up slowly and just stood there gazing at me, whilst relieving me of my jeans.

'Commando, Miss. Jones? I am impressed.'

'Yes some man stole my knickers last night,' I smiled up at him watching, as he lifted his T-shirt off and away from his fantastically hard body, I could just make out some bruising, probably from the rugby game. Was it only yesterday? I couldn't think any more. I watched as still in his jeans he bent down to pick up one of my feet.

He kissed each toe slowly and torturously on both of my feet, sucked each one individually into his mouth and ran his tongue in between each of my toes. The warmth of his mouth creating a flood from my pussy that felt like a running river.

Shit he was totally out of my league. If he could do this to me by sucking my toes, I would spontaneously combust before he even got up to my pussy or my nipples.

He kissed up each leg, stopping to pay a ridiculous amount of attention to the soft spots behind my knees. I was panting now, long drawn out pants. I was so turned on.

'Please,' fell from my lips.

'Please what?' His eyes met mine.

'I need you, and I need you now.'

'Where do you need me, baby?' His voice was so calm and in control.

Just then he slowly crawled up my body; I opened my eyes to find him inhaling from my pussy. I could feel his breath there as he questioned me.

'Do you need me here?'

He left my pussy, without me having answered and continued to lick up and over my stomach. My head, that had left the pillow to look at him, fell back with a thump and a moan escaped my lips.

'I don't know... I just know I need you.'

That bloody talented tongue of his, had found its way to the underside of my breasts and he was thoroughly enjoying running his hot, wet tongue around and around my nipples, but just not quite managing to touch where I needed him to be.

'I have been waiting so long, baby, to hear that you need me.'

He suddenly sucked my left nipple into his mouth, his tongue flicking it quickly. But it wasn't enough. My back had risen up and was arched just trying to find his jean clad erection. I needed some resistance against my clit and I was seeking it wildly, almost moving my hips around in circles. I realised I was following the rhythm he was creating with his tongue on my nipple.

Alex swapped nipples, sucking up my right one so quickly into his mouth I almost screamed out loud, such was the relief. He leant his body weight onto his right arm, and his left arm found its way down to where I desperately needed it to be.

'Oh my God...Alex.'

'You are so wet, baby.'

He was trailing his index finger through my folds and moving it over my anus and back up to my clit. It only took the pressure of his thumb on my clit and I began to fall apart. I squeezed my eyes together hard, trying to shut out the blinding white light that threatened to engulf me. My hands reached for my nipples and gently squeezed the tight buds. Wave after wave rolled over and over. Just when I was beginning to relax and feel my orgasm ending Alex moved suddenly. He went down, separating my legs and hoisting them over each of his shoulders. His mouth moved immediately to my pussy and he began to lap at me, sucking and probing. The orgasm that was fading away, suddenly leapt to life once again and I screamed his name, both of my hands now holding onto his head like my life depended on it.

Just when I felt I couldn't take anymore, I was that sensitive, his face appeared wearing a huge grin and wiping the back of his hand over his mouth.

I felt horrified.

'You taste divine, baby. In fact, possibly the best fucking meal I have ever had, so wipe that look off your face. This,' he blew on my clit as he spoke, 'from now on, will become one of my favourite places to be.'

Alex crawled up my body and pressed his mouth to mine. I had always thought the taste of me would be disgusting, but sharing it with him was so natural. Our tongues began to explore each other once again.

Just from him kissing me again my desire ramped. I found my hands running down his muscular back, feeling every piece of hard muscle and sinew I could.

He continued to kiss me, but I could hear his groans as I ran my nails over his shoulder blades. It felt almost heady realising in my inexperience that I could pull these sounds out of him. I pushed down towards the waistband of his jeans. Trying to divide us slightly to undo them and expose him.

He had felt huge before, but so far after all we had done, I still hadn't laid eyes on him and I had to admit I was beginning to feel a little desperate, even after two mind blowing orgasms. My pussy was soaked again and my clit was throbbing.

'I want these off,' I managed to get out.

With one swift movement, he broke away from me and stood at the end of the bed. His eyes captured mine as he all too slowly undid the top button, and then the next. Finally, he pushed them over that well defined arse, which right now I wanted to bite. His cock was exposed almost all at once and I felt myself take in a deep breath. He was a sight to behold; his cock was large and completely engorged. It went well with the rest of his well-defined body.

As Alex moved a step towards me his large cock bobbed. He crawled back up the bed to one side of me now.

'Just getting a condom, baby.'

Whilst he stretched over me I couldn't help myself and shimmied down a little. I just needed a taste of him.

'Don't!' I heard the command, but couldn't stop myself, my need was too great.

I opened my mouth wide and took in his large crown; I dubiously ran my tongue around the hot, smooth skin. He tasted so male and so Alex, obviously the cologne was also a body wash. Yummy.

'Enough, I want to cum in you and with you, not in your mouth this time.'

He rolled on the condom with an expert hand; just watching him roll it down his length was enough to have my pussy flooding again. He ran his fingers through my folds and closed his eyes, bringing his wet fingers up to coat his cock.

'So wet, Frankie, so goddamn wet. I love the way your body responds to me.'

After positioning himself above me for a few seconds, slowly the crown of his cock began to penetrate me. My pussy was on fire with need. But I now had the glorious feeling of being stretched beyond capacity, even if it was also slightly painful. After a final push all the way in, he slowed and stopped, his mouth regaining its previous hold on my nipple as one arm came under me to lift me off the bed.

'ALEX...ALEX I need you to move, this is killing me!'

With a noise of almost victory, he lowered me back down to the bed and began to rock in and out of me, rubbing my clit with every out movement. The pain had left me now as he quite obviously knew it would. I could feel my body climbing higher and higher as I grabbed hold of him tightly.

I looked into his eyes, just as I exploded with a force I had never felt before. Electric shocks travelled up and down every part of my body.

'Oh God...Yes...Yes!'

My explosion made the walls of my pussy clamp tightly together. As they contracted again and again he came almost immediately after me. I watched in complete awe as the beautiful man above me called out my name time after time. He rolled suddenly and pulled me on top of him. Tears fell down my face and onto his chest, to join the beads of sweat on him already. With a sure hand he removed the condom and dropped it to the floor.

'Holy hell, what you do to me, baby... sleep now, it's way past late.' His speech was so quiet it was almost a whisper. With that he kissed the top of my head and wrapped his arms around me tightly.

The sound of the rain awoke me the next morning. One of the many things I loved was the warmth and comfort of being in bed, whilst watching the rain hit the panes of glass outside. This feeling washed over me. The bed was beyond comfortable and huge. It took me all of a minute to realise exactly where I was. My body felt used and achy in places I had never ached before. Stretching my arms out wide over the blue sheets, it became very quickly apparent that I was alone, and even quicker panic engulfed me. Clutching one of the sheets to my bare chest I sat up suddenly.

*Where is he? Has he had what he wanted from me, and I've been discarded?*

Closing my eyes, I lay back down on the bed. It didn't feel anywhere near as warm and cosy now. I started to listen, in case I could hear him in the apartment anywhere. But unfortunately I could hear nothing over the rain.

*Stop it Frankie, you're over thinking.* But the truth was, I was shit at relationships, I didn't know anything about one night stands.

*Is that what this is/was?* I felt it was so much more. I must be more naive than I thought.

I decided it was flight time.

I jumped out of bed quickly and started to rummage around the floor looking for my few items of clothing. This seemed to be becoming a habit, me picking up JJ's rugby shirt off one of Alex's floors.

Just then I heard a loud 'Huh hmm' from behind me. I span around so quickly, in shock that I ended up on my arse. My limbs where in a tangle, and I held my few retrieved items of clothing.

But it was so worth it. My gaze lifted and found the absolutely captivating vision of Alex, leaning on the open doorframe to his bedroom. Hands tucked under his armpits and arms crossed over his chest. His sheer physicality took over the whole of the doorway. He was wearing the most gorgeous smile, full blown dimples in each cheek. His hair was messed up and very slightly damp. His eyes sparkled with their emerald green; once again I could not tear my eyes away.

*Jesus Christ have I got this bad!*

'Frankie, you look like an excerpt from Bambi, you OK?' He couldn't keep his amusement from covering the whole of his face. I smiled back. He started to make his way towards me. He was only wearing black gym shorts, and his body seemed to be glistening. Obviously, he had been working out.

*No shit Sherlock?*

Alex's bedroom was large,, and it took him a few steps to get over to me. Giving me the extra gawping time I needed just to appreciate this man. I expelled a small sigh and became conscious that the wonderful achy parts of my body, which I felt when I woke up, had once again become alive and were now throbbing with the need of him.

I accepted the out stretched hand he had offered to me. He pulled me up and straight, flush with his body. His hands went around and cupped each of my bum cheeks. I had the feeling of being right where I was meant to be, like I belonged with him and to him. My soft curves seemed to fit exactly against his large, hard frame. He buried his head into the crook of my neck and inhaled deeply.

'I was just checking on Nathan. Sorry you woke up without me being here. I had already checked on you a couple of times. You were fast asleep, in my bed... I liked it, seeing you there.' He removed his head from my shoulder now. Bending his knees somewhat so our eyes were at the same level and resting our foreheads together. 'Why were you getting your clothes together?' he asked.

I smacked my lips, and sucked in my bottom lip. I was just trying to think of an answer, that wouldn't make me sound like a childish, insecure wreck.

'Oh, I was thinking that I needed a shower, just picking up my clothes on the way and tidying up.' His eyes continued to seek out the truth in mine.

'Yeah, of course you were? Now, the truth?' He nodded slightly in encouragement.

'Oh... you weren't here and... well I just thought that perhaps that was deliberate. Perhaps we had done what you needed from me and it was time for me to leave?' Alex's face changed; his jaw was tensing in front of my eyes and the amber flecks had started to make a reappearance. I could clearly see he was not happy with my answer. He didn't push me away though, which had to be a good sign I thought.

'Right number one, I don't bring women back here. This is my space and I choose carefully who I invite into it.'

'Number two, I definitely don't fuck women here,' he inhaled deeply, almost as if to calm himself down.

'Number three, we didn't fuck last night, I made love to you. And number four...' his voice dropped now, 'Did you not feel that? If you didn't, baby, then I sure as hell wasn't doing it right. I obviously need to rectify that situation, NOW. THIS. VERY. FUCKING. MINUTE,' he started to gently nip my neck in between each word.

Suddenly he picked me up, my clothes fell once again onto his floor and he kicked them away. I had to accept I could get very used to this deliciously dominant male. He found my lips with his and began an onslaught of kisses that simply blew me away. He cleverly manoeuvred us into his en-suite and holding me up with just one arm he turned on the massive shower heads and steam began to fill the room.

I gasped in shock at being placed down on the cold tiles of the bench seat in his shower. I felt the goose bumps running up and down my body. He carefully left my face and grabbed both of my breasts to rest his face in the middle of them, turning his head from side to side to lick and suck at both of my nipples.

My hands grasped at the back of his neck, pulling slightly at his now soaking wet hair. He ran his tongue straight down the centre of my body, circling my belly button and then down to my pussy.

The embarrassment hit me, 'Alex... please you need to stop. I need a wee.'

He talked whilst still eating me out and laving at my clit. 'Uh uh baby, hold it... your orgasm will be more intense.' With a hand on each of my inner thighs, he spread me as wide as he could. The feeling was exquisite. The hot water was pulsing over my whole body, his talented tongue flicking, teasing and pressing on my clit. He didn't move it away at all, staying exactly right where I needed him, my whole body tensed up. Behind my closed eyelids I could see white light dancing. I felt myself convulsing against his face time and time again.

'OH MY GOD! ALEX...ALEX... I'm coming,' I could hear myself screaming as the waves of pleasure pushed sharply through the whole of my body.

He lifted his head up still holding my thighs. With his eyes closed, he leant his head back under the strong spray of the shower. Shaking his head now and running the one hand that had now left my thigh through his hair, he brought his focus back to me.

'Tell me you don't feel this, Frankie?' He moved his index finger backwards and forwards, from him to me.

'I do... but it scares me.' *There I've said it now; it's out there, with no returns. I lapsed into childish thoughts.*

'I will look after you; just give yourself to me... all of you. I have always looked after you.' His hands gently clasped each side of my face.

Our moment was disturbed by the phone. He started to stand up, leaving the shower and going to the door, where he picked up the receiver, abruptly.

''Yep... yeah, OK... We'll be there in ten.'

'That was Bella, I gave her my number, just in case she needed us... it seems she could do with some food,' he informed me, as he climbed back into the shower. 'I thought you needed a wee? Get it done now, Frankie, as I need to clean you.'

I hurriedly left the shower as a smack stung my bum cheek. I gasped and threw him a look. He smiled quickly at me and returned to rubbing that gorgeous smelling shower gel all over his body.

*Can I wee whilst he's here?* I didn't think twice I was that desperate. After all he had seen me up close, how could I be embarrassed about having a wee?

I felt cold as I got back in behind him and I ran my hands around his waist and hugged him tightly to my front.

'I have one rule, baby, about my bathroom. When you're in here I clean you. I want to look after you.' He began to fill a natural sponge with his cologne smelling shower gel. 'Turn around.' I turned and he directed me under the hot stream of water. Very gently he washed all of me down.

My gaze drifted to outside the shower cubicle and I saw my thong hanging on the towel hook.

*WTF?*

'You short on linen, Alex?' I smiled at him.

He moved his head and followed to where I was looking.

'They're mine now, for emergencies.' He grinned back at me.

'If I don't get rid of this soon,' he glanced down at his hard-on.... 'We may soon fucking have one, but now we don't have the time,' he grimaced.

'OK, jump out, baby. I need to turn the temperature to fucking freezing so we can go feed Bella and my asshat of a brother.'

# Chapter 20

I had to put on my old clothes, in order to make it across to our apartment. I didn't feel comfortable doing so, though. It came to my attention that Alex seemed to enjoy watching me do everything. As I pulled up my jeans he was already dressed and laying back on his bed. The smile on his face was captivating. I took in everything about him, just so I could remember him like a photograph, when needed. He was wearing an old, navy blue T-shirt, stretched across his chest. The slogan on it now faded, but it read "for those about to ruck, we salute you."

*An old rugby T-shirt then?*

As his hands were clasped behind his head, the T-shirt had risen slightly away from the waistband of his jeans. It was just showing the hint of a very happy trail leading down to his cock. Looking momentarily at the crotch of his jeans, I realised I could see movement.

*Oh God, he was getting hard again.*

'Well like what you see? Keep staring and you're playing with fire, baby... Frankie, if you stop fucking staring at it, hopefully it will die down again.' His face was alive with the amusement of it all.

I lifted up my gaze to meet his, smiling back at being well and truly caught out.

'Come on, before I jump on you... Stud.' I offered my hand, to help pull him off the bed. Of course it was a bad move. His hand grabbed mine and pulled me down on top of him; he expertly rolled me over and underneath him in one swift movement. His eyes were on fire and he devoured my mouth with such force, I felt breathless. I only just registered that his hands had moved down my sides. All of a sudden I felt like screaming. The bastard was tickling all over my ribs.

'Say you're mine and I'll stop. It's so simple.'

My knees came up the moment he lifted some of his weight up off me. I tried rolling from side to side.

'Enough... Stop... I can't breathe properly,' I heard the words I was saying, but only just over my giggling and the creaking of the bed underneath me.

'Say it, Frankie.'

'Yes...Yes... OK, I'm yours, now bloody stop it!' He lifted away from me, but stayed to hover over my gasping form.

'Right get your ass up, then,' he pushed my knees down to one side of the bed and smacked my bum with a resounding thwack. Then standing he went to make his way towards the closed door, throwing me a look and a grin over his shoulder as he opened it.

'Honestly, jumping a guy like that,' I could see him shaking his head as he left the room, laughing.

We parted ways in the marble hallway. He walked me over to the apartment Bella and I shared and placed a gentle kiss to the top of my head. He clasped me to him for the briefest of time.

'See you in five.'

I watched until he disappeared from view. I could still however make out his deep voice from the other side of the door and the laughter that followed it. The door opened again and Bella appeared.

'Well, Frankie, you look... erm how can I put it?' she stopped to pretend to think for a minute. 'Yeah well and truly, thoroughly bloody shagged.' She placed her arm around my shoulders and squeezed me tight to her. 'And now you need to tell your best friend all the details.' I looked at her and smirked. She was waggling her eyebrows at me and loving being able to take the mickey. Luckily we didn't have time for the heart to heart just yet, as apparently Nathan had given her the "ten minutes and we're outta here" demand.

I stripped quickly out of my God knows how many days old clothes, dropping them on the floor in my bedroom, such was my haste, and started rummaging in the closet for something that said comfy, casual, made no effort, but stunningly gorgeous all at the same time. Surprisingly there didn't seem to be anything that quite fitted the bill.

Finally deciding, I got into my solid black, skinny, ripped jeans, pulled on my good brown boots and stood staring into my drawers trying to find a decent long-line jumper. I finally found my aubergine one. I started to turn it the right way, in order to put it on. I had just got it over my head and was busy thrusting one arm in each sleeve frantically, when suddenly I felt the hairs on my body stand on end. My bedroom door clicked shut.

'Purple underwear, baby?' questioned the deep voice behind me. I managed to pull down the jumper to my neck and as my head appeared through the gap, I could see Alex behind me grinning, in the reflection from my mirror. He snaked both arms around my front and drew me to him quickly. He was still hard and it made me gasp.

'We need to eat now, you need to come back and shower again. I need you smelling like you, and not me... I want to be inside you again, this hard on is just about fucking doing my head in.' He smiled at my reflection, and lifted his eyebrows.

'Why, Mr. Blackmore, you seem to have an endless list of wants and needs,' I teased.

'Baby, I'm only just getting started, now come on. Put a brush through your hair and let's get outta here. Let's feed my asshat of a brother and your best friend and make our way back to my apartment."

'Yes, Sir,' I saluted him, taking the piss.

'Be careful what you wish for, baby, I could get used to... Sir,' he released me, winked and grinning he left my room. My body was on fire.

*Is that all it takes for him to do this to me? A hug and a bit of banter and I'm dissolving into liquid inside?* I laughed out loud at the realisation. Moving fast, I ran a brush through my hair, trying to tame the waves, applied some lip gloss and a very quick stroke of mascara.

I stood back to take a look at my reflection. Yep I'd do.

The four of us made our way down in the penthouse lift. I was not sure I would ever get used to the speed of the bloody thing. Although I was somewhat grateful today, as the atmosphere inside it was a little tense. Alex had hold of my hand and it was clasped behind his back, pulling me as close to his side as was possible, which surprisingly I loved. It was becoming very apparent that he still had a problem with Nathan though, as he continued to glare at him. Bella and Nathan were paying no attention; they just kept flirting with each other in their own little world.

'George is bringing around my Range Rover, I'm driving,' he said to no one in particular.

'Range Rover, huh? That's a bit English.' I smiled when making the remark and looked up at him. I felt his grip get a little bit tighter on my hand as he smiled back.

'Yeah, well that's what happens when you spend nearly ten years of your life in that country,' Nathan stated from the other side of the lift.

Alex stared at me intently, almost waiting for the penny to drop. 'We still need to do some talking, Frankie,' he whispered in my ear.

My face was obviously doing its normal thing, showing every bit of confusion that I was now feeling. Alex released my hand as the lift reached its destination. He clasped my face in both of his hands as he began to kiss each of the lines on my face making up my frown.

'I know, Frankie, we still need to talk,' he added in again. 'Let's get food inside us first though,' he grabbed my hand, and led us outside the lift, to a waiting Nathan and Bella.

The Range Rover had to be top of the range, of course. It was British racing green in colour, with blacked out back windows. I opened the backdoor, in order to sit next to Bella.

'No, Frankie, I want you in the front with me, please.' Alex actually seemed to be very aware that I was trying to recoil into myself. I was intending to go for a little space between us. Just so I could think things through. It seemed when we were in close proximity, thinking just didn't seem to happen.

'OK... I guess.' I walked around the car to the front passenger seat. He was watching me now, even more questioningly than before. Bella helped Nathan up and into the back seat. I heard them laughing together as they clambered in.

'Don't over think it, Frankie,' he shot over at me, as he pressed a button to start the engine.

'As if I would,' I muttered back sarcastically.

'Sarcasm doesn't become you, Frankie,' he added.

'You sounding like my bloody mother also isn't helping' My voice had risen now, silencing the giggling coming from the back seat. Great, the atmosphere in the car was now so thick; I could have cut it with a knife.

Alex turned on the music and I gazed out of my window, just trying to make sure my eyes didn't latch on to him. I wasn't sure why I felt so pissed off with him. I spent the time whilst we were driving, just trying to weigh up the new revelation. Logically we had only actually been in each other's company off and on for 24 hours.

*So I'm not going to know everything, am I?*

I watched New York go past my window and began to calm down a little.

'I thought we were off to Denny's,' suddenly came out of Nathan's mouth.

'We are,' answered Alex.

'Why the hell are we going out to Brooklyn, then? The nearest to us, would have been in Tribeca.'

'I thought we could do with the drive and change of scenery,' retorted Alex. As he answered I felt one of his hands beginning to lightly rest just above my left kneecap. I refused to move a muscle. The hand gently squeezed my leg and I knew he was questioning if I was OK. I really needed to snap out of it and slowly I began to turn my head back to face front. I placed my hand over his now, just starting to relax and actually listened to the music playing in the car.

'I never did tell you,' I said in a small voice, 'I loved the song you texted me yesterday.' I casually turned to look at him.

He didn't reply, or even take his eyes from the road, but squeezed my leg in response. The corners of his mouth began to lift, and a small smile spread over his lips. I spent the rest of the journey watching him expertly drive us through the busy streets. Thinking how wonderfully safe I felt with him.

Denny's all day breakfast hit the right spot. We spent a couple of hours, just the four of us, sitting in the all American restaurant, squashed into a booth. Laughing and joking and teasing. The previous atmosphere had long gone, thank God and I loved the relaxed one that seemed to have taken its place.

'Oh God, Frankie... don't forget about our date for Thanksgiving, will you. I know how much you're looking forward to it,' Bella suddenly burst out.

I wasn't sure what she was trying to do. I could see from the expression on her face it was something. I glared back at her.

Alex immediately tensed beside me. 'Date?' he forced out, placing his coffee mug back down on the table.

I was nicely cocooned in the crook of his arm pit. His arm rested casually around my shoulders. It wasn't feeling so casual now. Every muscle in his body had gone hard and his arm now felt like it was imprisoning me.

'Well it was just a casual arrangement,' I answered.

'Who with?' He repositioned his body a little, straightening up.

'Just some guys Bella works with, that's all.' I answered the question very calmly, trying to play the whole situation down. I was trying to get him to relax again. Bella was grinning like the cat that got the cream. I wasn't sure what game she was playing, but I sent her a look of total contempt. From the look on her face, I knew what she was playing. She was just setting him up, so she could read his expression. Checking him out, to see how much he felt for me or not.

I think he'd answered her question. She raised her eyebrows at me, obviously very pleased with her findings. I shook my head back at her.

'I was hoping we could spend Thanksgiving together, in fact I have rented out a cabin up in the Catskills. Haven't I, Nathan? Thought perhaps the four of us could go together?'

Nathan looked up from his second dessert of the sitting. His plan was to soak up what was left of the alcohol in his system, clearly by eating as much food as he could possibly stomach.

'I'm sure we're expected back in the Hamptons?' he questioned, looking at Alex.

'No,' replied Alex, staring him out.

Nathan lifted both eyebrows in a questioning reply. 'OK then big brother, if you say so?'

Bella was now jigging up and down in her seat with excitement. 'I have heard so much about the Catskills, when do we leave?'

I watched Nathan openly taking in the movement in her breasts.

'I think Wednesday evening will do it, it takes about three hours to drive up, depends on traffic. That'll give me time to tie up some loose ends at work,' he looked at me now, 'I know your boss; he'll give you the time off,' he grinned his perfect smile at me, making me melt.

'What do you think? Spend the weekend with me,' he whispered in my ear, I was sure he deliberately just made the scruff on his face lightly rub on it. My body instantly responded. I gripped a hold on the front of his T-shirt and pulled his ear down to my mouth. Feeling really brave I casually licked the rim of his ear, which caused him to inhale deeply.

'That depends on my boss being really open and answering some of the many questions I have for him, truthfully... like as soon as we leave here.' I smiled sweetly back, as I released the grip from the front of his T-shirt. Placing my hand firmly on his chest, I pushed him back against the booth backrest. I started to run my hand over his chest flattening out the creases I just put in it.

'OK everyone, time to cut and run,' as he spoke his eyes never left mine.

This should be interesting.

# Chapter 21

The ride home in Alex's Range Rover was so much quicker than the trip out. But doesn't it always seem that way; I remember thinking the same as a kid. The happy memories of my uncle's old car apparently must have crept over my face. Alex's hand was once again resting on my leg, just above my knee cap and he squeezed it slightly.

'Penny for them,' he asked.

'Oh I was just back home, thinking of a Sunday afternoon ride with JJ, my aunt and uncle,' I smiled back at him.

My tiredness was beginning to sneak up on me now. Yesterday had been a long day and night, what with one thing and another. It was Sunday, late afternoon and the heated seats in this luxurious car were beginning to have an effect on me..........

The fire was sending huge flames up. I could see their flickering reflection on the ceiling. I was tucked up on a huge, deep, soft settee. Alex had covered me with a fleecy blanket. On the low coffee table in front of me sat an equally huge glass of red wine. I rolled over onto my back and took in the room around me. It was decorated in blues and muted greys, very masculine. The furniture seemed to be heavy oak. On further inspection the room was similar to the living area that Bella and I shared, just on a much bigger scale. The view of NYC lit up was magnificent. Of course his apartment would have the best views. Floor to ceiling picture windows framed Central Park and the lights of the city behind.

*I must have fallen asleep, how embarrassing.*

'Hey,' came from the man, with the deep voice I loved. He was sitting in a chair, in the opposite corner of the room.

Slowly I brought my eyes into focus.

*God what must I look like?*

He of course looked like the Greek God; that I became more certain as time went on, that he actually was. He had reclined back into the chair, one leg crossed over, so his foot was on the opposite knee. He was just wearing blue sweat shorts and basically a smile. I knew that when he stood up, they would be so low on his hips I would have to resist the urge to pull them down. I felt myself lick my lips with the last thought. His smile grew wider as if he could read my mind. I watched him take a sip from the bottle of beer in one hand and turn the page of a book with his other.

*Dear God, he reads as well?*

'What's the time?'

'A little after seven. Are you feeling better now?'

I nodded.

He closed his book, after inserting a book mark and placed it down on the table next to the chair. Clasping his bottle of beer by the neck with his fingertips, he stood and prowled over to me. That was exactly the correct description. I allowed myself one quick look down and yes I was right, his blue shorts did hang low on his hips, God help me. He sat on the edge of the settee and brushed my hair away from my face using his fingertips.

'I poured you a glass of wine, I wasn't sure what you would like to drink, but as we need to have a talk, I felt it might help us to relax.'

'That's fine, thanks.' I managed to mumble in response.

I had to force myself to sit up now, as I knew our discussion was imminent. I wanted answers and I wanted the truth. I was just so afraid of them making me feel any different than I did right at this moment.

Alex reached out and grasped the wine glass from behind him; slowly he brought it around and to my lips. I sipped at the liquid, all the while staring into those deep eyes, the same eyes that just about pulled every available emotion out of me and then some. Alex put the glass back down on the table and moved to sit down on the settee behind me. With hardly any effort he lifted me up onto to his lap and wrapped both his arms around me tight.

'I need to feel you, Frankie.'

I nodded.

And he began, with my back to his chest.

'At eleven years old I was sent to England, to a private school in Kent, my stepfather could no longer bear to look at my face. You see I reminded him too much of my father, any picture shows how much we look alike.'

'Where is your father?'

'Dead, Frankie, he died when I was five.'

'Oh I'm sorry; I know what it feels like to lose your father.'

'Yeah... I know you do.' I could hear him take a sip from his beer and then he continued.

'The school was great. I really, I mean I really fucking enjoyed it. I was away from him, the fucker... People appreciated me for what seemed like the first time in my life, for what I was good at. But the best thing was I met some brilliant friends... my best friend came to the school when I was fourteen and he was thirteen, he had won a local scholarship because he was so fucking bright, he could pick up any language and just run with it. We became instant friends, you know the sort of thing you have going on with Bella, through thick and thin we stuck together. I didn't get home too often, the rather pathetic fucking excuse was "it's too far away," or "we're going on holiday." He made a feminine squeaky voice as if to take off, I can only assume, his mother.

'I loved the stories he would tell me of his home and his family.' I could hear his heart going ten to the dozen behind my head. 'God I miss him... You must know where I'm going with this, Frankie?' he breathed out. He had hold of my hands in his and was stroking them with his fingers.

I nodded, but made no sound. I just wanted him to carry on.

'I didn't get home to see my little brothers and my stepsister... I couldn't protect them from him, the fucking asswipe that he is,' Alex's voice was beginning to break slightly. I had questions I wanted to interrupt him with, but I just didn't dare throw him off course. He had opened this dam and it needed to come out. Too many questions and I just knew he would shut it down.

'Are you close to your other brother and stepsister, now?'

'Scott and Ruby, yep I would move the earth for any of them. He sent me away but he never destroyed our connection. I think that gets to him even now, after all these years.'

'JJ's best friend at school was called James, I think I saw him a couple of times at sports days and rugby matches?' I quietly added in.

'Yep... you did,' he whispered. 'Well here I am James Alexander Blackmore II, Lieutenant J Blackmore, otherwise known as Jabby. But I just prefer Alex; because all the people I love most... call me Alex.' His voice started off as hard and indifferent, slowly softening as the sentence continued. His arms enfolded me slightly tighter.

*I don't know if he's worried I will bolt at the news or what?*

*I am reeling, or am I? I think far down in the recess of my mind I knew I had always known him, almost like we were fated to be together.*

The synapses in my brain began to fire.......

'The beautiful flowers I received after I had been to visit my dad's grave for the first time, they were from you weren't they?'

'Yep.' He swigged from his beer.

'Thank you, the words on the card meant so much to me.'

The pain in his voice was apparent. 'I wanted to do so much more to help you, Frankie, but I'd just enlisted and couldn't get the leave.' He drew in a deep breath, and carried on.

'I first saw you; I mean really saw you, Frankie, when you were fifteen, only from afar. I knew I had found a kindred spirit in you. I knew all about the clusterfuck your life was and I recognised you, you know, like only another person who has felt your pain can. I don't have to add that you were the most gorgeous thing I had ever seen. I was twenty-one at the time and you had come to Cambridge to watch JJ play rugby. I had girls falling at my feet and all I could ever really think about was you.'

I had to look at him now and I turned in his arms. I placed a leg either side of his thighs and for a minute I knew he wanted to pull me up higher over his cock, but he resisted. I tucked my hands down onto his naked stomach and forced myself to look into his face. He really was the most beautiful man I had ever seen. Slowly I lifted up one hand to cup his hard, stubble-covered jaw line. The right words were so difficult to find. The information he had just bestowed on me was slowly filtering through. Alex closed his eyes and leant slightly onto my palm.

'Say something, Frankie... say anything.'

Taking a deep breath I started, 'I have felt so alone for so long, but you were always there weren't you?'

He nodded at me gently and his eyes opened to find mine again. My other hand came up to rest on top of his left pectoral muscle, just so I could feel the steady rhythmic beat beneath his ribs.

'I fell for you, baby, the first day I saw you. You were too young for me to do anything, so I waited and waited, hoping that by helping you in small ways as you grew up... well I hoped that someday our paths might cross again. Well either that or I would get over the beautiful girl that had captured my heart.' His heart shaped lips twitched at the corners and he offered me a small smile.

'You've wanted to be with me for...' I was mentally doing the maths, 'Nearly nine years... is that what you're saying?' My voice was starting to rise in tone at the sheer disbelief of what the man in front of my eyes, and under my thighs, was actually, owning up to. The only movement coming from Alex was the slow rise and fall of his feet. Lifting me too, up and down slightly every time. The rocking movement was almost comforting. I could feel tears coursing silently down my cheeks.

'Please don't cry, baby.'

'I have dreamt about you most nights since first seeing you at Coronado.' I laughed a nervous laugh through my ever increasing tears. 'All this time you wanted to be with me too?' Alex nodded urging me to continue. 'I've had a few lucky breaks in the last couple of years, scholarships and things... were they all you, too?'

'No, baby, they were all you, I just made sure that things you did got noticed by the right people. I've always been in the background, gleaning anything I could about you from JJ and then your aunt and uncle.' The deep breath he inhaled lifted my whole body up. I flung myself forward and onto his naked torso. My arms wrapped so tightly around him and I hung on for all I was worth. My face turned to nestle into his neck and I inhaled the cologne, the only cologne I ever wanted to smell again for the rest of my life. I lifted myself away and roughly wiped my cheeks with the back of my hand.

'I get it, your rugby club has the same colours you both used to play in at Cambridge and various things now are connecting in my brain. You need to tell me though, did you really want me as Nathan's physio, or is this all some elaborate plan to get into my knickers?' Humour was what we needed now and I needed to inject it into the conversation fast. I smiled at him.

'Well now, let me think?' He raised his fingers to his chin. The other hand sneaked behind my arse and he pulled me forward, onto his growing erection.

It felt so good to have some of the loose ends tied up. I had more questions but they could wait. We started to kiss, running our hands all over each other in a frenzy. It felt good just to relax once more into him and I started to look forward to a whole weekend of us.

# Alex

*What the fucking hell was that?*

The alarm on my phone was continuously fucking beeping. I needed to find an arm in order to reach it. But most of my body was entangled with her.

*Well fuck, I like it.* The heady realisation reverberated around my head.

I couldn't at this moment interpret which limbs belonged to me and which ones were hers. But with the noise obviously disturbing her sleep, she moved slightly away from me. It was all it took. I could now reach my arm over to the phone, to get it to shut the fuck up.

Fuck, it was 6am Monday, and time to get ready for work.

I rubbed my hands over my face. I could not remember the last time I had felt like playing hooky. So much had happened this weekend. I raised my head now onto my bent right arm. Just so I could look down at her.

She was lying on her front, arms pushed under her pillow. Her hair was messed up and fell everywhere around her. I gently lifted up the cover that was only covering her backside, just so I could see her, all of her. She was so fucking perfect. Her skin was smooth and I couldn't fucking help myself. I started to trace all her curves and dimples lightly with my fingertips.

It must have been tickling her, as she started to move. Instantly I froze not wanting to break this moment... just yet.

*I really am a lucky bastard.*

She was here in my bed. I couldn't believe it. What a lucky son of a bitch I was.

But fuck, I needed to talk to Nathan and soon. The asswipe had my balls on a plate and had nearly dropped me in it more times than I cared to think about over the weekend.

He caused the biggest clusterfuck on Saturday. He nearly destroyed everything.

My life wasn't ready for her just yet. I had always planned to have her in it, but not just at the moment. The shit was hitting the fan here. I didn't want her involved with it.

I threw myself back down on my pillow.

'Fuck it.' I placed my bent arm up and over my eyes.

Circumstances beyond my control back in England had forced my hand.

I fucking hated having my hand forced in anything.

Still she had understood last night, she had been fucking accepting about everything, and we'd ended up back in my bed. My cock went hard just thinking of last night. I gripped it with my left hand just trying to find a sense of relief.

*I won't lie to her.*

*I would never lie to her.*

*I just won't tell her everything, at this juncture in time.*

*Yeah... let's call it a need to know, basis.*

I lifted my body up and moved myself carefully over her, keeping my weight off of her and I began to kiss all down her spine. Slow wet kisses. I knew it affected her when I ran my fingertips down her spine. She pulls me in every time; it's like being fucking magnetised, her north to my south, and all that crap. Except for the first time in my life I didn't feel like it was crap.

*Pussy whipped prick.*

I shook my head, to rid it of that thought. A smile began to break out over my face.

I slowly began to part her butt cheeks with both of my hands and as I sat back onto my haunches, in between her legs, I leant over to lick deep into her cleft with my tongue, lapping up her arousal as it started to appear even in her half sleep.

'Up... Baby,' I demanded.

She started to shift now, getting up part way onto her knees and she began to moan. It was like fucking music to my ears. I lapped at her more enthusiastically. I fucking loved the noises she made for me, just for me.

My guilt lifted as I woke her up, the only way I ever wanted her woken up ever again, me inside her, me licking her, and only me.

# Frankie

I was having one of those out of body experiences. I couldn't believe the mind blowing orgasms Alex had just left me with. Bella was so right. I really did need a guy who knew exactly what he was doing. I began to chuckle slightly to myself.

*Need to rein it in Frankie; he's only just in the shower. He'll think you're one shilling short of a ten bob note.*

Lying on my back, I gripped the soft blue sheets in my fists and just had to burst into a 'Yes' as I pummelled my hands and feet into the mattress underneath me, really quickly. Holding in the squeals that I wanted to let rip from my mouth, sheer excitement and happiness overtaking me.

'I could watch you all fucking day, Frankie. You crack me up... I was going to ask if you were feeling OK... But watching you then, it's become apparent you are,' a loud laugh left his lips.

I threw the sheet up and over my head in my embarrassment. Slowly I took a peek out.

*He really is a Greek God!*

OMFG... I had seen everything now. He was slowly walking towards me wearing the start of what looked like was going to be a grey, three-piece suit. As he made his way towards me, he was fastening up a silver cufflink; his eyes never left my face. The pale grey of his suit was shining; it was quite obviously a very expensive material and by the way it fitted him so well, cut to order.

Underneath he wore a white dress shirt. Over his arm he was carrying a black tie and the suit jacket.

Alex in rugby kit, or old jeans and a T-shirt and he looked bloody fantastic. In a suit, he was killing me!

Every part of my naked body flushed hot and I could hear my pulse banging in my ear drums. Wetness started to cover the top of my legs.

*Oh my God! Really?*

The gorgeous man, who was staring down at me as he fastened his tie, had just brought me to two mind blowing orgasms and I needed more?

'I don't want you to work today,' spilt out of me.

*How needy do I sound?* I wanted to face palm.

'Frankie, I'd stay, but as we're going away on Wednesday night I have to get some work done this week,' he winked at me as he pulled his suit jacket on. His left hand was running through his damp hair making sure it was flopped to one side, just as he liked it.

'Baby you need to stop looking at me like that, otherwise I won't be going anywhere for a very fucking long time,' he adjusted the front of his smart trousers. Bending over to me, he kissed my lips softly at first and then with increasing vigour. I reluctantly let him break away.

'I like you here in my bed... stay with me tonight?' He whispered in my ear, no scruff today. I decided I liked him just as much clean shaven. As much as I wanted to, I knew Bella and I needed to chat.

'I have plans already.' At the furrow of his brow I quickly added, 'With Bella,' and I gently smacked his shoulder, chastising him. His lips had left my face and were now lightly brushing the underneath of my chin and down my neck.

'Are you sure I can't persuade you... Frankie?' His hands were wandering under the sheets, and I was finding it difficult to breathe, let alone talk. His cologne once again invaded my nostrils. I didn't know the answer to anything at that precise moment.

Alex's phone vibrated in his pocket. It was probably the one thing that could break our connection. He looked at it and then his eyes were back to mine.

'I gotta run... Edwards is downstairs with the car. I'll call you later; if I can get home early enough Tuesday perhaps we can do dinner?' He kissed my forehead gently.

'That sounds great.'

He stopped at the door, blew me a kiss and winked. I listened to every movement until finally the front door slammed behind him. I left him my purple knickers on the peg with my thong, just as a joke for him to find later, in case of an emergency, I smiled to myself. I pulled on the rest of my clothes and tidied the bed. I began to reluctantly make my way out of Alex's domain, when suddenly I had a girlish thought. Quickly I made my way back to his bedroom and picked up his T-shirt from the night before and decided to take it with me, it smelt of him. Not that I needed a reminder, but I borrowed it anyway. I felt as happy as I could ever remember.

# Chapter 24

I opened the door to the apartment just in time to see Bella pulling on her trainers.

'Good you're here, get changed quickly, I just have time for a run before work.' She picked up her water bottle from the hall floor.

'Yep OK, give me five minutes and I'll be back.' I moved swiftly through to my room.

Stripping fast I put on all the clothes I needed, including clean knickers. I tied my hair up and grabbed my jacket. It looked miserable outside and I might need it. Our run certainly re-energised my aching body. But it was difficult to talk to Bella this morning, as she was keeping up such a pace.

*Maybe that's her bloody idea?*

Finally, after having done our usual run in double quick time, we reached the front of the building. I downed some water to enable my throat to actually release words. We were just in time as the heavens opened.

'You and me! Girl's night in tonight?' I forced out in between gasps.

'Well?' I could feel her trying to squirm out of it.

'Not taking no for an answer,' I stood hands on my hips just staring her out.

Slowly she smiled. 'Yes OK, oh demanding one,' and she mocked bowed to me.

'Don't forget, when you get to work today, to cancel our plans with those guys?'

Bella put an arm around my neck as we entered our building foyer and she pulled me closer to her. 'Yeah OK, gorgeous... I'll talk to... those guys, no worries.'

We made our way up in the bloody ridiculously fast lift that I knew I would never quite get used to. I knew why now, it seemed to leave my stomach back down on the ground floor. Just as we were letting ourselves back in, the door opened from the inside. I stared into the mischievous looking face of Nathan.

'Hey ladies, how are we this fine morning?' he smiled his panty dropping smile at both of us, as he shuffled slowly backwards, placing most of his weight on his good leg. Bella brushed herself past him and I followed.

'Thought you were going to leave earlier, Nate,' she threw into the air.

'I know you did, sassy, but you don't always get your way, you know,' he grinned at her and she moved away sighing.

I grabbed a fresh bottle of water from the fridge and got myself back to the lounge area fast. I didn't want to miss anything. I needed to see the dynamics of this "fuck buddies" thing in action. I perched my backside on the back of the settee.

'I thought we had already discussed it this morning, Nate baby' she smiled at him sardonically.

I watched as Nathan closed his eyes slowly and exhaled. 'You decided, Bella, that I shouldn't be around when Frankie got back, not me darlin.... and do not call me Nate baby, I hate it coming from you.'

I watched as Bella almost tail in the air wiggled her way back to her room.

*What the hell was she playing at?*

Nathan ran his hands through his hair in exasperation, 'Women?' With that he turned to leave. 'See ya later for my physio, Frankie? What time?'

'Oh give me an hour, Nathan and I'll be around.' I watched as Nathan vacated our apartment.

*Well that's why we were in such a hurry to run this morning. What is up with Bella?*

I could hear her scurrying around in her room, and decided to wait. Finally, she emerged looking stunning as usual, in another beautiful, blue Chanel suit and nude heels. She looked at me waiting for the quip; I was so not going to give her.

'Come on then, what's going on? Why was he not allowed to be here when I got home? I'm a big girl. I know what's going on between you two.'

Bella looked at me, and for a moment I saw panic flicking over her face. She managed however to calmly pull herself back together as she wobbled around just trying to put on her final high heeled shoe. Her camel coloured swing coat grasped in her other hand.

'It's just easier, Frankie, easier to keep all things separate and in their place.'

I stopped staring at her now and I bent to pick up her coat for her, as it fell out of her arms.

'Bella, easier for whom, exactly? We all know what's going on here. I really think you and I need to have a good chat later and you can tell me what has got you running scared... I recognise it you know, my life has been spent running away,' I added the last bit and took stock of what I'd just said.

'Yeah... OK, I look forward to seeing you later then, oh wise one.'

I leant forward and quickly gave her a hug before she had to depart for work. I became conscious, that for the first time in our whole friendship, I seemed to have my shit together and she didn't.

It was a sobering thought. I made my way through to my bedroom. I was in need of a shower. I quickly folded up Alex's T-shirt and placed it under my pillow.

*Who am I kidding? I have so not got my shit together.*

I placed my face down to inhale the gorgeous smell that exuded from the soft fabric and laughed cathartically.

The physio session with Nathan was subdued to say the least. I knew why and knew that no amount of messing around from me or me telling him how much stronger his leg was feeling would relieve the atmosphere. I left him doing chin raises, hanging in the air under a door frame, legs off the ground. He really was a sight to behold.

*Why the hell was she pushing him away? I didn't know.*

For the first time since the "Jack Russell" incident, I was really pleased to leave his apartment and go back to ours. This was going to make for one interesting weekend in their company. I spent the rest of the afternoon doing laundry, ironing and preparing a tasty dinner for the evening. I was listening to my ever broadening taste of eclectic music. Suddenly a new one came on and I knew I was just going to have to text Alex with it.

> *Hi*
>
> *Thinking of you and listening to this*
>
> *Like I'm gonna lose you- Meghan Trainor*
>
> *Frankie*
>
> *Xxx*

Just after I pressed send I got a familiar feeling of panic and a worried hot flush ran through my body.

*Was it too much?*

Perhaps he won't listen to the words properly. I can only hope not. Not everyone is like me, analysing every lyric.

*Oh god what have I done?*

I hastily sent him another text.

*Sorry, don't worry about listening.*
*I know you are really busy today.*
*Looking forward to seeing you*
*Tomorrow.*
*Xxxx*

After a few worrying minutes, I heard my iPhone ping with a reply. I had deliberately left it in my bedroom and walked away from it.

*Like that was going to help me?*

Slowly I made my way back, hearing it ping again, just reminding me that I hadn't had the guts to pick it up and look at it. I placed my thumb to it and waited for it to register that it was me. I opened one eye at a time to read his incoming message.

*Thinking of you too Frankie*
*So fucking much you wouldn't believe.*
*Love you too, Baby*
*Not that this is the way I expected to*
*Tell you, the first time.*
*I also said once before, you obviously didn't take it in?*
*Do not expect me to let you go!*
*Love Alex*
*X*

I sat down on my bed and fell backwards clutching my phone to my chest. Oh my God!

*He loves me? My Greek God, he loves me.*

I just needed to be truthful with myself now.

*Isn't that exactly what I felt when listening to the song earlier?*

I had fallen for this man hook line and bloody sinker, in the very small space of approximately forty-eight hours and if I was truthful I had never felt happier in my life. Shit scared but so bloody happy.

I found the afternoon disappeared quickly enough. What with the chores I was doing and me literally dancing around the apartment. I had to get it together before Bella arrived home. She could see straight through me and I really wanted the chat to be focused on her. I heard the bang of the door as she stepped into the apartment. I could barely see her behind a colourful and huge bouquet of wild flowers.

'Let me see,' she said with a smile, 'I wonder who these could possibly be from,' she added with a not so subtle infusion of sarcasm.

'There's a card,' she said, waving the silver envelope under my nose.

I turned up the dinner in the oven, now she was home. I had to wait to grab the card from her, as I needed to dry my hands on the tea towel I was carrying with me.

'Is here OK, Frankie?' I watched her place the flowers on the side table.

'Yeah, lovely thanks.' I slowly pulled the card out of the envelope and ran my fingers over the words he had written.

*Frankie*
*I'm not good with words!*
*But I need to try to tell you how I feel, so.......*
*Play this please*
*Make you feel my Love-Adele*
*Love you Baby*

*Alex*


I ran back to my room, just to call up the song as I lay back on my bed.

*So this is what the giddy excitement feels like?* I replayed the song over and over.

There was so much I didn't know about him, I didn't even know his favourite colour. I had only met one member of his family, but I didn't care. I felt like he had been in my peripheral view for a long, long time, and now he was slap bang in the centre of my focus. I didn't care about all the things I didn't know about him. We had time to learn from each other. Those things were just negligible. My thoughts were broken by the smoke detector going off and Bella shouting from the kitchen. I ran as quickly as I could, just in time to see her removing the burnt offerings from the oven. She dropped the pan into the sink and turned on the taps.

'Take out it is then!' she exclaimed, watching the smoke rise from the pan.

She rummaged around in a drawer next to me and dropped all of the pamphlets onto the work surface. We both burst out laughing.

'Pudding will be OK, though' I said unconvincingly.

'Oh good, what is it?' she questioned, still laughing.

'Ice cream,' I dropped in with a big smirk on my face.

'Yep, gorgeous, even you couldn't burn that.'

'Oh come on! How many times do I burn dinner?' I opened my arms out to her in question.

She threw the oven gloves at me as she went to walk out of the kitchen. Looking me up and down in thought. 'Erm now let me see, every time you're in love I'd say.' I watched her eyes light up with the enjoyment of it all. I so needed to turn this conversation around, I wanted it to be about her tonight. I spun around and followed her out; I was still listening to her laugh at my expense. She walked towards the settee, stepping onto the soft carpet and wiggling her bare toes.

'I'm worried about you, Frankie, you're letting him in too soon.' She looked at me now, seriously.

I took on board what she was saying, our previous laughing and light heartedness gone in a split second.

'Why are you worried about me, Bella?' I asked, not wanting to really know the answer, but needing to know in order to neutralise her argument.

'It's fast and I don't want you hurt, gorgeous, that's all.'

We sat down together on the settee, with me still clutching the takeout leaflets and her holding my arms.

'They're a very powerful family you know, Frankie. I have been doing some research on them. They're way out of our league, that's for sure.' I dropped the leaflets and grasped her hands back.

'I'm not interested in them though Bella, I only need him.' I lifted my gaze up from our hands to her eyes now and I smiled. She nodded at me, not in agreement but with a modicum of understanding.

'What about you, Bella, I'm worried about you. You like Nathan don't you, I mean really like him?' she pulled her hands away from mine now and I could tell by her body language she was feeling uncomfortable.

'Oh you know me,' she said adding a laugh.

'Yep I do and that's why you're worrying me, you are allowed to actually like someone, Bella, you are allowed to actually let down the facade and let someone in. I know IT hurt you before. But that doesn't mean everyone is tarred from the same brush, Christ I should bloody know.' I could physically see her shrink back at the mention of IT, the bastard who shall forever remain nameless. She jumped up and with apparently now sweaty palms, as she wiped them down the front of her Chanel skirt. Now I knew I'd got to her and that wasn't what I intended at all.

'I'm just happier keeping the control, you know?'

'Well can I just say, and I'll say it only once. Please don't be so busy compartmentalising your life in order to stay safe, that you end up pushing away maybe the one thing that could make you truly happy.'

'Wow!... when did you become so....SO knowledgeable?' She looked at me smirking.

'When I appreciated, that for probably only the second time in our friendship, my bestie needed help.' I stepped towards her to close up the gap and embraced her in a squeezing hug.

'You do know that one day; somebody is going to hug you so tightly, that all of the pieces he broke will just fit back together.' I kissed her forehead.

She looked at me and pulled together a tight lipped smile.

'Right enough of this serious shit, let's order takeout and have a nice bottle of wine. By the way you'll be pleased to know, I didn't ruin the wine either.' I handed her the phone so she could make the choice of what we were eating this evening. An hour later we were settled watching an old black and white movie surrounded by chocolate wrappers and empty Chinese boxes. In that brief instant, we weren't concerned with anything other than where our next glass of wine was coming from.

## Alex

I knew that if my little brother peered through the spy hole and saw that I had come bearing gifts, he would let me in. I glanced down at the pack of beers in my right hand and I knocked on the door again using my ring. The door swung open with some velocity.

'I knew it was you,' Nathan let go of the door now and it started to swing closed. I just managed to get my boot wedged in the doorway before it shut in my face.

'Whatever you want, dude, just get it the fuck over with and leave.' He didn't even turn his head back towards me.

'Why wallowing today, asshole?' I questioned.

He moved stiffly around the furniture and flung himself back onto the couch, lifted out his bad leg straight in front of him and he rested it on the table. I watched him close his eyes and run his hands over and over again through his hair. After moving nearer, I could see the evidence of a couple of empty bottles of beer in front of the couch, yep definitely wallowing today then.

'Here,' I said, passing him a fresh one.

'I came over to talk about Frankie, but I can see your need is greater than mine. What is it? Trouble with your sponsors?... bike team? What the hell's going on?'

He opened his eyes and looked up at me. For a split second I could see trepidation there. I hadn't seen alarm in his eyes since we were small.

'Just this, fucking leg! I need out of here, I need it sorted so I can get on with my job. Just ignore me I'm just spewing crap. What do you need to talk about?'

'What is it, fucker? It sounds like pussy trouble to me.' I smiled at him ready for the onslaught of abuse that was bound to follow. Leaning back in the chair, I raised my right leg and hooked it over the arm. Taking the top off the beer bottle, I started to drink the cool liquid, and waited for him to answer.

'Bro, you know us Blackmore's never have any trouble getting pussy,' a trademark grin spread all over his face and I knew the moment had gone.

'OK, is it trouble with keeping pussy then?'

He sat up quickly and coughed on his mouthful with pretend shock, and then he flicked beer in my direction. Pointing the end of the beer bottle at me and shaking his head, 'Unlike you I haven't found any that's worth keeping. You know me, if it's worth a fuck, I'll do it. But then I force it to move on.' I could see he was enjoying getting at me so I let him continue.

'So come on then, Bro, let me have it. I know I caused you a lot of grief this weekend and I apologise. For once I just wanted you to have what you want, and need... BUT... if you hurt Frankie, then brother or not, dude, I'll kick your ass from here to the Hamptons.' He stared at me now, just trying to make me feel the depth of his intent.

'Nathan... I love her.' What surprised me was the ease with which I could say it; it was like I had been telling people my whole life. When in truth the only other people I had ever said these words to, were my siblings. I went to carry on, but stopped myself as he stood and made his way to the window. Considering he was injured he did it in pretty quick time. I watched as he lifted a hand to shade his eyes.

'Do you see that?' He questioned. 'That, my pussy whipped big brother, is a... fucking pig flying.' He loved his own jokes, and laughed his head off watching me smirk. He really was a prick, but I conceded a comical prick at that.

'I need a favour from you though; I need you to give nothing away about the shit that's going on at home.'

'Right... but I won't knowingly lie to her.' His face became serious once again, as he started to shake his head.

'I'm not asking for lies, Nate, just don't eagerly drop me the fuck in it... I need a little bit of fucking time, that's all. I am sitting on a knife edge here, trying to juggle my own life and at the same time keeping the warring factions at home on an even keel.'

'You know Al; you can't carry on putting us before yourself. If you really love Frankie, then shit, dude, you need to grab her with both hands and run.' He took a deep breath, 'I know what you promised dad... but that promise was made when you were five years old. We're adults now? Man you really have to let it go. Take Frankie as an example, I could have had a team physio, but no you wouldn't hear of it, so you pulled her over here... I'm still trying to work out who the hell that was for? I can probably guarantee it was for me or her, rather than you, Alex... I guess what I'm trying to say is, you have got to let the promise to dad go; you cannot seriously still think it's your job to protect us? I know we don't talk about it...' He was back sitting down now. I could tell he was going to go for it and mention what we never talked about. I could feel my fingers gripping the beer bottle tighter, my whole body strung so tight, I could probably be played like a fucking guitar. My head was beginning to thump with my rising blood pressure.

'Nathan... Don't fucking go there,' I threatened. I took a long drawn out swig of beer.

He lifted up his gaze and his eyes met mine, challenging me. 'Scott and I know what you went through to protect us... we know, dude. But you can't protect everyone all of the time, Alex you deserve a life.'

*Little cunt, you're weak just like your father.* I squeezed the fucker out, once again.

'Don't you think I don't fucking know that?' I put the beer bottle down before the inclination to throw it became all consuming. It banged the table, and fell over onto the floor.

I jumped up and started pacing. 'Really, don't you think I don't know?... I, better than anyone I know, KNOW.' I forced both my hands into my front pockets, almost scared of what they would do if I left them loose.

'I couldn't look after you three, once he sent me away. I didn't bring all of my men out of Afghanistan. The woman I have loved since she was a girl has had such a fucked up life and even now I'm trying to help her stay away from another goddamn awful situation at home. In doing so, I am bringing her into our fucked up lives.' I sat suddenly and grasped my head in both hands.

'I think it has to be said, my track record for protecting the people I love... seriously fucking sucks.'

The silence in the apartment was almost deafening.

'Since she was a girl, eh?... you have it bad, dude.' I didn't look at him but I could hear the smile in his voice.

'Really? All the crap I have just put out there and that's the bit you home in on?' I grinned at him, feeling my blood pressure starting to slow down.

'Alex, it's two more months' man, just two more months.'

I threw him another beer; we opened them and chinked them together.

'I'll drink to that, Nate, just two fucking more months.'

*I was a man who exuded control; surely I could keep all the shit up in the air for two fucking more months?*

# Frankie

The kettle slowly came to the boil as I listened to Nathan on the phone to his team manager. I couldn't help but earwig, I was born a nosy cow.

'Yep, that's what they're saying, Brock.....Yep........mm hmm.......So after the New Year it is then. OK I'll be seeing ya........yeah, really looking forward to it, I'm going stir fucking crazy here........See ya.'

I could hear him fist pump into the air 'YES.'

'So, good news then?' I shouted out.

'The best fucking news, everyone is happy with the progress, with more work from us,' he moved his head, gesticulating between me and him as he arrived back into the kitchen, 'And me focusing on my upper body strength, I go back into training after the New Year, and I couldn't be happier.'

'Well thank God for that, because you've been in a right bloody depressive funk, for ages.' I smiled at him quickly, and handed him his black tea. I'd managed to convert him to having a cuppa with me sometimes. I was pretty pleased with that.

He turned now and leant his backside onto the polished concrete worktop; he grasped his tea in both hands. 'So, chocolate drop, tell me about you and my brother, I'm ready for a good girlie gossip.' The grin on his face was infectious. I smacked his shoulder for good measure.

'Ow..... What is it about British girls? Always looking to inflict pain on me, me a poor injured man.'

'Get over yourself, in fact let's turn the tables to you my friend, how are you and my bestie getting on together?' He let out another sigh and let go of his cup, one hand came up to run through his hair. Exasperation I recognised.

'Oh, you know, she can't get enough of me,' he winked, and slowly made his way out of the kitchen. By moving away, it was like putting a full stop to the conversation. I followed him out.

'Alex was here last night,' Nathan offered as he dropped down onto the settee.

'He was? I was having a girl's night with Bella.'

I remembered the text I received last night when he obviously came across my surprise hanging on the hook in his bathroom. It was dirty and full of need.

*Inhaling your intoxicating scent, baby.*

*I need to be in between your thighs, licking away your arousal, now*

*X*

We had sent texts back and forth until I had been so turned on I had to resort to using my own hand in order to sleep.

*It was a gift that just kept on giving, so to speak.*

I brought myself back to the here and now after feeling the flush on my face.

'He's pretty complicated, my older brother. He carries a lot of emotional baggage. Whatever happens, have a bit of patience with him and know this, I have never known him to fall in love. In fact, he doesn't really do relationships.'

'OK.' I tentatively added, 'He told you he loved me then?' I couldn't help the teenage girl inside me, and had to ask.

'He sure did, and do you love him?'

I could only smile at him in response to the question. I sat down next to him on the settee and snuggled under his arm. I had got to be the luckiest person in the world right now. I had a gorgeous man I loved, a bloke that treated me like his kid sister and my bestie. Life didn't get much better than that.

After spending the afternoon at a local beauty parlour getting the essentials maintained, I made my way back to our apartment.

*What the hell was I going to wear this evening for our dinner?*

I closed the front door behind me and I couldn't help but wrap both arms around myself and squeal out loud. I then very quickly decided to do a Bella. I ran and jumped onto the nearest settee letting out a loud 'woohoo' as I plonked my bum down on it hard. Laying on the huge settee now I opened up my arms and legs doing a pretend snow angel. Maybe finally my luck had changed. The flowers he sent yesterday were filling the space with a gorgeous scent. On the way to my room I buried my head in them and inhaled deeply.

When I reached my room, I stood and stared into the walk in closet, it was hilarious really, my sparse amount of clothing barely took up an eighth of the closet. I didn't really have a lot of choice as my wardrobe was hardly extensive. I was trying to keep some things by for our weekend away. My underwear was even less promising as two sets had pieces missing now. I struggled to contain my laugh as it rumbled up inside of me. I thought tomorrow I would have to go out shopping, I wondered if Bella could join me and help. My bank account was unbelievably healthy as my wages had just gone in and I really didn't have many things to pay out for. For the first time in my life I could really enjoy a shopping trip and I believed some new underwear purchases were maybe just what were needed. But tonight I would have to settle for something in here. I pulled out my iPhone and quickly text Alex.

*Hi*
*Hope your day is going well?*
*Just a quickie (no pun intended)*
*Is our meal casual?*
*Or smart this evening?*

*Frankie*

*My day is shit. I didn't wake up*
*with you this morning.*
*I don't mind what you want to wear,*
*As long as you have on a skirt*
*or a dress.......*
*I thought we would go to a little Italian place near here, they have old fashioned table cloths and my hands could wander?*
*Love you Baby*
*X*
*PS I don't do quickies*

*My God what does this man do to me?* A simple flirting text message and I was on fire; my clit was throbbing with the need of him. But two could play at that game.

*Mr wandering hands*
*I thought perhaps I could wear a*
*Wrap dress and no underwear,*
*As some greedy man is withholding*

*my best knickers. Perhaps under the*
*Tablecloth, you could examine my*
*Newly waxed areas?*
*Love you too*
*Miss Smooth*


*Dear Miss Smooth*
*Jesus woman, what are you trying to*
*do to me?*
*I'm in the middle of a meeting*
*My cock is straining so hard against*
*My zipper, it's painful to sit, but I can't*
*Stand as my arousal is not what the*
*rest of the board need to see.*
*Lie down on your bed!*
*X*


*Lie down on my bed?* I questioned it but did it anyway.

*Lying down now.*

*Remove the bottom half of your*
*Clothing....*


Oh God I had started something now. But I did as I was asked. I must admit it was leaving me nearly breathless; I was already so turned on. I hoped Bella didn't come home early; my bedroom door was still open. I stifled a nervous giggle.

My phone began to ring. I knew it was going to be Alex but he wanted to face time me!

I touched the screen to allow the incoming call, the feeling of suddenly being way out of my comfort zone rushed over me. All at once his face filled my screen. His hair was slightly messy and his pupils were dilated, the green of his eyes had the tell; flashes of amber in them. It was empowering to see what kind of effect I had over him and it made me feel bold.

'Alex,' I tried in my best coy voice.

'Baby,' he replied, his voice having dropped even deeper, confirming what I knew already, just how turned on he was. 'Stop running your tongue around your lips and show me.'

'Show you?'

'I have suspended a meeting; I have approximately ten minutes..........SHOW ME.'

I could see a faint smirk on the corner of his lips, so I continued to play with him.

'You know I'm no good at selfies I just can't get the angle right,' I smiled back at him, 'I can show you this though.' I ran my index finger through my folds and over my clit, slightly grazing it. It caused me to take a sharp intake of breath and I closed my eyes momentarily, it felt so good. I heard him swear, I opened my eyes and I removed my now glistening finger. I held it up to the phone to show him.

'Put it in your mouth and suck it clean, baby.'

I did as asked and I heard him groan. Hearing that nearly made me orgasm.

'You're lucky I'm not there, you wouldn't be able to sit for a week.'

*Why does that statement make me flood the top of my thighs?*
'SHOW. ME.'

I decided to be a bitch and give him a very quick glimpse at what he was missing. I moved the phone down to my pussy and showed him my smooth mound and as I had decided to be a bitch, I went for complete bitch. I ran my index finger back through my folds several times.

'Holy HELL.....YES.....YES,' came out of the phone. I couldn't remove my fingers now after listening to him come, and I finished myself off easily with a few more rubs on my clit. After getting my breath back I lifted the phone back up. There he was in all his sated glory, the man I loved, smiling at me.

'Miss Jones, I do believe you have made me shoot my load at the office, AGAIN. That's a very bad girl, you shall be punished later,' he said in his best British accent. He winked and the call was disconnected.

I laid back on my bed feeling very pleased with myself. I was so looking forward to seeing him tonight and I clutched the phone to my chest. I must have dosed off, because I came to a bit later at the sound of my name being called. I jumped off the bed and hastily got into my clothing from earlier. I turned my head and checked the clock beside my bed, my one remnant of home. Bella was home early, I wondered if we could shop now.

'Bella, do you fancy hitting the shops for a couple of hours?' I enquired as I reached the lounge area. Just in time to see her taking off her coat and kicking off her shoes.

'Retail therapy... I'm all for it, just let me jump in the shower and get changed and I'm all yours.'

I ran back to my room and grabbed some jeans, boots, jumper and my parka. I brushed through my hair and put it up in a messy twist. Unbelievably she only took another ten minutes to get ready and we left the apartment. Outside our door we bumped straight into the awaiting figure of Edwards.

'Frankie,' he nodded his head 'Bella.'

'Alex has sent me to take you shopping. He thought possibly that you may wish to buy some clothing?' I didn't question his ESP.

'That's fantastic, we are so short of time... the first stop needs to be a lingerie shop please, Edwards,' my voice had become quieter, tinged with a little embarrassment. But he was a very welcome sight, as outside in the dimming natural light New York was becoming bloody freezing and I knew it would be so much easier being dropped around by the limo and then having him wait to pick us up. How time changed, I laughed to myself. Once upon a time I wouldn't have even been able to afford the bus fare. Now it seemed I could only think in limo!

He took us to a beautiful area, quite near Midtown and stopped outside a boutique looking lingerie shop. Just as we got out, Edwards handed me a black credit card. 'Alex wanted me to let you know, anything in here is on him.'

I could feel my eyes widen in embarrassment. But Bella grabbed it out of his hand, before I could answer. She pulled me towards the front of the shop, shouting over her shoulder to Edwards, 'Tell Alex I'll make sure she uses it.' I heard him chuckle as we stepped into the welcoming warmth of the shop. I had never been to a shop before, where you try on lingerie in a huge changing room complete with chaise longue and mirrors on the wall. They were all so beautifully framed; they were like works of art. I tried not to let it intimidate me too much, as the saleswoman handed me everything they had in my size. The material was exquisite, and with Bella's help I picked out six new sets in varying colours and designs... all with the thought of hanging the bottoms up outside his shower. Bella paid, as quite frankly I didn't want to see how much of Alex's money I had just spent. We ran out grasping the equally beautiful bags filled with coordinating tissue paper and jumped into the back of the limo. My phone pinged.

*Frankie*
*I was hoping to meet you at the shop.*
*The thought of surprising you and helping*
*You pick out new panties, is all that's*
*got me through the afternoon.*

*Can't wait until this evening, Baby*
*Love you*
*X*

Half of me was pleased he hadn't made it and the other part was disappointed. I hurriedly shopped in another local store for a couple of dresses, shoes and jumpers that would go with my jeans. If it was getting this cold here, God knows how much colder it would be up in the Catskills.

We made it back to the apartment by six o'clock and Bella, being the lovely friend she was, drew me a huge bubble bath, whilst I put away my new purchases. I had to laugh; even with some of Bella's clothes in there the closet was still so empty. I chose my new black dress for this evening with a long line cardigan for warmth and of course some new black underwear. I laid them out carefully on the bed, and made my way to my en-suite smelling my orange blossom bath oil and on the way I grabbed my bathrobe.

'Thanks, Bella, that is just what the doctor ordered and it's much appreciated.'

'It's OK, gorgeous, I'll leave you to it now and I'll listen out for Alex knocking, OK?' I smiled in answer.

I couldn't take too long luxuriating and I was in and out in fifteen minutes flat. My body was alive this evening, just with the anticipation of seeing him. The hairs on my body seemed to be on a heightened state of alert. After creaming my body and wrapping up my hair in a towel I made my way out of the bathroom.

There he was, laid out full length on my bed, with both hands tucked underneath his head, in all his Alex glory. No wonder the hairs on my body were on end, my body knew he was here even if I wasn't aware. His eyes were closed like he was relaxing so I took my time just to drink him in. Slightly damp mussed up hair, a bit of scruff. He was wearing blue faded jeans and a fitted blue T-shirt, which showed off his muscled physique. When I looked at the floor I could see he had kicked off his boots. I just wanted to jump him as soon as his cologne hit my nostrils.

'You're staring, Frankie, I can feel it.'

I didn't answer, but after checking my bedroom door was shut I dropped my cream robe into a heap at my feet, loosened the towel on my head and ran my fingers through my wet hair. His eyes were still closed as I began to crawl naked up his stretched out torso, breathing him in as I got closer. He still didn't open his eyes, but a smile started to make the corners of his mouth twitch and his dimples come out to play. He moved suddenly and rolled me underneath him. He looked at me like I was the only person he had ever cared about and right at that moment in time it was the only thing I wanted to believe. His tongue licked gently at the seam of my mouth to gain entrance. I opened and we began our dance, slow and exploring, teeth gently nipping at each other's lips. I would gladly lose my mind being kissed like this. We spent several minutes loving each other with our mouths. He finally broke the kiss and rested his forehead against mine.

'So, Miss Jones, you love me?'

'I do,' I answered in a timid voice.

'I love you, Frankie... I've been in love with you for so long, it's fantastic to hold you in my arms and finally say the words. I've needed to say them to you, so badly.' He closed his eyes, as if he was reliving the yearning for me. I wanted to cry with the emotion of being here with him now and hearing this beautiful man declare his love for me. A tear slipped out of the corner of my eye just as he opened his. The hand that was running through my wet hair moved suddenly and he wiped the tear away.

'One day soon, I'm going to ask you to be my wife, Frankie and you better be ready to say yes... I can't live without you and I will not let you go.'

'I love you so much, Alex, I think I have loved you since Coronado.' I hated saying the name, but we couldn't spend the rest of our lives just skirting around the issue.

'I don't blame you for JJ's death, I know now how much you loved him,' there I'd said it, it was out there. It was my turn to wipe a tear as it came running down his cheek. He buried his head in the crook of my neck, placing gentle kisses here and there as he held on to me so tight I could barely breathe. Right at this moment I didn't care and I held him back, like my life depended on it. He rolled us back over just as suddenly and released some of his grip on me. He had both of his hands on my naked bum cheeks now and he was rubbing them soothingly and simultaneously. I realised very quickly that coming over here naked was probably a big mistake as each hand took a turn to swat my arse, so hard both cheeks stung. I gasped out loud.

'That, baby, was for making me suspend a very important meeting, with the whole board, for ten minutes, just so I could shoot my load in a very cramped bathroom.'

He winked at me and rubbed my bare cheeks with both hands. Surprisingly the pain dissipated and was replaced by a very much heightened sense of awareness, in and around my pussy, and as usual when around this man, moisture started to pool at the top of my thighs.

*Who would have thought it? I like him smacking my arse?*

'OK, baby, we have a dinner reservation in thirty minutes, you need to put some clothes on, and quickly. I can smell your arousal...' He inhaled just to reiterate what he was saying was true. 'Before you ask I have placed your panties back in your drawer.' I looked at him questioningly, 'I need full access, Miss Smooth.' He laughed at the expression on my face. I was unsure whether playing him at this game would be to my benefit now, I was OK playing games in the safety of my bedroom.

*Can I play them in a very public restaurant?*

I really wasn't sure, but I could see by the look on his face I was about to find out. I dressed quickly and dried my hair, leaving it down and put on my normal makeup but with the added addition of some subtly smoked eyes. Alex watched, sitting at the foot of my bed, elbows pressed to his knees and hands clasped together. He caught me staring at him in the reflection of my mirror.

'My hands are clasped together, so I don't reach out for you and tear off the clothes you have just put on. I mean for us to make it out to that restaurant this evening if it kills me, and it probably will.' His face had lost all sense of playfulness and I could see the expression was one of determination. I just couldn't help myself. It had to be said I was my own worst enemy at times. I grabbed my black high boots and put them on my feet by placing a foot next to him on the edge of the bed. I knew that by doing that my wrap-around, black dress would open up somewhat and give him an eyeful.

*His fault, right? He put away my knickers after all.*

It was all I could do to not laugh at my cunning plan. The dress fell open and he inhaled again deeply.

'MINE... other boot on... NOW.' He jumped up from the bed and grabbed his leather jacket and my cardigan, holding it out to me. I quickly placed my arms into the held up garment and he whispered into my ear, using his scruff to its usual sensual effect.

'Teasing, baby... deserves an equal punishment,' his deep voice sent vibrations throughout the length of my body. 'Playing with fire will get you burnt.' He grinned now and his eyes were alight once again. I could feel my eyes open wide in astonishment. He took my hand and led me out of my bedroom and across to exit the apartment so quickly I didn't even hear Bella return my goodbye. This was going to be an interesting meal.

# Chapter 27

The drive was short to the restaurant. He was right when he said it was only a couple of blocks away. But I was grateful to be in the car, the night was that cold. I glanced down at our entwined hands, the only time we had not been connected to each other since the apartment was when he had shut my door and ran around to his. Automatic cars have their bonuses, so it seemed. No gear stick equals continuous hand holding. The warmth coming from his large hand was being soaked up by my cold one.

I wouldn't have ever noticed the restaurant, it was set back somewhat in a small side street. By the looks of the tired decor it was an old family run business. We pulled up outside and a young waiter hurried out, to open my door. Alex walked around to me and threw the Range Rover keys to the waiter, to park it I presumed. He took hold of my hand and led me in. The gorgeous aroma of herbs and fresh tomatoes hit my palette and my mouth began to immediately salivate. I hadn't realised just how hungry I was until that moment. An elderly waiter led us over to a darkened table in the corner, at the back of the room, much to my relief. I didn't know what Alex had up his sleeve, but the less visible I was could only be a good thing.

Alex helped me off with my cardigan and handed it to the waiter along with his leather jacket, which seemed a shame as I was enjoying the whole bad boy persona it was giving off. It went hand in hand with the feeling of vulnerability that was coursing through my nervous system.

'Frankie... relax,' he whispered in my ear as he ran his fingers down my spine. It made my hips react as normal and they jerked forward in response. He caressed one of my bum cheeks as we waited for the waiter to spruce up the table. The warmth spreading through to my skin was bringing the nerve endings alive again.

*Ok so hopefully the teasing was going to be restrained?*

I could hear his deep voice conversing with the waiter, but the only thing I could concentrate on was the movement of his hand.

'Sit, Frankie,' he motioned for me to slide in first. I did just that, consciously holding my wrap dress together for modesty. I could not believe how different my pussy felt, completely bare with no knickers on. It felt more aware of him, I didn't know if that was even possible. Right then I was embracing my inner tart, it seemed.

'Do you know this is the first proper meal we have ever shared, Frankie?' I glanced up at him now, and began to relax. He took both of my hands in his.

'I hope you're a woman who enjoys good food? I can't stand a picky eater, someone who just sucks on a piece of lemon.' He grinned at me now and I could feel my body just sinking into the comfy cushion on the corner seat.

'You're going to wish I was, Alex, I can eat like a horse, why do you think I run every day.' He put his fingers to my chin and lifted my head slowly. Gazing into my eyes he slowly tilted his head towards mine and kissed me chastely. But with so much meaning behind it, I felt I could have melted.

'I can think of a better way to exercise, baby,' he pulled away bestowing a wink on me.

We selected some dishes to share from the menu as the waiter left our drinks.

'OK,' I blurted out, 'I think we could do with sharing some information with each other. I mean I know more about Nathan than I do about you.' Alex leant back and exhaled.

'Yeah, good idea. Fire away.' His demeanour seemed somewhat guarded but his face was smiling. So I pushed ahead.

'Well you have me at a disadvantage, don't you? You seem to be aware of all my family's shortcomings and problems, even our bereavements. But I only know you and Nathan and that you lost your father.' He physically stiffened. I brushed over it. After a few seconds of silence, he began to let me in.

'Fair enough, Frankie. I am one of 3 boys, born to James and Margaret Blackmore. I'm the eldest; hence I am named after my father. I am 29 years old, soon to be 30. Stop me when you've heard enough won't you?' He looked at me laughing and picked up my hands again in his. 'Nathan and Scott are twins; they are 20 months younger than me. Our mother had it tough when our father died and unfortunately married the first man, and I say that loosely, that came along.' He stopped and took a drink. 'But we gained Ruby our stepsister and that was a blessing. You know about my schooling and military history and now I am CEO in my father's company. Oh and my favourite colour is anything you're wearing as underwear.' I looked into his eyes and could see the humour dancing.

'Do you enjoy your job?'

'Not really, it just came with being the eldest. I admire Nathan for doing what he's passionate about, he just up and left High School and went with what he wanted to do... unfortunately being the eldest comes with a level of responsibility.'

'So if you could do anything, what would you do?' I released one hand from his and started to draw the outline of a square on the tablecloth.

'I would build things,' a boyish grin took over his face and once again I felt captivated by the man. 'My degree from Cambridge is in structural engineering... So I would build things,' he lifted his hand and tucked some loose hair behind my ear. The touch sent electrical currents coursing down my body. 'My father's company buys other companies, strips them down and sells the pieces to the highest bidder. It's soul destroying really, but I am somewhat governed by the board.' Alex let out a deep sigh. 'What else do you want to know?'

'What does Scott do, does he work at the company?' I smiled in encouragement, as if I realised just how difficult it was for him to open up to me. I was finding it harder to concentrate on the interrogation; as his hand had now landed on my knee closest to him. I could feel the cold of his wrist watch and the burn of his fingertips as they made small circles on the inside of my leg. The two opposing temperatures were making this conversation extremely difficult to concentrate on. I stared at the green and white table cloth, and willed my mind and body to come back into the conversation I was trying so desperately to have. So that was his game, his huge hand was on the move now and was slowly and purposefully making its way up the inside of my thigh. Instinctively I started to press my legs tighter together, forcing his movements to at least slow down.

'Scott is an artist, he paints and he sculpts. Although he has been ill for a while, so he hasn't produced anything lately... I have no idea where his talent comes from. But it is an exceptional talent and I am really proud of him.' He didn't need to say the last sentence as I could tell by the way his face lit up, like a proud father.

*Did I really think that?*

It had just made my situation a whole lot worse, I would love him to be the daddy of my babies.... my God it was like my ovaries were exploding at the very thought and a further rush of wet hit the top of my thighs. I let out an involuntary moan and it was greeted with a pinch on the inside of my thigh.

'Ouch.' That brought me back to the conversation with a bump. I raised my eyes quickly to see him smirk. He leant towards me and closed the slight gap between us.

'Moans are for my ears only, baby,' Alex whispered into my ear, just making the whole bloody situation much, much worse.

*Saved by the waiter!*

The rather elderly man came back to our table, with an enormous amount of food. As I studied the serving trolley further, I could now see that it contained several small dishes of food. The food smelt and looked simply dazzling. My stomach rumbled in appreciation. Alex's hand started to move further up my thigh as he conversed with the waiter and thanked him for the spread now in front of us. I didn't miss the euphemism.

'I thought we could share all the dishes, and I have ordered one of everything on the menu, just so you could taste them all.'

'That sounds great, I can't wait to start. I hadn't appreciated just how hungry I was until he presented us with all this.' I smiled at him, just taking in now that I had no knife and fork to eat with.

'I'm feeding you, Frankie. There is nothing more erotic than being fed with mouth watering flavours and textures. There's nothing more loving than being looked after and loved by someone so much that they feed you. It's a primal thing.'

'OK... just as long as you don't start throwing me over your shoulder like a caveman when we leave, who am I to protest?' I said the words and shot him a huge smile but actually I was registering quite quickly that I would bloody love this gorgeous hunk of a man to throw me over his shoulder.

So the onslaught on my senses began, along with the torturous caressing of my inner thigh, getting higher and higher, towards the place I now needed him so desperately to touch. The marvellous tastes and textures entered my mouth via his hand; God forbid if a little was left on my lips because he gently wiped it with a finger and made me suck it off. I had several times tried to retain the finger inside the cavern of my mouth, but I was greeted with a small pinch of my inner thigh, and a raise of his eyebrows. My body started to move closer and closer to the edge and he still hadn't even touched me properly yet.

'So your stepsister Ruby, tell me about her?' I needed to normalise the conversation and quickly before I really lost it and started having a "when Harry met Sally" moment.

I watched as he smiled again, he could see exactly why I was trying to engage him in a normal conversation. He understood my body better than I did, already.

'Well she is a story unto herself. She's a real firecracker, a real force to be reckoned with. She majored in business at school; like me, she was also sent away to boarding school in Switzerland. She's more equipped to run my father's business than I am, but our family is very old and as a lady she has social engagements, charity commitments etc., that must be adhered to. She's allowed to sit on the board and advise, but that's it... One day though I know she will have had enough. I really want to be there when she tells my mother where to go. At the moment though she seems content to be at home and I am grateful, she keeps an eye on Scott for me.'

'And your mother?' I questioned. He just shook his head.

'No let's not go there; she isn't worth the time or the effort.'

The conversation was halted there, and I knew once again it was deliberate on his part. A very large finger had just made it to the folds covering my pussy. My teeth clamped down on the fork full of food that had just entered my mouth. I needed to do something; else the whole of this small quaint restaurant would be aware of exactly just what was going on under the very well laundered and starched, green and white tablecloth. I was now staring at it so hard; I knew I would be able to see the pattern in my sleep. Alex carefully removed the fork from my mouth and he kissed me chastely on the lips. His finger entered me and I felt him groan against me. 'So fucking wet, baby... so fucking wet.'

I was on fire. The blood in my veins had become molten lava. He slowly began to stroke the said finger backwards and forwards in a come hither movement. My mind was no longer on food; it was just trying to work out how the hell I could orgasm without disturbing the relaxed scene in front of me. Of all these couples in here and no one else seemed to have any hands under their tablecloth.

Just when I thought I could breathe again, I glanced at the delicious bad boy next to me. My want for him became all consuming, as I watched his Adams apple bob up and down as he struggled to retain his seat. I reached over and grabbed hold of his cock through his jeans and just like that it was game over, he pulled out his finger making me gasp in the process. No one heard though, as he stood abruptly and asked for the bill.

He whispered to me, 'Move quickly, baby... else I'll throw you over my shoulder.'

'You wouldn't?'

He raised his eyebrows, the start of a smile just teasing the very corners of his mouth, and licked his lips as he leant down on the table with both hands. His cologne was enveloping all of my senses.

'Try me, baby... please try me.' His eyes found mine. I smiled and stood up adjusting my dress. It had become very apparent that I also needed to get home quickly.

Alex drove fast and purposefully, who would have known that just watching him skilfully handle a car would turn me on more. After pulling up outside of the building, he helped me out of my seat and strode into the entrance. I felt very much like the little woman as I scurried along behind him. Normally I would have bawled him out, but I was just as eager to get where we were going as he was. He politely threw the keys at George in the foyer and said goodnight. Finally, the doors closed on the lift.

Alex pushed me abruptly against the wall, trapping me with the sheer weight of his body on mine. He used one of his large hands to hold both of mine above my head. His mouth lunged straight for my neck, the place that he knew he could find my inner tart button. He kissed, nipped and licked up and down until I could audibly hear myself gasping. I longed to run my hands through his hair. The more I pulled against his hold, the tighter he restrained me. That only added more heat to my already burning body. The lift sounded, letting us know it had reached its destination. Alex freed my hands just as the doors opened. He lifted me by the waist and placed me over his shoulder, in one movement. I literally squealed and burst out laughing, what the hell.

'I don't think I tried you, did I?' I asked, in between giggling. I was having a conversation with one hell of a fine arse.

'No... But I liked the idea. I'm in a hurry and let's face it, I walk faster.' His deep voice reverberated into my very core; I loved how his voice deepened when he needed me. Holding on to me now with one arm, he quickly walked across the hallway and gained entrance into his apartment with the other. The door shut behind us as he decisively strode over to the full length windows. He let me go slowly and I slithered down the entire length of his hard body. We didn't need words, our previous bantering fell away as he kissed and caressed me. My dress was quickly pooled around my feet after he undid the tie to the side of my waist. The only light coming into the room was the light from the city below. I felt wanton standing in front of him, in only my bra and high boots. He reached behind me with one hand and expertly undid my bra. I, in turn, shucked it off in my haste, I needed to feel his hot mouth around my nipples and quickly.

'You are like a vision, Frankie... standing there for the entire world to see... but for my eyes only.'

I seized hold of the bottom of his T-shirt and started to lift it up, as I did so I lowered my body. As his skin became visible, I pushed my face to everything I had managed to reveal and began to lick. It made me feel powerful as I heard him begin to moan into the silence of the apartment. Alex grabbed hold of my hair and twisted it around his hand, my face was pushed further into his tight abs and I begun to lick the undulations, following the sinew with the tip of my tongue. My hands snaked around and grabbed hold of his arse cheeks; he remained in my vice like grip. I became aware that he had pulled his T-shirt over and off his head.

'Do you know all the things I want to do to you, baby? I will possess every part of your body, and your mind. I will make you cum in so many ways; and so many times you will be begging me to stop.'

'I will own you... As you own me'

'I. WILL. NEVER. LET. YOU. GO'

'DO. NOT. EXPECT. ME. TO. LET. YOU. GO'

I started to release his belt buckle in my desperation to get to his cock. I absolutely loved that he always went commando. Alex helped me to push them over his backside and down his thighs; finally they reached the floor. After treading on the back of each of his unlaced boots and kicking them off, he pushed his jeans off one leg and then the other, using his bare feet.

I was not at all experienced in giving blow jobs, but I so wanted to taste this magnificent male presented in front of me and I once again started to lower my head. I flicked out my tongue and just licked up the bead of pre cum away from the eye of his penis. All at once he growled and the sound hit my core, I clenched my internal muscles involuntarily. He began to lift me up to his eye level.

'Legs around my waist, I need to fuck you and I need to fuck you NOW.'

I complied and he moved one step forward pressing my body in between the cold glass and his already sweat covered body. He moved his feet apart, to widen his stance. I heard the tell rip of foil, and my breathing hitched as he entered me in one movement. My pussy was so full of him and was stretched beyond belief; the feeling was wonderfully intense.

'Tell me when you're ready, baby.'

I knew what he meant; he was just waiting for my body to accept his girth. I looked into the eyes that I loved so much. They contained so many things, including the reflection of the city lights below us. I had never felt so alive. I allowed the amber flames in his eyes to burn into my very soul.

'Yes,' I managed to force out from gritted teeth.

He began to move then and started to vigorously fuck me against the window. My shoulders started to make a squeaking noise on the glass. The heat emanating from my body had caused the glass to slightly steam up. He really meant fuck, the speed in which he entered me and still continued to move was forceful yet controlled. His strong and well-muscled thighs supported us both. In my mind I thanked the Gods of rugby, for that very moment.

Moving my hands upwards, I hung on to him, with my arms around his shoulders, feeling the muscles constrict with his exertions. The speed of his movement was vigorous and in what seemed like a matter of a few short minutes we both fell over the edge together. Such was the need we had for each other. My body felt like jelly, how he was still standing up was some sort of a miracle to me, and with me still impaled on his cock. Which unbelievably, was already coming back to life; as he walked us into his bedroom. He started to lay me down gently on his bed.

'Alex, I need to take off my boots.'

'Uh uh, baby, you need to keep them on, I want them over my shoulders when I make you cum again.'

He laid me down on his bed and removed the used condom. He started from the bottom of the bed and began to climb his way up my prone figure, dropping the odd kiss here and there. Finally, our foreheads rested together.

'You are so beautiful, Frankie; you have a flush all over your body. I can't believe I'm the lucky bastard, who put it there,' and just like that we began kissing again. I knew it was going to be a long and very pleasurable night. I didn't want it any other way.

Our weekend away couldn't come soon enough.

# Chapter 28

We had been driving for about an hour now and finally the buildings were becoming less dense. We were leaving New York behind.

The atmosphere in the car was more relaxed than I could have hoped for. Bella and Nathan, who were sitting behind us, seemed to be teasing and laughing with each other. I pulled down the sun visor just to look at them really, but I pretended to touch up my lip gloss for good measure. They looked so good together; I didn't really understand why she kept fighting it and blowing hot and cold on him. Alex had reassured me that Nathan wasn't as vulnerable as he seemed and could fight his own battles.

Ah Alex, I turned my head to watch him drive his beloved Range Rover. He made me stop breathing every time I looked at him and realised the gorgeous man was actually mine. He was a show stopper even dressed as he was today in biker boots, dark blue jeans and another well fitting white T-shirt. The T-shirt had to be old; it stretched superbly across his muscles like he'd had it for years. A sigh must inadvertently have left my lips because he glanced across at me and the corners of his mouth lifted slightly. The large hand that hadn't left mine squeezed and then lifted so he could kiss each of my knuckles. Just at the very last moment he put my thumb into his mouth and sucked it hard. I didn't say anything to him but lifted my eyebrows in question, and shook my head at him. I loved the playful Alex part of his personality and loved it even more when it came out to fool around. The further we drove away from New York the more he seemed to be relaxing.

'We have another two hours to go you know, Frankie, you seriously need to stop staring at me like that, else we may have to pull over.' He let go of my hand and gripped the outline of his erect cock. 'You get my drift, Frankie?'

'Yep,' I replied, my eyes widening. I leant down to turn up the music in the car as it was one of my favourites of the year. *Shut up and dance - Walk the moon.* My eyes never left his hand.

As soon as Bella heard it she started to sing along with me and the boys just watched awestruck at the hideous caterwaul that filled up the suddenly tight confines of the normally spacious beast of a car.

I was enjoying watching the world go by my window, places that I never thought I would even see. What I was enjoying most though was the companionship in the car, the lively teasing banter and the underlying sexual current that flowed between me and the sex God in the driving seat next to me.

'How much longer do you think, Alex?'

'Probably about an hour, as the heavy traffic leaving NYC has added some time onto the road trip.' On answering he suddenly pulled into a road side diner just the other side of Liberty.

'OK everyone out, seriously in need here.'

'Yeah caffeine here we come,' I heard from Nathan as he started to exit the back seat, holding up a hand to help Bella out, too. They walked away from the vehicle towards the diner.

Their mother must have done a pretty good job, their manners were impeccable, whatever they seemed to think of her now. I watched as Alex ran around the car to open my door for me and I managed to do a fairly decent job of jumping into his arms. He twirled me around and then after slamming the door to his car, I was pushed gently but firmly into the metal. He ground his erection into my stomach and upon comprehending it wasn't quite where he had anticipated, I was once again lifted slightly as he bent his knees and he thrusted again. The excitement I felt made me close my eyes briefly. When I reopened them seconds later, I was gazing into his gorgeous pools, only further enhanced by the crinkles around them, which made me become conscious of the fact he was smirking.

'Ermm, I thought you were in need?'

'I am, baby... not of fucking caffeine though. I am badly in need of... YOU.'

'Oh, Mr. Blackmore, you say and do all the right things to a girl,' I whispered in my best piss-taking, demure voice.

His hands moved to my bum and he gripped both cheeks tighter.

'You better believe it, baby... and I've got many more things I want to do to you. But people are beginning to stare and while I don't care, you probably will.' He slowly let me come back down to the floor in that trademark way of his, by letting my body slip down the front of his. Just so we could feel every outline of each other in the process. After we broke contact he held out his hand for mine. I grabbed at the hand he offered and he pulled me closer.

'Come on, cup of tea time for you I expect,' he laughed out loud and placed his arm all the way over my shoulders and around my neck, pulling me closer to him so he could kiss the top of my head. I in turn placed my arms around his waist.

'Well, whatever you think of your mother, she has done an awesome job with you and Nathan, your manners are impeccable.' He didn't answer for a minute and I began to tense. All I could hear was our feet, crunching on the loose gravel as we made our way to the polished metal diner door.

'Nah, you've got that wrong, Frankie, we dragged ourselves up... we come from a hell of a fucked up family... We all felt the need for some control over our lives and gradually we all drifted in the same direction.' He took an intake of breath, 'The good manners come from the times Nate, Scotty and I spent at a few BDSM clubs we frequented in our formative years.' I stopped walking now and turned to look at him, he had to be joking, right?

I could see though, on further examination of his face, he wasn't joking at all. I had to stop my mouth from physically dropping open.

Alex helped by placing his thumb and forefinger under my chin and he gently brushed my lips with his.

'Really?... That surprises you?' His eyebrows raised in question.

'Well I thought you could be a bit dominant... and I sort of like that, but....' My voice trailed off now.

'You more than sort of like it, Frankie.' He bent his knees so he could look into my eyes.

'I don't think I want to be punished, though.' I could hear my voice getting smaller as my body began to inwardly flinch.

'I don't want to punish you, baby... Being a dominant isn't always about punishment, for me being with you, it's about putting your pleasure above my own... Being in control is what I get off on... Well that and making you cum so many times, you pass out through sheer exhaustion.' He was smiling at me again. 'I won't hurt you, Frankie. I just want, no, I need to own your pleasure and all you have to do is let me... It's quite simple. Sometimes I just want to make love to you, so it's not an all the time situation.' Inside my heart I knew what he was saying was true.

'Trust me?' He questioned.

'Do you know what.... I do.' As I said it, I think that the realisation was more shocking than the disclosure of him being a dominant. My body began to tingle remembering the smacks to my arse that I quite liked, oh who was I kidding, that I bloody loved.

Our moment was broken by a shout from the diner doorway.

'You guys coming?' bellowed Nathan.

'Not at the moment,' Alex shouted back as we made our way towards the grinning figure, which was shaking its head in pretend disgust.

After the brief reprieve in the diner, in which Nathan and Alex ate nearly everything off the menu and more apple pie than I have ever seen in my life, we were finally back on the road. I had my window open slightly as I could now make out the whiff of pine being carried into the car on the chilly breeze. In the darkening light I could just make out the shapes of the of the tall pine trees.  It reminded me of home.

The wooden cabin finally came into view. I was sure if I could've actually seen it all through the darkness, it would've been completely overwhelming. In the gloom all I could really see were the lights shining out of the floor to ceiling windows. Alex obviously liked a good view and I could thoroughly appreciate that. The cabin appeared to be resting on a steep side of a bank; the glass was mostly one sided, to take in the vista I presumed. From what I could make out, to keep the house on the horizontal it had stilts underneath it. I couldn't wait until tomorrow, to explore more thoroughly.

Alex's voice broke me out of my thoughts. We had pulled up in the driveway and he had jumped out and was starting to unload the car.

'Fuck, how much food do you have in this box, Frankie? It feels like enough to feed a small army.'

'Knowing you and Nathan well, it's probably nowhere near enough. Anyway I had to bring everything needed to do my first ever Thanksgiving dinner, didn't I? As well as some other bits and pieces, for the other days.' I was really looking forward to cooking a real Thanksgiving dinner, nervous but looking forward to it nonetheless.

I watched as Alex's huge arms gathered up the overstuffed box and he began to carry it into the cabin. Mentally I chastised myself, for not being able to tear my eyes away from his bulging biceps and triceps. They literally filled all the fabric of his T-shirt turn ups. I have to say I really appreciated this new fashion trend of rolling up the bottom of the arms on T-shirts. It meant you got to be so thankful for seeing even more well-defined muscles than normal.

190

*Perhaps that could be my Thanksgiving thanks? Frankie is thankful for turn ups on T-shirts.* I stifled a chuckle to myself.

I was right to bring warmer clothes up here, it was positively freezing. I snuggled further into my cable jumper. The light in the cabin seemed to be even more inviting now as the first of a few shivers found their way down my back.

'Come on, gorgeous girl,' came a holler from the doorway, 'You have so got to see inside this place.' OK that was more of a shriek now. I watched as Bella practically bounced up and down on the doormat. Watching Nathan was funnier as he couldn't peel his eyes away from staring at her bouncing rack. God that boy had it bad.

'Go inside, Frankie, I can get the stuff in. Even Nathan can help with some of the light stuff.' The deep voice sent even more shivers down my spine than the cold air.

'OK, but don't let him walk too much, it will put too much strain on his leg.'

'Yes Ma'am,' he answered grinning at me. He really was so much more relaxed up here. I decided I was going to love being here, even if it was for that reason only.

The warmth of the cabin hit me as soon as I crossed the threshold. Completely decorated in bare wood with a honey glow, I glanced around the space. There appeared to be an integral porch that led into an open plan room. The kitchen ran down one complete side, all units were in the same coloured wood with black granite worktops and lots of very modern appliances. I wanted to grab hold of myself at the sheer excitement of being able to cook in there tomorrow. In front of the kitchen was a very large island, which contained the sink and other necessities. There were large, very old looking, comfy brown leather settees and a magnificent wood burner slap bang in the centre of the vast room, which was blazing and throwing out welcoming heat. All the settees appeared to have chequered throws over them in various places; the effect was so cheery and inviting. Last but not least was an eight-seated dining table, which appeared to be even older than the mountains we were now in.

Bella was still running around the place, squealing. 'Wow! Would you look up here?'

I shifted my sight up to the direction of her voice, to see her leaning over the wooden balustrade above me. A loud thudding noise suddenly made my eyes move again to Alex, as he dropped the last of the bags on the floor. Nathan slammed the door shut behind him.

'Home sweet home,' came out of Nathan's mouth as he made his way to an extremely well stocked fridge. I could see him pulling out the beginnings of various meats and cheese, probably to make a huge sub roll.

'I did tell you the Goldberg's who own this place would be stocking up on food for us, didn't I, you didn't have to buy all the food you did,' Alex whispered in my ear. Somehow he had made his way up behind me and had pulled my back against his front, wrapping his huge arms around me tight. I in turn lifted my arms up to hang on to his, really enjoying our close proximity to each other after our journey.

'Will one of you guys come up here and look please?' The frustrated voice of Bella reached my ears again. 'It's really Wow!'

'Bella, unfortunately there is only one room up there, and it is the master, so it's mine and Frankie's,' Alex started to shout up to her. 'There are three more down here and out the back, as I wasn't sure what yours and Nathan's arrangement consisted of. I mean is it just fuck buddies in NYC, or does it cover fucking when away from the city.' I could tell he was just teasing her, but slapped the arms crossed over my chest for good measure.

'Asswipe,' came from the kitchen area, where Nathan was just about to place his jaws around a seriously mammoth looking sub roll, which literally could never contain another morsel of food it was that well stuffed. In fact, bits were already falling out of the edges as he manipulated it towards his mouth.

I watched as Bella jumped down the stairs two at a time. She sidled up to Nathan, just for effect. 'So what do you think?' She questioned.

Nathan span around on the barstool he was sitting on and placed his sub on the worktop. He grabbed her hands and pulled her to him, she rested in between his parted thighs, 'I think we need to give them a run for their money, what do you say, darlin?' He didn't give her a chance to speak and pulled her down to him for a kiss.

'Well fuck me,' I heard rumble in the chest behind me. 'You're pussy whipped, little brother, you put down food for a woman.' I watched as Nathan, not even breaking his kiss with Bella, lifted up his middle finger and gesticulated in our direction.

I could tell we were going to have some fun here, just the four of us.

I was standing in a breathtakingly beautiful master bedroom. It had a wooden four poster bed in the very centre of the room, which was decorated with white bedding and very simple but also very dramatic voiles that hung from the top of each post. The room was decorated in exactly the same way as downstairs, with all four walls just being exposed wood. The large windows had the same long, flowing, white voiles; they billowed all over the stripped wooden floor. The effect was so romantic. On the bed there were many beautiful pillows and what seemed to be an overly wadded quilt all in white embroidery anglais. The bedroom was just like I imagined a honeymoon suite to look like.

'I take it by the look of wonderment on your face, Frankie, you like it?'

'I more than like it, Alex, it's simply stunning.' I turned, ran and jumped onto the middle of the bed.

'Oh this is just sheer bliss; I can't wait to sleep here tonight.' I felt movement on the mattress as Alex's weight was put onto the bed and he began to climb up me. After he kissed my neck a voice caressed my ear 'Sleep, baby? You won't be sleeping much tonight, I promise you,' I could hear the laughter in his voice. 'I've been wanting to test out these bed posts since I saw them online, I can see you now spread out in the St. Andrews cross position.'

'Oh dear God, do you two ever give up? There are some pictures you cannot erase from your brain after imagining them, you know,' Bella's voice came from outside our open door. 'I am now trying to lose the very image of my naked bestie spread out like a bloody X marks the spot, and I can tell you it's grossing me out.'

Alex picked up a pillow and aimed it well at the open door, it closed over somewhat.

'Don't listen at doorways then!' he added for good measure before letting out a deep laugh.

'I only wanted to see if she's seen the hot tub on the balcony yet? That was all. Knock, knock, can I come in please?'

'I give up,' Alex threw himself down beside me now and was lying on his front, head to the side, looking at me. I could tell he wasn't really annoyed by the beautiful smile on his face. 'Yes, Bella, by all means enter our room,' he added sarcastically.

'By the way the pillow on the floor, which you've just lobbed, is one of yours and not mine,' I slapped his backside for good measure and leapt off and away from the bed quickly before he could grab me.

He moved quickly and I watched him jump athletically to his feet, on the other side of the bed.

'You wanna play, baby?' and just like that his eyes were on fire, I could actually see his pupils dilating.

'Oh bloody hell, here they go again,' I heard Bella shouting out to Nathan who was probably still downstairs. 'I'm closing the bloody door on you two.' I heard the click as the metal caught into place and so did Alex. It must have been like a starting gun in his ear as I

194

watched his nostrils flair slightly and he moved like I was his prey. I could hear myself giggling as we danced to and fro around the bed in the middle of the room.

*Oh so that's why they've placed it here in the centre. It's so much more fun.*

I managed to get myself around to the side nearest the closed door, and having gone around the bed several times trying to avoid being caught by the sexy man pursuing me; I quickly made a bid for freedom.

*I have no idea why?*

I wanted him to catch me really, but still I lunged for the door and just managed to press down on the handle to open it. I pulled it open and ran out onto the landing but stupidly away from the stairs. Once Alex saw where I was, he slowed and prowled towards me knowing he had me caught like an animal in a trap. A smile was widening over his lips and his arms hung to his sides, fingers flexing in his anticipation to touch me. I felt myself flood; I could not believe what he did to me without having even laid a hand on me.

He didn't speak. I watched him intently as I couldn't tear my gaze away. His eyebrows rose at me in question and he caught his bottom lip between his teeth. Lifting one hand, he beckoned me towards him using a crooked finger. I slowly made my way back to him and he gathered me in all at once to his hard body. One of his hands now held my arms behind my back and slowly, all too slowly, he kissed me. I struggled to control my breathing and he compensated for me, allowing breaks in between, where he lavished affection on my tart button, my exposed neck. I could feel my heart rate accelerating and I pushed my body harder against his erection.

'Holy hell, what you do to me, baby,' I heard him hiss through his teeth.

Just like that he pushed himself away and started to gallop down the stairs, laughing.

'Alex?' I held on to the balustrade for support and raised my other hand to my swollen, well-kissed lips.

'Anticipation... baby.' He gave me one more wink before he disappeared from view.

The teasing bastard.

I waited a few minutes and followed him down the stairs. All three of them were now busying themselves putting the food away and taking bags to various rooms. Music was playing in the background. I stopped at the bottom of the stairs just to take in the memory.

The beautiful room.

The glow, of the wood burner.

The laughter, of my best friend.

The man I love, laughing deeply with his brother, my friend.

I had done this since I was small. Happy times in my life had always been in such short supply. To try to preserve them I took a photograph in my head and recalled it later on when needed. I couldn't help the smile that took over my face. Without realising I had even done it, I was now aware of my arms tightly wrapped around my body, almost hugging myself.

'OK, boss... what food preparation needs to be done tonight, then?' I heard Nathan's voice breaking through my thoughts.

'Well the vegetables need peeling and cutting,' I replied.

'I think that's down to Nate then,' added Alex. 'He needs to rest that leg of his and the veg can be done sitting at the island, can't it?' He looked at us all with a crafty boyish expression. When no one immediately answered, he added, 'I've got the bags to carry to various rooms, haven't I?' He smiled and proceeded to pick up one of the many he had dropped just inside the door, when we had first arrived.

'Dude, why don't you just say... you're not interested in kitchen duty?' stated Nathan.

'Oh but I am... I'm really interested in eating all the food that comes out of the kitchen.' He shot a look over his shoulder to us all as he began to depart down a hallway towards, I could only presume, the other bedrooms mentioned earlier. 'It's really hard work you know carrying all these bags and I will get in a load of wood as well.' His voice started to trail off as he moved further away from the rest of us. I wanted to go and investigate the rest of the cabin, but didn't dare. I knew if Alex could lay his hands on me he would stir up my desire for him again. There was no way I was walking straight into the lion's den, well not quite yet anyway.

'So shall I unpack for you, Nate?' Bella questioned as Nathan began to seat himself at the island. 'Yeah, darlin, that'll be great and you can decide where I'm sleeping then, can't you?' I watched her smile sweetly at him and she then disappeared in the same direction Alex had previously gone.

'Pass us the veg then, Frankie and let's get to work.'

I stayed in the kitchen pottering around the beautiful space. The preparation had been done for tomorrow and apart from someone getting up at an ungodly hour to put the turkey in the oven, we were good to go.

Bella had nodded off sitting in a comfortable chair by the window, I knew she had been working really hard on something at work and was equally pleased to see her, as well as Alex, relax. Nathan slowly got to his feet and walked to her chair, I watched as he grabbed one of the many chequered blankets from the back of the settee. He placed it over her sleeping form and kissed her forehead. Alex's gaze met mine quickly and we silently acknowledged that Nathan did indeed have it bad. It made my heart swell with happiness, my bestie so deserved someone like him.

Alex and Nathan were having a friendly, but very competitive and loud, chess championship, over a few beers. I watched Nathan return to where he was sitting and heard him whisper, 'What, fucker?' presumably to a questioning look from Alex.

I had just spied my Kindle on the side table. I stared at Alex, waiting for him to look up at me, something he had been doing on and off all evening. In between the food preparation, I kept finding him gazing at me. I was unsure if it was in love or lust. I didn't care; I would take anything from him what so ever. It had done nothing but heighten my earlier desire for him and I began to shift the tops of my thighs together again, just to try to quell the building need inside of me. I was pleased to have the island to hide behind. Finally, he turned to observe me again, he licked his lips and a knowing smirk began to appear over his face. After shaking my head at him, I smiled my thanks to him for his thoughtfulness; he had obviously placed my Kindle there earlier, when he unpacked. It seemed the man will do anything to keep out of the kitchen.

I had been looking longingly for a while now at one of the huge settees, and carried my kindle and steaming cup of tea over to it. I placed my legs and feet underneath me, to get cosy and comfortable. My Kindle sprung immediately to life and I started to choose my next book. The book was highly recommended and I had been looking forward to reading it. It was the last one of a trilogy. I had been waiting for it forever and had downloaded it especially for our weekend away. But this evening things weren't going to plan. I couldn't get my head around it or into it and had reread the first couple of paragraphs several times. My mind was wandering. No matter how hard I tried, I couldn't shut it down.

It made me so angry with myself.

*Why should the feeling of complete joy and excitement be so hard to take pleasure in?* Somehow my subconscious always brought me back down on my arse, back down to relive previous pain. The trouble was, when all your life you have been fighting for acceptance, fighting to be loved and cared for, by the very people who should love and care for you by automatic default... it leaves a wide open chasm deep inside you. A chasm that constantly has to be plastered up. When you are never given acknowledgement that people love you, that the ones who should be closest to you are proud of you, or would walk on hot coals for you, very easily the plasters start to unpeel, almost like they have lost their sticky quality.

The wound inside me had begun to feel open and exposed. Probably because I was opening myself up to Alex.

I felt laid bare.

I felt vulnerable.

I felt defenceless.

I wanted these thoughts to go away; this was a happy room full of people that cared for me. But no matter how I fought to reason with my own thoughts, I couldn't stop the negative thinking. The beautiful man in front of me had told me he loved me. He had done everything in our very short time together to show me his true feelings, with his words, actions and that fantastic body of his.

*But why, when a striking, powerful man like him could have anyone, why would he have chosen me?*

I had always struggled to accept the unconditional love my aunt, uncle and JJ had given to me. It had taken years to accept they loved me for me. Years to accept I was worthy of such love. They didn't love me for what I could do for them, they just loved... ME.

I glanced again from my almost foetal position and found myself staring into Alex's deep pools. How long he had been carefully observing me, I didn't know. I could see his concern for me though. Almost as if he was able to read my mind. He patted his lap for me to go over, and I did so with no hesitation what so ever. I slid onto his large lap, feet on one leg and bottom on the other. I tucked myself up in a ball under his chin and placed my arms around his back. He in turn put his long arms around me completely, almost as if he knew I felt the need for his protection. I breathed in the smell of him and started to feel at ease. I could hear the groan of the old settee under both of our weights; somehow its old robustness was comforting. The steady rhythm of the heart that I loved so much began to erase the negative, worrying thoughts away. I really had to learn to go with the flow and accept things at face value.

'I can hear those fucking cogs in your head whirring again, Frankie.' He had moved his head down next to mine and softly spoke into my ear.

'Give yourself to me, Frankie; I WILL take care of you.' I lifted my head to find his lips with my own. Shifting my body's coiled up position; I lifted my hands up to his face. My fingers were now holding his face to mine in the desperation to get close enough to him. Each fingertip was reacting to the sensation of his stubble beneath it.

*Who knew?* Just the feeling of his scruff beneath my hands was enough to start my whole body yearning for his. In turn I could feel his cock starting to grow.

'Hey, Dude, this is so not cool, you know,' Nathan butted in, 'as much as I'm willing to watch a little porn here and there, okay I'll rephrase that, a lot of porn! I am not goddamn willing to watch my brother give his girlfriend one! Been there... you get the picture.' I heard him start to stand up out of his seat. 'Before you two carry on I think I'll call it a night and get sleeping beauty over there to bed.'

I broke off our kiss now and stared into Alex's eyes, just searching for any reason why I shouldn't trust him wholeheartedly. In turn he stared so directly and pointedly into mine, almost as if he knew what I was checking for. I was relieved when I couldn't find a reason. With a smile Alex moved out from underneath me.

Whilst Alex helped Nathan get Bella to bed, I moved to the floor and sat myself up as close as I could to the wood burner, waiting for him to return. I watched the flames consuming the wood and I tried to will them to destroy my negative thoughts.

'I should get Scotty to paint you; you are a vision sitting there cross legged on the floor. The light of the fire, reflected in your eyes, the heat of the fire, causing the flush on your cheeks. I love you, baby... so much... You take my fucking breath away.'

As I looked up I found him staring at me from the open doorway. He had both hands up above his head, holding on to the door frame. It caused his body to lean slightly forward. His T-shirt had risen up and it had left the top of his belted jeans, exposing the start of his perfect V and the bottom of his abs. He was so tall and broad he literally filled the whole of the void.

*I take his breath away?* He was perfection, from the scruff on his face and flopped over mussed up hair, to his always bare feet.

'You said you're not good with words?' I questioned him and smiled at his unmoving figure. 'That sounded bloody fantastic to me.' I watched as his lithe body slowly made its way to me, stopping on the way to turn up the music on the iPod that had been playing in the background all evening.

He stopped to one side of me, offering his hand out. 'Dance with me... Frankie.'

I stood and was immediately pulled into his body. Our bodies fitted together like they had been cast from the same mould and just been split into two. He held on to me like he couldn't get close enough of me. Listening I could just about make out the song playing was. *The One-Kodaline*

We began to slowly move around and he started to sing softly into my ear. The words couldn't be more relevant. He interspersed soft gentle kisses on my earlobe and just beneath it, on my neck. I felt a million miles away from anywhere and anybody else. I couldn't believe I felt this close to another human being and a gorgeous one at that. Right at that minute I became conscious that I trusted him with my whole being and for possibly only the second time in my life I felt like I was exactly where I was meant to be. I placed my arms up under his armpits and clasped tightly to his shoulders and closed my eyes.

We danced together, in just the muted light of the fire. Several songs later he pulled me down in front of the log burner. We went down gently together onto the rug. Tenderly my clothes were removed by his hands. Every piece of my flesh that he uncovered was licked, tasted, stroked and caressed. I had never been so aware of every hair on my body, every undulation on my skin. My senses had been heightened to an almost painful precipice. I loved the rough calluses on his fingers and palms; I could not get enough of his touch. His touch was fast becoming everything I wanted and desired. A feeling of desperation began to course up and down my body. Unwittingly I tried to manoeuvre various parts of my body into his hands, but with no luck as he kept me in place with his legs and his body weight. It seemed like it took him forever to remove all of my clothing. When finally he had me naked, I looked up at him through lust filled eyes, and I comprehended that Alex was looking at me as though he had never seen me before. I was kissed and touched to the point of incineration beneath him. When finally he brought me to orgasm, using only his hand, I came with my eyes wide open and staring into his beautiful eyes. No words were needed. The way he made love to me showed me everything I needed to know.

The world must be bright this morning. The white voiles did nothing to keep out the daylight. The beautiful bedroom I stayed in last night was almost bathed in white light. My senses began to come to. The movement that Alex was making obviously disturbing me.

'OH SHIT,' I sat up in bed abruptly.

A loud chuckle came from the gorgeous man by my side. He was looking up at me from his apparently comfy position when sleeping, laid out on his front, with both arms up, underneath his pillow. He was completely mesmerising. Hair tousled, sleepy but with still sparkling eyes and extra scruff on his face. I was sure it would be a beard by the time we got back to NYC.

'JESUS CHRIST! Here I go again; I am not going to look at you. I have things that need doing today and it looks like I'm already late. Stop looking at me! I have to get cooking.' My ranting and then throwing myself out of bed, was obviously completely entertaining as he had turned now on his side, head up on his bent arm, a beautiful smirk all over his face.

'Frankie, it's actually only 6.30am, quite early. I have just put the turkey in the oven. Yes, even I can just about fucking manage that. The reason it looks later is we had a very light fall of snow last night, its reflection has lightened up the early morning.'

I found myself moving quickly to the large windows.

*I FLOVE snow!*

It was true the world outside had, had a very light dusting. It wasn't enough to sledge or build a snowman or anything like that. The light dusting however was enough to make the outside look like a Christmas card picture. The tops of the trees looked like they had

had a shaker of icing sugar all over them. It made a beautiful silent image. Alex growled suddenly. The noise made me spin around on the balls of my feet.

'Did you growl at me?' For effect I placed my hands on my hips, but my face broke into a huge smile. I emerged from my position, half in and half out of the voiles.

'Do you have any idea what you look like stood there? Bathed in the white light from the window, with those fucking curtain things draped over your smooth skin. You look like every boy's fucking wet dream, an image that I would gladly wank to, even at my age.' With a smirk on his face he purposefully and slowly pushed the overly wadded quilt down his naked form to reveal his erect cock.

I just couldn't help myself. I crawled back up the bed, trying to do the best seductive prowl on all fours. It was all I could do to repress the laughter inside me. I bet I looked like a complete bloody idiot. Although, checking him out now, utterly exposed on the bed, I could see his eyes had begun to dilate, and that clever tongue of his had just flicked out quickly to wet his lips. I had very quickly learnt that both of these were a couple of his tells. I settled down on top of his lush body and began to kiss him. He didn't try to take over like most of the other times when we had kissed. I was just allowed to take control, something I know he didn't find easy. As his arms started to encircle me I allowed myself to be held for a short time. Then by just breaking our kiss slightly I uttered, 'Uh, uh.' I took his hands and pushed them up over his head. I tried to hold his huge wrists with one of my hands. It was pretty unsuccessful, but he played along. I sat up, on top of his hot erection and nestled my wet pussy down onto him. He closed his eyes briefly.

'That is the very fucking place I need to be now, baby.' He wriggled his hips slightly, trying to get deeper into my wet folds. I knew that it was now or never and I sprung up off him and the bed so quickly. Only four large steps and I pushed my back to the en-suite door as I locked it in place. My heart was beating like a wild animal. I glanced down at my clothes laid carefully over the chair in here.

Luckily in my preparation last night I decided that getting up early to cook would mean an early shower. The door banged behind me. And my heart flew into my mouth. I placed my hand over my mouth to stop any noise coming out.

'What game are you playing, baby?' I could tell he wasn't too mad by his tone of voice. I didn't answer.

'I could fucking break down the door, you know? Is that what you want?'

Oh crap, crap, crap. I hadn't thought of that in the few seconds I had run this through in my head. I silently shuffled away from the door. In my cowardice I was still not answering. This was better than any cardio exercise I had ever done before, my heart was pounding.

'I could probably break the fucking thing down using my cock alone. It's so hard now! This game you're playing is making me as hard as steel. My hand has never felt so good. Sliding up and down my pussy wet cock. I know you can hear me, baby?'

Unknowingly I was back against the door now, trying to make out the tiniest of sounds coming from the man on the other side.

*Bugger the bloody door why didn't it have an old fashioned key hole?*

The realisation that my own game was backfiring on me came when I heard his breathing start to accelerate; he was only strokes away from completion and moisture started to pool at the top of my legs. I was that desperate to hear the sound of his orgasm. Suddenly there were no more sounds to be heard.

'Anticipation, Alex... anticipation.' I felt almost stupid saying the words. I was now in a worse state than him.

A few seconds passed until he spoke again. The familiar deep voice that had dropped again in his lust filled state.

'I see, that's the game we're playing, baby. Until later then... when you're gonna be begging me to tie you to the four poster. Playing with fire, baby, is gonna get you burnt.' I could almost hear the chuckle in his voice. He was moving away from the door as his voice was sounding less effective. His laugh was still coming through to me though. I didn't move until I heard him leave the bedroom.

'Ok, Frankie... I'm heading off into the gym. I've left breakfast for you in the fridge.'

I managed to shout out a very weak 'thanks,' and was rewarded by his laugh. This game of mine had seriously bloody backfired! Half of me was pleased; the other half was mildly terrified.

Finally, I was reading the book I had been waiting to get into. Or at the very least, I hoped that was the impression I was giving off.

The other three were in the kitchen tidying up after our Thanksgiving dinner. I was sneaking peaks at them all, moving around each other, clearing plates, stacking the dish washer. I didn't go near those things, once bitten, twice shy. I was really pleased with how the dinner had gone. The boys had even had seconds and some dishes had even warranted thirds apparently. I didn't know where the hell they put it. Against tradition I had created a mixture of an English Christmas dinner and a traditional American Thanksgiving. We had turkey and cranberry sauce, mashed potatoes, sage and onion stuffing, vegetables, green bean casserole, which I didn't think was quite right, but they were too polite to comment, roast potatoes and pigs in blankets. Followed by a wonderfully, delicious, homemade pumpkin pie. Mrs. Goldberg was clearly a bloody good cook. A smile came to my face when I remembered Nathan picking up a pig in blanket and examining it closely. A very serious expression on his face when he had asked exactly why it was us English liked eating small penises. That being said after he tasted one, he devoured more and more. Bella had slapped him when he announced at the end of the meal, that his tastes were changing now and he clearly was now heavily into cock.

I could feel Alex looking at me again; I had begun to recognise the instant effect he had over my body, whether from a glance, the briefest of touches, or his eyes connecting with mine. Everything he did turned me into a ball of lust, it seemed. To be quite honest the end of the day couldn't come quick enough. I in turn had watched him do everything today; I couldn't turn my eyes away from him. My "game" this morning had bloody well not gone as planned and everything below my waist ached for him. He knew, the bastard, which was what he obviously meant by playing with fire, could I have ever thought in my inexperience, that I was going to get the upper hand? Even in my aching state though, it had to be said it was bloody fun trying. I was sure he had dressed deliberately too. He was in sweat shorts. They hung low of course and every time he moved I was greeted with peek-a-boo of his abs and his happy trail. The T-shirt had turn ups on the sleeves and I had been enthralled earlier, just watching his muscles flex. My gaze had drifted to him again and I watched him stretch to put the plates away. As he turned back I made sure my gaze left him.

'Seriously, Frankie, you need to reel your eyes in girl... they look like they are on bloody stalks. You're even making me feel uncomfortable and as you know that's genuinely saying something.' I raised my eyes to Bella's teasing ones and smiled.

'And you, big boy,' she had placed her hand on Alex's shoulder now, 'stop parading around in front of her, she's beginning to dribble.' I shook my head at her as they all laughed and finished up what they were doing. Slowly they began to filter back to the seating area.

'Ok I've got a plan,' Bella announced. Settling herself on the settee, as close to Nathan as she could get without inflicting pain on him. They were so good together 'This evening we are going to play truth or dare, after having a few drinks of course. What do you say?' She looked at each one of us in turn.

'Sounds good to me, darlin... keep the drinks flowing and I'll play along.' He was stroking her hair now. They both had it bad. I recognised it and so did Alex, but I was really not sure Bella and Nathan recognised it, or maybe it was because they didn't want to?

The sound of Alex's iPhone broke me out of my thoughts. My eyes darted over to him. He had been padding his bare feet over to me, but he stopped abruptly after casting his eyes down to see who was calling. A loud sigh escaped those heart shaped lips and he ran a quick hand through his hair.

'Ok guys, I need to take this, so I'm just going to step outside. I'm definitely up for the game; Bella... mines a whisky please.' He winked at me before turning around and making his way down to the back corridors.

'Hi, Ruby... Ok?' Was all I heard before he was too far away to make anything else out.

I met Nathan's strained look? I proceeded to look back at my Kindle. That was somewhat strange?

# Alex

I could hear by the way she was talking, the fast pace as she gabbled to get it all out to me, that things were not good back at the house.

*But then, when the fuck are they?*

A deep resonating, loud sigh left my mouth. I shut the door to the gym and tried to sit down to hear her out. It was no good; I reassumed my normal fucking pacing stride. At least now the door was closed behind me I could at the very least respond to her. I knew I shouldn't have tried to come away, this so called fucking Thanksgiving. It was a stupid forced decision, but I wanted Frankie. I was fucking adamant that neither of those butt wipes were going to have her. I had never very been good at denying myself, well not for long and I needed her all the time, desperately.

My body started to break into a cold sweat.

'Right... yeah got it.' I slowly but determinedly kicked out at the metal of one of the machines, in front of where I had stopped to think, tapping it hard enough with my bare foot to feel a modicum of pain. It kept me focused.

'They're leaving him alone though, aren't they?' She answered my question. I started to realise that all my shit was about to hit the fan. 'How the hell did they find out?' I became conscious that my pulse was rising. I struggled to remain calm, I needed to focus otherwise I would upset her more.

'I can't come back tomorrow,' I made my voice gentler now in a bid to calm her down. 'I'll cut short my business though and I'll be back on Saturday.'

'Yeah... I'm working,' I heard myself lie. I couldn't believe how fucking easily this shit fell out of my mouth.

She talked a bit more. I could hear now, that she was starting to calm down. Her voice was starting to lose its anxious desperation.

'No, of course not. Tell Scotty I'll be back on Saturday; tell him we'll sort it all out on Saturday. Tell him he doesn't need to panic.'

She answered in reply.

'Of course you can always call me, you know I am always here... of course I do... Yeah that's right other people are around.' I took a quick fleeting look around the empty room.

'Ok, see you Saturday... I won't call you as I'll be busy with work... Yeah, bye.'

This was going to take every bit of my control. I didn't move immediately, willing my pulse to calm down. I was clenching and unclenching my fists. My body language must be screaming tense. I used the shower room next to the gym to rinse off my face. As I patted it dry my gaze lifted to the mirror above the sink, I sure as hell didn't like the fucking reflection in it. I raised my fist in anger, smashing it on the mirror. The pent up aggravation started to leave.

'Well done Jabby,' I spoke to myself now, 'how the fuck, are you going to explain that?'

# Frankie

The warmth of the fireball drink was slowly spreading through my veins. I could hear myself gently sighing and I relaxed even more into the well worn leather behind me. We had all decided to sit on the floor, to one side of the log burner. Rugs and huge cushions had been moved to provide more comfort. Nathan was stretched out with his head on Bella's lap. I watched her playing with the longer messy strands of his hair, between her fingers.

The windows were showing that once again it was lightly snowing and at this moment in time everything felt right. We just needed Alex to return and our game could commence. Nathan had got an empty beer bottle to use as the pointer. I just hoped that the questions weren't going to get too personal.

*I knew Bella well!*

I heard him before I saw him, or did I feel him coming towards me? I wasn't sure which. Finally, he appeared in the doorway. He shot us all a quick smile. I could see it but it was the sort of smile that didn't quite reach his eyes, it was a flat, fake smile.

'Just gotta sort out my hand guys, sorry to keep you waiting.' He walked towards the kitchen area and opened one of the wall cupboards. I pushed myself up and walked over.

'Can I help?'

He looked at me but didn't answer for a few seconds.

'I lost my temper... I know I fucking shouldn't have, but I lost it anyway.' I looked down to see his bloodied knuckles, being presented in front of me.

'It stings like fuck... but at least I didn't smash the mirror I hit.'

'What the bloody hell happened for you to lose your temper and hit a mirror?' I questioned. 'The phone call was from Ruby, wasn't it?'

His undamaged hand came up and ran through his hair. 'Yeah it was... just some trouble with a bit of business we're dealing with at the moment.' He paused and took a breath. 'She was just keeping me updated.'

I gazed up now after rinsing off his knuckles and wrapping clean gauze over them. I loved looking into his eyes. But looking now, it would seem something had shifted, I couldn't tell what, but it was almost like a door had been shut as the light no longer reflected in them. The sparkle had gone. I could only presume it had something to do with him losing his temper.

'Come on, let's go and play,' he said as he put his hand out and ran his fingers down my spine. I was so in tune with his body that the slightest of touches such as this made me begin to ache for him. He steered me using his good hand towards where the other two were reclined. After he sat down, I watched as he opened his legs into a V. Alex pulled me down in between them and I laid myself back against his hard muscular chest. One of his arms came and wrapped itself around me, holding me to him tightly. He exhaled the breath that he had obviously been holding for a while; I felt his taut body begin to relax.

'Right Ok... So truth or dare then... Yes?' Bella questioned.

We all muttered our hesitant agreement. She sat up and pushed Nathan's head off her lap with the sudden movement, such was her excitement; probably due to her investigative journalism tendencies. I could feel a smile spread on my face and I lightly shook my head at her over exuberance.

'Well it's my game... So I say who goes first.' She didn't ask the question, she just stated it as a fact. 'Frankie my gorgeous babe, it's you, you're the youngest, spin the bottle.' I leant forward and spun the bottle, silently praying it wouldn't turn to me. My luck held and it landed on Nathan. He didn't even baulk as we began our onslaught of questions.

As the evening wore on, more shots were drunk in dares and the questions began to get more revealing. They started with things like who was your first kiss, gaining momentum up to who was or is your best lay. I began to have the piss taken out of me something awful when most of my answers came back to Alex. My life, it seemed, had been much more sheltered than anyone else's. The bottle didn't seem to land on Alex nearly as much as I wanted. Finally, my eyes were drooping in tiredness, or I suppose it could have been the amount of fireball I'd had to consume.

'Ok so last round then guys,' Bella spun the bottle again and it landed on Alex.

'Ok you've been avoiding truth most of the evening so I vote you don't get a choice now.' I felt him tense slightly underneath my body.

'So it's quite evident to me,' she winked at me in a drunken sort of way... so drunk it seems the little wink she offered me turned into more of a tic. I had, I hoped, a discreet little chuckle behind my shot glass. When she was like this it wasn't good to wind her up. 'You Blackmore boys are a little dominant,' she looked pleased with herself in her ability to read people.

'Darlin... you don't say,' Nathan grinned at Bella. She however was in her stride and it didn't even remotely cause her to stutter.

'So this question goes to Alex first and then to you, Nate,' Nathan slugged back a mouthful of beer and grinned again.

'Alex what's the most effective piece of equipment you have used, in your role as a dominant lover?' The question was so direct I felt if I looked at her, I might find she had brought out her notebook and pen, with which to take notes.

'Ermm... well... I would say any length of fabric,' he answered.

'Oh... OK. Not quite what I was expecting and now you, Nate... Same question, although I know some of the answers already, don't I?'

I closed my eyes now and shook my head. She was funny when she was a little bit pissed.

'Well, darlin... yeah you do, but the best piece of equipment I like to use is my Harley Davidson.' I watched her bend her head down over Nathan now and start to whisper to him. He in turn caught hold of her shoulders and pulled her down to him firmly and they started to kiss.

'Time to go, Frankie.' I felt his voice in my ear, more than heard it. We begun to stand and made our way to the staircase. We left the two of them kissing on the floor. They seemed totally oblivious to our departure.

Our bedroom was lit only by the fire that was gently burning in the log burner; it filled the room with a warm glow. The night was dark and cloudy and it had been snowing on and off all day. Still nothing much to write home about, but it made the scenery outside even more special. I heard the click of the bedroom door behind me and I slowly turned around to see Alex leaning against it with his arms folded. He lifted his eyes up from my feet; taking in, it seemed every part of my body, until they finally reached my eyes. Whatever part of me his eyes came in contact with, my blood rushed to. I felt the flush of heat consume all of me. I smiled at him shyly, I didn't know why I still felt shy in front of him but his perusal always made me feel the same way.

'I need to be in control tonight, Frankie... if that's not something you are comfortable with, just say and... I'll... I'll just hold you.' His eyes stared deep into mine.

'I can try,' left my mouth. I was so confident in my answer, I didn't even think once, let alone twice. I trusted him implicitly. I could see this was something he needed. I always wanted to be the person he turned to in the future.

'I won't hurt you, you know that don't you?' I nodded in agreement.

'But I will push your limits,' I nodded again.

'I need the words, Frankie,' his voice deepened.

'Yes... I know you won't hurt me.' I watched, frozen to the spot as he slowly peeled himself away from the closed door, his arms falling to his sides as he prowled towards me.

Finally, he was standing an arm's length away from me. I was watching his broad chest inhale deeply over and over again. It was almost hypnotic. Watching his eyes close as he took in my scent. My skin broke out in goose bumps, the hair on my body stood on end. He didn't have to touch me or even talk to me; such was his command over me. His eyes opened again alight with fiery amber flashes, as he took on his different guise. His tongue came out fleetingly to wet his lips.

'Strip,' he nodded at me.

Slowly and probably very clumsily I started to remove my clothes in front of him. I could see he took in every button I released; he was watching every push down movement and every shimmy I tried to add in, in order to try to put on a bit of a show in front of him. Finally, after watching his face come alight at the removal of some of my clothes, I felt the courage to strip off my sweatshirt with a bit of a flourish. I threw it down to the floor and shook out my long hair, and peered up at him.

'You are beautiful, baby... just beautiful.' I observed how he twitched his fingers in the anticipation of touching my bare skin; it gave me confidence holding this small piece of power over him.

'Lie down on the bed, on your back.'

I did so. There were no pleases just simply instructions.

'Arms and legs stretched open wide.' His voice had increased in strength, not volume but in potency.

I placed myself into the X position I knew he wanted and closed my eyes briefly. Listening to him move around the bed, I heard a loud and sudden rip, somewhat startled I opened my eyes to find him pulling voile away from the bed. I gasped and his eyes darted to mine. He lifted his finger to my lips to 'sssshh' my protest and he continued to shred the fabric with his bare hands. My arms and legs were quickly tied to the bed posts and he stood at the end of the bed admiring his handy work. I checked each limb to feel the bindings on them. They weren't uncomfortable or even too tight, much to my surprise. They did however hold me firmly in the position he wanted, open and available. I watched as he removed the T-shirt from his torso. His sweat shorts were tented at the front showing his very obvious arousal. All too slowly he made his way to my feet, dramatically dropping to his knees on the floor. Although my head was lifted up and away from the pillows, I could only really see the top of his head and eyes, but it was enough. His eyes spoke volumes to me. My pounding heart was starting to relax.

'You have no idea how much you intoxicate me, do you?'

'The scent of your arousal and the citrus orange you wear haunts me day and night.'

'Look at you, baby, tied up for me and only for fucking me, at my mercy.'

His long arms began to run up the inside of my thighs and I could hear myself gasping at the sensations his calloused fingertips created inside me. My legs instinctively pulled against their restraints. Completely bound and out of control, my gasps had turned into moans. I felt the bed dip as his hands left my thighs. He opened the lips of my pussy with his now out stretched fingers. I lifted my head once again to take in the view of him as he leant up on his elbows. I watched entranced as those heart shaped lips blew on my clit, and I shuddered as his breath connected with my flesh.

'You are so wet for me, Frankie... I can see it running out of you... I plan to lap up all of your juices.' His head dipped then and he licked from my anus all the way up and over my hard bud of a clit, in one long continuous sweep. The feeling was so intense the nerve endings all over my body sprung to life. His head lifted to look at me again.

'You are fucking exquisite,' he licked his lips just to reinforce what he was saying.

He left the bed again and I heard the balcony door open. What he was doing I didn't know but I felt the freezing draft blow over my already very sensitive skin. The door closed and Alex came back. I looked at him as he neared the edge of the bed. He was carrying two handfuls of snow.

'Close your eyes.' I did what he asked. I couldn't remember being more compliant in all of my life.

*But I want him, all of him and I want all he is willing to give to me.*

The first drip of the melting snow hit my closed mouth and it ran straight to the corner. It then continued its path, dripping onto my shoulder. Strangely it almost felt like I was being burnt by it, such was the change in temperature on my overly sensitive flesh. I moaned out loud.

'More?' he questioned, I nodded my head, enthusiastically. He slowly dripped more of the melting snow and I quickly flicked out my tongue and then took it deep into my mouth. I heard him growl beside me.

*So this didn't just affect me then?*

He ran the snow all the way down to my nipples and from the sensations they were receiving he had crunched the snow together to make ice. The ice was being run around and around both hardened nipples at the same time. The feeling was so immense I could feel myself pulling against all four pieces of the voile at the same time; my body was writhing with the movement. It was killing me that all I could feel was the ice on my body. He wasn't even near enough to touch; I could feel no heat radiating from him at all. My nipples were almost numb when suddenly he flicked them both at the same time.

'Oh fuck!' The initial shock and pain caused me to attempt to sit up. The pain quickly ebbed away and the pleasure flowed fast from my nipples, along every nerve ending I had.

'Lay back and close your eyes.' He quickly sucked up one of my nipples into his warm mouth, the other nipple was also receiving warm attention, from what I wasn't sure, but once again I was going from slight pain to deep, deep pleasure. Alex really knew what he was doing sucking, biting, licking and flicking. His ministrations were creating a ball of fire in my gut. I began to moan as my pussy started to convulse.

*Surely he can't be making me come with just his mouth on my nipples?*

All at once the feelings he was producing on my rock hard nipples set in motion a reaction between my thighs. If only he would just touch me once, just once on my clit, I knew I would explode.

'Please, Alex...'

'Please... Touch me. I need you to touch me.' I could hear the desperation in my voice.

He released my nipple at once from his mouth. It made a resounding pop as it was let go.

'Silence,' he demanded.

He moved, positioning his now naked self over me. I could feel the heat emanating from his skin. I needed to run my hands over him as he lay on top of me. I wanted to pull him closer to me. It felt almost requisite that our bodies should be connected; it was the most severe torture.

I could smell him, his masculine scent and his cologne all mixed together, like some addictive drug. He was my drug and I couldn't get enough of him. He wasn't stimulating me at all, in the traditional sense of the word, but just being near him, being able to smell him, was keeping me right on the edge of an orgasm.

I heard the rip of the condom packet. That and his sudden movement informed me that I was just about to be put out of my misery. He entered me at once and immediately stilled, filling my convulsing pussy. With just that one simple thrust of stimulation I came all over him. I squeezed my eyes together tightly trying to regain some control over my body.

'Open your eyes, baby,' I heard him demand of me.

That was my mistake; this wasn't my body to control, but his. The pleasure I felt was coursing through my muscles and nerves in waves. So strong was the surge, I considered for a brief time that it would never stop. As I began to come down from my high I looked down at our bodies together. The only parts of us that were touching were my pussy and his cock and I knew that was also deliberate. He winked at me and my heart leapt. He withdrew from me slowly, and gently, so not to hurt my still fluttering walls. After taking off the condom he literally dived in between my legs. Everything waist down became alive once again as he lapped at me and pushed his tongue in just the right way, and in no time at all I could hear myself screaming out his name.

'ALEX...ALEX...YES, YES...YES...'

As I began to descend once again his very talented tongue entered me and he licked up every trace of my orgasm, he growled and groaned whilst doing so. 'You are so tight, baby, so fucking tight.'

I was really tired now and my limbs began to ache in their fixed position. 'Alex untie me, please.' I lifted my head and took in the fact he was laying prone on one of my thighs.

He moved his head and looked at me, 'Uncomfortable, baby?'

'Yes, I'm just starting to cramp up.' He moved quickly once he heard and started to remove the ties from the bed posts, but not my limbs. I raised my eyebrows in question at him. He just smirked at me, giving me his answer without verbalising. I knew he hadn't allowed himself to come, so it was fairly obvious he hadn't finished with me yet. He rubbed all of my limbs and they began to slowly come back to life. He leant his head down to mine and started to kiss me; instinctively I placed my hands around his neck, in order to pull him closer.

'Let go,' he stopped kissing me and I once again had to relinquish my control and hand it back to him by removing my arms from around his neck. This instantly meant I was rewarded as he started to kiss me once more.

*Really his kisses should be bottled and sold. He puts every bloody thing he has into them.*

After breaking apart, I was aware that my hips were moving into him trying to rub his cock. With a smile he moved me suddenly away and flipped me over onto my stomach. His tongue was now running up and down my back.

'You need to rub on something, Frankie? Put one hand underneath you and find your clit, rock your pussy down onto your hand and fingers.' I couldn't refuse, so strong was the urge to come once more. The feeling of my hand in between my thighs was driving me insane. He was licking and biting places on me and just as that set in motion slight pain, I could feel him remove his teeth and lick my skin back to pleasure. My brain was mush. All I wanted was him. Moans and gasps left my lips; I tried biting down onto my bottom lip to contain some of my noises, but to no avail. I found myself in a rhythm, and I was rocking fast and hard into my hand.

'Stop.'

'Alex... I don't think I can, please.'

'Stop... The next time you cum it will be with me inside you.'

I slowed my hand but couldn't remove it. Suddenly my backside was on fire as he had brought his hand down fast and hard on my bum cheek, only to then rub the sting away using his warm palm.

'Remove your hand, Frankie; otherwise you will get no more of me.'

I really couldn't chance that, as I felt I needed him more than I needed my next breath. I did as I was told and showed him my hand. He grabbed it immediately and commenced to suck and lick all remnants of my arousal off my fingers. It was so bloody arousing and captivating all at the same time. Our eyes met as he finished cleaning me up.

'I want you, Frankie.' He moved abruptly off the bed and pulled me down with him, until I was on my feet, bum in the air. My naked body was laid out on the edge of the bed at a right angle, I watched him retie both of my hands to the nearest bedpost and I knew at last he was going to actually give me all of him. I heard the rip of foil again.

'Alex, we don't need the condom, I put myself on the pill a few weeks ago.' I had been waiting for it to become effective and finally that day was here. In fact, I had been OK for about a week. But even after all that we had done, it was still embarrassing to actually own up and say I had started it, knowing I was coming to NYC. It was like admitting I was looking for sex. Tonight though I knew for some reason, he needed from me as much as I could give him, and for whatever reason that was I needed to give him everything I had. My sudden statement was met with a few seconds of thoughtful silence.

'Baby, you never cease to surprise me.' His tone of voice was different when he spoke again. I felt him release my limbs.

'What are we doing?' I questioned as he picked me up in his arms and laid me gently back onto the bed.

'I've never gone bare back with anyone... let alone the only woman I have ever loved. I need to make love to you now, not fuck you. Do you understand?' He rested his forehead to mine and I nodded my head in understanding. I clung on to him, so enjoying the very basic pleasure of running my fingers and nails over and over his skin, feeling the sheen of sweat that covered him. Slowly he entered me. As normal he stopped and waited to check I was comfortable.

'Fucking hell, I've never felt anything like this before, baby, you feel like soft, warm velvet...You are just made for me... feel it, Frankie!' We started to make love. Staring into each other's eyes, it was passionate and intense and we showed each other everything we felt between us.

'I can't hold it anymore, baby; the feeling is too fucking extreme... Come with me... NOW.'

Clinging hold of his back I could feel when he had reached the point of no return as he started to shake. The powerful tremors shook me to my core.

'FUCK, baby...You are MINE.'

'FUCKING HELL.' As he exploded inside me I could feel his hot spurts hit the bottom of my cervix over and over again and it pushed me over the edge with him. I came, convulsing in his arms, and crying out his name.

'Jesus Christ I love you, baby, that was fucking amazing.' I could only agree by nodding my head. My ability to form coherent words had quite obviously left me, or had been fucked out of my system. I slowly began to fall asleep wrapped up in his arms, still wearing the pieces of voile around my wrists and ankles. I didn't care that the fabric was still tied on my bare flesh. I liked the way it felt.

I belonged to him.

I belonged with him.

I was his and he was mine.

# ALEX

*The smell invading my nostrils is acrid. Couple that with the hot, fucking dry air we're breathing in, with every uncomfortable breath and the weight of my equipment bearing down on me. I knew it was going to be a long fucking day. The men didn't complain around me though and I sure as hell wasn't going to be the one who started it. We entered the small village and all of my senses seemed to turn on to full alert. I took stock of where we were all positioned and I waved them all on.*

*The sudden blinding flash and ear splitting noise on our right flank made me instinctively go to ground.*

'FUCK.' I sat up and jumped out of bed almost in the same movement.

*Where the hell was I? Just breathe, breathe.*

My heart rate was pounding. My body was covered in sweat and I fucking stank. The nightmare that was part of my past, once again had entered into my reality. I moved quickly towards the bathroom. I needed to wash the filth away from my body.

'Alex?' questioned a voice behind me.

*Fucking hell!*

I couldn't answer her at the moment; I couldn't even fucking look her way. So like the weak little cunt I was always told I was, I walked even faster to the bathroom and closed the door behind me.

I turned on the shower to the hottest temperature I could stand and then some and I started to scrub myself raw under the omnipresent stream. My sobs came strongly and I hated myself even more, for my selfish emotion.

'Let me?'

*Fuck*

I could hear her behind me, but I didn't have the strength to turn around. I could however hear the sound of the bath tub filling up.

'God that water is boiling! What the bloody hell are you doing to yourself?'

Her hands reached in and turned off the flow of the water that had systematically been painfully trying to wash away my sins and the smell of guilt off my skin.

'Come in the bath with me, I'm going to wash you, and you're going to let me.'

Like a small child I followed her as she led me into the bath. She knew I couldn't look at her and she sat me in-between her opened thighs in front of her. My skin must have been red raw as even in a normal temperature bath I could still feel it burning. It was nothing less than I deserved. Time after time she filled up the natural sponge with water and soap. It washed and rinsed and wrung out over as many parts of my body as she could reach. She asked no questions and slowly, too fucking slowly, my mind started to clear. Finally, I lay back in her arms, it must have been a ridiculous sight to see, with our frames being so different in size, but I needed it and she was willing to give it to me, so there I stayed until the water started to cool.

'It was a nightmare, wasn't it?'

I owed her. I needed to at least answer that question.

'Yes.'

'Was it... Was it about when JJ died?'

'Yes.' I hated the answer, but owed her the truth.

'I love you... I love all of you, as my aunty said recently we both need to let it go. I do feel we were meant to be together somehow. We need each other.'

I took in her statement, exhaled and slowly stood up out of the water. For the first time since the nightmare had started, I looked at her face and stared into her forgiving eyes.

'I don't know if I will ever be able to lose the guilt completely... but for you I will endeavour to.'

I lifted her out of the bath and into my arms. This woman was a fucking wonder in more ways than one. As we stood, holding each other, I lifted both of her wrists to my mouth and kissed over the top of the voile, still tied there. After removing the wet fabric from her I swung her up into my arms and carried her from the bathroom. Personally I would've thrown her over my fucking shoulder, but felt that something more loving than fucking needed to happen now. We remade the bed together as my nightmare had destroyed the bedding with my sweat and apparent thrashing about.

Finally, the fog of oppression left me and I smiled as I gesticulated she should get back into the bed to get warm. She snuggled down immediately. Moving around to the log burner I rebuilt the fire over the top of the still hot embers and went to the kitchen to make us hot chocolate and whipped cream, I needed to find the packet of cookies I knew she had brought with us. Evidently I was in need of comfort food.

*Fuck, Nathan would have a ball with that info.*

The clock in the open plan room downstairs showed 2.45am. We had probably only had one-hour sleep tops, but I knew I wouldn't be sleeping any more tonight. Carrying our cups upstairs in both hands, with the packet of cookies between my teeth, I reopened our bedroom door with a push of my right foot against it and it swung open, banging slightly on the wall to one side of it.

'Sorry, baby,' I apologised as her heavy eyelids fluttered open at the sudden noise. I dropped the cookies from my mouth and let them fall onto the white bedding.

'It's OK... I was just resting my eyes; I wouldn't have slept until you came back anyway.' She smiled at me then and I clambered back into bed next to her, passing her the hot chocolate and offering her the cookies I had managed to find.

'It's not easy for me to talk about,' I offered, at the same time dunking a finger into the whipped cream on top of my drink.

'I realised, after watching you trying to expunge yourself in the shower. I don't mind that you can't talk about it... I just want you to know that I am always here to listen if and when you need me.' She turned and looked at me then, dipping a finger into her cream, then she dabbed my nipples with it playfully and after placing down her cup on the bedside table she licked at them both possessively. I knew what she was doing and welcomed the distraction. We spent the next couple of hours exploring each other's bodies and chatting. It was warm and comforting. We laughed and shared stories of our lives. I felt like I had never known anyone as well as I knew her now. Certainly no one knew the things I had willingly shared with her. I could have stayed wrapped up in our cocoon forever. I wasn't fucking looking forward to telling her and the others we were going to have to cut short our trip tomorrow. The crap at home needed my attention and there was only one way to avoid the clusterfuck that was brewing.

I had to sort it out. I would protect those I loved. I had promised.

# Frankie

Alex had taken me out that morning for a long walk. We needed the blast of the cold fresh air, just to clear our heads. Last night had shown me just how deeply he was affected by JJ's loss. He was quiet, really quiet, and nowhere near his normal self, but I put that down to our lack of sleep the previous night.

We had mostly walked in silence, just content to be with each other. Walking along holding hands and stopping frequently to hug and kiss. If it was possible the electrical connection between us was even stronger now. It was as if he had something to prove to me. Since last night's turn of events, he wasn't willing to be anywhere I wasn't, and that was made even better if it was just the two of us. Nathan and Bella had barely surfaced all morning. We had briefly seen Bella grabbing food earlier, but when Nathan had shouted through to her from the bedroom, she'd gone straight back to him giggling and waving at the two of us.

We made do with left-overs from the day before for lunch and I was currently curled up on Alex's lap reading. Bella and Nathan finally found their way out of their bedroom holding hands and laughing. I nudged Alex awake from his dozing and stared at them.

'Yeah, I see it too,' he whispered his acknowledgement.

I felt him start to manoeuvre himself slightly underneath me, as he rearranged his posture. He was leaning forward now over the top of me.

'Right as we're all here at the same time, I need to let you guys know that... well after speaking with Ruby last night... although I'm fucking reluctant to... I'm gonna have to cut this trip a day short. There's a problem with a business deal and it needs my attention.' After a somewhat hesitant start to the statement, the rest poured out quickly.

'Oh?' questioned Bella, 'That's sad, I love it up here, far away from world,' she looked at Nathan longingly.

I knew what Alex was doing without even turning to see. His hands had released me and were currently going through and through his black hair.

'You guys will never know how sorry I am, that we won't get to stay until Sunday. But after sleeping on it I know it's what I have to do. So we'll leave tomorrow morning. OK?'

'Well, dude, you have to do what you have to do... don't you?' Nathan was currently staring at Alex like he was trying to unpick his mind. Alex didn't answer, but looked at Nathan as if he was trying to move his thoughts into Nate's head by telepathic means.

'So one more evening everyone, we should make the most of it. What shall we do?' I jumped up and off his lap now and made my way to a cupboard that I knew from an earlier bout of my severe nosey tendencies, contained classic DVDs and began my inspection, to see what gem could be found.

'I vote girls' choice, what do you say, Bella?' I showed her the cupboard full of films.

She came and joined me then and between us we picked out some classic chick flicks just to make the men in the party groan with the torture of it all. Our last evening was full of laughter and banter. I took another photograph in my mind.

It was another wintery sort of day when we left our mountain retreat. The journey home on the Saturday morning was tedious as we seemed to meet up with all sorts of holiday traffic. Gone was the heady excitement I had felt on our journey up on Wednesday night. I was feeling guilty as I kept on falling asleep and jerking awake again. Alex had seen to it that we hadn't had a lot of sleep last night; I smiled to myself remembering the hot tub we had finally enjoyed together.

Alex on the other hand was doing fantastically, he didn't seem to be affected at all by the lack of sleep and this time, rather sadly, we didn't even stop at the diner on the way home. It seemed he was single minded enough to know he had to get back as quickly as possible, to sort out whatever the problem was.

Upon arrival at his building in NYC we drove straight into the underground car park. Expertly he drove into the tight space and switched off the engine. He turned his body to face mine and grabbed hold of my hands.

'Frankie, as much as this fucking kills me, I am going to have to drop you guys off now and get out to my mother's house... I won't be back tonight, baby,' a long sigh left those heart shaped lips and he closed his eyes in resignation. 'I hate to spend nights apart, but it's necessary... you don't know how much I regret that... it's fucking necessary.' His eyes found mine with the last sentence. Bella and Nathan had scrambled out of the car as quick as Nate's leg could manage. Almost as if they had already read the situation and wanted to give us some space.

'So will I see you tomorrow?' *God I felt like such a needy bitch.*

'I will have to work tomorrow, but I will find my way back to you at some point. I promise.'

I climbed over the centre console now and straddled his lap. Immediately we touched, I felt the by now familiar electric current coursing throughout my body. Alex in turn rocked himself forward with a deep moan and grabbed hold of my arse cheeks with both hands. I said nothing as I kissed all over his face and ran my fingers through the hair that I so loved to pull whilst we made love. His face was strained, and his eyes were a dark green with no light in them at all. Whatever was bothering him needed sorting out and fast as I wanted my playful, dominant man back.

'I will miss you, but it's a bit of luck I nicked one of your T-shirts previously. At least I'll have something to sleep with.' Without any warning his hands came up to mine rapidly and pinned them easily to my sides. My mouth was set about by his and my back was forced backwards onto the steering wheel. His tongue probed into my willing mouth. Once I had been kissed nearly breathless, he pulled away slightly and made straight for my tart button, my neck. He growled in-between licking and biting me.

'Don't make this easy for me will you, baby?' The voice I so loved had deepened with his arousal.

'No, Sir... I want you back ASAP.' I grinned and reluctantly started to remove myself from him. He didn't move from the driver's seat and slowly I got out of the vehicle.

'I will always find my way back to you, baby, always... I love you too much not to.' His eyes found mine when he said those words and he offered me a small smile and a wink of his eye.

'I love you too... so much.' I closed the car door, hating the finality of the click it made and began to walk towards the lift. Edwards was there trying to be discreet, holding the door open for me. As I reached the lift door I turned to watch Alex leave. I watched him drive up the slope and out of the garage until the red brake lights could no longer be seen and it felt like Coronado all over again.

# Chapter 35

I made my way quite sadly into the apartment Bella and I shared. A smile found its way to my lips to find Nathan there too.

'OK?' Bella offered.

'Yeah, I'm fine, just... oh you know... I would just prefer Alex to have still been here... you understand?'

'I'm always available ya know, chocolate drop.' I looked down at a spread-eagled Nathan stretched out on one of our settees.

Laughing and shaking my head at him, I gently tapped the bent knee of his good leg.

'Yeah... right. It's not quite the same you know?' I raised my eyebrows in question to him. He started grinning, using his full on bad boy smile to great effect. The relaxed atmosphere had at least brought a smile back to my face. I sat down with a jolt at the opposite end to Nathan. He deliberately put the bare foot of his good leg on my lap. I grimaced at him laughing. Bella was slowly wandering around the apartment unpacking. On the way past the telephone she pressed the answer machine button and the quiet of the room was broken by my aunt's voice.

'I know you're away, Frankie and Bella. I do hope you are having a wonderful time with those lovely men of yours.' There was a short pause then, 'Oh girls I don't know how to tell you, I don't want you to worry. But, well Uncle Robert let down his guard the other day. Well Karen had turned up on our doorstep asking about you. He let it slip where you were... we're both really sorry, I'm sure she won't turn up, but you know your mother, love.' She sighed, 'Anyway, sorry again. Phone soon OK. Let us know.........'

The answer machine shut off then, obviously the message had been too long and she had cut off at the end.

*Bloody hell, crafty bitch... what the hell does she want?*

My eyes found Bella's and we both sighed. Nathan had been watching us both.

'I take it, girls, this isn't a good thing?' He asked turning his head from one of us to the other, waiting for an answer.

'You could say,' I answered. I didn't really know where to begin.

'I have no parental relationship with her, Nathan... at all. All she ever wanted to be was a bloody kept woman, I was too much hassle for her... you know? I was too much of a commitment. I tied her down. She floats in and out of my life as and when it bloody well suits her, usually when she wants or needs something. It has never mattered if I wanted or needed anything.'

I lifted his leg up and away from my lap and stood up. 'God only knows what she's after this time.' I said almost as a thought to myself rather than a statement.

'You may never find out, chocolate drop, you're a long way away from England,' came from the voice on the settee.

'You don't know her, Nate... if she wants something, she'd fly over on her broomstick just to guilt Frankie enough to try and get it... OK enough about mutton dressed as lamb, otherwise known as Karen,' Bella added as she gave me a quick hug, 'Let's sort ourselves out and shouldn't you two be getting some physio done?' she glanced at us both.

'You are a slave driver, darlin,' Nathan smiled up from his still prone position. His hands tucked under his head, looking like a fairer version of Alex.

I started to leave the room to go and unpack. I had to stifle a giggle and was relieved my back was to them both as I heard, 'I need you back on that Harley Davidson, don't I?'

Nathan laughed and answered, 'You sure as hell do, darlin, you sure as hell do.'

We managed to do Nathan's physio that afternoon. The difference in the strength of his leg was amazing and I hoped that the end result would be so good that you would have to really scrutinize his leg and study hard, to see any signs at all of a lingering limp. Unbeknown to me, whilst I had been getting laundry done, Nate had been down to see the security team at the front desk. He had updated them all on the state of affairs regarding my mother and her possible arrival in NYC.

The next morning was chillier than ever. The presenters on TV had even been discussing the probable amount of snow due in between now and Christmas. I had wrapped myself up fully and had gone out for my morning run. Bella was nowhere to be seen and I thought it was extremely plausible she was in a bed somewhere with Nathan, tucked up and warm. My bed had held no such luxury this morning and I wanted to be out of it as soon as my eyes had opened in the winter's gloom.

The run was just what the doctor ordered; I ran fast and allowed my brain no time to think what I had possibly missed the night before. The run helped to erase the heightened sense of lust that seemed to occur every time I thought of Alex. I couldn't wait to be back in his arms. Upon finishing my run, I stopped to stretch out at my normal place, across the road from our building. The traffic was quite light being early on a Sunday.

After stretching out my hamstrings I stood back up. I could see Edwards talking to a woman outside the building. I hadn't needed to scrutinise the figure any further. It was her, but then I'd known she would come. To have turned up at my aunt and uncle's showed she was desperate for something. For once I hated being proven right. Now the question was did I cross the road and face the music or wait until she was turned away from the building. Edwards had noticed me there, but he was doing a fine and very polite job of keeping her from entering. Being with Alex these past few weeks had given me the confidence to face her. I stood tall and started walking, intending to cross the road as quickly as I could.

'Karen,' I spoke to her back and she turned around at the sound of my voice.

'Oh there you are, Francesca.' She turned slowly, everything she did and every movement she made was choreographed to absolute perfection. I had always been convinced that my mother had never played as a child. She would have practised her movements, hand gestures and expressions over and over, until she was entirely certain they had the desired outcome on all that she bestowed them on.

I was one of the few people that knew the bitch within. She just couldn't help herself and I saw her look me up and down in disgust. Sweaty running clothes and comfortable, well-worn trainers were simply not the sort of attire I should be wearing. I could hear her think it, so loud it was almost as if she was shouting. She would prefer me to not eat at all and then I wouldn't need to exercise.

'I was just telling this man here that I am your mother,' she bestowed a well used, but fake smile on Edwards and myself. I stopped a grin breaking out when I grasped that Edwards was the first man I had ever seen that was completely unmoved by the whole staged performance.

'Really? How obtuse of you,' I retorted.

*OMFG for the first time in my life, I didn't care what she thought of me, it was the most fantastic and exhilarating feeling.*

I'd secretly wished Bella was there to see it. I could mentally see her high fiving me.

'So what can I help you with?'

'Where are the manners I brought you up with, Francesca? Do you no longer invite people in out of the cold anymore?' She threw me a condescending look.

'Right first thing, you spent no time on my upbringing whatsoever. Anything good about me was definitely not shaped by you!'

*This felt damn good!*

'Secondly, I will invite you up, just to hear you out.' I nodded at Edwards and he side stepped his large frame away from the entrance of the building. I was sure of one thing and one thing only; I was in charge of this meeting, not her. I made sure that I led into the penthouse lift and that she, for once in our relationship, followed. Edwards squeezed in with us, making it fairly obvious he was here at my discretion, should she need to be shown the way out again. All too soon we arrived at the penthouse level. I could see she was impressed, well who wouldn't be? But to her material things like this, meant everything.

'Well I must say, Francesca; this is a turn up for the books. Who would have thought it, my little girl living in a beautiful place like this.' She had only seen the marble hallway and yes it was impressive, but quite frankly I was gobsmacked at the sheer audacity of the woman. I couldn't retort just yet, I was waiting until we had entered the apartment. I let us in and walked in front of her, making sure my body language still confirmed that I was in charge of this meeting, not her. The deep voice of Edwards reached through to me.

'Frankie, I'll be outside the door.' I nodded at him in understanding, and smiled my thanks to him. 'Can you tell me has Alex arrived home yet?' I knew it was a long shot, but hope was building up inside me as I wanted him to be around for what I knew was going to be one of the most difficult confrontations of my life.

'No, not yet. Sorry.'

'It's OK, I was just checking,' I smiled my answer, making sure my words conveyed my strength. I knew she would feed off of any form of insecurity.

The door closed and I was alone with her. Her tone changed instantaneously, the moment we were unaccompanied. She had walked herself over to the full length windows. She spun suddenly, a look of contempt now covering her expensively moisturised face.

'Well now... haven't we done well for ourselves?' She couldn't help the hint of jealous sarcasm pouring off her tongue.

I stood tall, for the first time ever; I wasn't going to break under her condescending look. My hands found the settee and behind the cover of the large cushions I gripped the back until my knuckles had quite possibly turned white.

'Yes I have, thank you for noticing.'

'So you are working here, I understand.' She ignored my sarcasm and carried on with her script.

'Yes I am... OK, enough of the twenty questions, we need to move away from the small talk and get to the nitty gritty of exactly why you have sought me out?'

'You haven't even asked me to sit.'

'You don't need a seat. Just spit it out.'

'My goodness, you have at last grown a backbone, my dear.'

I inhaled and fixed my eyes straight up to meet hers.

'The trouble is, Karen; you no longer have any hold over me whatsoever. There are only so many times your so called parents can push you away and turn their backs on you, before you decide to walk away from them altogether. I suggest to you now, that you tell me what you want from me this time, before I have you escorted from the building. Your time is fast running out.'

Movement came from the other side of the room. I became aware that Bella and Nathan had joined us. I looked up to see Nathan only wearing sweat shorts and showing off his bare torso and Bella wore his T-shirt from yesterday. The look of surprise instantly covered Bella's face, at seeing our house guest.

'Frankie, are you OK?'

I lifted my hand to her to get her to stop talking.

'Karen here is just going to explain exactly why she has come to see us.'

I watched my mother take in Bella and Nathan's state of undress. 'Arabella, how are you?... And this young man... I don't believe we have been introduced, but I believe you to be some sort of bike rider?'

Alpha males obviously ran in Alex's family; I could almost physically see the dominance exuding from the normally playful Nathan's pores. He stood himself unconsciously up to his full height and crossed his arms over his chest.

'Where's Edwards?' He growled.

'I don't need Edwards, Nathan,' I turned myself back to my mother, 'so? I'm waiting.'

She sat herself down uninvited on a corner of the settee. 'Well, so it's a brothel you girls have here is it?... albeit a very high class one.' I saw from the very corner of my eye Bella put out an arm to stop Nathan moving. 'Francesca you should come home.'

'What the hell for... just bloody well tell me what the hell you want from me?'

'I am getting divorced,' she finally admitted. 'Luke McMorran's father is my solicitor... He feels you two were so good together; he would love to see you back together... and well he feels he could get me a much better settlement if we were family.' Luke was my first and only ever boyfriend, before Alex. Momentarily I was stunned.

*Christ knows why?* This was typical of our relationship. I stared at her then, feeling like I could finally see her warts and all for the very first time. Before I knew what was happening I was laughing, I mean really laughing.

'So let me get this right... you accuse Bella and I of being prostitutes, which quite obviously we're bloody not and then you expect me to leave my life here and come home to sell my body, all so you can get a bigger divorce settlement?... You are not only delusional; you are the most selfish bitch I have ever had the misfortune to come across... I cannot believe... YOU... GAVE BIRTH TO ME!' I could see Bella grinning like a Cheshire cat out of the corner of my eye.

'I have a fantastic job here,' I waved my arms around the huge apartment. 'I am in love for the first time in my life, with the most fantastic and loving man... you really are under some sort of misconception,' I was shaking my head.

I watched her face change then, from manipulative cow to evil snarling bitch and I knew I had awoken the beast.

'I think you have to ask yourself, Francesca... why would a man like Alex Blackmore want you? Especially a fantastic and loving one, you are a mousey little thing. I am sure given a few weeks, when you have served a purpose, he will throw you away like the trash you seem to constantly dress in. Let's face it; the whole love thing could be simply a ruse, to stop a civil case looking into JJ's death, couldn't it?'

My wonderful new found confidence was slipping at her put down and her thoughts.

'My brother is in love with Frankie,' Nathan came and draped his arm protectively around my shoulders. 'Not that it has anything to do with you,' he looked my mother up and down with as much disdain in his expression as he could muster. I had to say I visibly saw her shrink somewhat.

'And I am in love with her best friend,' Bella recoiled slightly upon hearing that statement.

'As we're rich, talented, extremely successful, and very protective, I seriously doubt you will have anything you can offer either of them ever again, except maybe a heartfelt apology. But I know your sort, that will never happen.' Without taking his arm away from my shoulder we walked, him leading, without a limp, to the door. He opened it forcefully.

'Edwards, this woman is leaving.'

I watched as my mother stood and made her way to the door. My grip on Nathan's waist strengthened.

'Oh, Karen... just before you go.' We all turned to look at Bella questioningly. 'I just wanted to let you know... it's the sort of thing a friend should tell you... but of course you don't have any of those...

The fillers and Botox you must be paying a bloody fortune for... Well, they're not working. You are looking worse than the Mona Lisa and... She is...well, she is fucking old!'

My mother raised one hand to her face and disappeared quickly through the door.

She must have heard us cracking up with laughter at Bella's bitchy swipe and the sheer relief of her departure.

'So proud of you, my bestie,' Bella quickly made her way over to Nathan and I, the three of us hugged and I felt myself finally relax, for the first time since I had glimpsed her figure from across the road.

'It's a joke, isn't it?' Nathan was shaking his head and speaking to both of us, 'Family is supposed to be where we find the most support and comfort; more often it's where we find our biggest heartaches.'

# Chapter 36

It was Wednesday and I was staring out of my windows from the penthouse level, just watching the world go by. I still hadn't seen Alex; I had however woken up on Monday morning in my bed and by the indentation next to me in the bed, coupled with the smell of him and that cologne permeating from the pillow, I knew he had been there at some time during the night. Although I had taken some small consolation from that realisation, it didn't help with the ever growing feelings of loss and loneliness I was beginning to experience. The confrontation with my mother had started to put seeds of doubt in my head and I needed to extinguish them as quickly as possible.

We had spoken only once, properly. Nathan had reported to him about the meeting I'd had with my mother and straight away my mobile had rung. He had told me how much he loved me and how proud of me he was, the tension was still very evident in his voice, but he had assured me that the situation at home was now under control. He made a promise to be properly back, sometime this week. I needed him; I almost craved the sight of him. I knew this was palpable to those around me. In our last texting session last night, I was laid out on my bed touching the pillow where his head had been. I had told him how I took photographs of my best memories and kept them in my head. Under his scrutinising but sweet questioning, I had admitted to him that most of my happy photographs contained him. Today I had received an enormous bouquet of flowers. The card had read

*Miss you baby*
*It killed me waking up next to you on Monday.*

*Although we are apart at the moment, it won't be forever.*
*Remember I will always find my way back to you!*
*I Love you Frankie*
*Alex*
*Photograph- Ed Sheeran*

Every song we had messaged each other, I had on a repeatable play list. If anyone had been with me today, I knew I would have driven them up the wall. I had played it and played it and sung every word at the top of my voice, for quite a few hours whilst doing chores.

The front door to our apartment knocked suddenly and I flew over to answer it. The wonderfully animated face of Nathan stood waiting for his entrance.

'So?' I asked, 'How did it go?' He moved past me and into the apartment.

'Yeah really fucking fantastic, thanks.' He had attended a meeting with his bike team managers and sponsors today. I knew it had been playing on his mind. You're only a hotshot when you're actually winning and of course he hadn't even been racing for quite some time. I knew in the few conversations we'd had together on the subject that it worried him. Younger guys with no history of injury were queuing up to get their lucky break. But he had always hoped that his track record and experience would see him through.

'Well, Brock told them I was coming back into training in January and they're happy to continue my sponsorship.'

'Nathan, I'm so pleased for you. I know it has been in the back of your mind that they might not want you back,' I closed the few steps between us now and hugged him. He squeezed me back.

'They have asked me to talk to you as well... they are so fucking happy with my progress and the strength in my leg, that they wanted to know if the team could offer you a permanent physio position.'

'Really?' I was stunned. I knew that this job was coming to an end and that I was going to have to find a new one soon, but I had constantly been pushing that thought to the back of my mind.

We automatically went through to the kitchen and I filled up and turned on the kettle. He leant his jean covered backside on to the worktop edge.

'What do you think?... it would mean you would get to keep putting your hands all over this sexy body of mine.' His face broke out into full on bad boy, dimples and all.

'So I would have to travel with you, wouldn't I?' I looked at him questioningly, stirring the tea for far longer than necessary.

He nodded and took the cup of tea I was now offering to him. Taking my own I went back out to the living area. Falling onto the settee I brought my legs up underneath me and blew on the top of my tea to cool it down and to just give myself a moment.

'You do realise that you haven't damn well answered me yet, don't you?' He plonked his large and normally graceful frame down next to me. He started to drink the far too hot liquid.

'I know this job is coming to an end, Nate... and that I will need to move on to something else soon... but I'm reluctant to make a decision at the moment.'

*What I really wanted to say was 'Alex has said he's going to ask me to marry him soon, and I am waiting for that.' But how lame would that sound?*

'I know what you're thinking, you and Alex have just found each other and you're reluctant to leave... right?'

I laughed at him. 'Yeah, you're right,' I smiled and shook my head. 'I miss him, so much. Do you know if he has sorted out the business deal he and Ruby were discussing, yet?'

'Truthfully, chocolate drop, I haven't spoken to him... with everything that I've had going on this week. I did speak to Scott last night though and he is sounding really good, that is definitely a step in the right fucking direction... in fact he was sounding the best I've heard in ages. With him on the up that should hopefully release Alex a bit more. I will try and hold them off for a while on the job offer, at least to try and give you the time to speak to Alex.'

I was just going to start trying to ask a few more carefully worded questions when Bella burst through the door. I could hardly see her underneath all the bags she was carrying.

'A little help please, Frankie... Woman in severe shopping distress here,' her voice carried loudly into the apartment. She obviously couldn't have seen either of us sitting here.

Both Nathan and I jumped up to her and began relieving her of the ridiculous amount of bags. Slowly she began to immerge from behind the paper and plastic. Her eyes looked extremely panicked when she found I was not alone in helping her. The alarm bells were ringing in my head. In my extensive experience Bella only spent money like water when she was really, really stressed. She would just spend money on anything whether she liked it or not, she would spend money on things just because they were the colour she was looking at that day. All of these things put together, made me very concerned.

'There ya go, darlin,' Nate added as he placed the last of the bags on the floor. He took her into his arms now and ran light kisses over her collar bone.

'Thank you... I need to go and freshen up now.' With that comment she quickly and very effectively manoeuvred out of his arms and away to her room. In her wake she left Nathan and I looking at each other for answers, but unfortunately we were coming up with a big fat zero. I watched him as he pulled his face back together banishing the hurt expression and he tried to offer me a grin. It would have worked on anyone who didn't know him well, but I wasn't fooled.

'Nate... leave it with me...I'll go and check on her. I'm sure she is probably stressed about work,' I offered a reassuring smile to him. I wasn't wholly convinced myself. But I hated to see the hurt and rejection in his eyes. I wanted to do anything I could, to help take it away.

'She's been like this since our clash with your mo... Karen. She took offence to me declaring that I loved her and I've been getting the fucking cold shoulder ever since... FUCK!' He slammed his hand against the door. I could only stand and silently offer my solidarity. Unfortunately, I had seen it before.

'Tell her she knows where I am, if and when she wants to talk it through. But I won't wait forever.'

'Don't you think you should be saying that to her, not me?'

'Chocolate drop, if I thought it would make a difference I would, but honestly she's fucking shut down on me... for what reason? I haven't got a clue, and before you ask I have tried to get her to talk to me... OK?' I had to nod at him but I wasn't really OK. I knew what I would find when I got to her bedroom and the thought filled me with sadness.

I entered her room without knocking. I knew she wouldn't have answered me anyway. Bella was curled into a tight almost foetal like ball in the middle of her purple bed. I couldn't see her face as her blonde hair had fallen all over it. She reminded me of a colour wheel, the two most opposite colours colliding there on the bed, yellow and purple. It was a stark reminder that in life, the two most opposing emotions can come barrelling through at any moment in time, and cause utter destruction.

The sobs that wracked through her body, over and over again, made my heart ache. I could identify with her and knew that nothing I had to say at this precise moment, would offer her any sense of comfort or reassurance. I curled myself up exactly behind her and pulled her to me as tight as I could manage and there we lay. For what seemed like hours, in the same position. She muttered the same few incoherent phrases over and over again; her sobs died down and then escalated again. Tears ran silently down my face. I felt so utterly bloody useless, all I could do was to try and absorb her pain. Finally, as the afternoon light receded into dusk, she fell asleep in my arms. I peeled myself away from her. Now I needed to go and see Nathan.

The door to his apartment was open and I made my way inside. The open living area had no light on at all, but I could just make out his silhouette in the armchair in front of one of the huge panes of glass. His forearms were resting on his knees as he leant forward. I could see that he had been working out, as although he still had on his jeans his torso was bare and had a slight gleam of sweat on it. The lights of the city made it glisten.

'Frankie?' He questioned.

'Yeah, it's me.' I moved over to him. I couldn't properly see his face from here. His body language was coming across as extremely hurt, almost to the point of being distressed. I needed to see his face, in order to gauge him properly. Moving promptly, I sat down on the floor in between his bare feet. Nathan unclasped his own hands, which up to now had been wringing themselves and grabbed my own.

'How is she?' His voice was so small, almost as though he didn't want me to hear the question and then he wouldn't have to hear the answer.

'I haven't seen her like this in a long time, Nathan... for almost ten years she has kept a lid on her emotions and now for some reason they have resurfaced,' I was shaking my head at the reality of it all.

'It's my fault... isn't it?' He eyes met mine now in question.

'The fault isn't yours, Nate... You couldn't help falling in love with her, could you?' I squeezed his hands tighter trying to offer a modicum of comfort.

'I knew she wasn't damn well ready to be told though.' His hands left mine suddenly and started running through his hair, over and over again. 'I could just sense it, I could fucking recognise it, but still I had to go and say it.'

Nathan stood abruptly now and started pacing up and down in front of the windows.

'What happened to her, Frankie? What makes her want to run away?' He stopped and stared directly at me.

I froze for a moment.

*How could I decide between my friends as to who I helped? Of course it had to be Bella that I stuck by, even if it hurt to do so.*

'Nathan, I can't answer that... It is definitely not my story to tell. You don't know how much I wish it was. She needs to tell you and only her.' I watched as his head dropped forward onto his chest, just hanging there. He placed his hands into his front jean pockets, so deep down his arms were almost straight and the top of his Adonis girth peeped into view. My heart was breaking for my bestie asleep next door and for the beautiful man in front of me. I felt so utterly wretched at the fact it seemed that I couldn't help either of them.

'I'm so sorry, Nate, so, so sorry.'

He gathered himself now and stood taller. The tears, that had started to fall down his face at the veracity of it all, stopped suddenly as he pulled on another facade.

'Who else knows?'

'Just myself and Bella's sister, Jasmin... It's not something she has ever really wanted to share.'

I heard him inhaling one hell of a deep breath and he pushed himself off the balls of his feet into sudden movement towards me.

'Tell her I am here... waiting... I want to hear her tell me she doesn't love me to my face. I will wait for her until the weekend.' He left my personal space then and my gaze. He turned to stare out of the windows at the lights below. 'I will wait until then and only then.'

I knew he was upset, but the fact he was now offering Bella an ultimatum just angered me.

'So that's it?... She has until the weekend to talk or what... what will you do?' My voice had increased in volume; I wasn't sure if it was all in anger or just at the sheer undeserved finality of it all.

'I can't make her want to be with me, Frankie... I can't make her love me... and I certainly can't sit around here waiting for her either... it will fucking finish me!'

I slipped my hands around his waist from the back and hugged him.

'I will tell her, Nathan,' I whispered to his shoulder blade.

When I left his apartment, I left him staring out at the city below and I shut the door behind me. My eyes couldn't help but move to Alex's apartment and I found myself wandering over to it. I knew he wasn't in, but I was going to allow myself to wander around in there, I just needed to feel close to him at this moment. The door had opened with ease. It wasn't locked; I knew it wouldn't be as the whole floor was owned by his family. No one could gain access to the penthouse level without going through the whole security thing first or having a key card to swipe in the lift. The heavy door had pushed open wide and I stopped there on the threshold just to breathe in his scent. It was somewhat comforting and after the emotions of today I needed him, badly. I knew he was busy but had to make contact with him. Quickly I had made my way to his bedroom and placed my body beneath the quilt in order to envelope myself with his smell. Pulling up my phone I began to message him.

*Hi*
*I know you're busy.*
*I just wanted to tell you how much*
*I love you and how much I miss you.*

*I can't wait to see you*

My phone immediately pinged.

*Baby*
*I miss you too! I can't wait to feel you against me.*
*I want to hold you in my arms. I love you*
*I'll be home on Friday; we're going out on Saturday.*
*We're going to experience Christmas in NYC*
*X*

*That's great news*
*I CAN'T WAIT TO SEE YOU!*
*Frankie*

I laid back and sunk further into Alex's comfortable bed, clasping my phone against my chest as though it were a lifeline. The stress of the day had caused a feeling of absolute exhaustion to wash over me. Just after closing my eyes I felt my phone beginning to vibrate again. Looking at it I was brought back to reality with a bump. Bella was awake.

The next morning, I found my way back to Alex's. I was going to use his treadmill. Really I could have done with some fresh air, but Bella had gone over to speak to Nate and I didn't feel like I should be any further away than his apartment. We had lain awake last night chatting, stuffing our faces with chocolate and consuming copious amounts of wine.

Already I knew in my gut she wasn't going to open up to him. He would probably walk away. It was too much to comprehend. I didn't know who I was going to have to pick up first. The sheer emotion of it all was weighing heavily on my shoulders; I just hoped for both of my friends' sake I was strong enough to carry it.

Once I found the right position on the treadmill I slapped forcefully at the start button. I placed my ear buds in and turned up my music as loud as I could deal with. A small part of me desired to obliterate everything that was going on around me, just for a time, even if that time was short.

After I had run almost five miles my iPhone screen lit up in the holder.

The message was from Nathan, it was simple.

*Go to her*

I pulled out my ear buds, almost snapping the cable in my haste. My hand had slammed down onto the stop button as I simultaneously jumped off the machine and ran out of the apartment. Heading off in a diagonal direction, I manoeuvred myself around the central arrangement of plants in the marble hallway. I was moving quickly to get to her, but my movement was brought to a sudden halt when out of my peripheral view I had caught sight of Nate leaning onto the open doorframe of his apartment. His eyes lifted from the floor to mine. I started to move towards him then, even if just to offer my understanding in a hug. His hand moved abruptly, showing me his palm, stopping me in my tracks. His face had a hardened guarded expression. An expression I had never witnessed before on the normally playful Nathan's face and it broke my heart somewhat to see it there.

'She needs you, Frankie,' he started to move his feet to turn into his apartment. 'Look after her for me,' the door slammed suddenly behind him and with the sudden loud noise my eyes began to fill with tears for him and Bella. Rushing from my statuesque like position I burst through our door, screaming out her name. Hearing her, I found her in her bedroom on the floor, tearing at the carpet with her fingers in her anguish. The tears were falling so quickly down her face she was almost inhaling them back into her body as she gasped for breath. After I had fallen to my knees, I had just held her, rocking her slowly back and forth in my arms. After what seemed like a lifetime of hugging and crying together, she had finally turned in my arms.

'I couldn't do it, Frankie,' she finally managed to expel. 'I am going undercover to expose IT and I couldn't drag Nathan down there with me... I have let him go.' I had known she had been stressed over work and now that one statement had answered the question why. If we could have been clasping each other with any more force than we were exuding now, I felt we would have probably broken a bone or two.

'I love him, Frankie, and this is tearing me up... but I have to put this right before I can move on.' Her face was streaked with tears, snot and mascara, all mixed together. But looking into her pained blue eyes she was still painstakingly beautiful in her bravery.

'I got so lost in him, so lost in the two of us, so lost it was almost like being found for the first time ever,' she sobbed harder now and we continued to rock there on the floor.

'Don't you think that was his decision to make, Bella? I think he would move heaven and earth for you, if you would only let him in.' She shook her head suddenly and I knew she had already made up her mind. Nothing I said was going to change her mind; my heart broke for them. My fingers clutched tighter to her already dishevelled clothes and I sobbed with her and for them both.

'I'm sorry, Frankie, I can't stay here now.' I nodded my understanding at her reasoning.

'I understand but I don't think you will need to leave, I am certain Nathan is going, I saw him briefly and he looks... defeated... sorry I can't lie to make it sound any better.' We had started to stand up. Really I needed to check on Nate and didn't know how to put it out there into the conversation.

'Go and see him, Frankie,' Bella offered. She knew.

Nodding, almost relieved, I had run from one apartment to the other. I banged and banged on his door with both hands. My fists clenched in frustration.

'Frankie... he's just left the building.' Spinning around, I had found Edwards standing there. I must have been pummelling so hard on the door I hadn't even heard the bloody lift come up.

'He said he'll contact you soon.'

Light was starting to come through the windows in my bedroom. My head pounded and my shoulders ached with the tension in them. Even my skin felt on edge. I wanted to go back to sleep and get the two of them out of my thoughts. I found it hard to grasp that only a week ago we had all been so happy up in the mountains and how that happiness could have fallen apart so quickly. Turning over, I threw myself back under my covers and hopefully into oblivion, in doing so I found my body bumping into another familiar, naked one. He was asleep face down as normal, with his hands underneath the pillows. Moving quickly, I jumped on top of him and laid myself out flat on my front, pressing my needy skin tightly to him as I snuck my arms underneath his weighty, but extremely well formed, torso. My face nuzzled in the back of his hair.

*God I had so needed this. I hadn't understood just how much.*

'Morning to you too, Frankie' He was smiling, I couldn't see it but I could hear and feel it.

He moved an arm up to me and pulled me rapidly down to his side. My leg was lifted and wrapped around his hip and his arms closed around me like a vice.

'Missed you, baby, it's been a hell of a long week.' The scruff on his face was abrasive on my temple as he spoke, but I couldn't have cared less. I squeezed him to me, not wanting to ever let him go again.

'I can feel something has missed me.' I was referring to his hardening cock, protruding its way in between us.

'Ok I concede, baby, we've both fucking missed you.' He laughed out loud, released me slightly and clasping my chin with one hand he lifted my head up to meet his eyes. My lips were met with his as he brushed them lightly with a chaste kiss. 'Do you understand just how much?'

His eyes were sleepy but sparkling none the less; I moved one hand to the back of his neck and the other to his just fucked looking, bed hair and brought our mouths crashing back to each other's. Our teeth mashed together with the force of the kiss. The feeling of needing to consume him washed over me. Never one for losing control for too long, Alex rolled us over and I found myself underneath his hard muscular body. I needed to let him know what had gone on in the last couple of days, but not just yet. First I needed to lose myself in him and with him. He held me as he made love to me, holding me tightly and saying nothing. He stared into my eyes, trying to convey his love. The intensity I felt was palpable, almost like he was shouting out the words loud for everyone to hear. I was so worn out that afterwards I had started to doze again.

'Sleep, baby, I'll go and make us some breakfast.' That one sentence brought me to. For one thing I needed to be with him, I couldn't bear not to be near enough to touch him and then there was the obvious, that I needed to explain just what had happened here this week.

Grabbing the covers to my chest I sat up hastily, grabbing onto his arm. I started to shake my head.

'No, stop... I need to tell you about Bella and Nathan, before you walk out of here and possibly bump into her.' I proceeded to tell him what had gone on. What an absolutely hellish few days it had been.

He was sitting up slightly in bed and I was lying on his chest, tucked under his arm. I wanted this closeness as I told him all about my mother, from start to finish. Holding on to him I felt his heartbeat rise in anger, as I told him what she had wanted me to do for her. Next we discussed Nathan's mistake in saying he loved Bella out loud and the subsequent spiral downwards of their relationship. Obviously I said nothing of Bella's past to him and understanding as he was, he didn't question me. He placed kisses to the top of my head, in encouragement to carry on with the story I was telling, to carry on through the tears that were rolling down my cheeks and onto his chest.

'Sorry, Frankie... I couldn't have picked a worse fucking time to leave you, with all that going on.' He kissed the top of my head again. 'Before we even think about food, I have to contact Nate... Unbelievable, I just get Scotty on an even keel and then another one of my siblings crashes the fuck out. It's like trying to hold up a jelly with my hands. I keep running around pushing up the sides and the one I'm not pushing up, spills the fuck out... I must call him and then you and I are going to spend the day together, regardless for once of anyone else... OK?'

'Mmm Hmm.' I was still hanging on to him for all I was worth. 'You never did tell me how it went back home? Nathan did say Scotty was really upbeat and that it was a very positive thing to hear, he said it was something he hadn't heard in a while.'

'He doesn't cope well with Scotty's illness at all. Scotty has to, at times, cope with severe depression; I don't think I told you that before?' I could feel him shaking his head. Not answering him verbally, I shook my head against his chest.

'They often say, in lots of articles I have read on his illness, that the most brilliantly creative minds can often have some sort of mental illness to handle. We've dealt with a lot since our dad died......'

I hadn't realised, but I had pulled him tighter to me again. I already understood how difficult he found it to open up. It only made me feel more for him.

*If that was even possible?*

Every time he did, even if it only came in small snippets of information at a time, I appreciated him opening up and sharing with me. His hand was casually running lightly up and down my spine as he talked, it was sending electrical surges to every part of my body. We had to get out of the bed, otherwise as wonderful as it would be; the realisation was we would spend all of this beautiful day together between the sheets. Curious as I was, I needed to know what he had got planned for our day together. Moving quickly now, I sat up and over him, making sure I straddled his stomach and not his once again hardening cock. I began to tickle up and down all over his sides and ribs. Alex just leant back with his arms now behind his head, smirking at my evidently extremely feeble attempts to make him laugh.

'What are you up to, baby?' He raised both eyebrows and smirked.

'Apparently what goes around comes around... I seem to remember you tickling me before to get what you wanted... so here I am,' I gave him a huge grin. He really was the most beautiful man I had ever seen. His eyes lit up with fiery amber flecks, the surrounding green sparkled. His huge grin had brought out his dimples to play. His very evident overnight scruff just added to the amazing picture. He had tensed up all of his muscles on his torso, in a bid to stop my tickling make him laugh.

'There are easier ways to get what you fucking want from me; you must know that by now?' He continued to smirk at me.

My fingers sustained their movement all over him, but it was beginning to infuriate me that I couldn't find one area where he lost control, bloody control freak. He was laughing now, but at my ridiculous tickling that had turned into heavy handed prodding.

'What about here?'

'Here?'

'Oh come on... you must be ticklish somewhere?' I almost yelled at him.

His hands came down from his head suddenly and with very evident purpose. My hands were grabbed and pushed to my sides as he forcibly moved me back onto his now fully engorged cock. He winked as my eyes found his again at the surprise of the movement and where I now found myself. He flicked out his tongue to wet his lips.

*Dear God, I so wanted to bite that tongue.*

'Surely you must know by now, baby, what you have to fucking do to get your own way around here?'

'Look, Mister the second whoever you are... I have already done YOU this morning... I have no bloody intention of doing YOU again... for quite a while... Thank YOU.' As I spoke in my best school ma'am voice, I had also moved my arms, once they had been released, and they were now crossed over my chest. With a very noticeable result, as Alex was now having a conversation with my boobs. He continued to lick his lips, the consequence being that my nipples hardened too stiff, almost painful, points in front of his eyes. His large cock was flexing underneath me and I could feel myself beginning to flood.

'OK... thank you, that's good to know, baby... So you won't mind if I do this then?... as you've already... done me.' He mimicked the sound of my accent, stupidly, but it made me laugh. He contracted all his stomach muscles to sit up unexpectedly; placing his arms behind me he pulled my front and my nipples into his face. He began to lick and nip at each one simultaneously. My head threw back and I closed my eyes.

*OK maybe I could go again?*

That thought was brought to an abrupt end. The sound of a loud crack met my ears as Alex brought one of his large hands down onto my arse cheek with a resounding smack.

'Ouch!' I moved quickly at the intrusion and stood up; in doing so I released my captive from underneath me. Alex moved and got off the bed. He made it to my bathroom in only a couple of long strides, I watched as his heavy cock bobbed.

He turned as he reached the door, smiling at me now as I rubbed my bare arse cheek.

'Anticipation, baby... anticipation.' Then he stepped into the bathroom and out of sight.

'How do you do it?' I shouted, infuriated.

His gorgeous face appeared once again, smiling. 'They're called cold showers, Frankie, maybe you should try one yourself, either that or every time I touch you today, baby, you will be on fire for me... either way it's all looking fucking fantastic from where I'm standing.' His hot gaze swept up and down my naked form.

'You are a teasing bastard; you know that right?' I shouted, making sure my voice carried into the open door of the bathroom again. He reappeared, showing me once again his magnificent hard on. I must have looked a ludicrous sight, stood up on the bed naked, hands on my hips, glaring at him. My nipples were so erect I could have taken people's eyes out and my arousal was evidently running down my legs. All of those facts I saw him take in. Alex was cleaning his teeth, and was very slowly moving the toothbrush in and out of his mouth, it was having the desired influence on me and he knew it. I watched, unable to move my gaze away, as he beckoned me to him with a curled finger. After reaching the doorway I watched him spit and rinse.

'So, baby,' he winked at me, 'What's it to be?'

'Do you want to... as you put it... do me again, or shall we take a cold shower together?' One eyebrow rose at me in question. The steam from the hot shower began to claim the room. It was evident to me that he already knew the answer. I merely nodded and immediately felt myself being pulled to him and pushed up against the tiled wall. Alex dropped to his knees, spread my legs open and began to lick away my arousal from the tops of my thighs. Between that and the soapy shower sex, it was some time before we made it out to get breakfast.

# Chapter 38

It was nearly midday when we finally walked out of the building. Breakfast had been a quiet affair. Bella was already awake and sitting in the lounge when we had finally made it out of my bedroom. She was wrapped up in her purple quilt, and all around her prone figure we had picked up various pieces of debris, from her obvious pig out during the night. After talking to Alex using only my eyes, I had asked her to join us on our planned day out.

'You're OK, gorgeous... I am alright, enjoying my pity fest here... there are a whole host of cheesy black and white films on today and they have my name on them. I'm going to watch them until hopefully my body falls into a coma. I wouldn't be any company and you guys deserve some time together.'

I could hear the words she was saying, and knew how hard it was for her to say them, albeit in a bid to sound braver than she felt. We had known each other for years and she couldn't pull the wool over my eyes. But I also knew that she needed her own space for a while, just to get her head around what had happened between her and Nathan. She had been almost relieved last night when I had told her he had left the building, almost. Alex had phoned him during my chat with Bella. He had answered his phone, thank God. He was staying with a team mate, until pre-season training began, and he wouldn't be back.

Out on the pavement, I tried to leave my devastated feelings behind in the building. I was so looking forward to spending time with Alex. My feelings were obviously painted on my face like a tarts make up. Alex spun me around into him, crushing our thick winter coats together, one arm pulled me to him by encircling my waist and the other lifted my chin up so he could see into my eyes.

'Frankie, we need to leave it, I know it's fucking hard to not stick our noses in... I am the king of sticking my nose in,' he nodded. 'We will let the situation settle for a while and then see if we can help them... OK?' He started to kiss from my forehead down onto my nose and then finally our mouths met. So there we had been in the middle of the pavement kissing like our lives depended on our connection.

His kisses nearly always left me breathless. In this one, for the entire world to see, out on the bustling pavement, I could feel all of his love pouring from his mouth into mine. I could feel all of his want and need in the gentle but passionate way he stroked and nipped my mouth. In return I had tried to show him exactly all the good and wonderful ways he made me feel. A few boisterous shouts and laughter aimed in our direction made us reluctantly break apart, at the mouth only. We laughed good naturedly at the cat calls. He still held me tight in his arms and stared deeply into my eyes. I in turn gazed into his, watching his love and lust change the colour and dilation of them. The eyes that I had fallen in love with the minute we had met each other.

'We'll just give them both some space and try to jump in, if and when we feel the time is right... Yeah?' He spoke again.

'I know you're right; I just don't like being able to see people I love in pain and not being able to do a bloody thing about it.' I had hold of the sides of his heavy leather jacket, and was using them to pull him down to me. Just inhaling his comforting scent, and wondering how the bloody hell I had gone without it for the last week.

'I know, Frankie... I know.' He rested his forehead to mine and inhaled deeply.

'Things aren't always what they seem though... sometimes people just need a little time to sort out other fucked up stuff that's going on in their lives.' His eyes stabbed mine now trying to convey his message.

'Right, come on.' He broke apart from me and we started walking. He put his arm around my shoulders and hooked it around my neck, pulling me tight to his side. I placed my arm equally as tight around his waist.

'We're going on foot today; you can't take in the beauty of this place in a vehicle, especially at Christmas.'

'When did you become so poetic?' I joked with him, loving the easy feeling that swept over us as we strolled down 5ᵗʰ Avenue.

'Me, baby?... I'm always poetic, especially if it gets me in your panties later.' I light heartedly shook my head at him.

We spent our time, always connected in some way, casually strolling taking in the sights. The traffic was busy and horns went off left, right and centre. It's something that when you have been in NYC for a while you don't even really take any notice of. The smell of the many street vendors crept into our nostrils, especially the cones of roasted chestnuts. Eventually we both succumbed and shared one as we strolled around.

The window displays at Macy's and Bloomindales were amazing, it reminded me of being taken up to London once, on the train, with my aunt, uncle and JJ. We had stared into Selfridges' windows with our noses pressed up against the glass. Feeling a really silly, split second thought come over me; I pulled Alex closer up to the window and shoved his face up to the glass.

'What the hell are we doing?'

'This is the only way to take in a Christmas window display properly and to full effect. Spread your palms over the glass and peer in through the middle of your hands.' He looked at me but did as I asked.

'Ok... we reliving your childhood I presume?'

'Yep, one of my picture memories, stop gassing and start peering.' I smacked him on the shoulder for good measure. He had done what I'd asked even if he had been making comments about not being able to see everything properly around his hands.

Radio City looked wonderful; we had reached there just as the light was beginning to fade, and dusk was approaching. The Christmas decorations began to have a stronger presence. The street vendors were playing music; people had pulled their coats tighter around themselves. The Christmas atmosphere had been ramped up by the daylight receding. I felt like a kid in a sweet shop. My excitement was palpable. This in turn made Alex take on the more relaxed air I had seen up in the mountains.

'Hot dog and soda?' He questioned. 'Come on you know you want to? You can't be out here in New York and not have one.' I nodded my response, smiling at his boyish behaviour.

Alex quickly paid for four and brought them over to me. I was useless at eating and walking at the same time and had to stand still in order to try not to get the ketchup all over me. It was delicious; the wonderful crap in my mouth was just like I imagined eating expensive caviar to be, the tastes exploding all over my tongue. I heard Alex groan and immediately my eyes shot up to his. He closed the gap in between us now. I couldn't believe he had already eaten three hotdogs and I still had some left. I watched as he bent his legs so he could look me in the eyes. His tongue flicked out over his lips.

'Even eating a fucking hotdog you nearly had me making a mess in my jeans.' His voice was low so no one else could hear, he spoke into my ear. I felt myself being walked backwards and pressed into a building behind me. 'Holy hell, with your eyes closed guiding the fucking thing in between your lips like it was my cock, and the noises you made... seriously fucking killing me here.' He pushed his erection into me now and I smiled at him. Bending down slightly further, he started to lick up my exposed throat with one continuous sweep of his skilful tongue. I inhaled sharply. Finally, he flicked over my open mouth and broke away.

'Just cleaning you up, baby... just cleaning you up and making you dirty, all at the same time.' He stepped back and lifted my hand and the last remnants of my hotdog up to his mouth. He consumed it with a wicked gleam in his eye and proceeded to suck all of my fingers clean, one by one. He moved suddenly away from me as I was raising my other hand to slap him. We ran for a short distance, with me chasing him through the crowds, laughing. I loved the playful side of Alex as much as I loved the dominant one.

Dodging through the thickening crowds was getting to be a nightmare. The decorations had only really been unveiled a couple of days ago and the people of NYC were out in force with the tourists, just soaking up the happy atmosphere. Alex had held me close to his side at all times, sometimes using his body as a plough to almost push through the people. Once again I was grateful for his rugby skills.

We had stopped for quite a while to look at the Christmas tree at the Rockefeller Centre, and to absorb the atmosphere from the people around it. We had even managed to snap a few selfies and a couple of them weren't that bad. I had taken one with the tree behind us and Alex holding me tightly to him, he hadn't looked at the camera, but was staring at me. That one was my favourite and as we walked away I changed it to my screensaver. I had a few others of him that I had snapped previously, mostly when he wasn't aware and even when he was asleep.

*God, I had it bad!*

'OK... so I just want to look in a store with you on the way to Central Park... and the last thing we are doing today is ice skating.'

'You're bloody joking, aren't you?' I stopped dead in my tracks and restrained myself from saying more, but knew that he had taken in the horror that had quite obviously attached itself to every part of my face.

'Ermm... No, I wasn't... I thought it would be a great way to round off our day out.' His face took on a rather hurt expression. One of the few times I had seen an unsure Alex. His hand had come up to run through his hair.

*Shit, Shit, Shit... Note to self... think before you open your bloody trap!*

'Sorry... I feel terrified at the thought of ice skating... I mean if we were meant to glide around on a thin, sharp edge of nothing but possible throat slitting metal... I'd have them on my feet now, wouldn't I?' We both glanced down at my feet. I was wearing Dr Martens. Really comfortable and extremely flat and the emphasis was on flat! My nerves had overtaken me and had been joined by my galloping speech. My face was bright red.

'Sorry, you've taken time to plan today and I've just panicked over nothing and bloody ruined it.'

'It's OK, Frankie... let's just go up and look then shall we... it's nice up there now. Lights in the trees and stuff... the kind of things you women like.' He lifted his hands up in the air either side of his head, gesticulating an air quote movement with his fingers.

'It's pretty,' he mimicked sarcastically.

I made to slap him again but missed. 'You obviously enjoy me hitting you... don't you? As you just keep on giving me the ammunition to work with, don't you?'

'I just like you touching me, baby... anyway I can get you.' He pulled me into a quick hug and then we continued on our way. My panic had been momentarily diverted by holding on to Alex. We walked on for a while.

'This is the shop.' We found ourselves outside of a large regal looking stone built building. Looking up I could see it was Tiffany & Co.

He caught the look of shock on my face and grabbed me by the elbow to lead me in. Probably my mouth falling open like I was catching flies was a dead giveaway.

'We need to have a look at some diamond engagement rings... Please,' Alex spoke to very smart man in front of the counters.

'This way, Sir, Madam.' We were led further into the beautiful glass case filled, sparkling cavern, following the lead of the man in front of us. My brain was on repeat.

*Engagement ring? Engagement ring?*

Finally, we stood over a large tray of diamonds. I don't think I had ever seen so many beautiful pieces of jewellery. Square cut, circles, tear drop looking ones. I knew they had proper names but as my life had never involved having much money before, the proper names certainly didn't trip off my tongue.

'Which ones do you like, Frankie?'

'If I said all of them, is that too indecisive?'

He laughed slightly standing next to me, still holding my elbow. He was shuffling his feet, obviously a little nervous.

'Ermm... yep just a bit... come on help a guy out here... OK, just maybe you could give me a little help, say narrow the field.' I still hadn't taken my eyes away from the sparkling tray in front of me.

*OMG, OMG....he is going to ask me to marry him!*

'If I really had to pick... I don't know the proper names for them, but I really like the square ones and that one there that looks like a tear drop.'

'You have great taste.' He stopped fidgeting and pulled me closer to him, 'Come on then, let's go look at the "pretty lights" ... that's given me something to work with.'

He thanked the shop assistant for his time and we had made our way back out into the chilly evening.

After watching for a while at the skating rink, we had made our way home. We had decided that Bella had been on her own for long enough and instead of eating out we would order a takeaway and make sure she had some food in her, that didn't consist of ice cream, chocolate or wine.

My excitement was hard to contain as I sat cuddled up with Bella, watching another one of the movies she had on her list for the day. There was no way I could share what had happened to me today; normally I would have shared that sort of thing with her. But it would have been cruel to this evening.

Alex was still in the apartment with us. He was on his phone dealing with some business calls. My eyes never left him as he wandered around from room to room; he had changed into grey sweat pants and a fitted black T-shirt. More than once I found my eyes ogling him as he had a habit, when concentrating, of tucking one hand just inside the low waistband of his sweatpants. This moved the bloody things down further; knowing he was commando underneath was doing my head in.

*When did I ever get so lucky?*

'Are you sure about this?' I questioned Bella as Alex removed her case from the back of the car. 'I mean really sure?'

'I am... I just need to get home for a few days. I am going to have a chat with Jasmin, my mum and dad. They need to know before this thing blows up.' She shook her head from side to side, 'I can't believe we only got a few weeks together.' She hugged me to her now.

'Me neither... but we'll get together soon... Yes?'

'Of course we will... enjoy yourself with Alex and live a little... eh?' She stared into my eyes.

'I'll try,' I smiled back at her.

Alex opened the door.

'Ok?' He questioned, manipulating his huge frame to fit in the doorway.

Neither of us answered, but I offered him a grimace. We slowly walked Bella into the departures at JFK airport, made sure she got to the right check in desk and then we left. I couldn't hug her again otherwise I knew she would break down. I hated the thought of her flying all the way home by herself. It was one thing doing it when you have something to look forward to, but the thought of explaining her story to her parents must have been terrifying. They weren't bad parents, but I knew just how upset they were going to be.

With an audible sigh I clambered back into the car and proceeded to buckle up my belt. Just as I clicked it into position, Alex's hand came over mine and squeezed gently, offering his support.

'She'll be OK... You know that... right?'

'Yeah... my bestie... she's strong. I just hope she's strong enough... Have you spoken to Nathan again?'

'Today?' He questioned.

'Uh huh.'

'No, but I will... he asked me to keep him updated on how Bella was. I'll phone him and let him know she's gone home for a while.'

We settled back into the comfy seats and I watched as Alex masterfully weaved his way in and out of the airport traffic. Apparently it didn't matter what time of day, day of the week, or week of the year, this airport was always congested.

Reaching down I turned up the music playing, it was one of my favourites. *Stay-Sam Smith.*

Obviously feeling the atmosphere and listening to the poignant words as Sam sung his heart out, Alex reached across and took hold of my hand again, pulling it over and onto his leg. As he drove he caressed my fingers and sung along with the words. The feeling that had been in the car earlier lifted and my heart began to soar once more.

Alex stayed for a couple of hours with me. But as always business called and he had to pop out to the office. There was no way I was going to start to become the needy girlfriend, well anymore than I had already been. The life of a busy CEO, I assumed.

To keep my mind occupied I went across to his apartment, after all I had thought to myself, it wasn't really that I wanted to sniff his cologne again, no it was all really about using his gym.

*Who the hell was I kidding?*

After I had run for about five miles, done several sets of sit ups and leg raises, and even used the exercise bike for about thirty minutes, a level of boredom and tiredness was beginning to creep in.

The TV was on and I had music playing but I couldn't shift the feeling of tedium. I had no physio to do and no one to have a laugh with, the apartments were eerily quiet. I had never really spent too much time in Alex's apartment before and after a quick nose around I had decided to go back to my own. I could at least cook him a decent dinner to come home to. He had said he would only be gone a few hours at the most. That certainly seemed like an excellent plan and it would give me something to do. Making my way through the apartment, I was suddenly aware of voices in the hallway. The soundproofing was such that I couldn't make out if they were male or female. Being ever the nosy cow, I quickened my step towards the door and pulled it open fast.

I met the gaze of two women about to enter the apartment to the left of Alex's. One of them was an older lady, in her early fifties I would perceive and the other was a lot younger, probably just older than me. The younger woman had her back to me as she was attempting to gain entry to the apartment. They were beautifully dressed in long winter coats and boots, all very fashionable; it was very evident they came from money. I took in quickly that they had a small suitcase each with them and that they were obviously going to be staying a couple of nights. My face broke out into a wide welcoming smile. Although I wasn't particularly good about meeting new people, it was quite clear that these ladies had to be Alex's family; otherwise they wouldn't have been here in the first place. Rubbing my sweaty, work-out hands down the front of my leggings, I stepped my running shoes forward in haste, they squeaked on the polished marble. I wanted to make a good impression; I knew most of Alex's family meant a lot to him.

'Hello, I'm Frankie,' I offered my now non-sweaty hand towards the younger lady, she looked the less intimidating and it seemed the best place to start.

'Hi,' she smiled back, although her face had a curious struggle occurring on it. She was trying to work out who I was. She did at least shake my hand briefly. I wasn't left with it hanging in the air.

'Good afternoon,' I heard from the woman next to her. I made my gaze leave the younger lady and focus on the face of the older woman. 'I am Margaret Blackmore and this is my stepdaughter Ruby.'

*Of course! It had to be Alex's Mum. She had the same eye colouring as Nathan. Still, Blackmore?*

'And you are?' She questioned, her look sweeping over me in the space of a second. I could see that she was less than impressed with what she had found lacking.

This already didn't feel like it was going well. I found my insides switching into panic mode; I was starting to regret my hastiness.

*Oh God, not now...please don't let me... Not now.*

It was too late, no sooner had that thought left my brain, I felt myself intake a huge breath, just gearing my body up towards my oncoming spout of nonsensical words, which I was going to release due to my embarrassment.

'I'm Frankie.' Stupidly I offered the older woman my hand to shake. She just looked at it intently. This had made my face boiling hot with a level of blush that threatened to engulf the whole of my upper body.

'Yes, I believe you have already offered that small snippet of information... But who are you and why were you leaving my son's apartment?'

'Oh, I'm over from England. I'm Nathan's physio... I was just using the gym in Alex's apartment...as you can see by my state of dress.' I could see they had no idea Alex had a girlfriend. There was no way I was going to drop it in to the already stilted conversation. I had enough experience with my own family to know it wouldn't be a good idea. I knew he wasn't close to his mother, but I really felt he would have told Ruby about me?

'Oh Yes,' Ruby's face broke into a smile now. I started to feel a sense of relief coming over me, 'Yes, Nathan has told me all about you and the wonders you've done with his leg... You must be excellent at your job? He's not normally known for appreciating doctors or anything along those lines, is he, Margaret?'

'No, none of my children, especially James, generally appreciate any of those things.' She had manipulated her face in a frown now.

'I'm sorry Alex is at work at the moment. He did say he would be back in a few hours. Was he expecting you?' I felt nerves creeping over me now. His mother was obviously a hard woman to gauge, but being good at reading faces, probably because my own always showed everything I felt, I could see that she thought I was probably sleeping with one of her sons. She was giving me a look of total condescension.

'He didn't know we were coming down to the city. I know he is always so busy. We thought we would surprise him and do a bit of shopping while we were here, didn't we, Margaret?' Ruby seemed friendlier, now I had given an explanation for my presence.

'Yes, we have come down to do some shopping... we have a lot to buy.' I watched as Alex's mother's hand had dramatically appeared in front of me, by the removal of one of her leather gloves. I watched as she gently skirted over the top of the small but very apparent baby bump Ruby happened to be wearing along with her designer clothes. It had been previously hidden by her long coat

'Oh how lovely! Congratulations... how exciting for you.'

I watched as Ruby ran her hand lovingly over and over her bump. 'Yes, we're really happy, thank you for your congratulations.'

Alex's mother laughed now, she had relaxed slightly. Probably the most a woman like her would ever relax. In the background I had just made out the start of machinery whirring. It signalled the penthouse lift, starting to make its way up. I knew it was Alex; my whole body was on edge. It was the sort of edge that only his physical presence created within me.

'We have so much to buy, it's so very exciting. Ruby we must make sure he puts a diamond on that finger of yours this weekend... now mustn't we?'

I smiled at Ruby, she looked a little hesitant at this request, and I could imagine it must be bloody hard living with such a strong dominant character like her stepmother. I had known it well, all be it for a short time.

'We'll see, Margaret, he may be too busy this weekend to get an engagement ring. You know how busy his work keeps him.' I watched her silently raise her eyebrows and then quickly put her face back together.

'You have been engaged a week now, Ruby and some things need to be done in the correct way, even if others haven't been.' I was starting to feel a little uncomfortable now, perhaps it was the whole over sharing of Mrs. Blackmore's really *still Blackmore?* very evident disgust that Ruby was pregnant before being married.

*Oh dear!*

Finally, the doors of the lift opened. I didn't turn my head to look at Alex; I didn't want to give anything away to his mother. Not until he'd had the chance to tell her about us, on his own terms. I could feel him now behind me. I gave him a silly wave with my hand behind my back. I heard the lift door close.

'There you are, Alex.' I watched as Ruby smiled at the sight of him and they both moved their feet to look around me.

'We were just telling Frankie here, how you need to make sure your fiancée has a ring on her finger before we go back home this weekend.' His mother's face never turned from mine. I knew she was just checking out my response, 'We don't want anyone outside of the family getting the wrong idea, do we?'

Tick, Tick, Tick, Tick I could almost feel the time passing.

I had heard the words she had spoken. It was like I was going in slow motion as my brain filtered through them one word at a time.

271

Each word that I replayed over in my head felt like a knife stabbing into my heart. I had stopped breathing. I knew I had to move, but my whole body felt so heavy. I needed desperately to get away from these people, and quickly. My brain was running on overtime and a feeling of sickness was rising up from my stomach. I knew one thing and one thing only. Whatever happened, I would make myself walk away from here and to my door without showing my feelings. I would not break down; I would not make a scene.

None of these people deserved my feelings, not any of them, not any single one of them.

They had said other words to each other. None of which had trickled through to my brain. I was on shut down. I knew it and I'm sure Alex did, too.

I turned fast to see Alex behind me. What I really wanted to do was to fly into his arms and plead with him to tell me this wasn't true. I didn't need to; his huge body was racked with guilt, I could see by the way he held himself. One hand was running through his beautiful hair, his eyes were glazed over. It reminded me of his office at the rugby club all over again. Except I knew this wouldn't have the same outcome. His shoulders were hunched over and he was fidgeting his feet slightly.

'Congratulations, Mr. Blackmore, I hear you got engaged last weekend.' My eyes met his as I sucked my bottom lip in to stop myself from crying out to him, to plead with him. To ask him to tell me it wasn't true. His beautiful emerald pools came to meet my eyes. I fisted my hands to my sides, just wanting to touch the man in front of me. He was no longer mine to touch, I would never touch him again and he would never touch me.

'Thank you... it would seem that way,' his normally strong commanding voice was quiet. I couldn't listen to anything else that came out of his lying mouth.

I moved past him hurriedly and made my way to my apartment. I said no more to anyone, I simply couldn't trust myself.

Sod the pleasantries. I owed no one my manners now.

The weighty door slammed shut behind me and I locked it, probably for the first time in weeks.

I ran to Bella's room. I couldn't chance going to mine. His dirty clothes were still on my floor. His T-shirt was tucked into my bedside drawer. I knew I wouldn't cope with seeing any of it.

A recognisable sense of completely overwhelming grief brewed up inside me. I threw myself down on the same quilt that Bella had fallen apart on only a few days ago and screamed. I screamed until my voice was hoarse. My phone rang and rang until it finally stopped. I could only assume it had run out of battery. I had no concept of time, or anything other than the deep rooted pain inside me, and the audible sound of my heart breaking into a million pieces.

# Chapter 40

New York at night was a hard place to tell the time. It really was the city that never slept, as once it got dark outside it was still busy. I woke up in a wet patch of my own tears; my cheek was stuck to the cotton. At first I couldn't comprehend where I was or what day it was. My throat was killing me and I felt dehydrated. My head was pounding with an oncoming migraine. But it was the empty cavernous feeling inside me that immediately brought to the forefront of my mind the memory and pain of what had happened earlier, or was it yesterday?

I made myself get up off the bed. It was like I imagined cold turkey would feel, my whole body shook and ached with the sheer want to leave this place and to go and find him. Such was my addiction.

My mother's words rang around my head.

*Was it all just pretend?*

*Was it all a perfect plan on his part to make sure we never brought civil charges against him? Is that what had happened between us? I couldn't believe it had all been a ruse. Maybe that's how it had started and then it had become something more for him?*

I had made it slowly into our living area. Deliberately I forced my eyes not to look at the latest bouquet of flowers he had sent me. I moved carefully to the kitchen and found the light switch. To get the pain killers in the kitchen I needed to see, but this had meant turning on the bright white light out there. The noticeable increase in pain from my head caused me to cry out. I fell to the hard wood floor and gripped my knees to my chest tightly.

The phone in the lounge area started to ring. I knew who it was and didn't even consider getting up from the comforting position I had made myself fall to, the hard floor was a distraction, and it was an almost welcome pain. It took away very slightly from the pieces of my heart pouring painfully out through every pore and orifice of my body. Slowly I began to rock. I was bracing myself.

'Frankie... Frankie, I know you're in there. Please, baby, we need to talk...This isn't what it seems. I've been calling your phone, you've not answered. Please, baby... I need to know you're OK... Pick up, Frankie, I just need to talk to you... This wasn't meant..........' BEEP

I had put my hands up and over my ears; I couldn't listen to his voice anymore. Jumping up I charged into the lounge and ripped the bloody phone out of the wall and threw it with all my might against the wooden front door. It smashed instantly and fell into several pieces on the floor. Moving quickly, I ran as fast as my body would carry me, just managing to place my head over the toilet bowl before I threw up.

I spent the rest of the night there, either being sick or drinking water from the sink. The only good thing about having a migraine was the fact it took all my attention. I had no spare capacity to think about him.

The days went by slowly. I didn't leave the apartment. I went nowhere. I saw no one. Finally, on Wednesday, I decided I couldn't bear the smell of myself anymore. I needed to get up and move on. I showered and dried my hair, and for the first time in days I looked at myself in the mirror. My reflection showed pale, ill looking skin and sunken eyes.

*So this is what heartbreak looked like?*

I formulated a plan in my head and started to put it into action. I needed to go home. I recharged my iPhone now as I had to book a flight. While it charged I kept it on silent and forced myself into my bedroom for the first time since we had both left it on Saturday.

I carried all my things out of the room and packed my clothes up in the lounge; I couldn't cope with the strength of his cologne in my bedroom. I was taking with me only what I had arrived with and the letters and cards he had sent me. I knew at some point in time I was going to need to look at them again, even if it was only to get some closure on the whole situation.

*I don't know who I thought I was kidding, but it certainly wasn't me.*

In a couple of hours, I was ready. I had booked a flight back to Heathrow in London. I only had a couple of things left to do.

A sigh left my lips as I sat on the settee and grasped the iPhone in my hands. He had sent me forty-two messages. I opened none of them. My phone log showed a lot of missed calls. I closed my eyes and ran my finger over the wallpaper picture of us, which I had taken the other day, as it came into view.

*Surely a man that was pretending, a man that was engaged to someone else, couldn't look at another woman that way?*

I was almost unrecognisable in the picture on the phone, compared to the pale insignificant thing I was now.

I copied Nathan's mobile number into my old phone from home. I contacted George downstairs asking him to call a cab for me and my last job was to send Alex a text.

*You ruin me- The Veronicas*

I placed the iPhone face down on the table and took a deep breath. Slowly I moved my suitcases towards the front door. I knew he was outside, I could sense it. George was probably like everyone else in this building, on instruction from the control freak to let him know any information possible. This was the last thing I had to do; I just had to get past him and to the lift. I placed my eye to the security hole, he was there. His hand with his ring on was covering the hole to block my view. My heart was beating so fast, I needed to stop myself going into panic mode. This needed to be dealt with quickly before I lost my strength and determination.

After releasing the lock on the door I stood back, grasping the handles of my cases. The door flung open as I knew it would. I couldn't have prepared myself for the way I felt at that very moment. It was as though my whole body needed to see him, almost as if he was a fix, a fix that I had to have a part of. He looked like a complete wreck. My intake of breath, at the sight of him leaning heavily onto my door frame, made his eyes shoot up to mine.

'Please... I just need to talk to you, Frankie... please don't leave until you've listened to me.'

I said nothing as I moved towards him and the lift. I had nothing to say. He moved and I stepped past him making sure I touched no part of him. I couldn't touch him, it would kill me.

*What should I say? Have a nice life... let me know when you become a dad?*

It was best I just kept my mouth closed. The lift had begun to ascend up to us.

'I can't believe you can just walk away from us... you're really going to leave me aren't you?'

Finally, the lift pinged and the door opened. I moved quickly into the box like space and I turned to see a broken Alex standing in the hallway, tears streaming down his face. The doors closed and a loud sob left my mouth.

I heard him shout out 'DO NOT EXPECT ME TO LET YOU GO.' A loud bang vibrated on the lift shaft, presumably after meeting his fist.

The lift descended as fast as normal. I always knew I had hated the bloody thing and I realised I finally knew why. It wasn't my stomach it left behind, it was my heart.

# Alex

My fist was still fucking vibrating and although my nails were kept short, I was applying that much pressure clenching my fist, I could feel them cutting into my palm. The elevator whined its descent, taking with it the only woman I had ever loved. I couldn't help the anger that was firing around my body like fucking gun shots and I brought back my boot several times, kicking the closed doors in front of me. It served no purpose apart from creating a dent in the doors, but for a split second it had made me feel some sense of release.

Her face had been so pale and drawn; she had obviously lost weight. I could see how she had to concentrate in order to get around me to reach the elevator. Never once did her eyes meet mine, although I was so fucking willing her to, I knew if she had looked at me properly I would have stood a chance, a small one but still a chance. If only she had allowed our eyes to meet. Stopping her now would have proved to be no fucking good in the long run, but letting her go had taken every part of what little self-restraint I had.

Incredible how everything can come crashing down around your ears like a fucking house of cards, in the space of a few short hours. I was a stupid fucker to ever think I could keep all of my lives in separate places, away from each other.

*So fucking stupid, and so tired of all the shit in my life.*

I rubbed my face with both palms to wipe away my tears and went striding into the now empty apartment. I had kicked away the broken telephone, in order to walk further in. The orange blossom she used hung in the air, I inhaled it deep down to my soul, knowing it would be a while at the least before I smelt it properly again, if ever.

I walked around in a haze, room to room, not looking for anything in particular but looking for any sign of her I could take to memory. Fucking goddamn woman, she had me taking pictures now. My eyes went upwards. She had left the canvas on the wall. The one she had bought when she had first got here. I knew it was a cheap canvas, but it had meant a lot to her. She loved the significance of the heart being on the beach. JJ had told me that she always drove down to the sea when she was upset or hurt. He called it her flight place.

On her bedroom floor I saw my dirty clothes. It felt like a million years ago we had undressed each other in here. I closed my eyelids to try to stop the memories overwhelming me.

My eyes fell upon the bed we had last shared together. You know you have it really fucking bad when you inhale the smell from someone else's pillow, who the hell was I kidding, I knew I had it really bad, so I might as well just get on with it. Picking it up, I lifted the pillow to my face. It smelt so fucking good, but it did nothing to stop the burning anger inside; the anger was burning so fiercely I could almost smell it singeing my skin.

'FUCK!'

'FUCKING LOAD OF BULLSHIT!'

The bedding was coming apart in my hands and it felt so good. The rip of the expensive fabric eased my pain if only for a short time. Thrusting one hand into my pocket I pulled out a small square box, I lovingly rubbed over it with my thumb and then threw it as hard as I could against the window; it made a small, trivial noise and fell to the floor.

*Weak little cunt, just like your father.* As always I shook the bastard free from my head.

I hung my head low onto my chest, just trying to control my breathing and sense of utter fucking misery. I wasn't proud looking at the mess I had created, in more ways than one. I clenched my fists to my side and stared out to the city.

'I think you had better tell me what is going on Alex, don't you?'

Slowly I turned my head and lifted my eyes to the side. Standing in the doorway was my stepsister, Ruby. Her arms were folded and her foot was tapping on the floor. It would have been a comical sight with her arms crossed in front of her, in between her tits and her baby bump, if I had felt like laughing.

# Frankie

The journey home was painful. Although I needed to leave, it had made me feel physically ill doing it. The flight and subsequent train journey home seemed to drag. I didn't sleep, eat or even speak unless spoken to, and only when an answer seemed like the only feasible way out. Other passengers probably had their own ideas of what was wrong with me. I looked a mental and physical wreck.

Finally, my hand was on the old wooden gate of my aunt and uncle's house. I pushed it hard; to make sure it was wide enough to wheel in my suitcase, and I walked inside the breech quickly, before the spring returned it to its normal flexed position. My shoes made a familiar, comforting noise on the cobbled path. I hadn't made it two steps when the front door flew open and my aunt came barrelling down the path towards me, holding her soothing arms open wide. I stepped gratefully into them.

'Oh, my love.' She squeezed me tightly to her. 'Come on in, you look absolutely done in, the kettle's on. We can sit and chat.' It wasn't so much information as a set of instructions.

Thankfully, I moved with her and into the only place, other than when I was with Alex, which had ever felt truly like home.

'He's phoned you, hasn't he?' There could be no other explanation for the fact she was ready and waiting for me.

'Your uncle spoke to him yesterday.' I watched her nod and purse her lips together at me, as I fell down onto the settee of the old, bottle green, velvet three-piece suite. It was bald of velvet in some places, but what this home lacked for in expensive materialistic things, it made up for in its ability to love and protect all those who entered it. That was purely down to my aunt and uncle and their capacity for love, even to love what wasn't theirs in the first place.

In the kitchen, hung a little sign, I knew the quote off by heart.

"We may not have it all together, but together we have it all"

I couldn't think of a place anywhere, more deserving.

'How was he?' I questioned. I had promised myself I wouldn't, but what the hell.

'From what your uncle said, distraught. He wouldn't say what exactly had happened between you two though... So are you going to tell me?' She had moved out to the kitchen now to make our tea. The good thing about terraced houses was that being so small you could still communicate without raising your voice. I watched as she left the small kitchen, stepped up and through the dining room. Finally, she arrived back to where I sat. Aunty Jean passed me my hot drink and I started to blow on the top to cool it down. I stared as she placed the biscuit barrel down in front of me. She was most definitely ready for my arrival.

'I'm not sure I know quite where to start. I love him....' The tears started to fall and all at once she moved to sit next to me and gathered me up in her arms. I knew it would be a while before I was coherent enough to speak as the valve opened and everything came pouring out. Everything I had withheld on the tedious journey home. It felt so good to get it out and say it to another human being. Explaining about how he made me feel, the day trip out together and then the arrival of Ruby and his mother. My sobs finally stopped when I ran out of story.

'Karen did arrive out there. She turned up a couple of days after we came home from the Catskills.' I heard my aunt sigh. Her body language changed somewhat to irritated, but then my mother always managed to bring that out in her. 'I was so strong with her Aunty; you would have been so proud... but she did manage to get in a couple of snipes that I suppose have made this situation worse... if it could be any worse.' A sigh escaped my lips.

'We've always been proud of you. Let me guess... you weren't good enough for Alex, what would he possibly see in you? He could have his pick of other women.' She had her hand out and was counting her digits off with each reason she could list. I nodded at each reason.

'She's like an incessant dripping tap of bullshit, that bloody woman.' Never had I seen my aunt so riled up, and I had definitely never heard her swear before. It at least pulled a small smile to my face.

'The one thing that really got to me though, was... she said he was probably only with me to stop a civil law case being brought against him, in respect of JJ's death.' My voice had gone quiet as I looked up, searching for her eyes with my own.

'Well of course she did... She is a jealous bitch, so of course she did... just wait until your uncle gets home and hears all this rubbish.' She was shaking her head with absolute disgust.

'But even with all that... he is getting engaged to his stepsister, Ruby, and she is having his baby... I was stupid enough to believe we were sort of ring shopping for me.'

My aunt picked up my hand now in her own and then held the two of our hands together over my heart.

'Do you really believe that, Frankie, deep down in there... I know you're hurting... but really deep down inside, what does your heart tell you? The one thing he said to your uncle on the phone was that things aren't always what they seem and he would always find his way back to you. Now all we have to do is to work out whether you want him. Whether you love him enough to see around his mistake and move on?'

'I just don't understand why he couldn't have told me the truth? Why tell me he loved me if he loved her?'

'I know he loves you... I've said before, you two have a connection, it has been there for years... but you have to believe in

283

yourself too, in order to see that you are worth loving... and you so are, my love... you so are. Your uncle, me, JJ and Bella have always been able to see that... but that's no good if you don't recognise it in yourself. Whatever is going on with Alex and his family at the moment, I believe in that boy... he has had a lot of heartache in his life, too. I am convinced he never meant to hurt you... he knows we would never bring a case against him... he knows. So that thought has to leave your head... OK?' My aunt had always been a strong woman and I could see that even more now.

'I know you have been bombarded with hurt, my love, but I do need to tell you something else now.'

I could feel the panic rising up from my stomach and into my chest. I swallowed to help force it back down. My aunt hadn't moved away from me at all and the hand of mine that she clasped was squeezed just that tiny bit tighter. My pulse accelerated.

'Your uncle will be back anytime now and you need to know... you will see a change in him,' she took an intake of breath, obviously needing the brief second to regain some composure. 'Your uncle has been having chemotherapy, my love.' I watched as she brought her hand to her face and wiped away a lone tear.

It all fell into place then, with a bloody great resounding crash.

*So this was the reason she had almost pushed me on the plane over to my new job. But why?*

'My first question is how is he? Secondly, why didn't you tell me before, I'd have never left you both... does Alex know?' My voice was rising. I had so many questions flying around my brain right now. 'First and foremost, how is uncle?'

'He's really good... you don't need to worry, my love, he is really good. The tumour was removed and the chemo was just to make sure. He's lost his hair and a little weight... but he's good.' The relief I felt was all consuming.

'Why didn't you tell me? Alex knew, didn't he?' The relief I had felt only the second before was departing and was being replaced fast with anger. 'I could have coped, you know.'

My aunt's gaze left mine now and went to our conjoined hands. 'Love, I know you could, but you're so young and you have had so much to deal with in your life already... we all felt that... no I'll change that... I felt you didn't need to be here for this. I'm sorry if that hurts you. We had already seen a specialist before you left. He said the tumour could be removed and as long as there were no complications, the chemo would be sufficient treatment, and it has been. After what happened with your dad you didn't need to watch again from the side-lines, did you really? Alex needed a physio for Nathan and he was so happy at the thought of having you near to him... It seemed like the best option for all concerned.'

'Alex is a control freak... but I am a grown adult, I can't believe you didn't at least let me know what was happening, so I could make the choice myself.'

'Sorry, Frankie... I just thought it was for the best.' My aunt's posture sank down and I immediately regretted my harsh words to her. I pulled her to me and held on to her like my life depended on it.

'There are my best girls; do I get an invite into that hug, or what?' My uncle had entered into the room and we hadn't even heard him. As I looked up at him, I realised she had been correct. He had lost his hair and was looking extremely pale. My uncle and my dad had been brothers; there was no disputing the family resemblance. His skin and pallor now looked very similar to that of my dad, when he had first started his treatment for cancer, and they were so right, it was a bitter pill to swallow. I couldn't have coped watching him. I would have tried and given it my best shot, but looking at virtually the same face, would have made it so acutely painful.

I rushed out of my aunt's embrace and gently walked into my uncle's open arms. He smelt the same as he had always smelt; his cheap but clean smelling aftershave wrapped me in its memories. Although inside my heart was in pieces, it was so good to be home.

The first, of what was to be daily gifts, turned up at the house not an hour after I had. I opened the smallish box and found my old alarm clock, which I had been given one Christmas by my dad. In my haste to leave, I had left it behind. I knew Alex must have sent it, but there were no words included with it. I understood but somewhere deep down inside it hurt. I missed him terribly.

The next few weeks went by in a blur. I attended a couple of appointments with my uncle and was really pleased when the consultant said how well he was getting on.

I helped put up the Christmas decorations with my aunt. An old battered looking tree and decorations, that had certainly seen better days, but it contained such strong memories of JJ and me when we were younger; I knew she would never change it for anything fancy. It even had the childish decorations on it we had made in primary school.

*Surely this is what Christmas should always be about?*

Every day I received something from Alex. Flowers and chocolates were the normal, sometimes a few words written in a poem or a quote. The best and the worst things were the little personal reminders of our few short weeks together, a key-ring with a small plastic hotdog on it, a small teddy bear wearing a green and white striped rugby shirt and a picture in an ornate frame of the two of us. It had been taken from the iPhone I had left behind. All of these things I knew were being sent in order to remind me of just what we had between us. It was his way of not letting me forget. As if I ever could.

But nothing came from him about the situation we were now in.

Christmas day finally arrived and I was busy helping my aunty in the kitchen. Our neighbours from next door were going to share the day with us. I was grateful to them for helping my aunt when my uncle had been unwell; it seemed like a fitting way to repay them a little for their kindness. Slowly I peeled the vegetables, thinking back to the last time I had done this with Nathan, a smile crept over my lips thinking back to the fun we'd had together.

'I like that.' My aunty exclaimed. 'Keep that right there on your face... I have missed it so much.'

'As you're pointing a sharp knife at me I just might.' I smiled wider.

I watched her laughing as she turned back to the sink. Radio two was playing in the background. Christmas songs were the obvious choice of the day. She sang along at the top of her voice. I hadn't realised just how much I had missed listening to music, it was another thing I had simply stopped doing. I couldn't have trusted myself not to play our playlist.

Thinking back to Thanksgiving had unfortunately brought back the memory of his phone call from Ruby. My head was in a constant state of trying to work the whole situation out. Many nights I had spent awake talking to my aunt and even my uncle sometimes, when he could manage it, and neither of them thought that Alex had meant to hurt me. Neither of them thought that the baby was his. These disclosures were heart warming, heart warming that they thought so highly of him. The man himself continued to send me a gift every day, but never any words. He never rung me and he never wrote anything in his own hand.

*Whoever wrote that time was a great healer, had obviously never been in my bloody position. It hurt like hell.*

The Christmas lunch was a great success, my uncle had his appetite back and the easy relaxed feel around the table was palpable.

'OK, ladies and gents, with no further ado I bring you the Christmas pressies from under the tree.' My uncle was very gently tapping his knife against his pint glass in order to get our full attention.

'Frankie, as you're the nearest, love, please pass the presents up.'

Rolling onto one bum cheek and bending down and hanging off my seat, I kept my balance by holding on to the table corner. I passed up the presents as quickly as possible. The last one was quite big and I couldn't manoeuvre it up onto the table. My legs pushed the chair back slightly and I slipped down onto the floor. Crawling on my hands and knees I ducked under the branches of the fake spruce and looked at the written label. I felt myself breathe in as I became conscious of the fact the writing on it was Alex's.

*Frankie*

*I give to you, your happy place.*

*X*

'Come on, love, we're waiting,' my aunt demanded.

Carefully I pulled out the large parcel and placed it on my vacant chair. There was a smaller box too, also from Alex. Silence hit my ears as I raised my glance to the four faces sitting around the table.

'They're from Alex.' I told them all, but it was fairly obvious that they were already aware of that.

'We know, love... will you open them with us or somewhere private?' asked my aunt.

'Here, I definitely don't need privacy.' I was afraid of being alone with my feelings.

My fingers carefully brushed fleetingly over the beautifully wrapped gift, and I began to remove the paper. As it started to peel away I instantly recognised the picture underneath, it was the heart on a beach picture. The one I had bought at the second hand thrift store, in NYC, the same canvas that I had left hanging on the apartment wall when I had run.

It wasn't exactly the same though and on further inspection I could see it was the original print. My hand flew up to my mouth in order to stop the expletives that were threatening to fall out. I knew this had to have cost a fortune, but it wasn't the cost of the print that shocked me, it was the trouble he must have gone to, actually sourcing the print for me.

'Frankie love, take your hand away from your mouth girl, and show us what you're gawping at, eh?' I turned to see my uncle smiling at me and I very slowly lifted the striking print, and turned it towards them.

'That's stunning love... when you're born by the sea it always holds great significance in your life, doesn't it?'

'It always has to me, yes. I can't believe he has found this for me.'

'Well we have a packet from him, too.' I watched as my aunt wiped her knife clean with her napkin, and then slid the dinner knife into the sealed white envelope to open it. She pulled out some pieces of paper and having been unable to locate her glasses she passed them over to my uncle to read.

We all watched as he cast his eyes over the pages.

'Jean, we're going on a Caribbean cruise, my love.' He smiled.

'On a bloody what? We can't accept that!' She suddenly shrieked. Standing up with so much momentum her chair propelled backwards. It would have fallen over, but so small was the space in the dining room it just clattered into the old fashioned sideboard behind it.

'Alex has given us the gift of a cruise for Christmas; he says it's to celebrate the completion of my chemotherapy and to help with the recovery... and although I have always listened to you, my love... for once we are not turning down this opportunity to live a little.' He picked up the papers now and gave them to my aunty, who even without actually reading the words had tears running down over her cheeks.

'Frankie?' She looked at me now questioningly.

'Nope... you can leave me out of this... it has nothing to do with the situation between Alex and I... absolutely nothing. You can't turn it down; you haven't even been on holiday abroad, let alone the Caribbean. You two so deserve a break, you really do... So the question is not are you going, but what date do you leave?' I was holding up my hands in indignation.

'Hear, hear,' put in our neighbour Norah, 'When do you go?'

'Sixth of January we fly out to Florida, and pick up the cruise from there, everything is paid for even a luxury limo to the airport.' My uncle was still browsing over the pieces of paper spread out between him and my aunty.

My hands continued to move all over the second gift from Alex. I wanted to unwrap it badly, but I wanted to savour the moment. All around the table the four friends chatted about my aunt and uncle's good fortune. As the weeks had moved on I had missed Alex terribly, my body physically ached to see, touch and hear him, and the anger I had initially felt when storming away from him had dissipated. Although we never spoke he made contact with me every day, in some way or another, and I knew that this little box was going to be the last contact from him today. I needed to hang on to the feeling of pleasure for a little longer. Removing it from view, I tucked it into the pocket of the long line cardigan I was wearing, to save it until later. My thoughts of him were broken by my aunty.

'Did you hear what Nora just said, Frankie?'

'Oh no sorry, I was daydreaming.' I offered a small smile to everyone.

'We understand, love, but I think Norah has a great idea.'

'I was just saying, Frankie, that being this time of year our cottage in Dungeness hasn't been rented out; most people would find the place pretty bleak in the cold weather. But I remember how much you have always loved it down there. If you like, you could go down for a couple of weeks whilst Jean and Robert are away. It would give you the tranquillity you may need to think, and you'd be doing us a favour, wouldn't she, Bill?' She nudged Bill. 'The place could do with airing out, there's plenty of food in the freezer and fuel for the fires, isn't there, Bill?' After being nudged again Bill nodded enthusiastically and grinned at me.

'Do you know, I would love that, thank you for the offer.' Their beach cottage was in an almost cut off area of South East England. It had a small community of mainly fisherman, and it was as though time had almost stood still. The community was based around a small pub. There were no proper roads and all the cottages, which had stood for many years, were made out of reclaimed railway carriages, joined together. The cottages were all grouped together in-between the two lighthouses. Nora and Bill's was beautiful and old, yet it had modern conveniences and it held special memories for me. I had a couple of picture memories in my head of JJ and me when we were kids. The thought of revisiting those gave me a warm feeling.

That evening in my old bedroom, I sat crossed legged on a small twin bed. Slowly I peeled back the Christmas paper from the box I had kept safe in my cardigan pocket. I don't think I had ever unwrapped anything so slowly in my life. Normally I was the one frantically ripping it away with a child like exuberance. Tonight I savoured every tear. When the lid was lifted I could smell his trade mark cologne. I inhaled sharply as my fingers found the bracelet inside. It was a silver bracelet with several charms. I studied each one carefully, lifting them up with my fingertips one by one. I found a heart with an infinity symbol wrapped around it, a rugby ball, a pair of ice skates, a pine tree, a musical note and an apple. I had to think about the last one, but it finally dawned on me that it was the big apple. The charms he had chosen obviously signified the two of us. The whole bracelet had two different coloured gem stones interspersed. One of the stones I recognised instantly as blue topaz, my birth stone, but the other I needed to look up. After searching it out on my phone I found it was a garnet, the birthstone for January. Ridiculously I knew so much about Alex, but not his birthday. I could only assume his birthday was in January. I clutched onto the bracelet for hours turning all of the charms over and over in my fingers, I felt he was trying to speak to me without words, but what he was saying I didn't know. What had made me really happy was the fact that the charms had been put on the bracelet in such a way that a large part of it was still empty. I hoped it meant what I thought, that there was going to be other things to put on it in the future, that we had a future together.

Waiting on the cobbled path, I watched as the Limo driver shut the door on my aunt and uncle. The grins on their faces were enormous and it was positively catching. Jumping up and down waving and blowing kisses to them, I felt happier than I had in the four weeks I had been home. The thought of them going and enjoying themselves was definitely half of it; the other half of my happiness was a feeling that I was going to see Alex soon. At least that's what I hoped. I had spent days trying to work out the bracelet and the print I had received for Christmas. But it was his words, which he had said to me over and over again. All of them kept running through my head, he would never let me go and he would always find his way back to me, these were my constantly prevalent thoughts and I hung on to them for all I was worth.

My arms snaked around myself in a hug as I walked back indoors. All I had to do now was pick up my bag and check the house was locked, and I was good to go. Finally closing the door on my very ancient and hand me down Mini Cooper, I exhaled deeply.

'Right, come on Frankie, you can do this.' I started the engine and like a dream it fired up straight away. The little white car had once been JJ's pride and joy. After his death I found he had left it to me. My aunt had been using it whilst I was in NYC and had lovingly kept it for my return.

The journey was only going to take about thirty minutes; we already lived by the sea. Although Dungeness was nearby, it was almost as though time stood still on the small peninsular. Unmade roads, no shops and one pub were all its attributes, if you were describing the place. To me though, its beauty came in the things that were much harder to find words for. It certainly wasn't everyone's cup of tea and quite frankly for that I was grateful. My surrogate family had always loved it. Spending time down there together, most summers, was a child's dream; the freedom afforded to us was almost the same as children had in previous decades, and we had loved it. Dungeness had always been my flight place, when I needed to get away and think. The thrill of knowing I was actually travelling there now was humming through my veins.

*Let's just hope I had read all the signs properly and wasn't just grasping at straws.*

The journey went quickly and I remembered just in time to stock up on fresh food from the last local shop on my way. Opening the car door, the smell hit me all at once; the neighbouring shop was a fish and chip shop. My stomach was moaning like my throat had been cut. What the hell, it was lunchtime. If I had a big meal now it would save me cooking later. With my few provisions bought and loaded onto the back seat of the car, I sat in the car park outside and ate the fish and chips with my fingers, out of the newspaper. It was even better than the hotdog in NYC. I'm sure if the windows hadn't steamed up, several locals would have been able to see a shit eating grin spreading across my face.

The last few minutes of my journey completed on the very bumpy road, I pulled up outside the cottage and glanced around, some things it seemed didn't change and that was a wonderful realisation. I braced myself for the onslaught of the wind that I just knew was coming when I opened the car door. It was as strong as I thought it was going to be, and I hung on to the door handle fiercely. The wonderful smells down here, a mixture of sea salt and sea cabbage hit my nasal passages as soon as I got out of the car. Looking up I could see the sky was grey and heavy and the sound of the huge waves crashing on the pebbles was almost deafening. My heart however, was light, and although I missed Alex with every part of my being, I felt this was, without a doubt, the right place to be.

A couple of hours later I had unpacked my clothes in the main bedroom, placed all the food in the fridge, turned on the heating and lit a fire. I was sat in a huge armchair staring at the storm brewing up in the English Channel. I was drifting between dozing and reading a book, with my legs tucked up underneath me. My mobile ringing almost made me spill my wine and I hurriedly placed it down on the table to the side of me.

'Hello.'

'Chocolate drop, how are you? I know, stupid question, but I need to know.' I closed my eyes on hearing Nathan's voice; it had some of the same tones as Alex's. It was nowhere near as deep, but the sound had made me hope for a split second.

'I'm doing as well as can be expected, you know?'

'Unfortunately I do... yeah.' I could hear him pause in deep thought now and the silence of the conversation wrapped itself around me like a cold chill. 'He does love you, you know... he's a stupid fucker... but he does love you.' Tears were silently coursing their way down my cheeks and I ran my spare hand over my face to try to wipe it dry, to no avail.

'What's going on, Nate?' I managed to get out, albeit around a few sniffles.

'You know I would love to answer that for you sweetheart, but I can't... It's not my story to tell... I seem to remember someone I care about very much telling me the same thing not so long ago. Just have some faith in him. I know he will want to find you soon, whether you choose to forgive him is up to you... But I have a feeling you will; he really is a lucky fucker.'

'Touché.' I answered.

'I didn't not say what it is to get back at ya, chocolate drop, it's just that it needs to come from him and him only... How is she?' He put the question so quickly into our conversation that for a minute I thought I hadn't actually heard him.

'She's OK... not brilliant, but OK... I spoke to her at Christmas... You know she feels...' I was interrupted suddenly by Nathan.

'DONT... please don't say any more.'

I quickly found a different topic of conversation and we chatted away for another hour. I had really missed his companionship and quirky sense of humour. My relief was absolute when he made no mention of the job offer, as I still wouldn't have had an answer for him. When we said our goodbyes I realised, for the first time since being down in the cottage, just how alone I was.

That evening I decided to pull on some jeans and a jumper, tidy up my hair and apply just a little mascara. A visit to the local pub was a good idea, the locals gathered there most evenings, and although I was alone I wouldn't have to be by myself. The walk just across the road was freezing and so blowy that twice I thought about turning around and going back to my onesie and open fire. It turned out though it was a great idea. The publican, Charlie, an older and almost beer barrel shaped guy caught me up on the small community's latest gossip. The old chalk pits behind the pub had been turned into a wildlife reserve, a couple of the nearby cottages had been sold and someone was now doing up the old abandoned lighthouse. It was wonderful to spend some time with people I hadn't seen in a few years.

The sunrise was stunning, as I lay in my warm bed and watched it appear in the first window of the bedroom, and then slowly crawl its way around to the other larger picture window that looked out at the ocean. I watched the rays as they gradually spread their fingers over my entire bedroom. The storm had finally passed, it had taken a couple of days and I had spent the time reading, thinking and doing a small amount of crying.

It looked like the small peninsular was at peace this morning, that feeling in turn rubbed off on my mood. I hadn't had one sign that Alex knew I was even down here. Several times over the last couple of days I had resisted the urge to go back to my aunt and uncle's to check if any flowers or presents had been sent there. I was pleased to think I had resisted. Slowly, day by day, I was feeling stronger than I had in years, and less broken.

After grabbing some breakfast, I decided that a run was needed and being ever nosy I knew my run would take me past some of the old railway-carriage cottages that Charlie had said had been done up. My bloody nosy nature always eventually got the better of me. I wiped my face clean of mascara, deciding that my shower could wait until after I returned, pulled on an old tracksuit and let myself out of the backdoor. Before being nosy I wanted to have a run on the pebble beach, which would burn off the fish and chips and copious amounts of chocolate I had consumed in my solitude. I finally reached the cottages that had been done up. They were absolutely stunning, with a very modern turn of architecture being used on the old carriages. The old lighthouse was surrounded by scaffolding and plastic covering, I couldn't believe it was still up after the weather we'd had in the previous few days, not that you would have thought it now, the sea was like a mill pond and you could see for miles in every direction. I made a turn for home, just noticing a small heart made of pebbles on the path in front of me. I touched it gently with the toe of my running shoes. It brought a smile to my face; obviously some children had been creative. I jogged a little further and almost fell over another much larger heart, made entirely of sticks and bits of bracken from the beach.

I stopped now to stare. My own heart was beating so hard in my chest. He was here. I spun around now and checked to see if I could see anyone watching me, but as always the place was fairly deserted, it was cold and January, not the middle of summer, but I had to check. Disappointment filled me, but fleetingly. On the way back to the cottage I found two more hearts made of different pieces of beach debris, obviously blown in on the sea by the storm.

Alex was definitely here. My body awakened like it had been in hibernation, just waiting for him. Stopping at my back door I could see a small beautifully wrapped box, my aching body instinctively broke into a small run to cover the distance. Bending down I noticed it had a small card with it. I opened the door with trembling fingers, shut it quickly behind me and ran into my bedroom. I placed the small box down on the bed and removed the card. My body was shaking, with what I didn't know.

*Was it excitement or terror?*

Finally, I encouraged my fingers to open the card up and read.

*Frankie*
*I enclose a small charm for our bracelet.*
*Once you see it, you will know where to find me.*
*I hope you will come to me*
*I am here for you and only you.*
*Please give me this chance to explain.*
*I love you*
*X*

A loud cry escaped my lips, and I lifted up my hand to cup my mouth. My eyes read his words several times over. The box was lying on my bed. I fell to my knees and rested my elbows on top of the thick quilt; I needed to rest my arms in order to compensate for the shaking in my limbs. Swiftly I tore off the wrapping and opened the lid. Peering inside I could see a small silver charm, looking even more closely I could see it was a... lighthouse.

A couple of hours later I made my way towards the plastic covered building. I was wearing my warm coat over the one and only dress I had brought with me and knee high boots. My hair was done to fall loosely around my shoulders. I had bathed and shaved all over, my makeup was done to perfection, well the little I wore. Alex hadn't seen me in a month and I wanted him to see exactly what he had been missing, it was my semblance of being in control of this meeting. He had hurt me terribly, I knew deep down it was for a good reason, but I wasn't just going to bow down to him. I needed my facade around me. I didn't stop walking once; I wanted to show no hesitance. My traitorous body was on fire, as it always was whenever he was near, and my heart was pounding away in my chest, like I was out running.

The old wooden blue door flew open as I reached it; he had obviously been looking out for me. There he was, my Greek God, he was wearing dark blue jeans and a light blue button down shirt over a white T-shirt. I realised that I was casually and probably very slowly running my gaze over the entire gorgeous length of his body. I felt my lips start to lift as a smile took over my face. He was holding the door open with one hand and offering his other to me, I took it without thinking and the familiar pulse of electricity coursed between the two of us. My whole being wanted to fly into his arms. Somehow I stopped myself and walked around him and into the lighthouse.

It was beautiful inside, warm and inviting, and done out very similarly to the cabin in the Catskills, except the wooden walls were white washed instead. White and blue were the prominent colours with the very occasional accent of yellow thrown in for good measure. I wouldn't have picked anything different.

'Thank you for coming, Frankie... I was scared you weren't going to. Will you sit down?' I knew he was running his hand through his hair even without turning around; slowly I made my way to the deep comfy looking chair. I couldn't risk him sitting next to me at the moment.

'Can I take your coat?' His fingers grazed the tops of my shoulders as he relieved me of the garment. He threw it over the back on the settee, without ever leaving me. 'Please say something,

Frankie... speak to me.' His hands caressed down either side of my arms. They left goose bumps on my flesh. The hair on my body stood to attention. I pulled myself away from his embrace and sat down quickly.

'I think you are the one who needs to talk, Alex, not me.'

With a loud expel of breath he moved himself to sit on the arm of the settee. I knew why, it was closer to me than the actual settee. He sat and put his long muscular legs out in front of him and crossed his bare feet. He lifted his gaze and my eyes fell into his beautiful green pools.

'I was thirty on the sixth of January and with that coming of age, finally my father's Company and property became completely mine, no more fucking bowing down to the board, no more fucking curtailing to my mother and stepfather... finally they have no more say in any of our lives.' He said it with such complete and utter conviction, that I found it confusing.

'But I thought you didn't want the company?' He lifted his hand asking for my patience.

'On the seventh of January my mother and stepfather stepped down from their positions on the board and left the Blackmore family property in the Hamptons, and all of our lives, albeit somewhat reluctantly. We paid them off and they left to retire in Martha's Vineyard. I resigned as CEO after making my final decision in that position and my stepsister Ruby is now in charge of the company.'

I knew my face was pulling into a deep frown at the mention of her name.

'Also on the seventh of January, Ruby and my brother Scott were married, just a quiet affair with only Nathan and me as witnesses... They are very much looking forward to the birth of their baby.' The silence that followed was almost deafening as I filtered the information. He crossed his arms over his huge chest as he waited for me to catch up.

'So you aren't in love with her? It isn't your baby? What we had really was real?' I watched as he fell to his knees, and sat back on his haunches next to my chair. He made a grab for my hands.

'There's no WAS about it...I LOVE YOU!... I love you so fucking much!' He stared deeply into my eyes, trying to convince me.

'You are my extraordinary light in what has been a pretty fucking dark existence. Without you, Frankie, I am a sad excuse for a human being. I am just so sorry you got caught up in our fucking clusterfuck of a so called family, believe me it has fucking done me in being without you the past month. I hope you can forgive me?' He threaded his fingers in between mine. 'Please say you can forgive me?' Taking my silence as an opportunity to continue, he carried on with the explanation.

'I was only young when my dad died, but he made me promise to always look out for my little brothers.....' He was shaking his head from side to side.

'Ruby and Scott have been in love since she came back from university... She, like me, was sent away to school for looking too much like her mother, something my bitch of a mother wasn't willing to accept... they never grew up together.

'She is a strong lady, she can see past his illness, she sees him for the fantastic, creative man he is... his illness has meant we couldn't risk them being found out, as he would have been made to leave our family home... he simply couldn't have taken it, God forbid if they had found out she was pregnant by him... they see his illness as weakness, weakness that isn't allowed in our old distinguished family.' I could hear the disgust and sarcasm in his voice.

'Which of course, is a fucking load of complete shit.' he added with a strong vehemence.

I rubbed his hands with my fingertips, urging him to carry on.

'My stepfather physically and mentally abused me from when I was young; he hated us but loved the money and status the Blackmore's brought him.' Tears started down my face. 'That's why he got rid of me ASAP. While I was at home Nate and Scotty were safe, once I left they were in his line of fire... Nathan it didn't affect so much, but Scotty, well I think it has caused a lot of his problems... hopefully now they're gone he can get on with his life with Ruby.'

'I wasn't meant to meet you again so soon, was I?'

'Not if I'd had my way, Frankie, no... But make no mistake, I was always going to come for you... probably about now... but your uncle got sick and Nathan was injured... sometimes best laid fucking plans are thwarted by other circumstances. Please stop crying, baby; I am so sorry, so sorry for everything.'

I couldn't restrain myself anymore and snatched my hands out of his. My right hand smacked the side of his face with as much force as I could muster and then upon hearing the crack it made and with my palm still burning, I flew into his arms. A smaller man might have been bowled over, but not Alex.

He wrapped his arms around me as tight as I could stand and he began to kiss me. It was one of his kisses that made me lose my mind. Our tongues danced together and it became more and more desperate. We sucked and nipped at each other's lips in a bid to almost consume one another. Alex started to stand up, taking me with him, my arms were around his neck and I never wanted to let go again. Finally, we reluctantly broke free of each other. There was still so much to say.

'I totally accept that crack around the face, I fucking deserved it... but do you forgive me, baby?'

'I do... I understand,' I said resting my forehead on his, my feet not touching the ground as he held me up to his level. 'Once I had the time to think about it all, I knew there had to be a good reason for everything... but let me add... If you ever lie to me, cover up the truth, or manipulate me again, I will walk, even if it is done with the very best intentions. I never want to cry like I have in the last month ever again; never... do you understand me?'

I watched as the corners of his mouth began to curl as he broke out into a huge smile, his dimples came out to play and his gorgeous green eyes twinkled. 'Yeah, baby, I understand you,' and he winked at me.

*I was a seriously lucky cow!*

'Now before I carry you up those fucking ridiculous looking stairs,' I followed his gaze as our foreheads rolled against each other's a little. The stairs in the lighthouse were of course very narrow and wrapped around the inside edge of the building. I laughed cathartically out loud.

'Now this I've got to see.' I was rewarded with a smack on my bum cheek.

'First, baby, I need to give you just one more tear.' He let me slide all the way down the front of him in his trademark way, making me feel every hard part of him. My eyes never left his as I struggled to clarify what the hell he was talking about. My boots hit the floor and he released me, swiftly he went down on one knee, whilst delving in his front pocket for a box, which he now opened in front of me. Inside was the ring I had seen in New York, the beautiful tear-drop diamond one. My hands found their way into his hair, as his beautiful face looked up into mine.

'I'm a lucky bastard. Thank you for your forgiveness. I have carried this ring around with me since our last weekend together. It is the last tear I ever want to give you, baby. Please, Frankie, will you be my wife?

'Will you come with me and live in this lighthouse, which I bought especially for you? Even if it does have fucking stupid stairs.' He was laughing now, 'It's on your beach, and in your flight place. You will no longer have any reason to run. I will always look after your heart, I promise.'

'Yes... absolutely, YES!'

He took out the ring and pushed it onto my finger, chucking the box over his shoulder and behind him. I listened to his deep laugh as he stood up and picked me up easily into his arms, and twirled me around and around. We laughed as he tried to safely carry me up stairs that were never meant for passion. I watched in a mirror at the two of us in sync, I knew looking at us now we had always been meant for each other.

We were Fated to be together.

## JUNE FIVE MONTHS LATER

Tick, tick, tick. The time was moving on.

'Come on, gorgeous girl, you need to get a bloody move on.' Bella was peering over my shoulder, looking at my reflection as I put the finishing touches to my hair, and added a couple of blue sprigs of forget me nots. I had it piled up on top of my head with a few long loose curls falling down and around my neck.

'Oh, my love, you look simply stunning, I am so proud of you.' I found my aunt's eyes with my own in the mirror, and smiled at her.

'I'm going to go down now and take my place.' She grabbed my hand, squeezed it and blew me a kiss. I watched her until she had vacated our room.

Bella moved off towards the large balcony windows, which lit up our beautiful cream bedroom. She disappeared out onto the wooden balcony and I could just make out her elegant bridesmaid dress, the striking blue suited her so well. It had been a good choice. The style was exactly the same as mine.

I looked back at the mirror, 'Not bad, you'll do.' My off-white, Grecian style dress crossed over my now more than ample bust, underneath it fell like a waterfall to the floor. I was pleased with my choice. My makeup was simple as Alex preferred me more natural than heavily made up. I giggled a little at the thought of the lingerie I had chosen for this day. I was without knickers, all I had on was a supportive balcony bra in bright white, but the colour was the only thing that was innocent about it. It hardly concealed anything and was completely see through.

*Alex would love it!*

'Frankie, you really have to get a move on, I can just see Alex from here and he's beginning to shuffle his feet,' she laughed, even my bestie knew it was the only tell my husband-to-be had. He was starting to feel uncomfortable waiting for me.

'OK let's do it, I'm ready.' I turned away from the mirror to see Bella coming back into the room.

Bella handed me my bouquet, a simple bunch of blue and white flowers tied together with a white ribbon, she had one to match. We said not a word between us; we just smiled at each other in understanding.

My uncle waited for me at the bottom of the wooden balcony steps, he looked so smart and extremely proud. Before walking down, I glanced out over the beach. I could see Alex waiting there, with his back to me. The few people we had wanted to share our day with were also there. Nathan was next to Alex, sharing best man duties with Scotty. To one side stood my aunt and Ruby, who was holding hers and Scott's new born daughter in her arms. To create a balance Norah and Bill stood on the other side. Apart from the official waiting to marry us, that was it. It was more than enough, we had all the love we needed right there.

I started to make my way down the steps and towards my uncle's outstretched arm; the sun was just beginning its slow descent on the horizon. Nathan and Scotty walked away from Alex now and bent down to the ground lighting candles. I stopped my procession and watched as the candles in the sand began to glow. Being a short distance away I could see it was in the shape of a heart, it was stunning.

I quickened my step and took hold of my uncle's arm, he patted my hand, 'Your father would have been very proud, my love, I am so honoured to do this in his place.' I raised my hand and wiped at the tears just under his eyes. I nodded in understanding. He pulled me to him in a quick embrace.

'OK let's go, his feet are fidgeting more and more by the minute,' I smiled.

The moment my bare feet hit the sand I stopped again and gazed at the beautiful man that was just about to become my husband. He was wearing a smart white shirt, open at the collar and with the sleeves rolled up. It was tucked into a smart pair of navy blue trousers that fitted him like a glove. His almost black hair was flopped over slightly just as he liked it. Suddenly he seemed to sense I was there and he turned around. The expression on his face was priceless as he took in my wedding dress. He stopped shuffling his feet immediately.

I touched my hand to the bracelet he had given me, holding all of our charms so far; one had arrived this morning to be added later. It was a collection of three rings, engagement, marriage and eternity all in miniature.

My feet shifted all the time in the warm sand to stop them being consumed into the ground, and I placed one hand on my very pregnant torso, to touch the child that Alex and I had conceived on our last wonderful day together in New York. It seemed the pill didn't like migraines and the subsequent sickness that followed. This child, although it had been unplanned, would be born to two parents who loved and wanted it badly; it appeared my life had gone full circle.

The man I loved took one hand out of his pocket now, lifting it up and using just his curled index finger, he beckoned me towards him and my feet moved on command. As I started to walk towards him once again, he winked and held out his hand for me. The ceremony went by in a blur as I stared into his eyes. It was only when our small gathering burst into applause I realised we were finally married.

'Mine,' was the word he spoke for all to hear. I smacked his shoulder in embarrassment.

Alex pulled me to him quickly. His hands found their way slowly down my spine to my arse cheeks as he bent down to consummate our marriage with a kiss. It was a quick kiss and he broke away. His eyes took on their feral look; the green was being consumed by the fiery amber, his eyebrows raised in question. I couldn't help but smile, I knew he had found me sans knickers. His forehead rested on mine.

'Holy hell, what you do to me, baby.' He picked me up suddenly into his arms and started striding towards our balcony stairs. Our small gathering burst out laughing as I was carried off the beach so quickly, laughing and clinging hard onto the man I loved. I threw my bouquet over his shoulder and straight to Bella.

'Thank God we're in the Hamptons,' I whispered in his ear, 'At least the stairs are wide enough for you to carry me up,' I teased.

'Just you wait, Mrs. Blackmore, just you fucking wait...teasing baby deserves equal punishment, playing with fire will get you burnt.' He took off now running, with me in his arms shrieking.

*He makes me laugh.*

*He makes me want.*

*He makes me need.*

For the rest of our lives, I would always be grateful to the fate that brought us together.

**Thank you so much for reading FATED...**
**If you enjoyed being with the Blackmore boys, then my next book**
**may be for you...**

## INEVITABLE

Dirty talking, tattooed Nathan Blackmore has it all, at least that's what he wants everyone to believe. Six months ago the only woman he has ever loved walked out of his life. This super bike rider vowed never to look back and never to give his love again. Nathan's self-destruct button was pressed.

But that was then and this is now.

When Nathan and Bella Carpenter come face to face all the old feelings resurface. Bella, an investigative journalist, has a secret. A secret that has come back to haunt her, she needs to disappear, and disappear quickly. With her life possibly in danger the only person she can trust, no longer trusts her.

He wants the truth. She is determined to keep her secret.

But what they both feel makes their passion inevitable.

TO BUY LINKS http://amzn.com/B01HVGLCOM
http://www.amazon.co.uk/dp/B01HVGLCOM
Facebook page link http://www.facebook.com/A-S-Roberts-author-1482173865424420/

# IRREVOCABLE

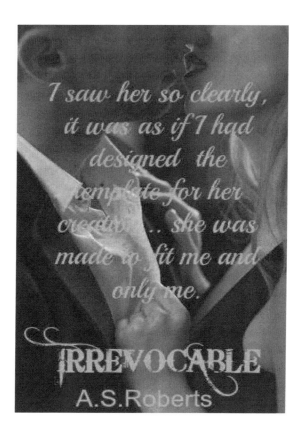

Head of security for a prominent American family, John Edwards is the epitome of the strong, silent type. With an all-work, no-play attitude, he guards his heart as fiercely as he protects his clients. John only allows himself casual fun with easy women, punishing himself for a past he can't redeem.

But when he meets Jasmin Carpenter, all bets are off. Suddenly, John is falling for the flighty and flirty British girl. Quickly marrying her under the guise of her safety, he's determined to make this sham of a marriage stick. While Jasmin desperately yearns for the security of marriage and the lure of unconditional love, she knows she can never give John what he deserves. Now, he must convince Jasmin that they are destined to be together.

He doesn't want more.
He wants everything,
Despite the irrevocable damage their pasts have created...

Made in the USA
Lexington, KY
08 April 2018